Charles King

Captain Close and Sergeant Croesus

Charles King

Captain Close and Sergeant Croesus

ISBN/EAN: 9783337022822

Printed in Europe, USA, Canada, Australia, Japan

Cover: Foto ©Andreas Hilbeck / pixelio.de

More available books at **www.hansebooks.com**

CAPTAIN CLOSE

AND

SERGEANT CROESUS

TWO NOVELS

BY

CAPTAIN CHARLES KING

U. S. ARMY

AUTHOR OF "THE COLONEL'S DAUGHTER," "MARION'S FAITH,"
"UNDER FIRE," ETC.

PHILADELPHIA

J. B. LIPPINCOTT COMPANY

1895

CAPTAIN CLOSE.

CAPTAIN CLOSE.

I.

THE conductor had eyed Lambert curiously as he punched his ticket. He held it a moment and edged his lantern around so that its feeble light could reinforce the glimmer from the bleared and smoky globe above Lambert's curly head. The train had started from the junction with that quick series of back-wrenching jerks which all veteran travellers remember as characteristic of American railways before the introduction of "coupler buffers." It was a shabby, old-fashioned train,—one whose cars had "seen service," and not a little of it, during the long and eventful war so recently closed. It had a baggage-car behind the wheezy old wood-burner that drew the rickety procession out into the dim, starlit aisle through the eastward forest, and, for the first time in a week, that baggage-car contained a trunk. It had a "smoker," in which three or four negroes were soundly sleeping on the worn cushions at the forward end, and three or four lank, shabbily-dressed whites were consuming tobacco and killing time under the single lamp at the other. It had a "ladies' car,"—so called,—in which no ladies were visible, and which differed in appointments from the smoker only in the facts that its seats were upholstered in dingy red plush instead of blackened canvas, and that both its lamps could be induced to burn, however feebly, instead of only one. It was a forlorn, hangdog, shamefaced sort of train, that seemed oppressed with sense of its own disrepute,—a train that kept in hiding during the broad light of day and ventured to slink forth only after nightfall, like some impoverished debtor, not loving the darkness better than light because of evil deeds, but hating it as it hated its own shabbiness, and accepting it as only one plane above total decrepitude, the junk-shop and the poor-house. Starting at dusk from a populous station on a north-and-south "trunk" line, it turned and twisted through red clay cuttings, jolted over mud-covered ties and moss-grown trestles, whistling shrill to wake the watchers at 'cross-country stations on the way, and finally, after midnight, rested an hour at a prominent point, a "State centre," where, sometimes at one o'clock but generally long after, the night express came glaring up from the South along the glistening rails of another "great northern" route, and three nights in the week, perhaps, gave it a sleepy passenger or two to trundle away westward towards the big river town it managed to reach by sunrise, once more to slink out of sight until dark, when again it crept forth and stole away on the return trip over its clanking road, unresentful of comment on its loneliness and poverty, and proud, if anything, of the fact that this way, at least, it ran "right end foremost," according to the American idea, with the baggage- instead of the ladies' car next the struggling engine.

It was a clear, starlit night, sharply cold, and the planks of the platform at the junction had snapped and creaked under their glistening white coat of frosty rime. The up train came in even later than usual,—so much so that the station-master had more than once asked his friend the conductor of the waiting "Owl" whether he really thought he could "make it" over to Quitman in time for the down express at dawn. "You'd better pull out the minute she gits hyuh," was his final injunction when at last her whistle was heard.

A lithe, active young fellow in a trim suit of tweed had sprung from the sleeper before the incoming train had fairly stopped, and, hailing the first man he saw, asked, "Train for Tugaloo gone yet?" which so astonished the party addressed that he simply stared for a minute without reply. A voice crying in the wilderness, apparently, was heard above the hissing of steam and the loud mouthings of the negro porters of the two rival hotels. "All aboard for Quitman," it said, and, abandoning his apparent purpose of repeating the question in sharper tone, the young fellow turned and ran nimbly across the dimly-lighted platform in the direction of the hail.

"Quitman train?—Tugaloo?" he asked of a dark form standing above the tail light of the car.

"Quitman it is. Anybody else thar?" And the interrogative went off in a shout. No answer.

"Aw, *Hank!* Anybody else?" Still no answer. Two or three dim figures were by this time clustered around the flaring torch of a coffee-stand at the edge of the platform. The conductor got off and walked impatiently towards them.

"Any you gentlemen for Quitman?" he asked.

"Quitman? Hell, no! What's any man want to go thar for night like this? Pull out with your old sneezer, Jimmy, 'nless you'll stop and take a cup coffee."

"Oh, that you, cap? Ain't you got anybody for us? Thought the judge was comin' up to-night."

"Warn't on *my* car," said the brakeman of the express, possessively. "Young feller 'n the sleeper all *I* know of."

"Got *him*," answered the conductor as briefly as possible for a man long attuned to the soft Southern drawl, and whose "got" was more like "gawt." "Reckon we might as well git, then," he continued, returning to the colloquial present indicative of a verb of manifold meaning and usefulness. "Tell Hank, will you?—Let 'er go, Jack," he shouted to the engineer with a wave of his lantern. A yelp from the whistle was the answer; the fireman crawled out from a warm corner in the baggage-car and shambled drowsily forward to the cab. Sudden jets of steam flew hissing out on the frosty air. One after another the three cars lunged sharply forward and then slowly rolled forth into the night. The conductor clambered up the rear steps with parting wave of his lantern, slammed the door after him, and came up the narrow aisle to look at his passenger. Before he had time to speak, however, his attention was attracted by a succession of yells from the track to their rear. Giving an angry yank at the bell-rope, he whirled about and hurried to the door. The train came willingly to a sudden stand, and Lambert, stowing his hand luggage on the empty seat before him, heard the following lively colloquy, as did everybody else who happened to be awake and within a radius of two hundred yards:

"What d'you want?"

"Come *back* hyuh, I say."

"What d'you wa-a-nt? I ain't goin' to back in thar now."

"Hyuh's a trunk."

"Wha-at?"

"A tru-u-unk."

"Why in hell didn't you sling it abawd *fihst* off?" sung out the conductor, disgustedly. "Ain't you felluhs got any brains?—Back up, Jack!" he shouted forward, signalling with his lantern again. "Somebody's left a band-bawx, by criminy!" And so, growling volubly, the custodian of the "Owl" swung himself out from the steps, hanging by the left hand to the iron railing and holding extended his green and white lantern with the other. A couple of stalwart negroes came panting forward to meet them, the offending trunk on their shoulders, and went stumbling up the sloping embankment towards the slowly backing baggage-car. The light from the lantern fell on the new canvas cover and on the fresh brown finish of the straps and handles, then on the inscription in bold black letters at the end:

I. N. LAMBERT,
U. S. ARMY.

At sight of which the conductor checked the half-jocular, half-resentful tirade he was composing for the benefit of the station-master, and abruptly asked,—

"Whuh's it goin'?"

"Tugaloo, suh," said the rearmost negro.

"Well, hump it abawd, 'n' be quick about it." Then, raising his voice, he shouted across the platform, "Shuah you ain't gawt a feedin'-bawtle or a cake o' soap or s'm' other truck to fetch me back again, Hank? Dawg gawn 'f I reckon we ever *will* get to Quitman, 't this rate!"

The darkies about the coffee-stand gave a guffaw of sympathetic rejoicing over the official's humor. The conductor was evidently more popular than the station-master. One of the two trunk-bearers came lunging in at the front door of the car, and, humble yet confident, appealed to Lambert:

"Little somethin', suh, fur totin' de trunk? Bin los', mos' like, 'f it had n' bin f'r us. Thanky, suh. *Thanky.*" And the negro's eyes danced, for the *douceur* handed him by the young owner of the vagrant baggage exceeded his hopes. He strove, indeed, to turn and renew his thanks at the rear door, but was collared and hustled unceremoniously off the car.

"*You* ain't goin' to git off at Tugaloo this time o' night?" asked the conductor, finally, and with that odd emphasis expressive of doubt as to a passenger's knowledge of his own intentions so often heard in our thinly-settled districts. Lambert interpreted it to mean "Anybody else, perhaps, but not you." He was already cogitating as to whether or not the conductor had intended some covert sneer in his recent reference to "feeding-bottles," for Lambert was but one-and-twenty, and youthful-looking for his years. The tone of this inquiry and the look which accompanied it after deliberate pause and study of the proffered ticket, however, were far from aggressive or discourteous, yet the unintentional misplacing of the emphasis, following an allusion equally hapless and alike unintentional, had given umbrage to the boy. "You must expect to hear no end of unpleasant things," he had been told at department head-quarters, where he had received orders to go on and join his company, then in camp at Tugaloo. "Everybody is mighty sore yet over the late unpleasantness. Hold your tongue and keep your temper," were the parting injunctions; and he meant to do both. All the same he did not intend to allow people to treat him with discourtesy,—certainly not a conductor of a public railway. Lambert was on his dignity in a moment. He looked the railway man straight in the eye and replied, with all the calm and deliberation he could master, "My ticket would seem to indicate that such was my intention," and almost immediately regretted it, for the conductor looked up in sudden surprise, stood one instant irresolutely, then saying, "Oh! All right," turned abruptly away, walked up beyond the stove, and, roughly shaking the elbow of a snoring passenger, sung out, "Coatesville," and let himself out with an emphatic bang of the door.

Two days later, when asked at Quitman what sort of a fellow the new lieutenant seemed to be, Mr. Scroggs, the conductor, himself a soldier of large experience and no little ability,—a man who had fought his way from the ranks to the command of the remnant of a regiment that laid down its battered arms among the very last, a man not five years Lambert's senior in age, but lustrums ahead of him in the practical details of his profession,—Mr. Scroggs, the conductor, promptly said, "He's a dam little fool," and never dreamed how much he should one day deplore it.

"Newt" Lambert, as he was known among his intimates, was far from being a fool. He had seen very little of the world, it is true, and, until this December night, next to nothing of the sunny South, where at this particular period in our national history it was not every man who could so conduct himself as not to fall into error. More especially in the military service was an old head needed on young shoulders, and a strong head between new shoulder-straps, for army life so soon after the great war was beset by snares and temptations it rarely hears of now, and many a fellow, brave and brainy both, in the

A *

days that tried men's souls 'twixt Big Bethel and Appomattox, or Belmont and Bentonville, went down in the unequal tussle with foe far more insidious than faced him in the field, but which met him day and night now that peace had come. It was at a time when the classes graduating from the Military Academy were being assigned mainly to the staff corps and to the artillery and cavalry regiments. Lambert fancied that he should prefer the associations and much prefer the stations of the artillery to those of any other corps, but an old friend of his father's, himself a veteran gunner, advised the young fellow to seek his fortune elsewhere. "If you are commissioned a lieutenant of artillery," said he, "it may be twenty years before you see your captaincy." And, though this was within three years after the reorganization of the army in '66, not one of Lambert's contemporaries who trusted to luck and applied for the artillery had yet come within hopeful range of the double bars. Lambert amazed them all when he asked for the infantry arm and took his commission thankfully.

He had been detailed for summer duty at the Point, as was then a custom, so that his leave of absence of three months did not begin until the 28th of August. He had been assigned to a regiment whose ranks were sadly depleted by the yellow fever, and which was still serving in the South. "You won't have to hoof it out to Idaho or Montana, anyhow," said a sympathetic friend, "and you'll have no end of fun at New Orleans."

But Lambert's company was not at New Orleans. Under recent orders it had been sent up into the heart of the country, where some turbulent spirits, so it was alleged, had been defying the civil officers of the general government, and by the time the short Southern winter set in more than half his regiment, together with three or four others, had been distributed by companies or detachments all over the Gulf States, and experienced officers were scarce as hens' teeth. The duty was unwelcome and galling. Lambert's captain lost no time in getting on staff duty, and "G" Company went into camp at Tugaloo under command of its first lieutenant. Arriving at New Orleans, Lambert reported himself at the head-quarters of the general commanding, who knew the boy's father, welcomed the son for old friendship's sake, and told his chief of staff to keep him there a week or so, that he might see something of the Southern metropolis and of his friends down at the barracks before going to his exile "up the road." Dining the very next evening at Captain Cram's, with Waring and Pierce of the light battery, and perhaps rather ruefully agreeing with them that he had "made a beastly fluke of it, going into the doughboys," Lambert was asked, "Who's in command of your company now?"

"Our first lieutenant," said he. "I don't know much about him, —Brevet Captain Close."

Whereupon Waring laid down his knife and fork. "Angels and ministers of grace!" he exclaimed. "Well, if that isn't the oddest *contre-temps* I ever heard of!" And then they all began to laugh.

"You evidently know him," said Lambert, somewhat nettled and a trifle ill at ease. "Why did you ask me about him? Somebody told me he had been commissioned for heroism—special bravery in action, or something of that kind—during the war."

"Gospel truth," said Pierce. "Close is the most absolutely fearless man I ever met. Nothing even Waring could ever do or say would ruffle him." And then, though Mrs. Cram declared it a shame, she too joined in the general laughter. Close was evidently a celebrity.

And now, as Lambert found himself within a few miles—though it might be several hours—of his destination, he was thinking not a little of the officer to whose presence he was so soon to report his own, and whose companionship and influence, for good or for ill, he was bound to accept for the simple reason that, so far as he could learn, there was absolutely no one else with whom he could associate,—except, possibly, the "contract doctor."

Quitting New Orleans after a long day's sight-seeing with his friends, he had sought a berth in the Pullman and slept soundly until aroused by the porter after two o'clock to change cars at the junction. Now he was wide awake, and, after the first few miles of jolting and grinding through the darkness, was becoming chilled and lonesome,— perhaps a trifle home-sick. Twice had the conductor bustled through the train, rousing sleeping passengers and seeing them safely off at dark and mysterious stations where hardly a glimmer of lamp or candle could be seen away from the mere shanty which served as a waiting-room and office. A heap of wood was stacked up near the stove, and Lambert poked the waning embers and piled on fresh fuel, whereat a young man who had got on at Coatesville with a shot-gun and a big bottle for luggage, and who had for nearly an hour been singing sentimental snatches to his own deep satisfaction, now smiled maudlin approval and companionably held forth the bottle. "'S good," said he, in loyal defence of the stimulant most courteously declined. "Bes' thing you can take these co' mawnin's.—Live 'bout hyuh an'where?"

"No," said Lambert, civilly, yet hoping not to be further questioned. He busied himself again with the fire, then, rising quickly, sought his seat.

But the young man with the flask was gregarious and bubbling over with the milk of human kindness. He promptly lurched after, and, flopping down into the opposite seat, sending some of Lambert's belongings clattering to the floor, held out his hand.

"'Scuse me, suh," he stuttered. "I hope I ain't—'fended you. My name's Potts,—Barton Potts. We ain't what we were befo' the wah, you know. But I know a gen'l'm'n—every time. Hope—I ain'—'sulted——"

"Not by any means!" protested Lambert, loudly and heartily. "Don't think of such a thing! I simply didn't feel like drinking; but I'm a thousand times obliged to you."

"Tha'z right. Tha'z all right," said Mr. Potts, grasping Lambert's hand and shaking it impressively. "I—hello! Wha'z that?"

Lambert's sword, encased in chamois-skin, had come in contact with the stranger's elbow and gone rattling under the seat. Potts made a precipitate dive and fished it out, regaining his equilibrium after some little struggle.

"Goin' to Quitman—too? Tha'z my home. An' I'm glad—meet you. I *know* a gen'l'm'n,—an' I'll stan' your frien'——I mean it. Missur—Missur——"

"My name's Lambert," said the lieutenant, quietly essaying to relieve Mr. Potts of the sword.

"Lammert? Glad—meet you—Missur Lammert. Where'd you say you b'longed?"

"I'm going to Tugaloo."

"Tu-gloo?—Tha'z no kin' of place. C'mawn to Quimman. Come to my house.—What 'n 'ell's thiz?" he broke off suddenly.

"My sword," said Lambert, simply.

"Sword?—*sword?*" exclaimed Potts. "You goin' Tu-gloo with sword? You—Yankee off'cer like that—wha'z name?—Close?"

"A Yankee officer certainly," laughed Lambert. "I've never met Captain Close."

The effect of this announcement on Mr. Potts was surprising. It well-nigh sobered him. He slowly drew back until he sat erect, his head wobbling a bit in spite of his efforts at self-control. Presently he began to speak, slowly and impressively at first, then winding up in a verbal entanglement:

"Missur Lam-p-bert, I didn't know I was talkin' to—Yankee officer—but—I'm a gen'l'm'n, suh, an' I stan' by wh-wha—I say. I mean to stan' *your* frien', suh; but as fo' that oth—felluh—*Close*—I'll see'm in 'ell first."

II.

It was sun-up and snapping cold when the brakeman shouted "Tugaloo," and gratefully Lambert stepped from the train and felt free air. Mr. Potts was sleeping soundly, doubled up in one of the seats. The only wakeful bipeds in sight were the conductor and his trainman. Unseen hands forward had shoved the trunk out upon the frosty boards. The sun was just peeping over a low wooded ridge before them. The track wound away among some desolate fields where tiny flakes of cotton still clung to the brown and withered stalks. In a cloud of steam the train pulled away, leaving Lambert and his trunk to look after each other as best they might, and as the cloud lifted the young officer looked curiously around him.

He was standing on a rude wooden platform whose shrunken planks left black, gaping seams between their upper faces, now, at least, beautiful in their thick coat of sparkling white. Except where the footmarks of the trainmen marred the smooth expanse, and where in two or three places the planks were gone entirely, this gleaming sheet stretched the length of the platform to where the white bulk of his trunk stood on end at the eastern edge. The charred and blackened relic of a flight of stairs led from the platform to the sloping ground some five feet below, but not even a hand-rail warned the unwary against a breakneck plunge into space. Part of the platform itself had been burned away, and some charred and blackened posts, sticking bolt upright from the ground in the shape of a narrow rectangle, showed that a wooden building of some kind had formerly stood along the rear of the rickety staging. Midway along its length, on the southern side, a shed with sloping roof had been loosely thrown together, and the end nearest him, boarded in and pierced for a door and a couple of windows, bore over the threshold in black stencil the legend "Ticket Office." Under the shed were a couple of ploughs

2

and some boxes. Out on the bare slope, midway between the track and a "snake" fence that paralleled it some twenty yards to the south, a dozen bales of cotton were huddled, three of them partially covered by old war-worn 'paulins and ponchos, the others entirely exposed to the rain of sparks to be expected from any passing engine when the wind happened to blow from across the track; and all of them, evidently, defenceless against the predatory hands of pilferers, for jagged rents were torn in the coarse sacking of each, and huge fistfuls of the white staple had been dragged from a dozen gaping wounds in every bale.

The red soil, showing here and there through the scant and withered herbage, was seamed with mule- and wheel-tracks, and a few rods away a broken-down farm-wagon lay with a spoke-bristling hub close by its shattered axle, while the tire, rolling away from the general wreck, seemed to have crawled off to die by itself, and leaned rusting against one of the charred timbers. The southward view was limited to a long, low ridge of ugly, white-flecked cotton-stalks. Eastward the sun was breaking a pathway through the fringe of trees along another ridge, and a faint line of mist, rising sluggishly in the intervening low ground, with the hollow rumble of the train crossing an invisible bridge, told of the presence of some slow-moving stream. Westward the track came into view around a thinly wooded hill-side, with a clearing here and there, in which some low cabins were scattered.

With this cheerful outlook to greet him at three points of the compass, Lambert turned him to the north. There was a siding with a switch at each end, but, as three or four rails were missing opposite the west end of the platform, it stood to reason that the railway company found the other all that was necessary to the traffic of so bustling a place as Tugaloo. A brown freight-car stood on the siding with wide-opened doors, and some household goods loomed in plain sight. "There is more honesty in this community than the United States marshal would give us to believe," thought Lambert, as he recalled the extract from a recent report which was shown him at department head-quarters. He laid his satchel and sword upon the platform, and, wrapping his blue circular about his shoulders, took a few steps forward and a peep into the interior of the car. From the midst of bedsteads, bureaus, and cheap, old-fashioned furniture, a quantity of bedding had been hauled out upon the floor, and from the midst of the bedding a woolly head protruded,—that of a negro fast asleep.

Beyond the car stood a dusty open square, bordered on three sides by dingy wooden structures, some of two stories, but most of them only one in height. A wooden side-walk framed the square in some places, and in others only indications of its former presence were to be seen. The side-walk was bordered by a rude railing, to which, it was evident, horses and mules were tethered during business hours, for at one of the rails, even now, sprawled upon the soft, hoof-pawed dust, a long-eared quadruped was half hanging by the bridle-rein, while the dilapidated saddle had worked around during the night until it settled upon the animal's side.

Judging from such signs or legends as were visible over the door-ways of Tugaloo, Lambert's impressions were that the vending of intoxicating drinks was the principal industry, as there were three saloons to one store devoted to general merchandise,—which establishment, painted white and with an air of prosperity and a flock of cotton-bales around it, bore the sign of I. Cohen, and told pathetically that the pioneers of a relentless and one-sided trade had already made their lodgement in the midst of a helpless community.

It was sunrise, and not a soul was apparently astir. A street led away northward at right angles to the main front of the square, and straggling houses lined it at intervals on either side. One of these, with a belfry, at the corner of the plaza, seemed to be a meeting-house of some kind, possibly the *pro tempore* substitute for the county court-house, thought Lambert, for the centre of the square was still heaped with charred and blackened beams and bricks where once the court-house stood.

As for the camp or quarters of his future comrades and associates, Lambert could see nothing that in the least resembled a military station, and, do what he could, the boy found it impossible to down the faintly heartsick, homesick feeling that speedily took possession of him. A dog would have been welcome as companion, but there was not even a stray dog. For a moment Lambert thought of arousing the negro, but after one glance at the wide, red cavern of his mouth and the emptied flask lying close to the frowzy head, he decided in favor of the mule.

A short walk brought him to the side of the prostrate creature, and a long pull induced his muleship to stagger to his feet, but in his struggles he snapped the old headstall, and the remnant of the bit and bridle dropped into the dust. It was not until the vagrant stood erect that Lambert discovered from the U. S. brand that he was, or had been, government property. The saddle, too, turned out to be one of the old-fashioned, black-skirted, pig-skin McClellans, so familiar during the war days. As the mule seemed only half awake and unaware as yet of his freedom, Lambert first essayed to reset the saddle, to which he submitted without objection, and then to replace the bridle, to which he would not submit at all, but with lowered front and menacing hoof turned him about and jogged over to where some wisps of hay lay scattered in front of a shanty labelled " Post-Office." For ten minutes Lambert exercised his arts in vain effort to recapture that mule, and then, in sheer disgust, threw the bridle on the side-walk, picked up an abandoned half-brick, and let the mule have it in the flank. He merely twitched his scraggy hide, raised one instant the nearmost hoof, but never lifted his head. The brute was hungry from long fasting, and did not mean to be disturbed, and Lambert, who had eaten nothing since the previous day, was presently in full sympathy. Once more he looked around in search of some human being, and found himself confronting a citizen in shirt-sleeves and a tangled head of hair, who, leaning out of a second-story window, was nevertheless not twenty feet away. For a moment each regarded the other without a word. Then the native spoke :

" What ye tryin' to do ?"

" I was trying to catch that mule."

" Want him f'r anything ?"

" No : only I found him tangled in his reins, and he got away after I loosed him."

The native regarded the new-comer curiously. Lambert had slung his blue cape over the hitching-rail during his brief pursuit of the ungrateful beast, and his neat-fitting suit of tweed was something new to Tugaloo eyes. So was the jaunty drab Derby.

" You don't b'long roun' yere, do you ?" queried Tugaloo next.

" I don't; and the Lord knows I don't want to; and I'd be glad to find some way of getting myself and my trunk, yonder, out to camp. Can you suggest any ?"

" We-ell, *you* might walk. Don't reckon your trunk kin, though. Know the way ?"

" No."

" Foller the track down thar a piece, an' you'll come to a path along the branch. It'll take you right in 'mongst the tents. 'Tain't more 'n a few rawds."

"Thank you, my friend. You're the first live man I've found. I suppose I can send in for my trunk."

"Reckon ye can. *They*'ve gawt mules an' wagons enough."

Lambert gathered up his belongings and trudged away. He did not mean to yield to the feeling of depression that was struggling to possess him, yet the blue devils were tugging at his heart-strings. Wasn't this just what his classmates had prophesied would happen if he went into the infantry? *Could* any service be much more joyless, uneventful, forlorn, than this promised to be? "Mark Tapley himself would go to pieces in such a place," he had heard some one at head-quarters say of Tugaloo, but he meant to out-Tapley Mark if need be, and nobody should know how much he wished he hadn't been assigned to this sort of duty and this particular regiment,—certainly not his classmates, and, above all, not the loving mother at home. Heavens! how unlike was this bleared, wasted, desolate land to the sweet and smiling New England vale where his boyhood had been spent, to the thickly-settled, thrifty, bustling shores of the Merrimac!

He had walked nearly a mile and had seen no sign of camp or sentry, but on a sudden the path left the brushwood beside the sluggish "branch," rounded a projecting knoll, and was lost in a rough, red clay, country road. A fence, with a thick hedge of wild-rose-bushes, was to his left,—leaves and roses long since withered,—and over the tops he caught sight of the roof and upper story of some old Southern homestead, at which he had a better peep from the gate-way farther along. A path of red brick led to the flight of steps, broad and bordered by pretentious balustrades. Dingy white columns supported the roof of a wide piazza. Smoke was drifting from a battered pipe projecting from the red brick chimney at the north end, and the morning air was faintly scented with a most appetizing fragrance of broiling ham. It made Lambert ravenous.

Somewhere around the next bend in the road, beyond the northward extremity of the old fence, he could hear the sound of voices and a splashing of water. Hastening on, he found himself overlooking a level "bench" surrounded on three sides by a deep bend of the stream and partially separated from the red roadway by a fringe of stunted trees and thick, stubborn bushes; and here, in an irregular square, Lambert came face to face with the encampment of the first company, outside of West Point, it was ever his luck to join. At that particular moment he was just about ready to resolve it should be the last.

2*

On two sides of the square, facing each other and perhaps twenty yards apart, were the " A " tents of the company, ten on a side. At the flank farthest from the road and pitched so as to face the centre of the enclosure was a wall tent, backed by one or two of the smaller pattern. Nearest the road was a second wall tent, used, possibly, by the guard,—though no guards were visible,—the white canvas cover of an army wagon, and a few more scattered " A " tents. Cook-fires had been ablaze and were now smouldering about the wagon. Several men in gray woollen shirts were washing their faces at the stream ; others, in light-blue overcoats, were sauntering about the tents, some of whose occupants, as could be easily seen, were still asleep.

Standing at the edge of the winding road, and thinking how easy a matter it would be to toss a hand-grenade into the midst of the camp, Lambert paused a moment and studied the scene. Resting on his sword, still in its chamois case, with his cloak and satchel thrown over his shoulder, the young officer became suddenly aware of a man wearing the chevrons of a corporal who, fishing-rod in hand, was standing just beyond a clump of bushes below and looking up at him with an expression on his shrewd, " Bowery-boy" face in which impudence and interest were about equally mingled. So soon as he found that he was observed, the corporal cocked his head on one side, and, with arms akimbo and a quizzical grin on his freckled phiz, patronizingly inquired,—

" Well, young feller, who made *them* clothes ?"

Lambert considered a moment before making reply. One of his favorite instructors at the Academy had spoken to the graduating class about the splendid timber to be found among the rank and file of the army. " They are like so many old oaks," said he, and some of Lambert's chums had never forgotten it. Neither had Lambert. " This," said he to himself, " is possibly one of the scrub oaks. I assume he doesn't imagine me to be an officer, and, in any event, he could say so and I couldn't prove the contrary. Ergo, I'll let him into the secret without letting him imagine I'm nettled."

" They were made by my tailor, corporal," said he. " He also made the uniform which I, perhaps, should have put on before coming out to camp." (" That ought to fetch him," thought he.) " Where will I find Captain Close ?"

"*He's* over there," said the corporal, with a careless jerk of the head in the direction of the opposite wall tent. "Then I s'pose you're the new lieutenant the fellers have been talking about?"

"I am; and would you mind telling me how long you've been in service?"

"Me? Oh, I reckon about two months,—longer 'n you have, anyhow. You ain't joined yet, have you?" And the corporal was nibbling at a twig now and looking up in good-humored interest. Then, as Lambert found no words for immediate reply, he went on, "Cap's awake, if you want to see him." And, amazed at this reception, yet not knowing whether to be indignant or amused, Lambert sprang down the pathway, crossed the open space between the tents, a dozen of the men starting up to stare at but none to salute him, and halted before the tent of his company commander.

Sitting just within the half-opened flap, a thick-set, burly man of middle age was holding in his left hand a coarse needle, while with the right he was making unsuccessful jabs with some black thread at the eye thereof. So intent was he upon this task that he never heard Lambert's light footfall nor noted his coming, and the lieutenant, while pausing a moment irresolute, took quick observation of the stranger and his surroundings. He was clad in the gray shirt and light-blue trousers such as were worn by the rank and file. An ordinary soldier's blouse was thrown over the back of the camp-stool on which he sat, and his feet were encased in the coarse woollen socks and heavy brogans with leathern thongs, just exactly such as the soldier cook was wearing at the hissing fire a few paces away. His suspenders were hung about his waist, and in his lap, seat uppermost and showing a rent three inches in length, were a pair of uniform trousers with a narrow welt of dark blue along the outer seam. They were thin and shiny, like bombazine, in places, and the patch which seemed destined to cover the rent was five shades too dark for the purpose. His hands were brown and knotted and hard. He wore a silver ring on the third finger of the left. His face was brown as his hands, and clean shaved (barring the stubble of two days' growth) everywhere, except the heavy "goatee," which, beginning at the corners of his broad, firm mouth, covered thickly his throat and chin. His eyes were large, clear, dark brown in hue, and heavily shaded. His hair, close-cropped and sprinkled with gray, was almost black.

The morning air was keen, yet no fire blazed in the little camp-stove behind him, and the fittings of the tent, so far as the visitor could see, were of the plainest description. Not caring to stand there longer, Lambert cleared his throat and began :

"I am looking for Captain Close."

Whereupon the man engaged in threading his needle slowly opened the left eye he had screwed tight shut, and, as slowly raising his head, calmly looked his visitor over and at last slowly replied,—

"That's my name."

III.

Newton Lambert has more than once in the course of his years of service been heard to say that of all the odd sensations he ever experienced that which possessed him on the occasion of his reporting for duty with his first company was the oddest. Accustomed during his four years of cadet life to behave with punctilious respect in the presence of officers, young or old, and accustomed also through his two months' detail at the Academy that summer to be treated with even the exaggerated deference which the old non-commissioned officers seemed to delight in showing to young graduates, Lambert was unprepared for the hail-fellow-well-met nature of his reception by the enlisted men and the absolute impassiveness of his one brother officer. That it was utterly different from the customs obtaining elsewhere in the regular service he knew very well. In visiting classmates already on duty with their batteries among the New York and New England forts, as well as during his brief stay at the barracks, he had noted the scrupulous deference of the veteran sergeants when addressing their officers. He could understand awkwardness and clumsiness among the recruits, but the idea of a corporal chaffing him on the cut of his clothes and—the idea of a two months' recruit being a corporal, anyhow! Never in the tales told of the Fire Zouaves of '61 had he heard of anything much more free-and-easy than the manners of this camp of regulars. Never in his wildest dream had he figured such a specimen of the commissioned officer as he had found in Captain Close. In the contemplation of this character the go-as-you-please style of the enlisted man sank into insignificance. Long years afterwards Lambert used to go over this meeting in his mind, and for two years, often importuned, he would convulse his brother officers by vivid description of it. But there came a time when they no longer laughed and he no longer told the story save to those he loved and trusted utterly.

Aroused by some unusual chatter among the men, the first sergeant of Company "G," smoking a pipe while working over a ration-return, stuck his head out of his tent and saw a young gentleman in a light-colored suit, courteously raising a drab Derby in his kid-gloved hand, while he stood erect with soldierly ease before the company commander. Sergeant Burns also noted that some of the men were tittering and all of them looking on. One glance was enough. The sergeant dropped pen and pipe and came out of his den with a single bound, buttoning his blouse and glaring about him as he did so. "Hush your d—d gab, you!" he fiercely growled at the nearest group. "Get into your coats, there!" he swore at another, while with menacing hand he motioned to others still, whose costume was even more primitive, to scramble back to their tents. In ten seconds silence reigned throughout the camp almost as complete as that which was maintained, for that time, at the tent of the commanding officer. Lambert actually did not know what to say in response to his superior's announcement. It was full ten seconds, or more, before he determined in what form to couch his next remark. He had intended to say, "I have the honor to report for duty, sir;" but a vague suspicion possessed him that this might be some game at his expense,—some prank such as old cadets played upon "plebes." He compromised, therefore, between his preconception of a strictly soldierly report and his sense of what might be due his own dignity. "My name is Lambert," said he. "And I am here for duty as second lieutenant."

Slowly the man in the camp-chair laid down his work, sticking the needle into the flap of the tent and hanging the thread upon it. Then he heaved up out of the chair, hung the damaged trousers over its back, and came ponderously forward. Not a vestige of a smile lightened his face. He looked the young gentleman earnestly in the eye and slowly extended his big, brown, hairy hand. Seeing that it was meant for him, Lambert shifted his hat into the left, leaning his sword against the tent-pole, and his dainty kid—a wild extravagance so soon after the war—was for an instant clasped, then slowly released. Captain Close unquestionably had a powerful "grip."

"How'd you come?" he asked. "Kind of expected you Monday evenin'—out from Quitman."

"The general kept me over a day or two to let me see New Orleans. He told me that you would be notified, sir. I hope you got the letter?"

"Oh, yes. That was all right. There was no hurry. I didn't know as they could get passes over the Northern. I s'pose the chief quartermaster fixed it for you, though?" And the brown eyes searched questioningly the young officer's face.

"Passes? No, sir; I bought my ticket through——"

"No! Why, you needn't have done that. The Quitman road's biddin' for all the government freight it can get now. They'd have given you a pass in a minute. I s'pose you want to be quartermaster and commissary?" And again the brown eyes looked almost wistfully into the blue.

"I? No indeed, sir: I don't know anything but a little tactics. What I most want"—with a glance around and an apologetic laugh—"is a chance to wash off the cinders—and something to eat. I'm hungry as a wolf."

The captain looked troubled. "I've had my grub; so've the men, 'cept those that come back late in the night—been up to Buckatubbee with the marshal. Did you try over at Toog'loo?"

"Everybody was asleep over there. I left my trunk at the railway and walked out."

"Why, I told the sergeant to send a mule in last night on the chance of your comin' by the 'Owl.' Didn't anybody meet you?"

"There was a mule, but no body," laughed Lambert, "except a darky asleep in a freight-car. The mule was lying in the dirt, and snapped his headstall when I tried to raise him."

"What became of him? He didn't get away, did he?" asked Close, in great anxiety.

"He didn't try to," answered Lambert, in some amusement. "Like the eminent head of the late unpleasantness, all he asked was to be let alone. I left him browsing in the public square."

"And the bridle an' saddle, too? Great Peter! That's bad. Some lousy nigger 's got him by this time, or his trappin's at least, an' he'll swear the Freedman's Bureau gave him the hull outfit, and it'll be stopped against my pay. *Sergeant!*" he called: "wish you'd go right down town an' catch up that mule an'——"

"*I* can't go, sir," promptly answered Sergeant Burns, his hand going up in unaccustomed salute in deference to the presence of the new officer. "I'm busy with them ration-returns. Here, Finney, you go."

"Go where?" said a young soldier squatting at his tent door and greasing a pair of shoes with a bit of bacon-rind. He hardly deigned to look up.

"The captain wants you to go and get that saddle-mule he sent up last night. Jake must have gone asleep and forgot him."

"Would it be possible to send a wagon for my trunk?" interposed Lambert at this juncture, appealing to his superior. Close hesitated and made no immediate reply. It was the sergeant who took the responsibility:

"*I'll* 'tend to it, if you please, sir. The wagon's going up in ten minutes to haul some grain.—Be lively now, Finney. Drop them shoes and start." And Finney, conscious, possibly, of some change in the military atmosphere, gathered himself together and vanished.

Meantime, in his anxiety about the government property thus placed in jeopardy, the captain seemed lost to all thought of the new-comer's comfort. It was Sergeant Burns who came forward with a camp-stool and proffer of further hospitality.

"If the lieutenant can put up with such rations, I'll send something from the cook-fire, sir," said he, doubtfully, looking at his commander very much as though he thought it high time for that official to suggest something better. Lambert said he should be most grateful if that could be done—and if there were no objections; and he, too, looked expectantly at the senior officer.

"I guess that's about the best we can do," said Close, slowly. "'Tain't what you've been accustomed to, but it's what *I* always eat. Send us up somethin', sergeant,—enough for two: I'll take another snack with the lieutenant."

And in less than five minutes Lambert and his new comrade were seated by a little fire on which a tin coffee-pot was hissing, and, with a broad pine shelf upon their knees, from big tin mugs and broad tin plates, were discussing a smoking repast of pork and beans, to the accompaniment of bread and syrup and creamless coffee. "It's the way I always prefer to live when I'm in the field," said Close, "and it only costs you nine dollars a month."

Lambert was too hungry not to relish even such a breakfast. He fancied he heard something that sounded greatly like a suppressed chuckle on the part of the soldier cook at his senior's remark upon the cost of living in the field, but sensations and experiences were crowding thickly upon him and there was little time for trifles.

Through the good offices of Sergeant Burns, a wall tent was pitched

that morning for " the new lieutenant" to the left of the domicile of
the company commander; a wooden bunk was knocked up in an " A "
tent in the back, and Lambert began unpacking his trunk and setting
up housekeeping.

"I suppose I can get what furniture I want in town," said he to
Close.

"Depends on what you want," replied the senior, warily, "and
whether you care to throw away your money. What'd you want to
get? They will skin the last cent out of you there at Cohen's."

"I merely want some cheap truck for camp, and some wash-stand
fixings," Lambert answered, falling into the vernacular of his comrade
with the ease of one just out of the national school, where every known
American dialect can be heard,—" things I can throw away when we
leave."

Close was silent a moment. "*I* can let you have everything you
need, 'f you ain't particular 'bout their bein' new. They're just as
good as anything you can buy, and won't cost you near so much."
Then, after a little hesitation, "They ain't mine to give, or I'd let you
have them for nothing."

Lambert had precious little money left, even after drawing his
November pay in New Orleans; but he had a big mileage account to
collect, for in those days nothing was paid to the young graduate in
advance, even though he had to find his way by the Isthmus to the
mouth of the Columbia. He thanked his comrade, and by evening
was put in possession of an odd lot of camp-furniture, some items of
which were in good repair and others valuable only as relics of the
war. A camp-mattress and some chairs bore the name of Tighe, and
the soldier who carried them in remarked to his chum, "They didn't
burn everything after the lieutenant died, after all, did they?" From
which Lambert drew the inference that the property in question had
formerly belonged to an officer of that name who succumbed to the
epidemic of the previous year.

But the principal question remaining unsolved was that of sub-
sistence. Waring and Pierce had told him that in all probability he
would find that Close was living on soldier fare and had no "mess
arrangements" whatever. This, as we have seen, proved to be the
case,—and Lambert inquired if there were no possibility of finding
board. "Yes," said Close; "Mr. Parmelee, the deputy marshal, lives
up the road about half a mile, and he told me to say he'd be glad to

accommodate you." Lambert lunched in camp at noon, and about three o'clock came forth from his tent buttoned to the throat in his handsomely fitting uniform, his forage-cap cocked jauntily over his right eye, and a pair of white gloves in his hand. A soldier slouching across the open space in front shifted to the opposite hand the bucket he was carrying, and saluted. Close surveyed his trim subaltern without changing a muscle of his face.

"What do they charge you extra for them buttons?" he finally inquired. Lambert said he didn't know. They were on the coat when it came from the tailor's. Would the captain kindly direct him to Mr. Parmelee's and permit him to go thither? The captain gravely said he need not ask permission just to leave camp,—even the men didn't do that,—and gave him the needed instructions, winding up by saying, "Got your pistol?" Lambert answered that he never carried one.

"You'll *have* to, here," said Close, "or be out of fashion entirely. I ain't got one to lend, but if you've a mind to pay less than cost I've got one that'll just suit you, strap and holster complete." In five minutes the trade was made, and Lambert had only eleven dollars left when he started to hunt up Mr. Parmelee.

Close watched the erect figure of the young fellow as he stepped briskly away. So did the first sergeant. Midway across the open space between the tents half a dozen of the men were squatting, in the bright sunshine, pipes in full blast, engaged in a game of cards that looked suspiciously like draw poker, a gray blanket being outspread and little piles of white field beans decorating its outer edge at different points. Surrounding the players were perhaps a dozen spectators, in various costumes more or less soldierly. At sight of Mr. Lambert in his trim frock-coat, some of the number faced half towards him ; some, as though embarrassed, began to edge away. The gamblers calmly continued their game. If the young officer had looked as though he did not notice them, the chances are that, though he passed within ten feet of the group, no one of the party would, in proper and soldierly style, have noticed *him*, but Lambert had seen enough "slouching" for one day, and his youthful soul was up in arms. He looked squarely at the two men nearest him as he rapidly approached, whereupon one of them nervously tugged at the sleeve of a third. Others, after one furtive glance, pretended they did not see the coming officer and became absorbed in the game. Ten strides, and he was opposite the group and

B   3

not a hand had been raised in salute, not a man was "standing attention." Then he halted short, saying not a word, but the two men nearest knew what was lacking, and, in a shamefaced, shambling way, brought their hands up to the cap visor. One of these was a corporal, and two other non-commissioned officers were among the players. For a moment there was an embarrassed silence. Then Lambert spoke,— rather quietly, too, for him:

"Corporal, have these men never been taught the salute, and when to use it?"

A sergeant among the players slowly found his feet. Others seemed to try to slink behind their fellows. The corporal turned red, looked foolish, and only mumbled inarticulately.

"What say *you*, sergeant?" inquired Lambert.

"Why, yes, sir," said Sergeant McBride, uncomfortably. "So far as I'm concerned, I can honestly say I did not see the lieutenant coming; but, to tell the truth, sir, we've got out of the habit of it in the company."

"Then all these men who are still seated here know they should be up and standing attention?" asked Lambert, as coolly as he could, though his blue eyes were beginning to flash. He had heard some tittering among the gamesters, two more of whom were now getting up.

"Yes, sir; at least most of them do. Only, Captain Close don't seem to mind, and——"

"That'll do.—I am waiting for you two," said Lambert. And the two who, hanging their heads, had been tittering into each other's faces, finding their time had come, slowly and awkwardly found their feet, but not the erect position of the soldier.

"So far so good," said Lambert, calmly.—"Now, sergeant, explain the rest to them, as they seem to be uninstructed recruits."

There was a general titter at this: one of the two was an ex-sergeant of ten years' service,—one of John Barleycorn's defeated wrestlers. His eyes snapped with wrath, but he knew the lieutenant "had the best of him."

"Don't make it necessary for me to repeat the lesson," said Lambert before moving on; "especially you, sir." And the ex-sergeant was plainly the man indicated.

Up at the end of the row Sergeant Burns brought his broad palm down on his thigh with a whack of delight, then glanced over to see how the captain took it.

The captain was carefully counting over the "greenbacks" he had just received, and, with these in hand, turned into the dark recesses of his farther tent. The episode in front was of minor importance.

"*You* got a rakin' down, Riggs," laughed some of the men as the lieutenant was lost to sight beyond the wagon, while the victim of his brief reprimand glowered angrily after him.

"Dam young squirt!" snarled the fellow. "I'll learn *him* a lesson yet."

"No, you won't, Riggs," was the quick rejoinder of McBride. "He was perfectly right, as you ought to have sense enough to know. I'm glad, for one, to see it, for this company has simply been goin' to the dogs for the last six months."

IV.

Lambert's nerves were tingling a trifle and his thoughts were not the most cheerful as he went away. That he should find his company commander a miser, a recluse, and something of a mystery, had all been foreshadowed. But that discipline should have been abandoned in "G" Company was quite another thing. Farnham, the captain proper, was an officer who had held high command in the volunteers,— too high, indeed, to serve with equanimity under the field-officer now at the head of the regiment, who had had no war service whatever. Farnham was within a few files of promotion to majority, and therefore despised company duty. So long as his company had been stationed in the city, furnishing guards and orderlies for the various officials then quartered there, he remained with it, and occasionally saw a portion of it on Sunday morning. Then, after two years of this demoralizing service, came the months of detachment duty up in the interior, and Farnham's friends at court were glad to get him out of such a mire as that. Ever since June, therefore, Close had been alone with the men and they with him, and no one in authority had the faintest idea how things were going. Inspectors were almost unknown in those days, and so long as reports and returns were regularly received at head-quarters, and no complaints came in from the civil authorities of negligence or indifference on part of their military backers, all went smoothly. Now, there had been not a few instances where civil and military officials had clashed, but "Captain Close and his splendid company" had been the theme of more than one laudatory report from the marshal on the score of what he heard from his deputies. The general commanding, indeed, had been much elated by high commendation from the highest power in Washington, all due to services rendered in running down Ku Klux and breaking up moonshiners by Captain Close of Company "G," —th Infantry. "It's just exactly what the old duffer's cut out for," said the adjutant-general of the department; "but I'm sorry to have to see young Lambert sent into such exile."

He could hardly have been sorrier than Lambert was himself as that young officer went briskly up the desolate road along the "branch." He had never seen a landscape so dismal in all his life. How on earth was he to employ his time? No drills, no roll-calls, no duties except the sending forth of detachments at the call of this fellow Parmelee; no books except the few in his trunk; no companions except this heavy, illiterate, money-grubbing lout who did not know enough to offer him a seat or a cup of coffee after his long night ride; not a soul worth knowing nearer than Quitman—and only the inebriate Potts there! Certainly, Mr. Newton Lambert felt at odds with fate this sunny December afternoon. He had tried to persuade himself that the laughable stories about Close were grossly exaggerated; but, now that he had met that officer, the indications were in favor of their entire truth.

It seems that Close had been on some detached service in connection with the Freedmen's Bureau, and had only joined his regiment late in the autumn of the memorable yellow-fever year, when, had he so desired, he could have remained away. His appearance at the stricken garrison when the death-rate averaged twenty a day, when the post was commanded by a lieutenant and some of the companies by corporals,—everybody else being either dead, down, or convalescent,—added to the halo which hung about his hitherto invisible head. There was no question as to his consummate bravery. Grant himself had stopped in rear of his regiment and asked his name after its dash on the works at Donelson, and the unknown private was decorated with sergeant's chevrons on the spot. Before he had opportunity to learn much of his new duties, "the Johnnies jumped the picket" one night and stampeded everybody but Close, who was given up for lost until he came in two days later full of buckshot and information. His colonel acted on the latter while the doctors were digging out the former, and Close got a commission as first lieutenant in a new regiment for his share of the resultant benefits. One bloody afternoon as they were scrambling back, unsuccessful, and under an awful fire, from the works at Vicksburg, the colonel was left writhing on the lead-swept glacis with no shelter but the dead and dying around him, and Close headed the squad that rushed out and fetched him in. Everybody at McPherson's side could see that the Rebs were firing high, when once the daring survivors of the six who started reached their prostrate colonel, but the bullets sounded just as deadly to the four who got back alive, and McPherson sent for Close and wrung his hard brown hand and looked admiringly into the sombre, impassive face with its deep-brown, almost dog-like, eyes. Some of the Thirteenth regulars were the next to report on Close, and these fellows, being at Sherman's head-quarters, had influence. In the midst of so rough a campaign Close looked but little worse for wear than did his associates, and when he brought in ten prisoners with only two men at his back, turned them over to the Thirteenth, and went in for more before anybody could thank him, "Uncle Billy" swore that man was one of the right sort, and asked him what he could do for him that very night. And then—so the story ran—Close said he guessed he'd like to be either a sutler or a quartermaster,—he didn't know which,—and for once in his life the popular general looked bewildered.

After Mission Ridge, where he got another bullet through him, and one that would have killed an ox, they simply *had* to put Close on quartermaster duty, he wanted it so much and had done such splendid fighting and so little talking for it. That was the end of him until near the end of the war. His train was captured by a dash of Forrest's cavalry, and, though most of the guards got away, Close went with his wagons. Andersonville was then his abiding-place for a time, but in some way he turned up again during the march to the sea, which he made on mule-back, and when Congress authorized the organization of sixteen regiments of infantry as a part of the regular army in '66, the great generals at the head of military affairs were reminded of Close. He wrote from somewhere far out West saying modestly that they had told him to let them know if they could ever be of any use to him, and the time had come. He had concluded to continue soldiering, and wanted to be a quartermaster. He was offered a first-lieutenantcy in the infantry, and accepted, though the examining board shook their heads over his ill-written papers ; was applied for by the colonel whose life he had saved at Vicksburg, and who was now on " bureau duty" in the South ; and on that work Close remained, despite some rumors of his unfitness, until the fever cut its wide swath in his regiment. The adjutant and quartermaster were both down when Close arrived and reported for duty. In his calm, stolid, impassive way, he proved vastly useful. Indeed, at a time when men were dying or deserting by scores, when even sentry-duty had to be abandoned, and when government property was being loaded up and carried away and sold in the city, it is difficult to say what losses might not have been sustained but for his tireless vigilance. He exposed himself fearlessly among the dying. He said he had had a light attack of the fever at New Iberia earlier in the season, and couldn't take it again. At all events, he did not. He was probably the only officer who remained longer than a week at the stricken post and escaped.

At last came the welcome frost, Yellow Jack's conqueror, followed by new officers and recruits in plenty, and Close's occupation was gone. He had helped to bury the adjutant, but the quartermaster proved tough, and—to Close's keen disappointment, as the boys began to say with returning health, appetite, and cynicism—recovered from his desperate illness and resumed his duties. When December and the new colonel came, drills and dress uniforms were ordered, and Close got leave of absence and tried to get back to bureau duty, where they did not want him. Then he appealed to Farnham, and through him to General Sherman. His wounds made him stiff and sore: he couldn't drill or parade. It transpired that he had no full uniform, and his first and only frock-coat had been let out to the last shred and was still too tight for him. Then some queer yarns began to be told. He was a *quasi* executor for three officers who had died intestate, and who had little to bequeath anyhow. He had nursed them in their last illness, and such items of their property as had not by medical orders been condemned and burned he had for sale. Under the regulations the major was the proper custodian of the effects of deceased officers, but the major was himself almost a victim and had been sent North to recuperate after a long and desperate struggle. On an occasion when he simply *had* to appear in full uniform, Close turned out in plumed felt hat, sash, and epaulets which, when questioned, he said were the late Captain Stone's, and so was the coat. If nobody could be found to buy them, he would, but he did not mean to buy "such truck" until it was absolutely necessary.

Respect for his fighting ability in the field and his fearless service during the epidemic prevented any "crowding" of the old fellow, though there was no little talk about the habits he was disclosing. The bachelors and "grass widowers" of the infantry and battery started a mess, but Close declined to join. He explained that he preferred to board with a French creole family a short distance away, as he "wished to learn the language." They gave a big dance Christmas week and taxed every officer ten dollars. Close had nursed Pierce through the fever, and Pierce was treasurer of the fund. Close was accounted for as "paid," both for the original ten and the subsequent assessment of five dollars that was found necessary, but it came out of Pierce's pocket, for Close begged off one and refused the other, and Pierce would not tell until it was dragged out of him by direct questioning months after. It transpired that Close went only once a day to the humble dwelling, four blocks away, where he preferred to board. He assiduously visited the kitchen of Company "G" at breakfast- and dinner-time to see that those meals were properly cooked and served, and there could be no question that he personally "sampled" everything they had. He wore the clothing issued to the men, until the colonel insisted on his appearing in proper uniform, and then had to rebuke him for the condition of the paper collar and frayed black bow that were attached to the neck-band of his flannel shirt. He wore the soldier shoe, and swore that no other kind suited his foot. He had to write letters occasionally, but when he did so he repaired to the company office or that of the post quartermaster, and not one cent did he spend for stamps.

Indeed, it became a subject of unofficial investigation whether he spent a cent for anything. He bought nothing at Finkbein's, the sutler's, where indeed he was held in high disfavor, his war record and fever service to the contrary notwithstanding. He never touched a card, never played billiards, and never invited anybody to drink, even when his brother officers called upon him in squads of two or three to see if he would. That he had no prejudice against the practice, then as universal in the service as it is now rare, was apparent from the fact that he never refused to take a drink when invited, yet never seemed even faintly exhilarated. "You might as well pour whiskey in a knot-hole," said the sore-headed squad of youngsters that with malice prepense had spent many hours and dollars one night in the attempt to get old Close "loaded."

He had to go to town occasionally on board of survey or similar duty, and always sought a seat in somebody's ambulance to save the nickel charged for a six-mile ride in the tram-car. When he *had* to take the car he would wait for some of the youngsters, well knowing they would pay his fare. Once when three of them "put up a job on him" by the declaration, after they were well on their way, that not a man in the party had less than a five-dollar bill, he offered to change the five, but refused to lend a nickel unless they gave their word, on honor, that they were not striving to make a convenience of him.

But the "closest" figuring he had ever done was that which he carried out for several months at the expense of a certain bank. Most of the officers on getting their pay check towards the end of the month would take it to the nearest bank or broker and get it cashed. Those were easy-going days in the pay department. Many a time the impecunious subs would prevail on the major or his clerk to let them have their stipend a week before it became due, and it would be spent before it was fully earned. Close never spent a cent, that any one could see or hear of, but he was on hand to draw it as early as any of the rest. He would take his check and vanish. The total footing up of his pay, rations, servant's allowance, "fogy," and all, was one hundred and some dollars and sixty-eight cents. They used no coin smaller than the "nickel" (five cents) in the South in those days, and it was the practice of the banks and money-changers generally to give the customer the benefit if the check called for more than half the value of the nickel, otherwise to hold it themselves. If the amount were fifty-two cents the customer got only fifty; if it were fifty-three cents he was paid fifty-five. Those officers who kept a bank account, and there were three or four, perhaps, who did so, simply deposited their check for its face value and had done with it. It was supposed that such was Close's custom; but he was wiser in his generation, as was learned later. Close took his check to the paying teller and got one hundred and some dollars and seventy cents. Then he deposited this cash with the clerk at the receiving window and was two cents ahead by the transaction. When it was finally discovered and he was politely told that hereafter he would be credited only with the sum called for on the face of his check, Close got it cashed elsewhere and deposited his seventy cents regularly as before. "But what he does it for is a mystery," said the bank official who let this sizable cat out of the bag, "for he never has more than a few dollars on deposit more than a week. He checks it out through some concerns up North."

No wonder the fellows wondered what Close did with his money.

A soldier servant made up his room and blacked his boots; a company laundress washed the very few items sent to her each week, and declared that the captain stopped the price of two pairs of gloves out of her wages because she wore the thumb off one of them scrubbing the dirt off the other. He never went to theatre, opera, or other diversion; never took part in any of the gayeties of the garrison; never subscribed for a newspaper or magazine, but was always on hand to get first look at those service journals which were intended for the post library. He smoked an old black brier-root pipe, which he charged with commissary plug tobacco, preferring it to all others. He chewed tobacco—navy plug—and did not care who knew it. He shaved himself, and when his hair needed trimming it was done by the company barber. He had no bills. He would be neither borrower nor—well, there *was* some talk about his lending money on unimpeachable security and usurious interest, but to those officers who applied, either in jest or earnest, he said he never had a cent to lend and wouldn't lend it if he had.

Then what on earth *did* Close do with his money?

Much of this was told to Lambert in New Orleans. More of it he learned later. On this particular day he was destined to have another peep into the peculiarities of this most unusual character.

He had walked perhaps half a mile, revolving these matters in his mind and keeping occasional lookout for Parmelee's (which was evidently farther away than he had been led to suppose), when he heard some one shouting after him. It was a soldier, running hard, and in a moment Lambert recognized in him the affable corporal who was the first to receive him that morning. This time the corporal saluted as he came, panting, to a halt. Possibly Sergeant Burns had been giving the company a " pointer."

" Did anybody pass you, lieutenant?—anybody on horseback?"

" No," answered Lambert, wondering what might now be coming.

" Well, cap says—er rather—the captain wants you to come back. Didn't *nobody* go along here a-horseback?" And the corporal was evidently perplexed as well as nearly breathless. " By gad, I thought 'twas takin' chances, even for the two of us. Two of 'em rode in an' sassed cap right to his face an' were off before a man of us could draw bead on 'em."

" Who are *they?*"

" Some o' the very crowd Parmelee nabbed last night. They must

B*

have cut across at the ford. They've finished *him*, I reckon, for one of 'em was ridin' his horse."

In ten minutes Lambert was back at camp, where all was bustle and suppressed excitement.   Close was seated at his tent, smoking imperturbably, and listening to the tremulous words of a tall, sallow civilian who was leaning against the shoulder of a panting mule. McBride, rifle in hand and equipped for field service, was closely inspecting the kit and cartridge-boxes of a squad of a dozen men already formed.

"Lieutenant," said Close, "I've got to send you with a detachment over to the county jail. How soon can you get read*y* ?"

Lambert felt a sudden odd, choky sensation at the throat, and was conscious that his knees were tremulous.   It was his first call, mind you, and it was sudden and vague.   The symptoms made him furious.

"I'm ready now," he said, reaching for his handsome sash and belt, and disappearing an instant within his tent door.

"Ain't you got some ord'nery things?   You don't want to wear such trappin's as them.   I've got a sash an' belt an' sword here plenty good enough ; and you can have 'em for half what they cost."

"I prefer using these, captain," said Lambert.

"Why, you may not get back in a week," persisted Close. "There's no tellin' where those fellows have run to.   You ought to have some suitable clothes for this sort o' work—like mine."

"I've got something different, but I thought we were needed at once."

"So you be, 'cordin' to what this gentleman says.   It looks like they must have stirred up quite a row ; but you needn't worry. There'll be no trouble once they see the regulars, and if there should be, you've got me an' the hull company to draw on."   And Close's face fairly brightened up for the minute.   "There's your squad ready. Parm'lee 'll tell you what he wants done.   Reck'lect, if there's any trouble you draw on me."

"I shall need some money, I'm afraid, if we're gone any time. That's the first thing I'll have to draw for."

Close's countenance fell.   "Ten dollars ought to be 'nuff for you anywhere here.   I could get along with fifty cents," said he, slowly. Suddenly he brightened up again.

"Just sit down an' make out them mileage accounts o' yours. —Here, sergeant, you and this gentleman go on with the squad.   Take the county road. The lieutenant 'll overtake you.—Sit right down over there in Sergeant Burns's tent, lieutenant: he's got all the blanks and things. Never made out a mileage account? Here, I'll show you."

And while Close slowly began his calculations, the squad under Sergeant McBride tramped out upon the dusty red road, most of the men following as though to see them around the bend, while Lambert, vaguely troubled, and feeling, somehow, that he ought to be with his detachment even though his superior officer called him back, stood looking anxiously after them.

"I thought you had twenty or so left in your wallet, lieutenant," said Close. "Just look, will you? *You* needn't be in any hurry. McBride knows just what to do. I'd change them clothes if I was you."

Lambert had slipped his hand into his breast-pocket, then began searching the others. All in vain: the little, flat pocket-book was gone; and now it flashed across his mind that he must have whisked it out with his handkerchief, which he carried, after the West Point fashion of those days, in the breast of his coat, just after he started on the run back to camp. Even as he began to tell of his loss the men came springing down the bank and bursting through the bushes in their haste to reach their arms and equipments.

"What's up *now?*" hailed Close, still slowly writing and never moving from his seat.

"Firing over near town, sir," called a sergeant.

"That so?" asked the veteran, imperturbably. "Get 'em under arms, sergeant.—Guess you'd better ketch up with McBride, lieutenant," said he to Lambert, whose boyish face could not but betray his excitement. "Hold on a second," he called, for Lambert had darted at the word. "*Wait*, lieutenant!" shouted Burns, and, wondering, Lambert looked back. Close was holding out the pen to him.

"Sign these, first off, will you?" said he.

V.

Long before they reached the public square the firing had ceased. Overtaking his little command, which the sergeant had wisely halted "for orders" as soon as the shots were heard, Lambert led them at double time.

"Put a stop to anything they're at. I'll be after you with the hull company," Close had shouted after him. The deputy marshal had disappeared.

"Mr. Parmelee somewhere ahead?" panted the lieutenant to the sergeant trotting by his side.

"Somewhere *behind*, sir. He'll come gallopin' in after we get there,—perhaps."

The road led into town from the northeast. Lambert could see the railway embankment and the old wooden bridge before they rounded the turn from which they came in sight of the belfry and the roofs. Somebody had begun to ring the bell, and there came the sound of shouting, with an occasional shrill yell. Then more shots, a short, sputtering fusillade, and more shouts, suggestively derisive and farther away.

"What's going on, do you suppose?" asked Lambert of his bulky second in command ; and McBride, with one hand steadying the absurd long-sword then worn by our sergeants, and the other clamping his rifle at the right shoulder, puffingly answered,—

"Havin' some fun with the sheriff. He had a nigger posse guardin' the jail. Folks wouldn't stand it."

Another minute of running brought them to the outskirts of the straggling town. Women and children could be seen peering excitedly towards the square. Two very small boys, hearing the heavy tramp, tramp of the infantry, turned and scuttled away for the shelter of an open door. Three hundred yards ahead a man in his shirt-sleeves popped around a corner, looked keenly at the coming squad, and popped back again. When Lambert, leading his men by a dozen paces, came dancing around that same corner and found himself at the northeast angle of the plaza, this same citizen was seated on the nearest porch, placidly smoking a corn-cob pipe and reading a newspaper, his boots braced against a wooden pillar and his chair tilted back against the wall. In similar attitudes of exaggerated calm, farther along in the direction of the post-office, were one or two other gentlemen of Tugaloo. Only around Cohen's mercantile emporium was there faintest sign of excitement. There one or two trembling, pallid clerks were bustling about and putting up the shutters. The gang of negroes ordinarily loafing around the plaza had totally vanished. Lambert, expecting to find himself in the presence of a surging mob, came to sudden halt in sheer surprise. The squad "slowed down" at a sign from their sergeant, and then, closing up their rank, marched silently ahead in quick time.

"Where's the jail?" asked Lambert of his subordinate.

"Round there behind the next corner, sir,—where the bell is."

Three or four prominent citizens came strolling out of the saloon nearest the post-office, their hands in their pockets and quids of exaggerated size in their cheeks. The bell, under the impulse of unseen hands, was still violently ringing: otherwise an almost Sabbath stillness pervaded the town of Tugaloo. At the corner lay a gaunt quadruped, blood trickling from its nostrils and from a shot-hole in the side,—sole indication of recent battle. The jail door stood obligingly open to the declining sun. The barred windows were tightly closed.

"'Put a stop to anything they're at,'" repeated Lambert to himself. "But what *are* they at?, How on earth can I find out?"

Like those of the jail behind it, the windows of the little meeting-house were closed, and apparently boarded up from within. The double doors in front were tight shut and decorated in one or two places with bullet-holes. The bell kept up its furious din. "Hammer the door with the butt of your rifle," said the lieutenant, annoyed to see that such of the populace as began to appear were looking on in unmistakable amusement.

"Guess they're all down in the cellar, lieutenant," said a tall civilian. "Want any of 'em? Reckon they'll come up 'f you'll tell Squire Parmelee to shout. Don't seem to see him, though." And the grinning countryman was presently joined by one or two of his friends. Lambert simply did not know what to make of the situation. Sergeant McBride was going around hammering at one shutter after another and muttering something about "dam fools inside." A corporal with a couple of men had explored the two rooms of the primitive building used as a jail, and now came out to say there was nobody there, which seemed to tickle the fancy of the rallying populace. Still the bell kept up its deafening clamor, and Lambert was waxing both nervous and indignant. The absence of the civil officer of the law—the deputy marshal or sheriff—rendered him practically powerless to act. He could not pitch into the people for standing around with their hands in their pockets and looking amused. There was nothing hostile or threatening in their manner. They were even disposed to be friendly,—as, when they saw Lambert take a rifle with evident inten-

4

tion of battering in the door, they shouted to him in genuine concern, "Don't do that, lieutenant. Those fellows will be shootin' up through the floor next. The squire'll be along presently. Let *him* do it."

Presently the squire *did* come, still "white about the gills," as the sergeant muttered; and him Lambert angrily accosted :

"What do you want us to do, Mr. Parmelee? We've been here several minutes now with nobody to report to."

"I s'pose my poor fellows are murdered to a man," cried Parmelee, sliding off his mule and handing the reins to a soldier, who coolly transferred them to the nearest post. "Can't you make 'em hear, McBride?"

"Not if they're all dead," answered the sergeant, disgustedly. "Which corpse is pullin' the bell-rope?" At this unfeeling remark the populace again began to laugh.

"Oh, you'll pay for this, you fellows!" tremblingly shouted Parmelee to the grinning group across the street. "If there's law in Washington and power to back it, you'll ketch hell."

"*Whawt's* been the matter, squire?" asked a citizen, soothingly. "Ain't anybody hurt, is there? I ain't heard nothin' of any row."

Parmelee pointed to the carcass of the mule and to some significant shot-holes at the corner. "I s'pose you'll deny shootin'—or hearin' any shootin'—next."

"Shootin'? Shootin' roun' *hyuh?* Why, doggone 'f that ain't the queerest thing! I *thought* I heard somebody pullin' off a pistol awhile ago. Don't you remember, major?—I reckon 'twas you I was talkin' with at the time,—I said there was a shot fired. P'r'aps that's what killed Potts's ole mule out *yuh.*"

"For heaven's sake, man," muttered Lambert, "stop that infernal bell and your own jaw. Can't you see they're just laughing at you?" And Parmelee evidently did.

"My God, lieutenant! they've mobbed the jail, let loose three of the worst scoundrels ever went unhung, and killed the officers of the law. They ought to be arrested right here,—every one of them, —'stead of standin' there insultin' the United States government. If Captain Close was here *he'd* have 'em in in less than a minute."

"He'll be here presently, if you want any arresting done. Meantime, the only row is that which your people seem to be making. Can't you stop that?"

Parmelee looked helpless and despondent. "Somethin's got to be done," he said, "or these rebels'll ride right over you. Why, every man you see's had a hand in this jail delivery. We had great trouble 'restin' those three scoundrels: the marshal's been after 'em a month, and he ought to have met us here, 's I telegraphed him. We fetched 'em here at four o'clock this mornin', an' not a soul in Tugaloo knew anything about it, an' the soldiers ought to have stood by us until the marshal came. 'Stead of that, they went on to camp and left us all alone, and just as soon as these people found out who were jailed an' saw we had no soldiers to guard 'em, why, I couldn't do nothin'. They just took my horse and—they'd have hung me, I s'pose, if I'd been fool enough to stay. I just 'scaped with my life. You've just got here, lieutenant. You don't begin to know what a hell-hole this is. These people are the worst kind o' rebs. Capt'n Close—even he wouldn't b'lieve it, but I reckon he does now, after the tongue-lashin' them fellers gave him——"

But Mr. Parmelee's description of the situation was interrupted by the coming of Captain Close himself. Dressed precisely as when Lambert had last seen him at camp, with no more semblance of rank or authority than was to be found in a weather-beaten pair of shoulder-straps on his cheap flannel blouse, without sash or sword, but with a huge army "Colt" strapped about his waist, the commander of the company came strolling around the corner of the jail, looking curiously about its door and windows as though in search of signs of the recent affray.

"Thought you told me they'd shot the door into tooth-picks," said he. "I don't see no signs of bullets."

"Come round here an' you'll see 'em. *I* wasn't goin' to let my men be shot like cattle in a pen. I got 'em out o' there soon 's we saw the crowd a-comin'."

"Then you didn't even show fight,—didn't even attempt to hold your prisoners?" exclaimed Close, in high dudgeon. "Why, great Peter! man, your birds just walked out without any one's helpin' 'em. You and your cowardly gang walked off and let 'em go; an' they've taken our mule. That's the worst of it,—taken our mule to replace that dam carcass there, that b'longed to the father of one of the boys you brought in this mornin'. He told the truth 'bout it then, when he rode into camp an' said your posse had shot his mule an' threatened to shoot him. What sort of a sand-heap were you raised on, anyhow? Why, 'f a *baby* in the town I come from had shown as little grit as you and your folks have, its own mother would have drowned it in the mill-race."

The effect of this unexpected tirade was remarkable. The knot of civilian listeners, who had come to get such fun out of the situation as the circumstances would permit, and who had been indulging in no little half-stifled laughter, were evidently amazed at this new side to the Yankee officer's character, and stood silent and decidedly appreciative listeners to his denunciation of the luckless Parmelee. The soldiers, who had for some months been tasting the comforts of military service under civil control, and trudging all over Chittomingo County, day in and day out, on the mysterious mission of " serving process," were evidently tickled that their commander should at last have seen for himself what they had more than half suspected all along,—that Parmelee was an arrant coward, who had held his position and made his record for efficiency in enforcing the laws only when a big squad of regulars was at his back.

As for Lambert, whose sole knowledge of affairs in the South was derived from the accounts published in the Northern journals and inspired almost without exception by " carpet-bag" politicians, and who fully expected to find himself pitted against a determined array of ex-Confederates engaged in the slaughter of Federal officials, white and black, the young New-Englander began to look upon the whole affair as another practical joke devised by his new associates simply " to test his grit or gullibility." This, at least, was his first impression, until the sight of the main body of the company swinging into the square under command of the first sergeant, and another look at Close's burning brown eyes and Parmelee's hangdog face, convinced him that so far as they were concerned there was no joke.

But how about the chuckling natives now augmenting their number every moment? Certainly there could be no doubt as to the contempt they felt for " the Squire," as they facetiously termed Parmelee, or the ridicule which Close's appearance had excited until he had well-nigh finished his denunciation of the civil officer. Then for an instant there was almost a ripple of applause. They watched him as, in his uncouth, ill-fitting, unsoldierly garb, the commander strode angrily back and began searching the walls and window-shutters of the jail for sign of bullet-marks.

Meantime, gradually recovering confidence or hope, the besieged in the cellar of the meeting-house began to parley. The bell ceased ringing, and humble voices were heard asking who were outside. A brusque order in Close's gruffest tones to " Come up out of that hole and account for your prisoners," seemed to cause unlimited joy. There was sound of unbarring doors and scrambling on wooden stairs, and presently the portals opened an inch or two and cautious peeps were taken. The sight of the blue uniforms was enough. The defenders, white and colored, to the number of six, dusty but uninjured, came gladly forth into the afternoon sunshine. "By gad, fellows, we had hard work standin' off that crowd till you come," began the foremost, another of the Parmelee type. "There must ha' been half Chittomingo County in here, and the bullets flew like——"

But here a guffaw of derisive laughter from across the street, the crestfallen face of Parmelee, and the quizzical grin on the sun-tanned features of the soldiers, put sudden check to his flow of words. There stood Close, glowering at him.

"Flew like what, you gibberin' idiot? The only bullet-hole in the hull square that hasn't been here for six weeks is the one in that wuthless mule there. You dam cowards ran for shelter an' let your pris'ners loose : that's plain as the nose on your face. I don't care for the pris'ners,—that's *your* bus'ness ; but what I want's *our* mule.— Lieutenant Lambert," he continued, addressing his silent junior, " I'm as ready as any man to fight for the flag, but for six months now I've been sittin' here furnishin' posses to back up these fellers makin' arrests all over the country, because them was my orders. *I* haven't seen a nigger abused. *I* haven't seen the uniform insulted. *I* haven't seen a sign of Ku-Klux : nothin' but some contraband stills. I've obeyed orders an' helped 'em make arrests of people I don't personally know nothin' about, an' you see for yourself they dasn't lift a hand to hold 'em. I'm tired o' backin' up such a gang of cowards, an' I don't care who knows it. March the men back to camp, sir. I'm goin' after that mule."

VI.

With the going down of that evening's sun Lieutenant Newton Lambert had finished his first day of company duty in the sunny South, and found himself commanding the temporary post of Tugaloo. The responsibility now devolving upon him was the only thing that enabled him to resist an almost overwhelming sensation of depression and disgust. Marching at route step back to camp, he had held brief and low-toned conference with Sergeant Burns and learned something of the circumstances that led up to the events of the day. "Old man Potts," said the sergeant, was a character. He owned a place half-way over towards Quitman and so near the county line that nobody knew whether he rightfully belonged to Quitman or to Chittomingo. When he was "wanted" in one he dodged to the other. Two of his sons had been killed during the war, and the two younger were prominent both as citizens and "skylarkers," for "there was no mischief or frolic going on they weren't mixed up in." Sergeant Burns didn't believe in Ku-Klux thereabouts, but the colored folks and the deputy marshals did, and so the soldiers were kept "on the jump." Old man Potts had "cussed" Parmelee off his place two weeks previous, but had ridden in to Quitman and reported himself to Brevet Lieutenant-Colonel Sweet, commanding the two-company garrison there, and said that any time he or his boys were "wanted," just to say so and he would come in and account for himself and them to an officer and a gentleman, but he'd be damned if he'd allow that sneak Parmelee on his premises. Then he had had high words with the marshal of the district himself. His boys had harmed no one, he said. They were full of fun, and perhaps of fight—he wouldn't own 'em if they weren't : but they did not belong to the Ku-Klux,—if there were anything of the sort around there at all,—and they only fought when interfered with. They might have expressed contempt for Parmelee, but *that* wasn't law-breaking. The marshal told him that very serious allegations had been laid against both him and his boys, as well as against friends with whom they forgathered, and warned him that arrest would follow if more "outrages" occurred ; and the result was that only the interference of Colonel Sweet prevented a shooting scrape on the spot. Ever since then Parmelee had had some one watching the movements of Potts and his boys. There was a young lady over at Clayton's plantation to whom one of the boys was devoted, and Parmelee's spies reported there was to be a dance there. That's how he came to go over to Buccatubbee with the squad, but they only got Harry Potts and two of the Scroggs boys ; Barton Potts wasn't there. They were riding home to Quitman County after the dance and "making some racket, as young fellers will, and Parmelee laid for 'em on the road." They were brought in to the jail by Sergeant Quinn and the squad and there left to Parmelee and his people. As for the rest, the lieutenant knew as much as the sergeant, except that "old man Potts" with his boy Hal suddenly rode into camp just after Mr. Lambert had walked away, and the old man had given Captain Close a piece of his mind, after which he and Hal with a couple of friends rode back townwards. All the shooting that took place was probably a *feu de joie* to the accompaniment of triumphant yells.

It was a fact that when old Potts with his friends, not more than half a dozen all told, came riding in to offer bail for the boys, armed only with the customary revolver, they were followed towards the jail by a party of inquisitive and interested townspeople, at sight of which array Parmelee's posse on duty at the jail had fired one volley from that building and then rushed for the shelter of the cellar under the meeting-house. They had killed Potts's mule and wounded another, in exchange for which the Pottsites had ridden off with the first two animals and all the prisoners they saw. There was no one to claim the latter, and old Potts had coolly offered the former to the inspection of Captain Close: one proved to be government property, the other Parmelee's. " I'll just *baw*row these two to take us back home, an' then you gentle*men* can have 'em as soon as you'll send for 'em ; but you'll hardly expect us to call again, after the reception accawded us law-abiding and peaceable citizens to-day." This was the majestic conclusion of Potts's remarks to the surprised but stolid captain. Then they rode away, and, crossing probably at the ford, made a circuit back through town, where they doubtless had a Tugaloo jubilee with their friends and fellow-citizens, to the continued alarm and dismay of the bell-ringers in the meeting-house, until warned that the troops were coming, when they deliberately withdrew across the railway track, firing off a parting salute and a volley of the characteristic Southern vocalisms known to fame as the "rebel yell." This was injudicious. It was all well enough to ride away in company with prisoners whom nobody claimed or appeared to care to hold, but they should not have rejoiced thereat with riot and ungodly glee. It was human and by no means divine. It gave the opposition too much to tell about in the startling reports that went broadcast over the North that very night and appeared with lurid head-lines in the morning papers on the morrow.

Parmelee had not been seen from the moment of the initial appearance of Potts and party until he came scrambling into camp on a borrowed mule. Later that afternoon, when matters had measurably quieted down, he made his way westward in time to tell at the State Capitol his story of the riot to his properly indignant chief, while, all alone, Captain Close was jogging over to Potts's on the "day accommodation," little dreaming of the ill repute in which he and his youthful subaltern would stand before the unthinking of their Northern fellow-citizens on the morrow; for, as was only natural, the deputy marshal had squared accounts with Close by laying the blame for the escape of the prisoners, the peril of the beleaguered posse, and the riot and insurrection in Chittomingo County upon the captain and his lieutenant, who, he said, though wearing the uniform and holding the commission of the United States, had refused to come to the aid of the officers of the law.

"I ought to be back by nine o'clock," was the message the captain told Corporal Cunningham to take out to camp; but Cunningham was the ingenuous youth who first accosted Mr. Lambert on his arrival that morning, and Burns had nearly shaken the life out of him when he heard the story the men were passing from lip to lip. Cunningham was a young fellow with a better opinion of himself than his employers seemed to entertain, and, though fairly educated in the public schools and in a business college of his native city, a fondness for Bowery life and association with Bowery boys had undermined his usefulness. He enlisted after losing his situation, and, coming to Close's company when clerks were hardly to be had at any price, was put into the company office instead of the awkward squad. Then came a vacancy among the corporals; the young fellow, being a new broom, had swept clean, and was so helpful about the books, papers, and the like for six weeks that Close gave him the empty chevrons and gave Burns abundant cause for another outbreak of blasphemy. There might have been some way of licking Private Cunningham into shape, but there was none whatever of reforming Corporal Cunningham. He was not all bad, however, for by evening he began to realize the extraordinary solecism of which he had been guilty in the morning; so he was actually ashamed to go near the lieutenant, and never even repeated his message to Burns until nine o'clock had come and the captain hadn't. Then Burns went over to the lieutenant's tent, where that youth sat wrapped in his overcoat, trying gloomily and with stiffened fingers to write some letters by the light of a single candle.

"I suppose, sir, the captain meant to ride the mule back himself. He could have got to Potts's place before six and back here by eight, easy. 'Tisn't likely they'd ask him to stay to supper. I'm only afraid of his gettin' into a row, and him all alone."

"I wish he could have been content to send for the mule instead of going," said Lambert. "Any of the men could have gone, I suppose."

"Well, sir, the trouble is that he'd have had to send the men on mule-back, or else pay their fare over on the cars. The captain has a pass, and it doesn't cost him anything; and he's afraid to let the mule be gone over-night. It's mighty easy losin' 'em among all these niggers, and they might charge it up against the captain's pay. The captain has stuck close to camp so far as these night posses have been concerned, but he'd hunt the whole State for a lost blanket or bayonet. And he always goes alone—and gets what he's after, and he's had no trouble worth mentionin'; but that fellow Potts was impudent to him to-day, and he was slow 'bout seein' it at first; now, though, he's got his mad up and gone over there to get the mule and satisfaction both: that's what I'm afraid of, sir. He lashed Parmelee to-day for bein' a coward, and—beggin' your pardon, lieutenant—though the captain ain't much on military, he fires up like a flash at anything like insult to the flag."

"Do you think it advisable to send after the captain?" asked Lambert, after a moment's reflection.

"There's no way we *can* send, sir, 'cept afoot or behind a four-mule team in an army-wagon. We only had that one saddle-mule."

Lambert stepped to the tent door and looked out. The sky was overcast and the darkness thick. A wind was rising and whirling the sparks from the cook-fire over by the road, and from the pipes of the men sitting smoking and chatting in little groups about camp. Some had come to him at nightfall and sought permission to go in to the village, and he had felt obliged to refuse. After the events of the day it seemed wisest to hold them at camp, and he had so informed Sergeant Burns. As he stood there now looking uneasily about, first at the dark and threatening sky, then at the darker shadows about camp, Lambert thought he caught sight of three or four forms, vague and indistinct, hurrying along the bank beyond the fire.

"Who are those men?" he asked.

"I don't know, sir. I warned the company to remain in camp. I'll see." And Burns turned quickly and made a run for the opposite end of the company ground. Some of the men started up and stood gazing expectantly after him, and the chat and laughter suddenly ceased. The shadowy forms had disappeared: so, by this time, had Burns. Then there came the sound of his powerful voice, out by the road :

"Halt there, you men! Come back here!"

Then followed a rush and scramble in the bushes, and the sound of footfalls, rapid and light, dying away in the darkness. Then some low laughter and comment among the men. Then Burns came back, and, without waiting to report, sternly ordered, "Fall in!"

Knocking the ashes out of their pipes and buttoning their overcoats,—a thing they might have overlooked before the lesson of the day,—the soldiers slowly obeyed the unusual summons. Burns got his lantern and quickly called the roll. Four men failed to respond. Leaving the company still in line, the sergeant hastened to the tents for the absentees. Two of the number were found placidly sleeping. Two were away entirely,—Privates Riggs and Murphy.

"If I'm not mistaken I saw three shadows," said Lambert, as the sergeant made his report. "What would the captain do if he were here?—send a patrol?"

"The captain never had a night roll-call, sir; but he wouldn't send a patrol. That's only a good way of *not* ketchin' men, unless they're too drunk to run. It wouldn't be of much consequence, only for that man Riggs bein' one of 'em. He's a troublesome case. If the lieutenant approves of it, I'll send Sergeant Watts and a couple of good men without arms. They can find whoever's out. What I don't like about it is that somebody jumped the fence and into the Walton place."

"The old homestead across the road?"

"Yes, sir. There's been some trouble between the captain and the Walton family. He ordered the men never to enter the enclosure on any pretext, the old lady made such a row 'bout it."

"Who live there? Surely they ought to welcome our sending responsible men over to drive off our renegades."

"Well, I don't know 'bout that, sir," said the sergeant, with a nervous laugh. "If there's anybody on earth the captain's afraid of, its old Mrs. Walton. She's a terror. Nothin' of the unprotected female about her, sir, though she and her daughters live alone there. Both her sons were shot during the war: one was killed, and the other's in Havana—or Mexico ; said he'd never surrender, and won't come home. I reckon they're pretty hard up there, sometimes, but you should see how the old lady rides it over the captain, sir. I wonder she hasn't been over to pay you a visit. Shall I send after Riggs and Murphy, sir? It's a little like sendin' good money after bad. They haven't a cent, either of 'em, and if town was their object there's no use in their goin'; nobody would trust 'em."

Then came interruption,—the sound of a horn, an ordinary tin horn, too, floating through the dark and muttering night.

"That's her, lieutenant. That's the old lady herself. She reads prayers reg'larly at half-past nine every night, and some of the niggers are out yet. They used to have a conch shell that sounded pretty, but Parmelee said they had to sell it. They've had to sell pretty much everything, tryin' to keep alive."

Again the sound of the cheap and despised tin. Lambert recalled it as a necessary concomitant of the street-boy and straw-rides about the Christmas holidays, and its summons, he thought, was never to prayer: it called for many a lively malediction.

"Send Sergeant Watts, if you think it advisable," said he, briefly. "I'm going up on the road a moment."

Again the blast of the horn, short, *staccato*, imperative, and then an impatient, querulous voice at the north end of the porch,—a voice calling, "*You* Elinor! you wuthless black gadabout! wh' *ah* you?"

And as Lambert scrambled up the steep path and reached the road, another voice, low, tremulous, eager, close at hand, whispered, "Oh, I thought you'd never come! *Hyuh!* quick! Leave the money, *shuah*, and the pail, t'maw'ow night."

And then, with a rustle of feminine garments, bending low, a slender, girlish form shot across the beam of lamplight falling from an east window. Another form, also feminine, scurried away from the hedge-row, and something came rolling out into the road-way, clinking against the stones. There was sound of voluble reprimand and flustered explanation at the north end of the building, a quick, kitten-like patter of little feet up the rickety old steps in front, and in an instant the girlish form seemed perched on the window-sill. There a second or two it hovered, motionless, until a door slammed around at the north side of the house. Then in popped the slender figure, out went the light, and, but for the sigh and complaint of the night-wind in the rustling branches of the old trees about the veranda, all was silence at Walton Hall.

VII.

It was after ten when Captain Close returned, and barely eleven when he again set forth. This time a sergeant and ten picked men went with him, nobody but Close knew whither. "I may be gone two days, lieutenant," said he, in the laborious use of the title which among regulars "to the manner born" had long been replaced by "Mr.;" and had not Lambert asked for instructions, none, probably, would have been given. Of his adventures during the day he said not a word. He brought back the mule, and that was enough. The first thing Lambert and Burns knew of his return was the sound of his voice at the wagon, informing the guard that he wanted coffee and something to eat. Then, paying only vague attention to Lambert's congratulations on his safe return, he told Burns to get a detachment ready at once, then disappeared within the dark interior of his tent, leaving Lambert standing in some embarrassment and chagrin outside. "Looking to see if his strong box is all safe," whispered the first sergeant as he came up. "It's under the boards—under his cot—and he never lets anybody come in, not even the marshal."

It was full five minutes before the captain reappeared. He struck no light meantime, but could be heard fumbling around in the darkness. When he came forth, he had some papers in his hands. "We'll go to your tent, sergeant," he said. "Your desk is handier.—How've you got along, lieutenant?"

"Two men are out, sir; Riggs and Murphy——"

"Dam blackguards, both of 'em,—'specially Riggs; almost the oldest soldier in the company, too," said Close, wrathfully, seating himself at the desk and beginning to arrange the papers for signature.

"I had been told I should find some splendid old oaks among the rank and file," hazarded Lambert, after a pause, and thinking his commander should give some directions in the case.

"Old oaks? Old *soaks*, most like," was the disdainful answer,— "'specially Riggs. He come from the cavalry. Why, I've had them two fellows tied up by the thumbs three times since last March; and it hain't hurt 'em no more 'n if they was cast iron. Better keep a guard over the mules while I'm away, sergeant—or, rather, lieutenant: you see, I ain't used to havin' anybody but the sergeant. Oh! Now 'bout them mileage papers o' yourn. You said not to send 'em. Why not?"

" You've made out a charge of some sixty-five dollars for transportation of a servant, sir : I brought no servant with me."

" What's the difference? The law 'lows it. Every officer's entitled to a servant. And if he does his own work he's entitled to what his servant would get. You didn't black your boots on the way, did you? You had a servant do it. He was with you on the train,— porter of the sleeping-car, wasn't he? I never go in the durn things myself, but you did, I'll warrant. Well, you paid him out of your pocket, every time you changed cars or boat."

" That may be, sir ; but I can't sign any such claim as sixty dollars for transportation of servant when I paid no such sum."

" Then how're you to get your money back?—the dimes and dollars you've given to porters and waiters on the way? Every officer I know would sign that certificate without question, and every quartermaster would pay it. Captain Warren came with you to headquarters, at least. What d'you bet he hasn't drawn servant's transportation? You think it over, lieutenant. There's no sense in you robbin' yourself this way. Write down to barracks, 'f you like, and see what they say at head-quarters. They'll tell you just what I do."

" I'll sign the accounts without that, and get the mileage for myself," said Lambert. " I need the money. Then if it's allowable and proper I can collect for servant later."

" Not much you can't. There's where you show your ignorance. Then the government would make you fight ten years for it, even if you'd brought a servant with you. The way is to get it first and let them stop it if it's wrong. But here, I can't fool away time arguin' a simple thing like that. I've got to be miles away before midnight, and, no matter who comes and inquires, you don't know where we've gone. Now you won't need any commissary funds or anything while I'm away. Just pay cash and take receipts if you buy vegetables for the company."

" You forget, sir, that my money's gone."

" Sure you hadn't anything but what was in that pocket-book?— Then, sergeant, you do it, and keep account."

" But, excuse me, captain," said Lambert, flushing, " I myself will need money. I must find some place to board. Keep those mileage accounts as security, if you like, but let me have twenty dollars——"

C   5

" But you hain't signed them : they're no good."

" I'll settle that," said Lambert, sharply ; and, taking a pen, he drew a line through the item for transportation for servant and altered the figures of the total accordingly, then, still standing and bending over the desk, slashed his signature with a sputtering pen upon the paper. Close carefully scrutinized the sheet, compared it with its duplicate when that, too, was similarly finished, and stowed both away in a long envelope. " Sure you've got to have twenty ?" he asked, as a soldier stuck his head inside the tent door, retired precipitately at sight of the junior lieutenant, and then, from without, announced that the captain was served. " Well, I guess I can get it for you—before I go." Slowly he finished, slowly signed, after close study of their contents, the papers placed before him, then slowly left the tent without another word. Not until he had buckled on his pistol-belt—he carried no sword—and was about to start with his silent and yawning squad, did he seem to awake from his fit of abstraction, and then only when Lambert appealed to him for orders.

" Oh, yes. Well, just have an eye on them mules, will you, lieutenant? Everything else, almost, is under lock and key. The quartermaster sergeant is pretty solid."

" But in case of disturbance, or demands for more detachments, or men wanting to go away ?"

" There won't be nuthin' now fur a week. Do's you like about givin' the men a little liberty. They've had a good deal. Everything around here will be quiet enough, and you'll hear what I'm after—well, when I've got it.""

That night, though worn and weary and downhearted, Lambert could hardly sleep. At eleven the little detachment had trudged away into the blackness of the night, and the tramp of their march was swallowed up in the rustle of the crisp brown foliage and the creak of overhanging branches. The men remaining in camp crawled back to their blankets ; the cook-fire smouldered away, only occasionally whirling forth a reluctant flight of sparks in response to some vigorous puff of the restless wind ; the sentry yawned and dawdled about the wagon and the store tent ; even the mules seemed so sympathetic with their recovered associate that no whisper of a bray came from their pen on the bank of the stream. Lambert had received the assurance of his sergeant that the missing men would surely turn up before breakfast on the morrow, and had given permission to that harassed and evidently disgusted official to go to bed. Then, after a turn around his sleeping camp, the young fellow went to his lonely roost "to think things over."

In the first place, as he lighted his candle, there was the tin pail which had rolled out from the Walton hedge-row, and which, on inspection, he had found to contain about two pounds of fresh butter, very neatly packed in lettuce-leaves. That proved that the Waltons still had something of their old garden left. Lettuce could surely be raised only under glass at this inclement season. He had hitherto had no time for close inspection of the contents. Now as he turned over the leaves he found a little slip of paper on which, in a girlish and somewhat "scratchy" hand, were penned the words, "Please send small currency. It's so hard to get change. You can have buttermilk to-morrow night if you'll bring a pitcher. Due, $5\frac{10}{100}$. You *must* pay it this time. *I must* have it."

"Now, who on earth is this young lady's customer?" thought Lambert. "Surely not Close. He never spends a cent on butter. Nobody else lives nearer than Parmelee's to the north or town to the south. Can it be that some of the sergeants have been buying supplies from this quarter and running up a butter bill?" Burns had spoken of trouble between the captain and the old lady and of all hands being forbidden to enter the Walton grounds on any pretext whatever. That, of course, did not prohibit the men from buying what the Walton servants offered for sale outside the fence, and if they were so straitened in circumstances they might be glad to find a market for their surplus produce even among the Yankee invaders, provided Madam Walton were kept in ignorance of the traffic. She was uncompromising. No intercourse with, no recognition of, the barbarians, was her rule to kith and kin, and the few negroes who still hung about the crumbling old place repeated her words with the fear born of long-continued discipline under her roof and rod in the days of their enforced and unquestioning servitude.

These and other items of information as to his surroundings the young lieutenant had obtained from Sergeant Burns in the course of their evening watch together. He had no other means of studying the situation, and was but one of many new and comparatively inexperienced officers thrown upon their own resources at isolated posts among "the States lately in rebellion." Not yet twenty-four hours on duty with his company, he had been ordered to proceed with an armed force to the succor of officers of law supposably besieged by a rebellious mob, and now, at midnight, in the heart of a strange country and far from the heart of its people he was commanding officer of his company and camp, without definite instructions of any kind and only his native common sense to guide him.

Lambert has since told two women—his wife and his mother—how his thoughts wandered back to the peaceful old homestead in the far Northland, and to the teachings of his boyhood days. He made a sturdy fight against the feeling of loneliness that oppressed him. He wished the wind did not blow so sulkily, in such spiteful, vicious puffs. It seemed as though nature had combined with old Lady Walton to give him ungracious welcome to this particularly shady side of the sunny South. The wind itself was whispering sarcastic and withering remarks to him, like those the sergeant repeated as coming from Madam Walton to the defenceless captain; and even Burns's sense of subordination could not down his impulse to chuckle over some of them. What would Lambert do or say if the prim and starchy dame were to call upon him, as she occasionally had on his superior, driving him at last to the refuge of the nethermost depths of his tent, whence, as Burns declared, "the captain couldn't be induced to come out till the old lady was back inside her own door"?

The last time he "tied up Riggs"—a punishment much resorted to in the rough war days and those that closely followed them, especially by those officers who were themselves graduated from the ranks or the volunteers—it was for trespass on the Walton place. The fellow had climbed the fence and was pilfering among the old fruit-trees when caught by Madam Walton. That was bad enough, but he had been impudent to her, which was worse. The men themselves would probably have ducked him in the stream—the old, self-respecting soldiers, that is—had the captain not ordered his summary punishment. Lambert was wondering what steps he should take in the interests of discipline, when he finally blew out his candle, determined, if a possible thing, to get to sleep. It was just a quarter-past twelve when he wound his watch and stowed it under his rude pillow. His revolver, the day's purchase, lay, with some matches, close at hand. He had even placed his sword and belt at the foot of his cot. The last thing he thought of before closing his eyes was that he would have to get a lantern on the morrow, even if he bought it of Cohen; but it was also the last thing he thought of when the morrow came.

Was it the wind again, whispering ugly things, or the ghost of Lady Walton, with her acidulated tongue, that roused him, he knew not how many minutes—or hours—later? Something was whispering, surely. The wind had been doing a good deal of that sort of thing all the night long among the leaves, a good deal of snarling and growling at times, and there was muttered snarling going on around him now. That might be the wind; but the wind would not trip up over a tent-rope and say such blasphemous things about it, even if it *did* nearly pull the flimsy structure down. In an instant Lambert was wide awake.

"Who's there?" he challenged, sternly.

No answer,—not in words, at least,—but there was sound as of stealthy yet hurried movement, more straining at the ropes on the side nearest the captain's tent, and heavy, startled breathing.

"Who's there?" he repeated, reaching for the revolver. "Answer, or I fire."

Then came a mighty strain, a jerk, a stumble and plunge, the sound as of a heavy fall, followed by instant scramble and a rush of footfalls around the rear of camp. Lambert was out of bed and into his boots in half a minute; but in his haste he upset the chair on which lay the matches, and the box went rolling to the floor. Pistol in hand, he darted out into the night, and found it black as Erebus. Quickly he ran to the first sergeant's tent, but Burns was hard to waken after the long day's work. Once roused, however, he was soon out, lantern in hand, while Lambert hastily dressed, and then together they scouted camp. A glance at their tent showed that Riggs and Murphy were still absent. A peep at the watch showed that it was almost two o'clock; a search around Lambert's tent revealed nothing beyond the fact that the corner peg to which the tent-fly was guyed was torn from the ground, and the soft, sandy soil showed that heavy boot-heels had made their imprint. Then Burns, still lantern-bearing, went crouching low around the back of Close's tent, while Lambert, with straining ears, stood stock still an instant in front, then, of a sudden, tore like mad through the rousing camp, out past the dim white canvas of the wagons, out past the startled sentry, up the steep pathway to the hard red road beyond, down which he ran on the wings of the wind till he reached the gate-way to the forbidden ground, for a woman's agonized shriek had rung out upon the night, and the sound of blows, of crashing glass, of fierce and desperate struggle, of

5 *

muttered oaths, of panting, pleading, half-stifled cries, of wild dismay and renewed screams for help, all came crowding on the ear from the heart of the Walton place.

VIII.

As he rushed around to the southern side of the old house,—the side whence all this uproar proceeded,—Lambert came suddenly upon two dim, swaying figures. The one nearest him—that of a man—was clutching, throttling, apparently, a slighter form in white, a woman. The butt of his revolver straightened out the dark figure with one crack, and then for a moment everything was darkness and confusion. A lamp, held by some screaming female at a neighboring window, was dropped with a crash. The screams subsided to scurry and chatter and Ethiopian protestations and furious demands: "You Elinor! you black nigguh!—you let me out this room *instantly!*" Then rush of footsteps to the window again, and tragic appeals: "Mamma—*ma-am-ma*! Whut's happened? *Do* answer! *Do* make Elinor let me to you, or Ah'll jump out this window. Ah'm coming now." And indeed a dim, slender form could just be descried, arrayed in white, bending low from the casement, when Burns with his lantern came tearing around the corner. Then a majestic voice, imperious even though well-nigh breathless, was heard: "Katherine, return to your bed *instantly.* Do you hear? *Instantly!* And send Elinor to me."

That Katherine shot back within the sheltering blinds was possibly due not so much to the impetus given her by those imperative orders as to that imparted by the sight of a pair of shoulder-straps and the face of the young officer gazing in bewilderment about him. Well might he look amazed! At his feet on the pathway Private Riggs was sprawling, still half stunned by the blow he had received. On his back, amidst the wreck of a glass hot-bed, Private Murphy was clutching at empty air and calling on all the saints in the Hibernian calendar to rescue him from the hands of that old beldam. On the pathway, in a loose wrapper, her bosom heaving with mingled wrath and exhaustion, one hand firmly clutching a stout cane, the other clasping together at her white neck the shreds of her torn and dishevelled garb, her dark eyes flashing fire, her lips quivering, stood a woman certainly not fifty years of age, despite the silver in the beautiful hair streaming down upon her shoulders, and the deep lines of grief and care in her clear-cut and thoroughbred face. She leaned heavily on the stick an instant, but raised it threateningly as the luckless Murphy strove to sit up and stanch the blood trickling from his lacerated hands and face.

"Don't you dare to move, suh," she panted, "unless——" And the uplifted cane supplied, most suggestively, the ellipsis.

"Oh, fur the luv o' God, ma-am, don't hit me ag'in! Sure I'd niver prezhoome, ma'am——"

"Shut up, Murphy!" growled Burns. "It's easy to see what brought *you* here.—Shall I let Riggs up, lieutenant? He's bleeding a good deal."

But Riggs didn't want to get up. He flopped helplessly back upon the grass-plot. Burns bent over and held his lantern close. "The man's drunk, sir," he said,—"and cut."

"*I* did that, I presume," said Lambert, still a little out of breath after the dash to the rescue. "I found him daring to lay hands on this lady.—Madam, I sincerely hope you are not injured. It is impossible for me to say how I deplore this outrage. These men shall suffer for it, I assure you."

With rapid step the corporal of the guard, bringing with him a couple of men and another lantern, came hurriedly to the scene and stood silent and alert, glancing eagerly from face to face. Two or three frightened negroes had crept around the rear portico and hung trembling behind their mistress. With a shawl thrown over her head and shoulders, a quadroon girl halted half-way down the steps from the side door, her eyes dilated, and her lips twitching in terror, until a low voice from within bade her go on, and a tall, dark-haired, pale-faced girl in long, loose wrapper fairly pushed her forward and then stepped quickly to the elder woman's side.

"Go back to the house at once, my child. This is no place for you. Go to Katherine and tell her I say she must not leave her bed. Go!" And silently as she came, but with infinite and evident reluctance, the tall girl turned and obeyed. Mrs. Walton had spoken slowly and with effort. Of Mr. Lambert and his party she had as yet taken no notice whatever. Again Murphy began to squirm in his uncomfortable couch of mingled mud and broken glass and head-lettuce, and the crackling accompaniment to his moaning once more made him the object of the lady's attention."

"Lie still, suh," she said, low and sternly. "You have broken moh glass now, suh, than youh captain can replace. Lie still whuh you are until my suhvants lift you out.—Henry!" she called.

"Ye-assum," was the answer, as one of the negroes came reluctantly forward, humbly twirling a battered hat in his hands.

"Go fetch your barrow."

"Indeed, Mrs. Walton," interposed Lambert, "you need not trouble yourself. The guard shall carry these two scoundrels to camp, and prison life at Ship Island, or Tortugas, will put a stop to their prowling. It is on your account I am distressed. We have no surgeon at hand ; I will send at once for the doctor in town——"

She raised a slender white hand, relinquishing her grasp upon the cane, which now went clattering upon the gravel of the walk. It was a sign to check him, and respectfully he broke off in his hurried words. Then again she turned to the negro, who stood with twitching face, irresolute, beside her.

"Did you hear me, Henry? Go."

Again Riggs began to groan and stretch forth feeble hands. Burns looked appealingly to his young officer, then as appealingly to the lady. Clearly, she was the mistress of the situation. Lambert had quickly stooped and picked up the cane, but she did not see, apparently, that he wished to restore it to her. In the light of the lanterns the mark of Riggs's clutch was plainly visible at her white and rounded throat.

"Two of you lift this fellow," said Burns to the corporal ; and between them Riggs was heaved to his sprawling feet. "Get him over to camp now and bathe his head. Put a bayonet through him if he tries to bolt. I'll be there presently."

And of Riggs, her assailant, and of Riggs's removal under guard, the lady of the Walton homestead took no note whatever. Rebuffed, yet sympathetic, Lambert again essayed to speak, but the rattle of the barrow was heard, and Henry once more loomed up within the zone of lantern light.

"Lift that—puhson—out," she said. And when Burns would have lent a helping hand, she interposed : "No, I beg you. My suhvants will attend to this." And neither Lambert nor his sergeant made further effort. Murphy, lifted from the wreck of the ruined hot-bed, abject and crestfallen, scratched and bruised and bleeding, yet neither so deadened by drink nor so stunned by the rain of blows which he had suffered as not to appreciate the humiliation of his position, was squatted in the barrow. At an imperious gesture from Madam Walton, Henry started to wheel him away, the corporal of the guard in close attendance.

And then, with calm dignity and recovered breath, the lady turned to the boy officer:

" I have not thanked you yet——"

" Oh, Mrs. Walton, I beg you not to speak of thanks. If you knew how—how ashamed I am, and my regiment will be—that any of our men could have dared——" The very intensity of the young fellow's indignation choked him, and gave her the floor.

" Once before this they came, and then I warned. This time, having no men to call upon" (negroes, it seems, could not be counted as such), " I was compelled, myself, to chastise. May I ask the safe return of our barrow,—it is the only vehicle the war has left us,—and that we may now be permitted to retire?" And she swept a stately courtesy.

" But, madam——" began Lambert, utterly chagrined at the attitude of cold and determined avoidance in which she persisted, " you have been brutally handled; I insist on sending for our contract doctor: it is the best we can offer to-night——"

" Neither to-night, nor at any other time, would his suhvices be acceptable, suh. I need no doctoh. We learned—we *had* to learn—how to do without luxuries of every kind during the war; and Dr. Hand—I think that is the name of the physician you refer to—would be too much of a luxury at any time. I regret that your men should need his suhvices, but they brought it on themselves."

" They will need him more before the captain gets through with 'em, ma'am," said Sergeant Burns, seeing that his young superior was at a loss what to say. As he spoke, the tall, dark-haired girl once more appeared, and swiftly, noiselessly stepped to her mother's side. " There'd be no need of a court-martial or of your having to testify, if Captain Close could settle this—or let us do it."

" Mother, come in,—*please* do,—and let these gentlemen go," said the girl. " Indeed, we are very much obliged to you," she continued, addressing Lambert, " for coming so quickly. That one, who seemed intoxicated, might have killed mother, who is far from strong. They had opened the cellar door, you see." And she pointed to where the broad wooden leaf had been turned back, leaving a black yawning chasm.

C*

"Your mother is faint," cried Lambert, springing forward just in time, for, now that victory was perched upon her banners, the foe soundly thrashed and driven from the field, nature—woman-nature—had reasserted herself, and the lady of Walton Hall would have sunk to earth but for the strong young arms that received her. Then came renewed outcry from within-doors. Miss Katherine could not have obeyed the maternal mandate, for there she was at the window, insistent, clamorous. "Bring her right in *hyuh!*" she cried. "Do you *hyuh* what I say, Estuh? Oh, who *day*-uhd to lock me in this room? You Elinor! open this do' *instantly*, I tell you!"

A moment later, when, by the light of Burns's lantern, now in Miss Esther's trembling grasp, the two men bore the limp and nerveless shape into the nearest room and laid it reverently upon the sofa, a wild-eyed and dishevelled young woman threw herself at her mother's side and began chafing and slapping the slender white hands and begging all manner of absurd and impossible things of the prostrate, pallid, death-like form. Elinor, who had obeyed orders and locked that impulsive damsel in, had now released her and then collapsed.

"Do not try to raise her head," said Lambert gently to the frightened child, who, having exhausted one effort, was now striving to revive her mother with passionate kisses. "We must restore the circulation to the brain. Pardon me: have you a little brandy? or whiskey?"

"There isn't a drop in the house," answered Miss Walton, piteously. "We had some, that had been in the cellar for years, that mother hid during the war; but—but—it was being stolen, or something—and she sold what was left."

Burns quickly left the room. When he returned, a few minutes later, he held forth a little flask. Mrs. Walton still lay senseless, and her condition was alarming to one and all. Lambert poured out a stiff dose. "Make her take it all, little by little," he whispered to Miss Walton, and then, with calm decision, stooped, and, encircling the slender waist of the younger girl with his arm, quickly lifted her to her feet. A tress of her rich red-brown hair was caught in his shoulder-strap, but neither noticed it. Such was the patient's prostration that for a moment even brandy failed of its stimulating effect. Not until several spoonfuls had been forced between her blue lips did there come that shivering sigh that tells of reviving consciousness. The white hands began feebly to pluck at her dress and the heavy eyelids to open slowly. " We will fall back," whispered Lambert. " I'll wait in the hall."

But when he turned to tiptoe away, a very touzled, tangled, dishevelled, but pretty head had to come, too. There was too much of that fine, shining, shimmering tress to let go. Burns was already creaking out into the dark passage. Miss Walton was absorbed in her mother's face. Miss Katherine's rounded cheek had flushed as red as the invalid's was white, and both her tiny hands were madly tugging and pulling at the offending tendrils ; but who could work to advantage with the back or side of one's head practically clamped to the workbench ? Miss Katherine could not tear herself loose except at the risk of carrying away a square inch or more of scalp, for the strap would not yield, and its wearer could not help so long as her own hands were tugging. There was every likelihood, therefore, that the tableau on which Madam Walton's opening eyes should gaze would be about the very last she would care to see,—the bonnie head of her precious child reposing, to all appearance, on a shoulder in Yankee blue,—when Lambert, alive to the desperate nature of the situation, quickly cast loose the two or three buttons of the flannel sack-coat then so much in vogue, and, slipping out of that and into the hall, rejoined his imperturbable sergeant.

" I hope the lieutenant will pardon my taking his flask. I saw it in the tent this evening, sir, and the captain didn't leave the key of the medical chest,—with me, leastwise."

" You did right. That was some good cognac they got for me in New Orleans. I hope it will revive her. Ought we not to send for Dr. Hand ?"

" No, sir," whispered Burns. " She wouldn't have him for one of her niggers—and be damned to them. I know now where Riggs had been getting his liquor, and where our coffee and sugar has been going. He's bribed these thieving servants of hers to steal that precious brandy, and those dam scoundrels broke into the cellar to-night to get more."

" But they must have been drinking in the first place. Where could they have got *that* liquor? Hers was gone,—sold."

" In town, somewhere. I'll find out——" But here the lieutenant checked him. A feeble voice was just audible in the adjoining room :

" Have they gone? Have I been ill? Esther—daughter, see that—No! *I* must see that young officer, at once."

"Not to-night, mother," answered the elder girl, pleadingly. "Not to-night. To-morrow: you'll be rested then."

"That may be too late. Whatever happens, there must be no court-martial. He said *I* should have to testify; so would you. *You* saw, Esther, and if under oath we should *have* to tell——"

"Quick! Come out of this!" whispered Lambert, hoarsely, and dragged the sergeant after him to the dark and wind-swept shadows of the yard.

IX.

Sunday morning came, gloomy, cloudy, with the wind still moaning among the almost leafless branches and whirling dust-clouds from the crooked road. After a night of so much excitement camp slept late. Lambert was aroused somewhere about seven by a scratching at the tent-flap, and Sergeant Burns, answering the summons to "come in," poked his freshly shaven face through a framing of white canvas to ask if he might send the lieutenant some breakfast from the cook-fire. It was barely twenty-four hours since his arrival in camp, and so crowded had these hours been with event, experience, and novelty that the young officer seemed to feel he had been a month on duty. There lay his blue flannel blouse at the foot of his cot. Unseen hands had tossed it from the window at which on his first appearance the previous night a slender, white-robed form had been piteously crying for help. He drew it to him and searched the left shoulder-strap. Yes! Even now three or four long curling hairs were twining like the tendrils of a vine about its dead-gold border and across the field of sky-blue velvet,—another vogue of the day. "She had time to disentangle the mass, but could not see these fine filaments in so dim a light," he laughed to himself. "Only fancy what my Merrimac *madre* would say if she were to hear that a pretty head—a Southern girl's head—had been resting on my shoulder the very first night I got here! Only fancy what the damsel herself would say, if she had a chance to say anything! And as for *her* mamma—well, what *wouldn't* she say?"

Lambert had lots to think of as he made his soldier toilet and came forth into the gloomy, moisture-laden air, for the southeasterly wind was sweeping the rain-clouds up from the distant gulf, and nature looked bleak and dismal. Two items occurred to give him comfort.

No sooner had he stepped out into the open space than the one sentry at the other end of camp shouted, "Turn out the guard—commanding officer!" which was unnecessary at the distance and under the circumstances, yet clearly proved that the disposition among the men was to "brace up" in recognition of the arrival of an officer who knew what discipline meant.

And then, looking suspiciously as though he had been waiting for a chance to undo the ill effect of his blunder of the previous day, there in front of Burns's tent stood Corporal Cunningham, company clerk; and the salute with which he honored the camp commander was as pregnant with good intent as it was clumsy in execution. Somebody had placed an empty clothing-box by the side of his tent, covered it with canvas fly, and set this improvised table for one with the best tins the company mess afforded. Somebody else had carefully blacked the lieutenant's boots and shoes, and presently up came a young German soldier bearing the lieutenant's breakfast on the company cook's bread-board, which was covered with a clean white towel.

"Burns is one of the oaks, at any rate," thought Lambert, as the sergeant followed to see that all was in proper order. Ham and eggs, "soldier coffee," a can of milk, corn-bread and hard-tack, were set before him with pardonable pride, and Burns explained that they bought eggs, milk, and corn-bread of an old darky who came over from the village almost every day. Then Lambert bethought him of his captured pail of butter, and brought it from the tent. "This does not belong to me," he said. "It rolled out from the Walton hedge last evening. Do you know who their regular customer is?"

"I don't, sir. Yet I know McBride and others have sometimes had butter,—good butter too, like this. The captain doesn't buy any, and wouldn't allow the company to buy any *there*. Not that he cared, sir; only the old lady was so uppish and made such a row when any of our fellows were seen even talking to her people that he gave regular orders forbidding it. No one from the Walton place dare set foot inside camp, and he'll make it hot for Riggs when he gets back. Murphy is less to blame, but will have to go to Ship Island all the same, I reckon."

"How are those two this morning?"

"Riggs is stupid drunk yet, but Murphy swears he'd only gone to try to get Riggs out of trouble: he'd hardly been drinking at all. He begs to see the lieutenant, sir. He says he can explain the whole thing."

6

And so, later that morning, after Lambert had given his men a further lesson by inspecting both company and camp and pointing out no end of things which could not, he said, be tolerated in future, Murphy was brought to his tent. His face and hands were badly cut in places, but his bruises were of little account. With the best intentions in the world, the good lady had not the strength for the trouncing the fellow had deserved at her hands. The story he told was hardly credible. Lambert could have ordered him back with sharp rebuke for his falsifications, but a glance at Burns's war-worn face, clouded and perplexed, gave the young commander pause. "Do you really expect me to believe this?" he asked, and Murphy answered, "I'm ready to make oath to it before the praste, sorr."

And this, in effect, was the Irishman's tale. He had known his "bunky"—Riggs—only since that worthy's enlistment in the company the previous winter, but this much of Riggs almost everybody knew; that he had been a sergeant during the war days, and was serving an enlistment in the regular cavalry when deprived, for persistent drinking, of his chevrons. The troop to which he was attached had been stationed at Quitman and in this section of the South for a year or more, but was ordered to the Indian country just about the time of Riggs's discharge by expiration of term of service. Then, after a protracted spree in New Orleans, he turned up at the barracks and "took on" again in the infantry, and in the very company which, oddly enough, was so soon ordered up to the region he knew so well. Indeed, Riggs claimed when drinking to have acquaintance not only with the Walton ladies, but with some of the most prominent men in Quitman County, and frequently boasted of the good times he would have could he only get over there. Another thing about Riggs: he had twice got Murphy to go as his substitute on certain detachment or posse duty, offering as excuse that marching wore him out, yet admitting to Murphy that there were other reasons. "There are men in this section who'd shoot me on sight,—get the drop on me,—pick me off from the woods or fences," he had explained. Murphy believed him, and believed, too, his statement that he had powerful friends even among officers and gentlemen who had fought through the war on the Southern side. "He got money when he needed it, and spent it like a gentleman," said Murphy; which, being interpreted, meant that he liberally squandered it on his comrades.

But Riggs had of late been out of money: he "couldn't hear from his friends," said Murphy, and was getting in trouble. He owed poker debts in the company and liquor debts in town. He couldn't get a drink on trust, and the men were shy of playing with him; but he had always been liberal to Murphy when in funds, and Murphy stood by him now. About nine o'clock, therefore, the previous evening, he noticed that Riggs was greatly excited when an old darky came shambling in and gave him a little note. The negro had occasionally come before, and did not seem to belong either in town or at the Walton place. Riggs stole out to the road, despite Murphy's warning, and came back in less than ten minutes, bidding Murphy in eager whisper to be quick and come with him. It was evident even then that Riggs had had a drink or two. Murphy reminded him of the lieutenant's orders and begged him to run no risk; and then Riggs broke out and told him that, come what might, he'd simply got to go to town, and Murphy with him. He would explain when they got out of camp, but there wasn't a minute to lose; and Murphy went along, "just to keep him out of trouble." Out in the darkness a stranger joined them, gave Riggs some low-toned orders, but refused to let him have another drink. They were stealing along the road together, trying to dodge the flickering firelight, when it suddenly flared up and must have betrayed them, for a moment later they heard Burns shouting after them. Then the stranger "lept the fince" into the Walton place; Riggs darted away and ran like a streak: so he followed Riggs.

When at safe distance from camp Riggs slowed up and told what he had agreed to do. At Cohen's store was a box containing some expensive wine and cordials which had been prescribed for Mrs. Walton two weeks before by their old family physician and ordered sent from New Orleans. It was one of the sad cases common in the South in those hard times. Miss Walton, who wrote the order without her mother's knowledge, had no money to send, and the firm had none to lose. She explained that the wine was needed at once, and the money would be at hand in the course of ten days. The wine was sent, care of Cohen & Co., with instructions to collect first; and not until this night had there been money enough to pay for it. Now "a gentleman," whom Riggs knew well, had brought them help; but he himself could not go to Tugaloo because of certain past events with which he was intimately connected, and none of the Walton servants dared go, because of the tremendous stories in circulation concerning the events of the day. The gentleman had come a long distance at big risk to see the lady, Riggs declared, and must get away that night.

In this dilemma Riggs was called on for help. His chivalric nature was aroused—presumably ; or possibly " the tiger had tasted blood" and needed more. Riggs had got the gentleman's last drink, and the money for more was now in his hands. But the gentleman had stipulated that a reliable man must go with him to fetch the precious packet in case Riggs "got full ;" and Murphy was the man. "We got the box, sorr, an' Riggs his bottle of liquor, an' come back all right, an' we stole in there as we were bid, an' raised the cellar door, an' I carried down the box to the fut of thim slippery steps meself, for Riggs was gettin' noisy-like. An' thin we stole away, niver disturbin' anybody, sorr, only doin' the poor leddy a kindness, as we were towld. We didn't see or hear annybody. It was *afther* it all the throuble came."

There was pathos in Murphy's description of the "throuble." Their task accomplished, Murphy sought to get Riggs to his tent, but the man had drunk just enough to be rabid for more, and in the struggle the bottle fell with the gill or two remaining and was smashed. This was indeed a catastrophe. Riggs had that fearful craze for alcohol which is satiated only when the victim lapses into drunken stupor. Murphy got him to the tent and to bed, and thought he had him safe, but awoke later to find him gone,—gone for more liquor ; but where? None was to be had in camp, unless he broke into the captain's medical stores, which, Murphy argued, he wouldn't dare attempt with the lieutenant lying there alongside. All of a sudden it flashed over him that his wretched "bunky," after having faithfully acquitted himself of his trust before the fatal whiskey-logging of his moral sense, had now stolen off in the darkness to rob the very household for whose sake, or that of the bribing liquor, he had braved punishment. Riggs had gone back for that wine.

The Irish soldier has his faults, God knows, but desertion of his fellow, even in face of torture, is not one of them. Murphy stole away, hoping it was not too late to recapture Riggs, and came upon him, just as he feared, tugging at something at the foot of those dark and slippery steps. Then came a struggle that, after at last he had borne his fiercely battling comrade up into the night, left Murphy breathless and exhausted. And then came the rain of blows that toppled him, crashing, into the ruin of the hot-bed.

"She came upon me that sudden and furious-like, sorr, I couldn't explain; an' it was tryin' to pacificate her I was, backin' off, an' niver see the hot-bed behind me fur the hot batin' I was gettin' afront. An' thin whin she had me down on the flat of me back, an' graspin' at thim glass works, poor Riggs, niver knowin' what he was doin', sorr, only to help me, grappled with the ould lady for the purpose of expostulatin', an' thin that naygur wench run screechin' into the house, an' the young lady came shriekin' to the windy, an' the stranger—the gentleman—lept to the side door, an' I a-callin' to him to come an' square me an' Riggs, whom he got into the scrape, an' there was more screamin', an' he niver so much as axed to shpake, but run fur his life when the lieutenant jumped in an' batthered Riggs, who was only askin' a chance to explain."

"Do you expect me to believe that any gentleman stood there and saw Riggs grapple that poor lady and never raised hand to stop it?" asked Lambert, almost angrily.

"It's God's thruth, sorr. He was makin' motions, crazy-like, but he niver came outside that door-way until he saw the lieutenant, an' then the lamp wint out, wid him a-runnin'."

The lieutenant pondered a moment. Had Sergeant Burns ventured on an expression of doubt, the interview would have come to an end at once, with Murphy in disgrace; but Burns looked full of honest perplexity and yet belief.

"You ought to have had sense enough to know I should be glad to send to town for anything Mrs. Walton needed," said Lambert. "Why didn't Riggs ask permission?—or why didn't you?"

Murphy was certainly frank. "Sure we both knew it would be anybody but Riggs the lieutenant would send. We were guilty enough of going to town without permission, an' drinkin'; but it was charity, not thavin', sorr, that we entered the garden for."

"You may send Murphy back, sergeant. We'll have to hold him until Riggs can tell his story. Of course," said Lambert, as the Irishman was led away, "if there's anything in this story about the stranger, it helps their case materially. There was certainly something queer about the agitated words Mrs. Walton used just before we came away, —words about their testimony and preventing court-martial. You heard, did you not?"

"Yes, sir,—a little, anyhow."

"Can you imagine who the man is, or account for his strange behavior?"

"I can't, sir. It might have been one of those three or four that Mr. Parmelee hauled in,—one of the Potts crowd ; but the idea of his standing back and letting the old lady have that tussle all to herself! That couldn't happen, sir, North or South, unless——" And Burns stopped short.

"Unless what?"

"Well, sir, unless there were reasons he daren't let her know he was there."

X.

At noon that Sunday it began to rain, adding to the gloom of Lambert's surroundings, and he sat listening to the steady downpour drumming on the tautened canvas of his tent, thinking of the odd contrasts brought about by army life. This was his first Sunday with his company, and in every possible way it was about as unlike every Sunday of his previous life as it well could be. He was trying to write to the mother far away on the peaceful banks of the Merrimac, where the rolling hills were by this time wearing their early mantle of snow, and old and young, farm-hands and mill-hands, a reverent populace, had obeyed the summons of the solemn bells that found no echo among these dripping woods, these desolate fields.

At intervals during the moist and chilly morning little squads of negroes had hung about the westward end of camp. Something of the events of the previous night had been put in circulation with the dawn, and, growing as it rolled, had attained huge proportions by the time it reached the outlying plantations five and ten miles away. This, coupled with the tremendous story of the jail delivery at Tugaloo, had been sufficient to draw the bolder of their number towards that centre of interest, the Yankee camp,—though farther they dared not go. At times there would be some rude soldier chaff between the men at the guard-tent and these curious visitors ; and no matter how poor the wit, it never failed of its reward of abundant guffaw. The Southern negro needs no visit to the Blarney stone : his flattery is spontaneous.

When Lambert had finished his conference with Burns, and, as in duty bound, went over to the Walton place to inquire how its *châtelaine* had passed the night, he marched forth through a little congregation of shining black faces and obsequious and tattered forms, and had to run the gauntlet of a chorus of personal remarks, all in high degree complimentary, as to the style and fit of his uniform, as well as his general appearance. In less than five minutes he returned, but with such chagrin at heart that it must have been reflected in his youthful face. Serene in the consciousness that he was doing a perfectly conventional and proper thing, he had bounded lightly up the broad wooden steps and knocked at the door. It was opened almost instantly by the colored girl whom he had seen the night before and heard apostrophized as "*You* Elinor." The eager expression in her eyes gave way at once to something of disappointment and certainly of doubt.

"I thought—I thought it was Mars'r Potts, suh," she stammered. "I—I don't reckon the ladies can see you."

"Will you say to Miss Walton that Mr. Lambert—Lieutenant Lambert, if you choose—has called to inquire how Mrs. Walton is to-day, and that, if possible, he would be glad to speak with Miss Walton a moment?"

Elinor stood peering through about one foot of gap, the door she had so promptly thrown wide open having been as promptly closed to that limit. Lambert could not but hear other doors opening within,—could almost swear he heard the swish of feminine skirts, the whisper of feminine voices, low and eager. The fact that the girl stood there, barring the entrance and apparently afraid to go, added to his theory that she was being prompted from behind.

"Ah dunno, suh. Ah'll see," she said at last, slow and irresolute. "Whut, mum?" she continued, involuntarily, an instant later, turning her turbaned head towards some invisible presence in the hall beyond; and that settled the matter in Lambert's mind.

"Ye-assum," and slowly now the yellow-brown face returned to light. "Mis' Esther ain't very well, suh, an' she says—er rather—Mis' Walton sends her compliments to the gentleman and begs he'll 'scuse her. Dey don't need nuffin'," she continued, in her own interpretation of messages telegraphed from the dark interior.—"Ye-assum. Mis' Walton rested very well, considerin', an's all right to-day, but she don't want nuffin', suh."

"I had hoped to be able to see Mrs. Walton, if she were well enough, or else Miss Walton," said Lambert, firmly, intending that his words should be their own interpreter at the court within. "There are matters of importance on which I desired to speak."

Again Elinor, mute and irresolute, turned to her unseen mentor. There was evidently a moment of conference. Then the girl was suddenly swept aside, the door was thrown wide open, and there, while other and younger forms seemed to scurry away from both sight and hearing, there with a gray shawl thrown over her shoulders, calm and dignified, her silvery hair fluttering about her temples, and the lines of care seeming even deeper in the sad, clear-cut face, stood Mrs. Walton, leaning on the stout cane which had dealt such trenchant blows the night before. With a voice that trembled just a trifle despite her effort at control, she slowly spoke:

"You mean to be courteous, sir, in your inquiry, and for this I beg to thank you,—to renew my thanks for your prompt service of last night. But now may I say, once for all, that we need, and can accept, no further assistance, and, if you are sincere in your desire to be courteous, you will not again seek to enter my door?"

Lambert flushed to his very brows.

"It is a more important matter than you have perhaps thought, Mrs. Walton, that has made me ask to see you. One of the men who broke in here last night——"

"I know what you would say," she promptly, firmly interposed, again uplifting, with that almost imperious gesture, the fragile white hand. "I am framing a letter to be delivered to your commander upon his return to-night—upon his *return*," she quickly corrected herself. "It will cover the case so far as we are concerned. Meantime I beg to be excused from further allusion to it." And the stately inclination with which she accompanied the words was unquestionably a dismissal.

Lambert stood speechless one instant. Then, simply raising his forage-cap, he whirled about, and left.

The boy was thinking of his own mother when he tripped so lightly up that worn old gravel path on his way to inquire how he could be of service to one whose dignity and sorrow and suffering had so impressed him. He had donned his best uniform for the mission, and little dreamed how in so doing he had rendered himself much the more *persona non grata*. He, who could not war upon women and children under any circumstances, had not begun to learn how bitterly the recent war had borne upon the women of the South, or how, even so long after, they suffered from its effects. He had gone to offer the aid and protection of a loyal heart and a strong arm, and had not realized that it was the very last succor a Walton would seek, so long as both heart and arm were draped by the Union blue.

Not ten minutes after his return, discomfited and dismayed, there rode up the muddy, red bridle-path—for it was little more—a broad-faced young fellow who was attired in the clumsiest of "store clothing" and whose lean and long-necked steed looked dejection itself as his vigorous rider dismounted, slung the reins over the gate-post, and, after one sharp and warning survey of the silent negroes still hovering about, swung cheerily up the walk. To him the old doors opened wide without a summons, and eager hands were thrust forth in welcome.

Lambert, hearing the first heavy drops come thumping on his canvas roof, thought it was the rain that so quickly thinned the group of darkies on the road. He could hear the mule-hoofs sputtering away through the mud as the rain came quicker and faster, but not until several hours later did further explanation dawn upon him. Then he heard Burns and Watts in conversation at the first sergeant's tent.

"Did you see how the niggers kind o' lit out when he came?" asked Burns. "I haven't seen him round here since August. Reckon he knows captain's away. He hates him like poison ever since cap interfered in that row he had with Parmelee."

"Looks like a pleasant enough fellow. I'd rather back him than Parmelee any day, 's far as looks go. What's he doing here?"

"He's some kin to the old lady,—they're all related hereabouts,—and she's sent for him to come, probably, after last night's row."

"But they're talking all over the company about Murphy's yarn,—about there being some relative there—some man—last night. *You* heard it when he talked to the lieutenant."

"Oh, yes," answered Burns, evasively, "I heard what he had to say, but Riggs shut him up short as soon as he was sober enough to know what Murphy was saying. Wait till Riggs tells his side of the story to the lieutenant. Then perhaps we'll know what brought Mr. Barton Potts over here."

Lambert was up and at the door of his tent in a minute. "Did you say that Mr. Barton Potts was at the Walton place now, sergeant?"

"Yes, sir," answered Burns, whirling about in the mud and promptly saluting.

"Then have some man let me know when he comes out. I wish

to speak to him. And if Riggs is sober enough now, send him here."

Presently, looking moist, blear-eyed, and dejected, the ex-trooper and sergeant was marched up through the pattering rain, and, with the big drops trickling down from the visor of his old war-pattern forage-cap, stood sullenly at the tent of his young commander. The guarding sentry, after the fashion prevailing among some of the regular infantry at the time, allowed his rifle to topple forward from the "carry" into the grasp of the left hand, a foot or so in front of the right breast, and with this well-intended effort at the "rifle salute" of the '60's, Private Mulligan reported,—

"Prisoner Riggs, sorr ; to spake to the lieutenant."

It was the first time Lambert had conducted an investigation of the kind, and he had no precedents to guide him.

"Riggs," said he, "Murphy tells me your going to town last night was at the instance of some relative of Mrs. Walton's, who asked you to do them a service. Was that true?"

"It was, sir."

"Then he will doubtless be glad to come forward and exonerate you, or at least explain your conduct in the early evening. Your later conduct only a court-martial can properly consider. Where is this gentleman?"

"I don't know, sir."

"What is his name?"

"I——can't tell, sir."

"You know it, do you not?"

"I suppose I do, sir, but——I can't tell it."

"In the event of your trial he is the only man who can help you, and the report I have to make of your misconduct is most serious. Drunkenness only aggravates housebreaking and attempted robbery, as well as assault."

"I broke no houses, sir, and attempted no robbery. As for assault, the lady herself will say I meant no harm."

"But your own comrade admits he found you in the cellar entrance at the foot of the steps, on premises you were forbidden to enter, to all appearances stealing wine, and he was striving to get you away when the noise brought Mrs. Walton upon you. The case is flagrant."

Riggs threw his hands forward in a despairing gesture, dropped them again by his side, and stood silent.

"Do you mean you have nothing to say for yourself?—that you cannot disprove the charges?"

"I have plenty to say for myself, sir, but nobody to say anything for me. The worst any one can ever prove of me is that I've been a drinking man. I'm no thief; I'm no burglar; and I'd burn me hand off before I'd lay it to hurt a woman, old or young. I never knew what I was doing, if I grabbed the lady by the throat. But I'd be a worse man than the lieutenant thinks me if I'd do what he asks."

"This is nonsense, Riggs. What have I asked you to do that would be either criminal or wrong?"

"To defend meself at the expense of a friend, sir," said Riggs, with melodramatic gravity. "I'll never betray the man that's trusted me."

"Take him back to the guard-tent, sentry," said Lambert, hardly knowing whether to be amused or disgusted. "The man isn't sober yet."

And then for the first time the young officer became aware of the presence of a horseman at the side of his tent. With his hat-brim pulled down over his eyes and the rain dripping from bit and boot and bridle-rein, there sat his acquaintance of the owl train,—Mr. Barton Potts.

"One of your men said you wished to see me, lieutenant," said Mr. Potts, with a courteous wave of his hand. "I was coming anyhow, but rode round from the bahn yawnduh and came in 'long the branch. Excuse me if I've stumbled on something I wasn't expected to hear."

"Certainly, Mr. Potts. Can you dismount and come in? I much want to talk with you."

"And I want to have a talk with you, lieutenant,—*ve'y* much,—and I'm coming for the purpose, but not just now. There are some matters I must 'tend to in town for my aunt, Mrs. Walton, at once. But let me add my thanks to hers—and much more than hers—for your prompt assistance last night. I know that man by sight. I've seen him around here befoh, and it's Gawd's mercy I wasn't there last night. I'd 'a' shot him dead."

"You can be sure he shall not escape justice, Mr. Potts; though your aunt seems to refuse to see me with regard to the matter."

"I'll explain all that later, suh," said Potts, lowering his voice. "I've simply *got* to go at once. But I'll see you to-night; and mean-

time let me repeat what I said. You shan't lack for a friend round
heah, suh. You treated me like a gentleman when I was drunk and
possibly offensive,—though I hope not, suh,—and you've behaved like
a gentleman to my people, and by and by they'll see it. Just you wait.
By the bye, you remember Colonel Scroggs?"

"I don't think I do. Some of that name were among the prisoners who escaped yesterday, I'm told."

"Yes, suh. The same family, suh; Colonel Scroggs's brothers.
I can't discuss *them* just now, but if the colonel should come here to
see you before Captain Close gets back, if you'll take my advice, you'll
listen to him. He wants to speak about that arrest, and square things;
and—well, I know a gentleman when I see one, just as I know a
rough—like that soldier you were examining. The colonel was conductor of our train night before last. Now I've got to ride like hell.
Good-day, suh."

And, pulling off his hat and sticking spurs to his mud-covered
steed, Mr. Potts galloped away along the Tugaloo road into the gathering darkness.

Soon after nightfall the rain ceased and the wind died away. For
the first time since he had turned in the night before, Lambert bethought him of the lantern he had purposed buying, even if he had to
send to Cohen's on a Sunday. Burns sent some candles over from the
company stores, and the young German "striker" set two of them
alight in his tent, with empty whiskey-bottles—off which he had deferentially washed the labels—as candlesticks.

One thought led to another. The proposed purchase reminded
Lambert that all the money in his possession was now the twenty-dollar
bill borrowed of Close, and this reminded him that he wanted five
dollars in small currency,—"shinplasters," as the miniature greenbacks were called at the time. Since hearing Murphy's story he better
understood the straits to which his neighbors were reduced, and he had
determined that the aid he had proffered in one way should, despite
Madam's high-spirited rejection, be rendered in another.

At eight o'clock he had secured the amount he needed through
the good offices of the first sergeant, and he was wondering how
soon he might expect the visit of Colonel Scroggs and what could
be its purpose, when all of a sudden the chatter at the other end of
camp told him of the return of the detachment sent out the previous
night; but it was Sergeant McBride, not his company commander, who
met him at the tent-door.

"The captain's compliments, an' he'll be back by an' by, sir. He stopped over to have it out with somebody that fooled him."

"Stopped over where, sergeant? Not alone, I hope?"

"No, sir; the sheriff was along, an' two others. They were talking with Mr. Scroggs—or Colonel Scroggs—and a young fellow they called Potts, who met us across the track on the Quitman road. The captain said you wasn't to worry about him, but we didn't get the parties the sheriff was after, and the captain thinks he knows who threw us off the scent."

Manifestly nothing was to be done but await the captain's return, and nine o'clock came without him. Lambert had determined to investigate the butter market, however, and time was not hanging heavily upon his hands by any means. Throwing a light-blue overcoat, such as was worn by the rank and file, over his uniform, he sallied forth just after nine o'clock, made his way around the camp until he reached the road, and followed it to the gap among the rose-bushes whence had rolled the tin pail on the previous night. All was dark and still. Setting the pail just within the hedge, he patiently waited. Presently voices—feminine voices—became faintly audible. "Elinor" had evidently been pushed forward *en reconnoissance*, and, after her recent nerve-racking experiences, didn't like the detail.

"I tell yo' dey ain' no one 'bout, Mis' Katie. I done felt fur de pail, an' 'tain't day-h," was her protest. At this Lambert saw fit to give a low whistle, at sound of which Elinor, with prodigious rustle of skirts, bolted back towards the house, and her unseen companion, after emphatic and scornful reference to "bawn cowuds," came hurriedly forward, but paused at discreet distance.

"You're theh, ah you?" was the semi-assertive, semi-interrogative remark in disdainful and truculent tone. "Ah hope you've got that money at last."

For all answer Lambert reached in and shook the pail. The combination of "shinplasters" and small coin within gave a reassuring rattle. Eagerly the girl bounded to the hedge. He could just discern the slender little form and the tumbled head of hair as she dropped the enfolding shawl and stooped to take her prize,—which the unprincipled young man had by this time cautiously withdrawn. He could hear her eager breathing and the patter of her hands among the rain-laden branches.

"Whuh on earth" (*who* on earth can spell the word as a real

D 7

Southern girl says it?) "did you hide that pail? Ah've no time fo' *nawn*sense."

Silence a moment.

"Look *hyuh*, Mr. Yankee! Ah'm not accustomed to being made a fool of, 'n' Ah want that money. Ah've had to wait too long already."

A sound as of something shaking in a tin vessel, but farther away, towards a broader gap in the dark hedge.

"Ah'm not going up *thuh*. Ah told you twice befoh. You bring that pail back hyuh" (indignantly). "Ah don't believe you've gawt the money at all" (tentatively). "If you had, no gentleman would keep me waiting—when we need it so much." (Symptoms of vanishing nerve, and again a tempting rattle.) "Ah *can't* go there" (pleadingly now). "Please bring it hyuh, Mr. Riggs. Brothuh Floyd would be fuyious if he knew" (pause)—"an' we had such awful trouble las' night, —all on account of some of your rascally——Oh! whut's that new lieutenant's name?" (Sudden change of theme and tone.)

"His name's Ike," was the response in a hoarse whisper across the dripping rose-bushes.

"Ah don't believe a wuhd you say. Whut's his *real* name?"

"Ask Mr. Potts if his name isn't Ike; and come and get your money."

"Ah don't have a chance to ask Mr. Potts anything. They don't allow me in the pahlor when Mr. Bahton Potts comes. Ah'm too much of a child to be trusted with family secrets, it seems; though Ah'm not too young to find out how much we need money.—Whuh's that pail?"—suddenly coming down to business again.

Lambert gave it a shake, this time within reach of a little hand that darted in among the bushes and firmly closed upon his own.

"You let go that pail!" was the imperious demand from within.

"I can't—till you let go my hand," from without.

"Ah don't *want* your hand. Ah want——"

"I didn't offer it, but, since you like it so much, here's the other." And through the darkness another hand, with soft warm palm and long, slender fingers, closed in upon the hot little paw straining and tugging at the original occupant of the handle. Instantly, with indignant force, the enfolded member was snatched away, and the stooping girl sprang to her feet, wild-eyed and alarmed.

"Wh' *ah* you?" she panted. "That's not Sergeant Riggs." A window was suddenly raised back towards the house; the mournful toot of a tin horn began. "Quick! Ah've *got* to go. Roll that pail through. Why didn't Mr. Riggs come?"

"He's detained,—on duty; but it's all right. Where's the butter-milk?"

Through the trees behind the girl came Elinor at top speed: one could hear the rustle rods away. "F' Gawd's *sake*, Mis' Katie, come quick. Mis' Walton's callin'."

But Kate was fumbling for something in her pocket and bending forward to the hedge. The next instant, with brilliant flash, the glare of a parlor match leaped out one second on the night and fell full on a laughing, handsome young face peering in from under the visor of an infantry forage-cap. One second only, and down went the match, and with stifled cry away bounded the youngest daughter of the household of Walton,—even the precious pail forgotten.

Ten minutes later a horseman came galloping up the muddy road and inquiring eagerly for the lieutenant. Lambert recognized him as one of the deputies or assistants engaged in Saturday's affair at the jail. He handed a folded paper to the young officer, and, in low, excited tones, began some explanatory comments.

"Wait," said Lambert. "Let me read."

Tearing open the paper, by the dim light of Burns's lantern he made out the following:

"LIEUTENANT LAMBERT:

"Post guard at once around Walton place, so as to prevent any men from getting in or out. Take half the company if you need it. I'll be there in half an hour.

"CLOSE,
" B'vt. Capt. Com'd'g."

XI.

At ten o'clock that dark and gloomy Sunday night Mr. Lambert stood in front of his tent, leaning on his sword and listening in silence to the conference going on between his commander and the civil officers of the law. Close had come home in high dudgeon, and was, as usual, slow and cautious, but more than usually reluctant and suspicious. Fuming over the failure of the mission on which he had started so confidently, believing himself "tricked by the enemy," and now offered ample revenge and assured of success through the information tendered him, he nevertheless faltered. Lambert, returning from the round of his sentries, was taken unawares by the sudden question,—

"This gentleman says the old lady knew just where we had gone and just when we would get back. What do *you* think of it?"

"It's a matter I know nothing about, sir," was the answer, "except that she did say she was writing a letter to be given you on your return this evening, and instantly corrected herself by saying on your return."

"Yes. Here's the letter, by Jove, and it's a worse puzzle than before. And here's the deputy marshal back with increased powers, new orders, search-warrants, and God knows what all.—I'm willing enough to back you in dealing with men, Mr. Parmelee," said the captain, turning again to the eager civilian, "but the lieutenant has had these sentries posted forty minutes and there hasn't been a sound. I don't want any searching of a house that holds nothing but women, because you think some of your jail-birds are there——"

"I tell you, captain, there's no room for doubt. The negroes have seen them. *They* told Mr. Jarvis, here, and told him the mules were to be there before ten o'clock to carry 'em off out of harm's way. Your man Murphy admits he saw one last night,—one of the Scroggses, sure, by the description, and his brother is with him there, I'll bet a hat."

"I don't believe it," sturdily answered Close. "Only last August she turned Walton Scroggs away from her door with such a tongue-lashing as *I* never heard; an' that's saying a good deal. She forbade his ever setting foot within her gates again. I heard her; so did half the men in this company."

"I know all about that. He has been in love with his cousin, the elder of the Walton girls, as long as I can remember, and because of his shiftless habits the old lady wouldn't listen to it. Then they took to meeting by stealth, and she found it out. She discharged old Rasmus for no other reason than that he carried letters for them. I've tried to bribe him twice to tell where Wal Scroggs was hiding, but the old nigger's a dam fool,—with a starving wife, too. They tell me he was seen round here a day or two since, asking for Riggs, and he's been carrying letters again. The old lady wouldn't have him there before, perhaps, but she would shelter him now, when the government demands his surrender. But, even if *she* wouldn't, Esther Walton would. I tell you they're *there*, captain, and they'll be off and out of our reach this night if you fail to take them now."

Close was pulling on a soldier's overcoat at the moment, and stopped to listen to some sound down the dark recesses of the "bottom" along the winding stream.

"It's the mules now!" began Parmelee, excitedly, but Close held up a warning hand.

"If it is, my men will nab 'em, that's all. Now you've been the means of my takin' the men on more'n one long wild-goose chase afoot —that telegram of yours was enough to give the whole scheme away— and of my bein' invited to be dam fool enough to fight two duels this afternoon. Both Colonel Scroggs and Mr. Barton Potts, by thunder, want me to go out and be shot because I preferred to satisfy myself Mr. Wal Scroggs wasn't in the old Gibson place, 'stead of takin' their word of honor for it. There's a sick lady there who was scared of Yankee uniforms; but I'd rather search all Tugaloo and Quitman and hell together than rout out old Mis' Walton to-night. They can't get out past my sentries. They're sure to be nabbed if they try. Let 'em try, I say. It's the easiest way to settle the whole business. Then they can be arrested without disturbin' anybody in the house."

But Parmelee was dissatisfied. He had been chaffed, jeered at, maddened over the escape of his prisoners. Two of them—the worst of the lot, so far as he could judge—were here now, within his grasp, if he could but persuade Close to act. He had still a card to play, and it was a trump lead:

"I *did* send you a telegram steering you to Gibson's, and I did it because the marshal himself so directed; for it was he who was sure that was where they had taken refuge. Scroggs and his precious kinsman, Potts, probably got warning in time to send their two refugees away, and now they've had the cheek to hide them here, right under your nose. Talk about the record you've made as a preserver of the peace down here: how'll it read all over the North that, after being released from jail in the presence of Captain Close's company, the worst of the gang—men under indictment for murderous assault on United States officers in discharge of their duties—came and took up their residence across the road from Captain Close's camp and dared him to take them? That's the way it will read, by God, if you don't act to-night."

7*

For a moment Close simply stared at the man. Parmelee was no fighter, man to man, steel to steel; *that* the war veteran knew well; but the Yankee school-master of the *ante bellum* days had learned to use his wits and tongue. He could argue, if he couldn't face a bullet. The stalwart soldier who, single-handed, had captured a squad of as-tonished trench-defenders before Vicksburg and had faced the blazing battle-line with dauntless front a score of times, looked helplessly a moment into the face of this keen fencer, then turned appealingly to the young West Pointer, as though to ask, "Isn't there something in your education to answer this?" But Lambert was silent. From first to last the lesson taught him at the National Academy was sub-ordination of the military to the civil authority.

"Well, go ahead. You're boss, I s'pose. I can only follow. What d'you want me to do?" said Close.

"I want you to search that house and get those men," was Parme-lee's answer.

And then there was another moment of oppressive silence; then sudden start and alarm.

Down the Tugaloo road to the south, at the farthest corner of the fence which surrounded the Walton place, there was a pathway leading through the brush to the level "bottom" below. Somewhere in this direction, but beyond the corner, only a few seconds before, had been heard a sound like that of a bray nipped suddenly in the bud,—of a mule's essay at vocalism checked summarily with a club. At this point where road and pathway came together Lambert had posted Private Green, a reliable soldier of many years' experience, and when Green challenged there was reason for it. Low and stern his voice was heard distinctly at the listening camp,—"Who comes there?" followed almost immediately by the sharp order, "Halt! *Halt*, or I fire."

Waiting for no order, Lambert was off like a dart, Burns following with a lantern. Again came the cry "Halt!" but the promised shot was not heard. Even when running at speed past the gate of the Walton place, the young officer could not resist a quick glance at the dark façade of the old homestead. Already a light was dancing along the portico, another gleaming at an upper window.

"What's the matter, sentry?" he panted, as he came upon the dark figure at the turn of the road. Green, with his rifle at "ready," was peering into the gap in the tangle of shrubbery.

"Some one was coming up there, sir, and ran the instant I challenged. I ought to have let him get up to me and then halted him, but I had regulations instead of sense in my head," said Green, a New-Englander with a propensity for talk. "He's out o' harm's way——"

But Lambert waited to hear no more. With Burns at his heels he sprang down the dim pathway, and had not gone thirty yards before he came upon some struggling objects crashing into the brush towards the stream. "Halt!" he shouted, and, while something halted, other somethings, with muttered oaths, went plunging on. He heard a splash, hoofs clattering over gravel, the lashing of a whip, and then all was still across the dark open space through which flowed the sluggish "branch." But here among the bushes were two wondering quadrupeds, one a mule with broken bridle-rein, the other, as Burns's lantern speedily showed, a Cherokee pony,—both saddled. A corporal came running to join them, and in a moment the beasts were led back to the road-way, where Close and Parmelee by this time stood ready to receive them. One glance was all the latter needed.

"What did I tell you, captain?" said he, in triumph. "That is Wal Scroggs's own pony, and the master's hiding there at the Walton place."

Ten minutes more, and a strange, solemn scene was being enacted at the head of the steps leading up to that broad, vine-covered old porch, whose dingy white columns loomed dim and ghostly in the glare of lantern and candle. The door was thrown wide open, and on the worn coping-stone, calm, dignified, erect, even though leaning heavily upon her cane, a lighted candle held high over the shimmering gray of her well-poised head, her stately, slender form garbed in some dark clinging robe, stood the mistress of the house, the clear-cut, pallid face standing forth against the black background of the hall-way like some exquisite cameo, the thin, sensitive lips quivering just a trifle at the drooping corners of her firmly-set, almost colorless mouth. In front of her, his brown head bared, his burly form nearly concealed in his light-blue overcoat, an almost pleading look in his soft brown eyes, was Close, the hero of a score of battles. On his right, folded and formidable-looking documents extended in an unsteady hand, also with uncovered head, stood Parmelee, representing the majesty of the law. To the left of the commander and a pace retired, buttoned to the throat in the uniform of his rank and girt with sash and belt, stood young Lambert, obedient to orders. Behind them, and almost at the top of the steps, armed and equipped, a sergeant and two soldiers of the guard. Back, farther down the steps, still others were grouped, the fixed bayonets gleaming in the light of the two lamps, one held by the amazed woman at the threshold; the other swinging from the gloved hand of the sergeant of the guard.

"What you say, sir, is absurd,—impossible. At no time, under no circumstances," Mrs. Walton was saying, "could the gentleman you name be secreted in that room."

"Madam," replied Close, his deep voice trembling, "nobody can feel more sorry about this than I do. I'd rather go through the whole war over again than be here on such an errand to-night, but—a soldier must obey his orders. I *saw* him, madam, at that window. These gentlemen saw——"

"*Gentlemen!* Gentlemen, sir, never could connive at such an outrage. That is my daughter's room,—Miss Esther Walton's."

Dead silence for a moment, solemn and impressive indeed, for Close turned helplessly to the supporter on his right, unable to face such majesty of confidence and conviction, unable to say the words that could sound only like insult intensified. It was Parmelee whose sense of duty rose superior to exalted sentiment.

"Madam," he began, stepping forward, "these papers are full warrant for my action. I know two men to be secreted here. I, too, saw one at that window, and the law must take its course."

"*Stop!*" she cried. "I have said that was my daughter's room. One of your party, at least, has the appearance of a gentleman. Lieutenant Lambert, is it possible that you—that *any* graduate of West Point—can stand here and permit such outrage as this? Would you allow your sister's room to be searched for—oh, my God! nothing we have had to bear was comparable to this. I give you my word of honor no such man is, or has been——"

But she got no further. Out from the dark hall-way, with bounding step, tall, slender, and athletic, sprang a young fellow with the warning cry, "*Mother!* not another word."

She strove to check him as he pushed his impetuous way past her. With a wail of anguish unspeakable she threw aside her cane and seized him by the arm. Down went the candle sputtering to the floor. "Floyd—Floyd! Oh, my boy, what have you done?" she moaned, and bowed her gray head upon the broad young shoulder.

And then, with just a touch of the melodramatic in his bearing, the youth folded his arms and stood erect before the astonished group of officials.

"I reckon, gentlemen, *I'm* the man you want."

Close looked at him in bewilderment, then turned to Parmelee, whose face, whether through fear or excitement, was twitching nervously, and who stood staring blankly at the stranger. From the hallway came creeping hurriedly forth a girlish form, misery in the streaming eyes and dishevelled hair, and Katherine Walton threw herself upon her brother's arm, sobbing convulsively. "Hush, Kate," he whispered, in almost stern reproach. "Hush, child. Go back to your room;" and though now he enfolded his mother in the embrace of his left arm, he strove to free the right. But Katherine would not go.

And still, though here apparently was the sought-for prisoner, no man stepped forward to claim him. Officers and men, the nocturnal visitors looked blankly at one another, at the stricken group upon the threshold, and were silent. Then with sudden gesture, as though he could no longer bear the strain, the young man broke loose from Katherine's clinging arms, and, gently unclasping his mother's hands, once again addressed himself to Close:

"I say, suh, I reckon you've come for me. I'm ready to go with you at once."

And then, with wonder and relief in their faces, with sudden check to sobs and tears, mother and sister lifted up their heads and stared at the embarrassed officer. Lambert gave vent to an audible gasp of delight, for Close, turning slowly upon the silent and astonished deputy, and with a world of suppressed wrath in his deep tones, growled forth,—

"You've got no warrant for this gentleman. I never saw him before in my life, and never heard of him as being mixed up in any trouble.—This is young Mr. Walton, isn't it?" he suddenly inquired of the stranger, over whose pale face a look of bewilderment was creeping, and who for a moment seemed unable to reply. It was Madam Walton who, with quivering, ashen lips and with hope, fear, yearning, anguish in her eyes, found voice to say,—

"This is my youngest son, suh,—Floyd Walton."

"You say," she continued tremulously, "you have no warrant—no cause for his arrest. Then in God's name go, and leave us in peace. I am not well; and, on my word of honor, no other man is hidden——"

"*Mother!* Hush!"

D *

A door hastily opened within,—the door leading to the room to the left of the entrance, the room at whose window Close and Parmelee could swear they saw the dim figure of a man peering forth as they entered the gate. A heavy footfall resounded through the hall. A light streamed forth from the opened room, and a woman's wailing, shuddering cry followed the tall powerful form that came striding to the front. With utter horror in her eyes, Mrs. Walton staggered, would have fallen, but for the clasping arm of her son, upon whose breast she now leaned, panting for breath and glaring at the new-comer, to whose side now sprang Esther, her long black hair streaming down the white wrapper in which her tall figure was enveloped,—Esther, who strove to drag the stranger back from before her mother's eyes.

"*You* here? *You?*" was Mrs. Walton's gasping cry. "And in—that room?"

"Mother!" wailed the elder daughter, throwing herself upon her knees before the fainting form,—"mother, listen.—Oh, make her hear me, Floyd!—Mother, I am Walton's wife."

But the words fell on senseless ears. The lady of Walton Hall slipped swooning, till they caught and bore her within the open doorway.

"Well," said Close, a moment later, "what do you want done with your man,—Walton Scroggs? One's enough for this night, I suppose."

"One's enough for me, as things have turned out. Now what are you going to do with the other?"

"Leave him here, with his mother, where he ought to be, of course. You've got no cause to arrest him."

"But you have, anyhow."

"*I!* What, I'd like to know?"

"Because he is a deserter from the United States Army."

XII.

The Christmas holidays were coming on at Walton Hall, where, sore stricken, its mistress lay hovering between life and death. Two weeks had passed since the eventful night of the arrests, and, though no change had come over the landscape, and days of sunshine were few and far between, some odd alterations had taken place in and around the old homestead. Of these the most remarkable was the appearance three times a day of a young officer in Yankee uniform at the family board,—a young officer who often prolonged his visit until late in the evening. Mr. Isaac Newton Lambert, though occupying his tent in camp, had become otherwise an inmate of the Walton establishment, for, unknown to the beloved invalid, her daughters were actually "taking boarders."

Another boarder, who had come and moved a modest bachelor kit into one of the up-stairs rooms facing the east and overlooking the little camp, was Mr. Barton Potts, better known to all the inmates as "Cousin Bart." Indeed, it was due in great measure to his advice and influence that Mr. Lambert was admitted. Impoverished as were the Waltons,—in dire need, as it turned out, now that the resolute woman who so many years had managed the family affairs was stricken down, —nothing but prompt action and the helping hands of kinsfolk and friends stood between them and starvation. Squire Potts—"Old Man Potts," as he was generally called—had urged on Mrs. Walton in November the propriety of her abandoning the place entirely and taking shelter for herself and her daughters under his roof. Even though in desperate need, she had declined,—for one reason, because that would bring Esther and Walton Scroggs together again ; for another, because she could not bear to think of the old home becoming the abiding-place of all the houseless, shiftless negroes in the neighborhood. She had offered the house, garden, and cotton-fields still remaining in her hands to any purchaser at almost any price ; but who was there to invest in such unprofitable estate at such a time?

In the midst of these cares and troubles, which she could share with her daughters, were others which she could not. She durst not let them know on how slender a thread her life depended. That was one secret, held as yet by their old family physician and herself alone, because the knowledge of it would bring such grief to "the girls." There was another, which she prayed they might never know, because its very existence brought such grief and shame to her : Floyd, her youngest son, her darling, who had fought so bravely by his brother's side through the hottest battles of the war, had "abjured the faith of his fathers," as she bitterly expressed it,—had become intimate with the Federal officers and soldiers, instead of sticking closely to reading law in the office of her old friend Judge Summers at Quitman. And then, worse than all, she learned through his own desperate letter that he had enlisted in the cavalry. That within a week thereafter, repenting of his "mad folly," he should have deserted the service and fled the country, was in the poor stricken woman's eyes no crime whatever. That he should have enlisted, sworn to defend the flag which was to her the emblem of insolent triumph over the fallen fortunes of the land she loved, the only land she ever knew, the once happy, sunny South,—*that* was infamy.

Not until weeks after her boy had taken the step that made him a fugitive from justice did she learn, or begin to imagine, the chain of circumstances that led to it all. While occupying a desk in the office of Summers and Todd, Attorneys and Counsellors-at-Law, Floyd also occupied a seat at the table of a widowed relative who, left penniless at the close of the war, had to struggle hard to keep body and soul together. The efforts of Judge Summers had been sufficient to save the house in which she dwelt, and "taking boarders" became her vocation. But paying boarders were scarce, and even when her table was crowded with homeless people her pockets were often empty. When Sweet's squadron of the —th U. S. Cavalry marched into town and took station there, the application of some of the officers for "rations and quarters" under her roof was coldly declined. They went to the hotel, and suffered, as they deserved, the pangs of indigestion. Later it transpired that two of them went to church, and this put an unlooked-for factor into the problem of how to treat these conquering but unpopular heroes. The Reverend Mr. Pickett, of St. Paul's, might condone his parishioners' refusal to supply them with bodily food, but it was impossible to refuse to minister to their spiritual necessities. Their religious faith was identical with that of his flock; it was in political faith that they differed. One *might* decline to sit at meat with them, but could hardly decline to sit with them at worship. They could be forbidden to eat with the elect, but the elect would not forbid them to pray. Even in the sanctuary, however, only hostile or averted looks were vouchsafed to Colonel Sweet and Captain Vinton when first they sought its doors; but in the course of a few months the women found that their soldiers—their husbands, brothers, or lovers, whom the war had spared—were actually fraternizing with the Yankee invaders, and that between those who had done hard and honest fighting on either side there was springing up firm and honest friendship. The irreconcilables were limited, apparently, to the non-combatants. When the squadron was ordered elsewhere after a six months' sojourn at Quitman, the populace was astonished to find how much the troopers were missed and really needed; for even Yankee custom had been acceptable in the stores and Yankee contributions welcome in the church. Business had brought Colonel Sweet to Summers's office, and in the course of frequent visits cordial relations were established, and Floyd Walton could hardly treat with disdain a soldier and gentleman whom his patrons welcomed, even had he long retained the disposition to do so.

The command had not been gone a week before men were unaccountably wishing it back, and when it reappeared, with certain additions, it was actually welcomed by people who would have scouted the possibility of such a thing the year before. This time Colonel Sweet announced to the rector that his wife and daughter would speedily follow, and were even then in New Orleans, awaiting his instructions to come. The hotel was no place for ladies in those rough days: the rector went to Mrs. Tower, and Mrs. Tower no longer resisted the inevitable. Floyd Walton, going to tea one hot June evening, was astonished to find himself in the presence of two ladies, one of them a pretty girl of perhaps eighteen, and to be presented to Mrs. and Miss Sweet. Within a week the young fellow was spending his evenings at the Towers', and within the month was hopelessly in love. Then came trouble. He hadn't a cent in the world. She was a soldier's daughter, and presumably poor. Whether she was poor or not, he, at least, had nothing to offer, and, having nothing, held his tongue, though he could not hold his peace. That was gone.

That was a wretched summer and autumn. The fever raged along the Gulf, and cholera swooped upon the garrison. Sweet got his wife and child away to the mountains. They left suddenly, while Floyd was on a brief visit to his mother and sisters. It was December when they came back. Meantime, Judge Summers had abandoned practice and gone to live at his old home at Sandbrook. Mr. Todd could offer young Walton no help; there was no money in law business just then. Matters at Tugaloo were going from bad to worse, and Walton found himself absolutely without money to pay his board. That made no difference to Mrs. Tower. She told him his mother's boy was as welcome as her own, and *made* him welcome where fascination all too strong already held him. Something in Jennie Sweet's gentle manner had changed. She was nervous, ill at ease, and sought to avoid him. Something in her mother's manner, too, was very different. And one day the truth came out. The frequency with which

8

letters began chasing one another from the North explained the whole thing. Jenny had met her fate that fatal summer among the Virginia mountains, and was engaged to be married. Mrs. Sweet referred to the happy man as "a wealthy gentleman from Philadelphia, a few years older than Genevieve, but a most charming person." Genevieve herself said little or nothing, but looked none too radiant. Colonel Sweet said less, but looked much at her.

Then Floyd Walton found another boarding-place, and one where the influences were worse. He threw up his position in the law-office and took a humble clerkship at a store. It paid him enough to board and lodge him, and here, from serving his customers with drink, he got to serving himself, and to associating with a reckless set, some young townsmen, some soldiers. There were stories of gambling and quarrel even before Colonel Sweet found that Jenny, the apple of his eye, was drooping in that Southern climate, and sent her, with her mother, North "for good." The next thing heard of Floyd Walton was that he had gone to New Orleans with a discharged soldier; and, even while grieving over her boy's infrequent letters and evident hopelessness and depression, Mrs. Walton received a missive one day that left her prostrate. She went alone to Quitman as soon as able to move, and came back within forty-eight hours looking years older, and both the girls soon knew that she had parted with the diamond ear-rings that were their father's last gift to her in the happy, prosperous days that preceded the war. Floyd had written that, starving, drunk or drugged, and desperate, he had been led by his associate before a recruiting officer, had been sent with others as reckless as himself to sober up at the quarters of a cavalry command near the city, and that, the next thing he knew, he with a squad of seven recruits was on his way to join a troop stationed within a few miles of his home, instead, as he had been assured would be the case, of being sent to the Fourth Cavalry on frontier duty against the Indians in Texas. "They broke their contract," he said, "and I broke mine." He had deserted, and, if captured, would be sent to hard labor at Baton Rouge Penitentiary or to the Dry Tortugas.

Such stories leak out despite every effort to conceal them, but not until just before Lambert's coming to join Company "G" did Mrs. Walton dream that Esther knew of her brother's peril. A sudden outcry in her garden one day brought her in haste to the spot, and there were a drunken soldier and her quadroon maid Elinor,—he demanding liquor and she the return of a pitcher which he had evidently snatched from her hand. Madam Walton's stately presence and her imperious order that he leave the premises at once only partially sobered him. He gave her to understand that if she reported him he could bring shame upon her head,—he knew more about her affairs than she dreamed. His insolence tried her temper, but could not alter her tone and bearing. It was not until he was gone that Esther, trembling and in tears, came and begged her to lodge no complaint against the man, as he indeed knew more than she supposed. And then, in reply to her mother's demand, Esther brokenly admitted that she had already heard of Floyd's enlistment and desertion through this very soldier. He had been at the house before. What she did not tell her mother was that the news first reached her through Walton Scroggs.

And then, without warning, Floyd suddenly came home. So troubled had he been by the condition of his mother's health and affairs as confided in Esther's letters (sent under cover to an old family friend now serving as a surgeon in the Juarez army) that, having earned a little money in Vera Cruz, he hastened back and appeared there late at evening, worn and weary, before those loving yet terrified eyes. He had ridden miles on horseback that day, as he feared recognition by officers or soldiers still at Quitman if he came by rail that way, or by Federal deputies if he came the other. Esther alone had received him on his arrival, for she, poor girl, was watching at the old arbor near the south fence for the coming of her lover-husband, that day released from the clutches of the law. Then, after hearing her recital of their needs and sorrows, he had sent old Rasmus with a message into camp, while she had gone to prepare her mother for his coming.

Late that night Mrs. Walton, kneeling by the bedside of her sleeping boy, became suddenly aware of a scuffle going on underneath the window, and, noiselessly descending the stairs, unfastened the side door and came at once upon the intruders, with the result already known. Not until aroused by the screams of Elinor and his sister Kate did Floyd know anything of the affair. Half asleep, and bewildered, he had jumped into boots and trousers and rushed to the rescue. One glance explained the whole thing, but it was Esther who in desperation seized and held him back when he would have sprung to release his mother from Riggs's drunken grasp,—Esther who, hearing the coming rush of Lambert's footsteps, realized that what meant instant rescue for her mother meant equally instant peril for him,—Esther who actually ordered his hurried retreat at Lambert's appearance. Not until the following day did it occur to her mother to ask how it was or why it was that she was up and dressed at that hour of the night. At any other time, perhaps, she would have found it far more difficult to frame plausible excuse, but almost anything would answer now. For hours she had been listening for the tap upon her window that should tell her Walton had not been spirited away to a place of safety until he had come to bless and comfort her with his love-words and caresses. To her, at least, despite the wild oats of his earlier days, her cousin-husband was all that was true and tender and fond. For him she had dared her mother's wrath, her younger sister's indignation, and Floyd alone was her supporter in the secret marriage that took place during her brief visit to the Claytons in the early spring.

With the dawn of Sunday, his signal at last was heard, and she stole out to meet him,—to tell of Floyd's return, and to plan with him for their joint escape, for Floyd had told her that it would be folly to attempt to remain in hiding there. Already certain negroes of the neighborhood had seen him, and it could not be long before the military authorities were informed. Walton was all helpfulness and sympathy. His brother, the conductor, had planned to send his horse to the Walton barn at ten that night, and "Wal" was to ride 'cross country to a friend's in Barksdale County, leave the horse there, and be at the point where the railway crossed the county road at eleven-thirty, when the "Owl" would stop and take him on the baggage-car, —unless some of Parmelee's spies or deputies were aboard. There would be no trouble at the capital, where the Owl often waited an hour for the express. The engineer would slow up just east of town. Walton could drop off in the darkness and make his way around to the west side by a brisk tramp of a couple of miles, and there be taken on again about one-thirty A.M. and jostled away to the river. Once there, all the sheriff's posses in the South couldn't find him. Walton promptly urged that Floyd go with him. Rasmus was routed out from slumber in the barn and sent away with messages for Colonel Scroggs and "Cousin Bart," and then the voice of Kate was heard, calling for her sister. Instead of being asleep, as they hoped, Mrs. Walton was painfully awake and planning a diplomatic letter to be sent to Captain Close. For hours the only refuge they could offer Esther's husband was the cellar, for Mrs. Walton had insisted on being up and dressed to meet Cousin Bart, whom now she desired to send for and consult.

The letter which had so bewildered the company commander was brief enough. It bore neither date nor place, but went straight to business:

"Mrs. Walton presents her compliments to the officer in command of the Federal troops here in camp, and begs to say that she finds upon investigation that the two soldiers who visited her premises last night did so at the request of a member of her household, who sought their aid in bringing certain supplies from town when her servants proved too ungrateful to be relied upon. Mrs. Walton deeply regrets that the soldiers referred to are now in danger of further punishment, and, while utterly disapproving the action which led to their employment in violation of her express orders, she nevertheless accepts the entire responsibility, and begs that no further steps may be taken against them, as she will not only positively refuse to appear as a witness in the case, but will prohibit any of her household from so appearing.

"Sunday morning."

And very possibly the lady of Walton Hall felt quite assured that her mandate would overrule any subpœna the Federal authority could draft. One thing is certain, when Close read it over a second time he handed it to Lambert, saying, "So far as I'm concerned, that blessed old lady shan't have any trouble on account of them two scallawags. She's got too much of her own. Unless you want to make an example of Riggs, you can release him in the morning. Murphy ought to be let off anyhow."

But when morning came it was found that Riggs had released himself. How he managed to cut his way out of that guard-tent without disturbing anybody, no one could explain. He was gone at daybreak, leaving not a trace behind.

XIII.

Confined to her bed and room as was Madam Walton, and only vaguely alive to what might be going on in the household,—for there were days when she lay dull and apathetic, yet mercifully spared from

8*

suffering,—it was Esther's duty and fondest care to minister to her mother's needs even at a time when her heart was torn with anxiety on account of her husband, now a prisoner in the hands of the United States marshal at the capital, and of her brother, who, under the orders of the general in command of the department, had been sent under guard to New Orleans, there to await his trial by court-martial for the crime of desertion. The visits of the old family physician were frequent, for the invalid had had too much to suffer and seemed incapable of further struggle. Floyd was twice permitted to visit his mother during the two days that elapsed before telegraphic orders came in his case. She knew him, clung to him, yet seemed unable to realize that he was going from her. She once or twice asked if Judge Summers had been heard from, for Cousin Bart had written full details of Floyd's trouble, and the family united in urging him to make an appeal to certain influential friends of the *ante bellum* days, who had scandalized the Waltons by their loyalty to the old flag. Then Lambert wrote a letter which Close signed and sent to department headquarters, and the boy, remembering some kind words said to him by his father's old friend, ventured on a personal letter to the general himself, pleading Walton's cause and portraying the family's distress. It was this letter that overcame Esther's objection to the advice of Mr. Potts to the effect that they take Mr. Lambert in as a day boarder. And within forty-eight hours of his initial appearance at their table Mrs. Scroggs, as he was the first to address his blushing hostess, was more than reconciled to the step.

But if she was, Miss Kate was not. The wrath and indignation of that young lady can hardly be described. It was one thing, she declared, for her to sell eggs and butter to a gentleman who was a friend of Floyd's, who told her he despised his captain as much as she did, who had enlisted only because he had been promised immediate promotion to a captaincy, and who never would have done so even then, had he known that soldiers could be used to persecute the people of the South. He was only waiting for his commission to come—or his discharge—to tell Captain Close what he thought of his conduct. It was all very well to make friends with gentlemen like Mr. Riggs, who had been dear brother Floyd's friend at Quitman before he fell in love with that horrid designing Yankee girl who had lured him on to "cohtin'" her when she was all the time engaged to that rich ragpicker—or whateveh he might be. Mr. Riggs had behaved like a

*puh*fect gentleman. (She had forgotten the little bill he had been running up and was so long vainly importuned to pay. She also attached
slight importance to Barton's statement that "Brother Floyd said
Riggs was a fraud and a liar, and responsible for much—though not
all—of his trouble.") As between Mr. Riggs and this new Yankee
lieutenant who had dared to disguise himself and seek to make her
acquaintance, she had but one opinion : Riggs was driven to drink and
desertion by having had to serve under such brutes. She declared she
would starve rather than eat under the same roof with Lieutenant
Lambert, insisted on staying in her mother's room and being served
there, and was conspicuous by her absence from the table for the first
forty-eight hours since Lambert's admittance, despite Esther's pleading
and Barton's ridicule. " *You* may think it fine to take money from
such people, Mrs. Scroggs," she declared, with high disdain ; " but you
never would, if Moh was well enough to know whut was going on."
(*Moh* is the only alphabetical combination I can think of which even
approximately represents Miss Katie's pronunciation of the term by
which she was accustomed to refer to her mother.) But if Miss Kate
were indignant before, she was simply furious when her married sister
responded, with exasperating calm,—

"And yet *you* took Mr. Lambert's money in payment for your
butter, Katesie."

"Ah *didn't!* How day-ah you say so, Esthuh? It was Mr.
Riggs's."

" Floyd says it wasn't. Floyd says that man had not had a cent
for three weeks. You know yourself it was Mr. Lambert there at the
fence both nights, and you know why that wretch couldn't have been
there."

" Ah'll wuhk every finguh to the bone, then, till it's paid back,"
cried Miss Walton. "An' it was mean an' contemptible an' cowuhdly
in him to fawce it on me as he did,—to listen to whut wasn't meant fo'
his *yuhs* at all." By his " yuhs" Miss Walton meant those organs of
hearing that lay so close under the brown curls on either side of Mr.
Lambert's shapely head,—ears which she could gladly have pinched, or
tweaked, or even banged, in her wrath at that moment. The hard-
earned, long-expected five dollars had been sent to town and expended
before this sisterly conference took place, or beyond doubt Miss Katesie
would have hurled it back at the donor when he came so springily up
the walk that crisp December evening.

Two days later brought a long letter from Floyd, written from the barracks at New Orleans. He was not confined in the guard-house, as he had feared and expected to be. The prisoners awaiting sentence were there, but those yet to be tried were kept in an old storehouse that was not uncomfortable, and on the evening of his arrival an officer, Lieutenant Waring of the artillery, took him into a separate room, "treated me like a perfect gentleman," wrote poor Floyd, leaving his readers to divine whether this lavish descriptive were to apply to the lieutenant or himself, listened to Floyd's story from beginning to end, and told him to keep up his spirits. "Lieutenant Lambert had written urging him to do all he could to help me, and had asked old General Ducannon to restore me to duty without trial, in view of the way I had been tricked. If he does, and will send me out against those infernal Indians in Texas, by heaven I'll show them I can fight as hard for the flag to-day as I did against it three and four years ago. All I ask is officers and gentlemen like him—or young Lambert—to serve under, and I'll *earn* my pardon."

They had been utterly blue and hopeless on Floyd's account since his transfer to New Orleans, and this letter was a revelation. Esther took it up to her mother's room and strove to make her understand its purport, "Katesie" sitting silently and, at first, scornfully by. Mrs. Walton's faculties seemed too dazed to follow, and Esther had to reiterate and explain. Then the doctor came, and the hale old gentleman's eyes filled as he read. "That young fellow is a trump," said he, referring to Lambert; and he, too, bent over the gentle invalid and whispered hope and courage. Later, when Kate was wanted, it was found she had quitted the room. Esther discovered her after considerable search, shivering in a room up-stairs. She wouldn't talk, but, that evening, came to tea.

For several days Miss Kate contrived to hold aloof from the general conversation; but it was a hard fight against every natural impulse. Before the end of the week her resolution had failed her utterly, and time and again her ready tongue had challenged Lambert to debate; and now, to her chagrin, it was he who declined. When formally presented to "My sister, Miss Walton," by Mrs. Scroggs, the young gentleman had bowed very low and had striven to be civil. As they sat facing each other, and only the width of the table apart, her downcast eyes and determined silence proved embarrassing, even though long, curving, sweeping lashes and flushed cheeks appeared, perhaps, to dan-

gerous advantage. " Aw pshaw !" said Cousin Bart that evening, as
he and Lambert were smoking the pipe of peace, and the young fellow
ventured a fear that he had offended the damsel in the butter business,
"just you pay no attention to that child for a day or two, an' see how
quick she'll come round. She just wants to be huffy. She'll be haw-
bly cut up when she finds you don't notice her." Potts had not a little
worldly wisdom when he wasn't drinking, and since his installation as
ex-officio head of the house he hadn't touched a drop. Lambert was
beginning to like him very much, but couldn't induce him to come
over to camp. " I can't stand that captain of yours," was his sole
explanation.

From frigid silence on Katesie's part to occasional monosyllable
and thence to brief and caustic comments on the remarks of her sister
and cousin, the transition was easy ; but now that Lambert addressed
no remarks whatever to her, yet chatted smilingly with the others, the
girl's position became exasperating. She was willing enough, at the
start, to keep at wide distance, but that anybody should presume to
hold her there was a very different matter, in fact, simply intolerable.
Esther noted in silent amusement how the girl began to display unaccustomed solicitude as to the fit of her gown, the effect of such poor
little efforts at ornamentation as her simple store of lace or ribbon
afforded. Such quaint, old-fashioned bows and flounces as came forth,
such queer combinations of shade and color ! Esther caught her more
than once glancing up shyly from under the long lashes and looking
furtively at her *vis-à-vis*, for Lambert, with malice prepense and afore-
thought, began telling Mrs. Scroggs of the belles and beauties of last
summer at the Point, and one evening when the verbal blockade had
lasted perhaps three days he turned to Esther as they were rising from
the table,—and if it wasn't taking a mean advantage of a defenceless
foe, what would be ?

" I brought over these two to show you, Mrs. Scroggs," said he,
producing some carte-de-visite photographs from an envelope. " This
is Miss Fordham, who was considered the prettiest girl at Cozzens's this
year, though that fashionable street suit is perhaps less becoming to
her than evening dress. And this is Miss Torrance. I think I told
you that our ladies are no longer wearing crinoline, and that these
short dresses are worn even for calling in the daytime."

And Katie Walton was halted at the threshold as she would have
left the room. What woman could resist a peep at these pictures of

reigning belles garbed in the height of the fashion of the day,—a fashion these fair Southern sisters had never seen, and had only vaguely heard of! Cousin Bart could have laughed outright when he caught a glimpse of Katesie's face, but mercifully refrained. She flushed, stopped, bit her lip, turned and fairly ran up-stairs, but came down five minutes later, as Lambert knew she would, "looking for a book;" and Esther, yearning over her, called her sister to her side. Looking at Northern girls' pictures wasn't making friends with their friends, anyhow! "Ah don't see anything pretty in that one," was Katesie's prompt comment. "And Ah couldn't be hi-uhd to weah a gown like that." But Lambert felt that he had won the day, and the next evening fetched over a whole album-full. " *Ce n'est que le premier pas,*" etc. Miss Walton, having looked at two, concluded she might as well see the others, but she never meant to ask questions about them—as she had to when Esther went in to see what Moh would like for her tea. Cousin Bart had brought in a bag of plump and tempting "partridges" that evening, and it was beginning to puzzle Esther very much, when she remembered how impecunious a person Bart had ever been, to account for the supplies which he began to fetch from town.

And so things were going a trifle better at the old homestead towards the end of December. Hopeful letters came from Walton. The Parmelee party were having difficulty in getting reliable evidence against him; his friends were making him entirely comfortable in his confinement, and his lawyer assured him that his release would be effected in a very few days. Floyd wrote that an aide-de-camp of the general commanding had come with Lieutenant Waring to see him, and to say that his case was being investigated and that, as yet, no charges had been preferred by the commander of his troop. Little delicacies and luxuries in the way of tea, jellies, preserves, and wine—things to which they had been strangers since early in the war—were finding their way in and greatly comforting the invalid mother, and, could their doctor but say the dear lady was really mending, the girls would have had hope and courage, but the doctor *could* not say.

"I've got to go to Quitman for two days on business, Esther," said Cousin Bart one keen morning, "and I reckon I'll ask Dr. Falconer to come back with me, 'f you don't mind, and have a day at the birds. They'll all be gone in a week 'f this weather keeps on."

"You have deeper reason than that, Barton. I saw you with Dr. Coleman when he went out last night. It's a consultation, is it not?"

" Why, of co'se I want Coleman to have a chance to talk it over with Falconer, and *he'd* like it, too. Falconer's more up to date, the old man says, and he thinks perhaps the new school knows something wuth tryin'. You see, Cousin Lou ain't pickin' up fast as she ought to."

" I see it all too plainly, Bart. What I don't see is where all the money is to come from to pay for doctors and consultations and—and——" Big tears began welling in her soft, sad eyes. " Bart, where does it all come from now ? How do we get all these dainties ? *You* can't spare it. It *mustn't* be Mr. Lambert's——"

" Now just don't you bother 'bout that, Esther. I made a raise, I tell you. There's old Uncle Pete and that no-'count nigger Frank been owin' your mother on last year's crawp o' cawt'n all this time. I made them pony up, an' I told Hicks I'd sell out his mule an' cart 'f he didn't pay,—made him *bawwo* the money——"

" That wouldn't begin to cover the cost of what you've been having sent up from New Orleans,—the expressage even——"

" Now just don't you bawwo trouble." (One *r* in a sentence wasn't too much for Potts. When they doubled up on him he confessed judgment.) " Lambert 'tends to all that. Uncle Sam, he says, pays freight on commissary stores. Just do's I say, and we'll fetch Cousin Lou round all right yet, and find somebody to rent the old place and send yo' all down to Biloxi for the winter. But I'll tell you what I *do* think, Esther : y'ought to have Lambert over to sleep in my room while I'm gone. He'll come."

But when Lambert came to tea that night half expecting to be welcomed to Cousin Bart's place in his absence, a surprise awaited him. Esther, with joy in her eyes, blushingly told him that her husband would be with them before nine o'clock. A telegram had announced his release and speedy coming.

" There's no train over before morning, is there ?" he asked.

" No—but—Mr. Scroggs took the stage at noon for Vernon, up north of here, and will get a horse there."

And, as it was evident that she looked any moment for that longed-for coming, Lambert decided to slip back to camp instead of spending an hour in chat or reading as he usually did. At this Miss Katesie's big blue-gray eyes were opened wide in surprise, then lowered in confusion, for he turned to look at her.

" Oh ! Good-night, Miss Walton," he laughingly exclaimed. " I had almost hoped you would ask me to stay."

"Ah don't know wh'a Ah should," was the prompt and pouting reply. "Sister Esthuh can if she likes."

"She doesn't like, to-night—as a matter of course. I couldn't expect her to. But as your good mother is sleeping and Mrs. Scroggs will be able to leave her to welcome her husband and you will be—well —rather superfluous, I thought I might profit by the situation to the extent of having an hour's chat with you,—about your fair compatriots up North, for example."

"Ah don't know of any subject that would interest me less. And they're *not* my compatriots, as you call them," answered Miss Kate, with fire in her eyes.

"Ah, true," said Lambert, with provoking coolness, and a mischievous smile twitching the corners of his mouth : "I recall your indifference to their photographs the other evening. Will you kindly say good-night to Mrs. Scroggs for me, and tell her——"

"Ah'll tell her you were simply hateful and Ah thought you'd *never* go !"

"Well, I won't, if you think I ought to stay," said Lambert, returning smilingly to the door and proceeding to hang his forage-cap upon its accustomed peg. She promptly snatched it from his hand.

"Ah wish you and your photographs wuh freezing up Nawth, whuh you b'long, 'stead of coming down hyuh ty'annizing over people——"

"Now do you know I was wishing that too? It's so much nicer freezing up North than being frozen here ; and then next week's Christmas. Oh, you don't have any mistletoe here, do you?"

"We did, before *you* all came. You Yankees ruined everything nice you didn't carry off."

"Now what am I to say, Miss Katesie? If I *don't* say you're nice you'll think I'm ungallant; and what Yankee would ever dare try to carry *you* off?"

"Lieutenant Lambert, Ah think you're simply horrid, and Ah wish you'd go, 'stead of standing there pulling your moustache in that silly way."

"Now, Miss Katesie !—the idea of your being the first girl to set her face against this struggling moustache ! I never should have thought it of you. Or was it the mistletoe put you in mind——"

"*Will* you go?" she cried, with flaming cheeks and stamping foot.

"How day-uh you stand there laughing at me? Oh, if I were a man——"

"If you were a man nobody would think of such a thing. As I'm one, I can't help it."

"Ah wish Ah could help you down those steps and back to camp," she retorted, trying hard to look furious.

"You could, easily, but you don't want to, or you would have given me my cap long ago."

" *Oh!*" and the jaunty *képi* went spinning into the darkness of the night, and the little lady stamped in fury at her own blunder. " *Take* your cap, and go."

"We-ll," said Lambert, with provoking coolness, "if I'm to follow my cap it hasn't gone towards camp at all. It seems—excuse me if I come back for a light—it seems to have dropped close to that old arbor of yours among the rose-bushes, where you sit in the summer moonlit evenings. Suppose we leave it as an excuse for me to drop around next time you go there."

But now she seized a candle and went bounding down the steps. A moment's search among the bushes, and she had found it,—also him, for he calmly followed.

"There's your cap," she said, "and yawnduh's the gate!"

He looked up in affected pain and astonishment.

"Why, Miss Katesie!—I supposed you were simply acting on my suggestion, and we were going to have such a lovely time at the bower. That's why I followed."

"Oh, Ah should like to tay-uh your tongue out. You know Ah hate the very ground you stand on——"

The gloom in his face gave way instantly to radiant joy. "You do?—*really?*" he cried. "Oh, I never hoped for that! I thought you loved every inch of this ugly old State and that I never could coax you to leave it. Do you really hate it so?"

But now, fairly beside herself with vexation, the girl had turned and fled, her little feet seeming to fly up the worn old steps that groaned and creaked under any other touch. He stood gazing after her a moment, the teasing, merry smile still hovering about his lips, then picked up the cap she had hurled to earth, and walked blithely away.

Not ten yards from the gate came Corporal Cunningham on the run. Captain Close desired to see the lieutenant at once. A negro stood by the camp-fire in front of Close's tent, trembling from either fear or excitement or both, his protruding eyes fixed on the form of old Rasmus, who was eagerly jabbering to the company commander.

"Do you know anything 'bout this, lieutenant?" asked Close. "These darkies say there's been a big row over towards Vernon, and that Walton Scroggs is among the killed."

XIV.

The first Christmas a young fellow spends in the army is one he is apt to remember. What he did in years before, or of what nature were the festivities in those that followed, may, in course of time, become but vague and shadowy pictures before the mind's eye. After something like twenty years of service as a commissioned officer Mr. Lambert was heard to say that never, even when a homesick plebe at West Point, had he passed so forlorn a Christmastide as that which immediately succeeded his graduation.

The rain was beating down in sullen shower upon the bare and dripping woods and sodden fields; the roads were deep in mud; camp, of which he was once more commander, was wet and cold and cheerless; in the adjoining tent lay his senior officer groaning on a bed of pain, hands and face blistered and bandaged, hair and eyebrows gone, while over across the way a pile of scorched and blackened timbers, a couple of brick chimneys, and the stone foundations, were all that was left of Walton Hall.

The story brought in of the big row at Vernon, though exaggerated, had been sufficiently confirmed in the course of an hour or so that wintry evening of Lambert's last visit to the homestead, to warrant his being ordered thither with half the company to "support the civil authorities in restoring peace." Close reported the situation by telegraph to department head-quarters, and the action taken by him, his despatch reaching the general commanding the next day an hour or so after that official had been ordered from Washington to send full particulars of the disturbance in his bailiwick, for the Federal officials in the South and the partisans of both sides of the political questions at issue had worked the night wires for all they were worth, and the early morning papers were lurid with details of the tragic outbreak.

It was midnight when Lambert started on his march with two excited deputy marshals for guides. Five miles out they met some horsemen convoying an old carriage containing Walton Scroggs, seriously wounded, and a doctor. With the escort Lambert held brief parley, also with the wounded man, who, though weak, was full of pluck and spirits; his sole anxiety seemed to be on the score of his wife and the shock the news would cause her. The account given the young officer of the circumstances leading up to the fracas differed radically from that with which he and his commander had thus far been favored. This was to be expected, as, up to this point, their sole informants were either negroes or a couple of whites of the Parmelee stamp. In the North, as a rule, the affair appeared to have been a wanton and unprovoked attack by Walton Scroggs and his friends upon some negroes who had been instrumental in securing his arrest,—nothing short, in fact, of a red-handed act of vengeance, as was evident from the fact that immediately on his release he and his party, armed to the teeth, had ridden over to Vernon, instead of going home, and, without warning or warrant, had begun the indiscriminate shooting down of certain unpopular whites and their luckless negro supporters.

In the South, except among certain journals published in the interest of the "radical" Republican party, the other side of the story was promptly circulated. "Captain" Scroggs and a friend, endeavoring to reach home by a circuitous route so as to avoid trouble after his release from jail, where he had been incarcerated several weeks on baseless, trumped-up charges, were set upon in the streets of Vernon by a blackguardly pack of loafers, insulted, abused, and assaulted, and finally compelled in self-defence to draw their revolvers, not, however, until they had been fired upon. One odd circumstance connected with these perennial shooting scrapes in those days was the fact that in footing up the score it was always found that five negroes to one white was about the proportion of casualties. This may have been due to the fact that the ratio of black to white in every scrimmage was about five to one, or else that the Caucasian, being cooler and long skilled in the use of arms, was more effective in close combat. At all events, when impartially investigated, it was found that this Vernon difficulty differed from its fellows in no important particular except one,—that it "had no political significance whatever." Walton's friends, rejoicing with him in his release from durance vile, did so after the fashion of the day, and more or less bad whiskey was consumed before the stage reached Vernon,—where more friends were met, more treats exchanged, and where, as the devil of mischief would have it, he happened into the bar of the old tavern just at the moment when two or three others, all white, were happening out. One of these was an old-time admirer of Esther Walton, a man with whom Scroggs had been at odds for years. There was a jostle,—unintentional,—a sneer in the careless apology, and a rankling word or two. Peacemakers drew the principals apart. Indeed, Walton was too happy, too eager to continue his journey home and Estherwards, to care to quarrel. But his rival's heart and brain were burning; and more liquor made matters worse. The horses were being brought around from the stable with the troop of vagrant negroes loafing after, when, despite the efforts of his friends, the half-drunken man came lurching out of a neighboring saloon and with savage oaths rushed at Walton, "demanding satisfaction." Weapons were drawn and shots exchanged on the instant, and one of the scattering mob of negroes fell dead with a bullet through his heart, while for a moment Walton, with smoking pistol, stood alone looking down at his assailant writhing on the sidewalk. Friends rushed in, carried one man into the drug-store, and crowded Walton into the tavern bar. It was "fair fight." He had drawn only in self-defence. His assailant was to blame, and there was no man to suggest arrest. But he stood there pale and unnerved now, covered with sorrow at the disaster to the man who, even though no friend, was popular, well and widely known, and, according to the somewhat accessible standard of the State and day, "a perfect gentleman." It was characteristic of the time and place that nobody present happened to think of the dead negro.

Among these poor people Walton Scroggs was, perhaps deservedly, unpopular. The other man, open-handed, generous, easy-going, had won not a little of their unreasoning yet enthusiastic regard. It was while Scroggs, with two advisers, was seated, sad and trembling, in a little room of the tavern awaiting the result of the doctor's examination of his fainting foe, that a citizen came rushing in. "Scroggs, you'll have to get out of this,—quick. There was a meeting of that old Grant and Colfax Club going on up the street, and the niggers have rushed in and told 'em you killed Pete Jackson. The whole gang of 'em are coming."

Coming? They were already there. With furious yells and vengeful threats a surging crowd of negroes came tearing along the village street, stopping only a moment to verify the death of their friend, and —too late now for explanation or denial—they swarmed madly into the office, demanding Walton's body. The battle was on in an instant, a battle for life, a sixty seconds' war of races, white against black, as it had to be, since none would listen to reason, and superior nerve and aim told. Pistols and the office were emptied about the same moment, but five more darkies had gone to join Pete Jackson at the mercy-seat, and the proprietor of the Southern Star had died like the soldier he was, defending the life of his guest. Scroggs himself, seriously wounded, was borne away on the dark Tugaloo road, and far and wide the affrighted negroes were scurrying over the country, carrying tidings of riot as they ran.

It was all a miserable blunder, but the end was not yet. Lambert and his detachment took station at Vernon, whence the negroes had fled in terror, and all warring was at an end. Such were his orders, and he had no choice; yet it would have been wiser counsel to recall him and his party within twenty-four hours. They could have done better service nearer home. How it happened none could ever surely say. Among the whites it remained for years an article of faith that desperate and determined negroes had followed Walton Scroggs to his refuge and there wreaked vengeance for the blood of their fellows. Among the negroes it has never been looked on as other than a direct manifestation of divine wrath upon their enemies and persecutors. How the house could have so suddenly burst into flame every one could theorize and no one explain; but at three o'clock in the morning the few men remaining with Captain Close in camp were startled from their sleep by the report of the sentry's musket and the yell of " Fire !" and, springing from their tents, were greeted by the sound of crackling wood-work and screams for aid and the sight of Walton Hall one glare of flame.

Some men got there quicker than others,—none were slow,—but even the foremost of the soldiers were appalled and bewildered by what they saw and heard,—Katherine Walton and the quadroon maid Elinor wringing their hands and imploring them to save the bedridden mother, while Esther was making vain effort to drag a helpless form through the blazing hall-way. It was at this juncture that Close came laboring up the path. He was slow, heavy, had a longer distance to run, and was panting hard, but he burst through the squad already scrambling up the steps, sprang through the fire-flashing portal, and with the strength of an ox heaved Walton, groaning, upon his shoulders, tumbled him out into the arms of his men, then turned on gasping

Esther. "Where's your mother's room?" Almost fainting, she could only lean upon the pillar for support and point through the vista of smoke and flame. Close leaped in like a tiger, with Cunningham and Murphy at his back. An instant, and these latter reappeared, blind, staggering, their faces hidden in their hands, and burst out into the open air, stumbling heedlessly down the steps. A groan went up from the men : their captain was gone. In vain Burns and McBride strove to rush in to the rescue. Mortal man could not stand such heat. And then, in the midst of the wild wailing of the terrified and helpless women, came from around at the north side of the house an exultant cheer. Those men who had had sense enough to strive to reach the side windows were rewarded by the sudden thrusting open of the shutters and the appearance of the well-known burly form of their captain with some blanket-shrouded shape in his arms. The flames leaped forth from that very casement but a second after Close and his precious burden were lowered to the walk below.

And this was the story of a brave man's deed he heard from every lip, said Lambert later, as he hastened back on receipt of the news ; and this was the response made by the brave man himself, when his lieutenant bent over his senior's seared and bandaged face next day and tendered his soldierly congratulations. Turning slowly over on his side, Close pointed to the wreck of a pair of uniform trousers, scorched and burned in a dozen places and irretrievably ruined.

"Look," said he, mournfully. "Them was my best pants."

Then it was found that not only had the strange old fellow lost his hair and beard, and not a little of the cuticle of his face and hands, as well as those patched but precious "best pants," but that his eyesight was threatened. The good old doctor who had for so many years attended the Waltons, and who had come at once to renew his ministrations under the humble roof in town that was their temporary refuge, listened to the story of Close's heroism with quickened pulse and kindling eye. He and Mr. Barton Potts, who had hastened back from Quitman, came out to camp to see and thank the prostrate soldier, Potts being ceremonious in his expression of gratitude and admiration and most earnest in his apology for what he had said and thought of Close in the past. The doctor stayed longer by the silent sufferer's cot, carefully studying his face so far as it could be seen. Professional etiquette prevented his saying anything that might be a reflection on the treatment and practice of the "contract surgeon," yet it was plain to Lambert, and to Potts too, that he was disturbed. Close, however, seemed to think less of his own plight than of that of the Waltons, who, except the little patch of fields about the ruined homestead, had lost everything they owned in the world, and who were now in sore anxiety and distress. The terrible shock and exposure had been too much for one so fragile as the lady mother, and Mrs. Walton was sinking fast. Walton Scroggs, too, was in desperate case, though soothed by the knowledge that the cause of all the row at Vernon—that is, the human cause of it all—was already out of danger. Close begged the doctor for full particulars not only as to how they were but how they expected " to git along through the winter," and at last said he wished to speak with him alone, whereat Potts and Lambert, wondering, left the tent.

It was long before the doctor came forth, and when he did he called the young officer aside, a quiver in his voice and a queer moisture about his spectacles. " Have you no expert on the eye and ear in the army ?" he asked. " The captain should have the benefit of the best advice without delay."

Lambert said he would report the matter at once to department head-quarters, and, while they were still talking, two men came riding out from town,—" old man Potts," beyond all doubt, and with him Lambert's railway friend the conductor, and these gentlemen, too, had come to "surrender." Close could have had his fill of triumph and adulation that dull December evening, had he been so minded and the doctor more complaisant ; but that practitioner said that, while he was not in charge of the case, he should strenuously advise against further disturbance of the patient. When at last they were all gone and Lambert could address himself to the little packet of mail stacked up on the office desk, he was rejoicing to think how the good in his queer comrade was winning due recognition at last. " He's a rough diamond," he said to himself, " but brave as a lion and true as steel."

And then as he opened the first letter from department head-quarters, addressed to Brevet Captain J. P. Close, First Lieutenant, —teenth Infantry, Lambert's face paled and his eyes dilated. It was a brief, curt official note directing Captain Close to turn over the command of his company and post and report in arrest to the colonel of his regiment at New Orleans, for trial. " Acknowledge receipt by telegraph."

What a Christmas greeting !

XV.

Those were the days which but foreshadowed the *lettre de cachet* episodes of the winter of 1870–71. Never an ornamental, never a social, and often an embarrassing feature of garrison life, the first lieutenant of Company "G" had been laboring under the further disadvantage of a six months' absence from the post of the regimental colors. There were many to speak against and none to speak for him. His singular habits and characteristics, the rumors in circulation with regard to his "saving" propensities when on Bureau duty, and the queer "yarns" in circulation as to his disposition of the property of the officers who had died on his hands during the fever epidemic, had all received additional impetus from the publication in Northern papers of the Parmelee side of the Tugaloo stories, and Close's name was on the regimental market at low quotation, even before the announcement of his arrest. But this was not all. For months the regimental commander had been the recipient of frequent letters from two despairing widows, relicts of the late Captain Stone and Lieutenant Tighe, which letters claimed that their husbands had died possessed of certain items of personal property—watches, jewelry, money, martial equipments, etc.—of which Captain Close had assumed charge and for only a very small portion of which had he ever rendered account. They, with other ladies of the regiment, had been sent North when it became apparent that an epidemic was probable; they had never met Captain Close, but were confident, from the unsatisfactory nature of his replies, and from all they could learn about him from the letters they received from the regiment, that he was robbing the widow and the orphan, and they appealed to the colonel for redress.

Now, old Braxton knew almost as little of Close as did they. He asked his adjutant and one or two captains what *they* thought; he had a letter written to Close telling him of these allegations and calling for his version of the matter. It did not come, and another letter—a "chaser"—was sent, demanding immediate reply, and nearly a week elapsed before reply came. Close wrote a laboring hand, and for all official matter employed the company clerk as amanuensis. This being personal, he spent hours in copying his reply. He said he was tired of answering the letters of Mesdames Stone and Tighe on this subject. He had sent them inventories of everything of which their husbands died possessed, and had remitted every cent he had realized from the sales thereof. Only one of them had a watch. If either had ever owned diamond studs, as was alleged, he, Close, had never seen them, nor the hundreds of dollars alleged to be in their possession, nor the company fund for which Stone was accountable. In point of fact, he, Close, was compelled to say he did not believe the ladies knew what their husbands did or did not have. He was ready to make oath as to the truth of his story, and Hospital Steward Griffin and Dr. Meigs could also testify that the deceased officers had hardly any effects to speak of—could they only be found. But thereby hung a tale of further trouble. Meigs himself had died of the fever, and Griffin, after a fitful career, had been found guilty of all manner of theft and dishonesty as to hospital stores in his charge, and was himself languishing, in dishonorable discharge, a prisoner at Ship Island. Here Close thought to end it all, but the widows—sisters they were, who were born in the laundresses' quarters of old Fort Fillmore and had followed the drum all over Texas and New Mexico before the war—had wedded strapping sergeants and seen their spouses raised to the shoulder-straps in the depleted state of the regular army during the four years of volunteer supremacy—the widows were now backed by a priest and a pettifogger, and, mindful of the success achieved by such proceeding when led by a name of their own nationality, were determined to "push things." When December came, such was the accumulation of charge and specification against the absent and friendless officer that old Brax took the simplest way out of it and applied for a court-martial to try the case.

The day after Christmas, therefore, and before the official copy of the order was received at the barracks (as, oddly, often happened in those times, until the leak was discovered and duly plugged), the New Orleans evening papers contained the following interesting item:

" A general court-martial of unusual importance is to be held at the barracks, the session to commence at 10 A.M. on the 2d of January, for the trial of Brevet Captain J. P. Close of the —teenth Infantry on charges seriously reflecting upon his character as an officer and a gentleman. The detail for the court comprises officers of several other regiments, as it is conceded that there is wide-spread prejudice against the accused among his comrades in the —teenth. Even the light battery has been drawn upon in this instance, an unusual circumstance, as officers of that arm generally claim exemption from such ser-

E *

vice in view of the peculiar and engrossing nature of their battery duties. Brevet Brigadier-General Pike, of the —th Cavalry, is detailed as president, and First Lieutenant S. K. Waring, of the —— Artillery, as judge advocate of the court. The latter officer will be remembered as the hero of a remarkable adventure in connection with the recent *cause célèbre*, the Lascelles affair."

"Well, may I be kissed to death!" exclaimed Captain Lively, of the Foot, as he burst into the mess-room that evening. "Just listen to this, will you! Old Close to be tried by court-martial—with New Clothes for judge advocate!" "New Clothes," be it understood, was a name under which Mr. Waring was beginning to be known, thanks to his unwillingness to appear a second time in any garment of the fashion of the day.

"By gad, if I were the old man I'd object to the J. A. on the ground of natural antipathy!" said Mr. Burton; and among the men present, some of whom had been the colonel's advisers in drawing up the charges, there were half a score who seemed to think that poor Close could hope for no fair play now. It was then that Major Kinsey, red-faced and impetuous, burst in with the rebuke that became a classic in the annals of the old barracks:

"Fair play be damned, and you fellows too! What fair play has the man had at *your* hands? It's my belief that he never *would* get it, but for the fact that Waring is detailed."

The sensation Kinsey's outbreak created was mild compared with that caused by Close's appearance before a grave and dignified court in the week that followed. On the principle of "a clean sweep," it had been determined to arraign him on charges covering the allegations as to his official misconduct in failing or refusing to support the Federal authorities during the late disturbances. "Might as well get rid of him for good and all," said Old Brax. And so the array of charges was long and portentous. So was the bill for transportation and *per diem* of civilian witnesses the government afterwards had to pay. So was Braxton's face when, the evidence for the prosecution exhausted without proving much of anything, the testimony for the defence began to be unfolded. It transpired that Mr. Waring had gone up to headquarters on the evening of the 1st of January and formally asked the general commanding to be relieved from duty as judge advocate and allowed to defend the accused. The general was astonished, and asked why. Then Waring laid before him piece by piece the evidence he had collected as a result of his investigation, and the chief ripped out something Old Brax and his adjutant might have been startled to hear, but, after thinking it all over, told Waring to go ahead, try the case, " exhaust the evidence," and never mind the consequences. He sent his aide-de-camp down to say to Close that any officer whose assistance he desired should be assigned as *amicus curiæ.* Close replied that he " reckoned he could git along without any amycuss curious, whatever that was,—he'd talked it over with Mr. Waring and Mr. Pierce ;" and the trial went on.

Parmelee was the first witness to flatten out and go to pieces, and the *only* one who had anything but " hearsay" to offer on the score of the official neglects. The widows were the next. They began truculently and triumphantly enough, but the cross-examination reduced them to contradictions and tears. It became evident that most of Stone's company fund went North with one of them, that the alleged diamonds were paste, and that both Stone and Tighe had been gambling and drinking for months previous to their fatal seizures. It was established that, so far from having defrauded the widows of their money, the old fellow had sent them each one hundred dollars over and above the proceeds of the meagre sales, besides accounting for, as sold at fair valuation, items he never disposed of until Lambert bought them.

Then when it came to testimony as to war and other service, Close sat there, blind, bandaged, scarred, and little Pierce, who had volunteered as " amycuss" anyhow, unrolled one letter after another and laid them on the table, and they went the rounds of the court until old Pike choked them off by saying they couldn't well attach the accused's scars and wounds to the records, any more than these letters : *he* was ready to vote, unless the gentleman himself desired to say something, —had some statement to offer. How was that, Mr. Judge Advocate? And Waring turned to Pierce, who was beginning to unroll a batch of manuscript, to which he had devoted two sleepless nights and in which he had lavished satire and sarcasm by the page upon all enemies or accusers of his client. Pierce meant it to be the sensation of the day, and the court was crowded to hear him read it, despite the significant absence of Brax and his now confounded advisers. Braxton already was in deep distress, the victim of overweening confidence in the statements of his associates. " Upon my soul, general," he had said to Pike, " the result of this trial already makes me feel as though I, not Close, were the criminal." And Pierce fully meant to "show up" the scandal-mongers in the case, placing the blame on them and not their colonel.

But it was not to be. Old Close put forth a bandaged hand and restrained him. "I've been thinking that all over," he said, "and I'll just say a word instid." With that he slowly found his feet and the green patch over his eyes was brought to bear on the court. The silence of midnight fell on the crowded room, as, leaning on the back of his chair, the accused stood revealed in the worn old single-breasted coat, the coarse trousers and shoes, so long associated with him. He cleared his throat and then faltered. He did not know how to begin. At last the words came—slowly, and with many a hitch and stumble:

"You see, it's this way, General Pike and gentlemen of the court. I never knew anything about what was expected of a regular officer, 'r I wouldn't have tried it. All I knew was what I'd seen durin' the war, when they didn't seem to be so different from the rest of us. I was bred on the farm; never had no education; had to work like a horse ever since I was weaned, almost, not only for my own livin', but—but there was the mother, and, as I grew up, the hull care of the farm fell on me, for my father never was strong, and he broke down entirely. When he died there warn't nothing left but a mortgage. There was the mother and four kids to be fed on that. For twenty years, from boy to man, there never was a time a copper didn't look as big as a cart-wheel to me; and when a man's been brought up that way he don't outgrow it all of a sudden. I've built the mother a home of her own, and paid off the mortgage and stocked the farm, and educated the youngsters and seen them married off, and now I 'low they'll expect me to educate the children. When a hull famb'ly grows up around one bread-winner it comes natural for the next genera-tion to live on him too. I couldn't ha' gone to the war only Billy —he's the next boy—was big enough to take care o' things once the mortgage was paid, and afterwards I jined the army—the riggle-ers— because it looked to me like they got bigger pay for less work than any trade I ever heard of out *our* way. I'm sorry I did it, 'cause so long's there's no more fightin' I seem to be in the way; but I don't want to quit,"—and here the rugged old fellow seemed to expand by at least a foot,—"and I don't *mean* to quit except honorable. There ain't a man livin'—nor a woman either—can truthfully say I ever defrauded them of a cent."

And then Close felt for the chair from which he had unconsciously advanced, and which Pierce hastened to push forward to him, and abruptly sat down. Court adjourned *sine die* just at luncheon-time, and some of the officers of the infantry mess invited the members to come over and have a bite and a sup. They all went but Cram and Waring, Cram saying he had asked a few friends to his quarters, and Waring audibly remarking that it would take away his appetite to have to sit at meat with so and so; so and so being the officers who were mainly instrumental in working up the case against Close. The telegram sent by Mr. Newton Lambert that afternoon was on his own responsibility, because neither judge advocate nor member of the court could reveal its finding, but it bore all the weight of authority and it brought untold relief to an anxious household; not, as might be expected, to the immediate friends and relatives of the accused in the distant North, for never until days afterwards did they know anything about it, but to a little family "lately in rebellion" and holding in abhorrence Captain Close and all his kin; for the despatch was addressed to Mrs. Walton Scroggs, Pass Christian.

XVI.

The honorable acquittal of Captain Close proved, as was to be expected, a thorn in the flesh of certain of his accusers, and stirred up trouble in the gallant —teenth. This was a matter Close didn't much mind. He was granted six months' leave on surgeon's certificate of disability, which meant on full pay, and he took it very hard that some means were not devised to send him North under orders, so that he could draw mileage. He and Lambert went back to Tugaloo together and packed up, for "G" Company was ordered relieved by another, and Close was there made the happy recipient of a pass to Chicago, while the old company, after seeing their ex-commander safely aboard the sleeper, went on down the road to New Orleans and took station once more with regimental head-quarters.

Here Mr. Lambert found means of getting occasional brief leaves of absence and of employing his two or three days in visits to his erstwhile neighbors of Walton Hall, now comfortably domiciled in a picturesque but somewhat dilapidated old cottage close to the tumbling waves of the gulf. It had been the property of a near relative before the war, and was reclaimed and put in partial order for their use, apparently, through the efforts of their old physician and the energics of Mr. Barton Potts. Here the warm, soft, salty breezes seemed to bring new lease of life to the beloved invalid, though it was plain to one and all she could never be herself again. Scroggs, her kinsman son-in-law, was rapidly mending and eagerly casting about for employment. Floyd, restored to duty without trial, was serving patiently and faithfully with his regiment in Texas, bent evidently on making good his words. The two events which seemed to bring general cheer and rejoicing to the household were those which three months before would have been promptly derided as absurd and impossible: one was the weekly letter from a trooper in the Union blue, the other a much rarer visit from a Yankee subaltern, whose profession was not to be disguised because he came in " cits." On the occasion of his first appearance in that garb Miss Walton did him the honor to say, " Ah never *did* like you, but Ah do think *those* clothes *wuhse* than the others." This was rather hard, because, as the spring came on, Lambert's lot at the barracks was not as pleasant as it might have been, and his comfort consisted in running over to see how Madam Walton was doing.

Cram and his battery, with Waring, Pierce, and all, had been ordered away, and then for the first time Lambert realized, what his regimental comrades had marked for months, that he preferred the companionship of the battery men to that of the men who wore the bugle, the badge of the infantry in those benighted days. Old Brax concluded he had had enough of garrison life, and sought a long leave. Major Minor took command of the regiment and post, and the adjutant and quartermaster took command of Major Minor. It had neither been forgiven nor forgotten by these staff officials that Lambert had been equally outspoken in defence of Close and denunciation of his accusers, and the further fact that he preferred to spend his leisure hours with his fellow-graduates of the artillery rather than his uncongenial brethren of the —teenth gave the offended ones abundant material to work on. Minor was a weakling,—a bureau officer during the war days, a man who could muster and disburse without a flaw, but never set a squadron in the field without a " fluke." Lambert was a capital drill-master and tactician, and " G " Company, under his instruction, was rapidly overhauling every other in the regiment, even those of Kinsey and Lively, the two real soldiers among the captains. Minor hated the sight of a page of tactics, and never even held dress parade. Lambert had a clear, ringing voice, and Minor couldn't make himself heard. One morning the orderly came to Lambert at company drill with "the major's compliments, and please to take Company 'G' outside the garrison, or make less noise." It was the adjutant's doing, as things turned out afterwards, but it angered Lambert against his commander. Then, when May came round and he asked for three days' leave, Minor hummed and hawed and looked at his staff officer and finally requested that it be submitted in writing; and "it" came back with a curt endorsement to the effect that Lieutenant Lambert would be expected hereafter to show more interest in matters connected with his regimental duties: the application was disapproved.

All this time he had written every few weeks to Close, and got a very nice letter in reply, written by a young fellow who announced himself as the captain's brother Wallace. The captain was getting better,—very much better,—but the eye-doctor's bill was a big one, and he thought the government ought to pay it. He had bought some land up there six years before, and, what with schools and roads and bridges, the taxes were awful. What he wouldn't mind doing would be to come back to the regiment as quartermaster; but in those days there was no four-year limit to staff positions, and the incumbents, both adjutant and quartermaster, proposed to hang on as long as possible, and Lambert replied that he feared there would be no chance.

And then, one day, there came a telegram to the commanding officer of Company "G" at the barracks with the brief announcement that a soldier serving in the 26th Infantry under the name of Roberts had been identified by Corporal Floyd Walton, 4th Cavalry, as Private Riggs, a deserter from the —teenth. Please send charges and descriptive list. Two weeks later Lieutenant Lambert was summoned to Austin as a witness before the general court-martial appointed for his trial. The Morgan line steamer would not sail until Saturday night. There was time to run over and see if the Waltons had not something to send to their soldier boy in Texas, and Lambert sent his trunk to the Morgan wharf while the Mobile boat paddled him away through the Rigolets and out into Mississippi Sound and landed him at the familiar pier at Pass Christian just at twilight of a lovely May evening. Ten minutes' walk along the shore brought him to an enclosure wherein the moonbeams were beginning to play among the leaves of the magnolia and to throw a huge black shadow, that of the grove of live-oaks, over the veranda of an old, white-painted, Southern homestead bowered in vines and shrubbery at the end of the broad shell pathway leading from the gate. Somewhere among the foliage a mocking-bird was carolling to the rising moon, and the music of soft, girlish voices and subdued laughter came drifting out on the evening air. Lambert's heart gave a quickened throb or two as he recognized Kate Walton's unmistakable tones. He had to traverse the length of the moonlit walk. She, with her unseen friend, was in shadow, so there was no possibility of trying the effect of surprise.

"Well, whayuh'n the wide wuhld 'd *you* come from?" was her nonchalant greeting. "Ah supposed you were dayd'n buried." (There *is* no such thing as spelling that word as pronounced by the rosiest, sauciest, and possibly sweetest little mouth in creation. He could not take his eyes from it, and she knew it.)—"Miss Awgden, this is Mr. Lambert. Ah think you've heard sister Esthuh speak of him.—Ah suppose you want to go right in to see *huh*. Ah'll call huh down."

So Lambert made his bow to Miss Ogden, who had her own womanly intuitions as to the extent of his eagerness to see sister Esther, and who presently declared she had to go home, and went without much delay over the leave-taking, in spite of Katesie's voluble remonstrance and well-feigned disappointment. Miss Walton, in fact, hung on to her all the way to the gate and made every proper and apparent effort to detain her there; but a wise head had Miss Bettie Ogden : she *would* not delay. She *had* heard sister Esther talk of Mr. Lambert time and again, and had read in Katesie's significant silence or simulated scorn a whole volume of information. She went tripping lightly, laughingly away, and Katesie watched her until she was out of sight, then came dawdling slowly back. She well knew it would be unlike Esther to come down inside of twenty minutes.

Lambert was seated in the big wicker chair, amusing himself with a kitten. He did not even look up when she finally returned.

"Hasn't Esthuh come down yet? Ah told huh you wuh hyuh, ten minutes ago."

"No. Possibly she didn't understand. I didn't hear her answer. Indeed, I could hardly hear you call."

"That's because you were listening to Bettie Awgden." (Pause for reply or denial : none offered.) "*She* doesn't like Yankees any better'n I did—do."

"Then it was on my account she left so suddenly. Where does she live? I'll run and call her back and tell her—what shall I tell her?—that I only wanted to say good-by to Mrs. Scroggs?"

"You haven't said how-de-do yet."

"I haven't? How utterly stupid of me! You see, between Miss Ogden and the cat, you were so engrossed that I deferred that ceremony until you should have time to devote to me. Permit me." And, carefully depositing pussy on the chair, he quickly bent low and seized Miss Katesie's hand, which he raised towards his lips: "Miss Walton, I am *so* glad to see you again. This fortnight has seemed a year."

Indignantly she snatched her hand away.

"*Fawtnight!* It's five weeks to-day since you were hyuh." Then, suddenly conscious, "Not that *I* cay-uh."

He started up in feigned astonishment. "*Five* weeks? You amaze me! and how sweet of you to keep count!" (Something more than mere teasing and merriment now in the sparkle of his eyes and the twitching about the corners of his handsome, sensitive mouth.) "Those five weeks have been five years."

But she had sprung to the door-way, wrathful at being so artfully trapped.

"Ah *didn't* keep count. It was Moh; 'n' Ah don't cay-uh *how* long you stay away, or how soon you go. *Esthuh!* ain't you ayvuh coming down? Mr. Lambert says he's got to go."

"You haven't told me how Mrs. Walton is, and Mr. Scroggs, Miss Katesie. And how's Cousin Bart?"

"Cousin Bart's up at Quitman; so's Walton; and Moh's 'bout the same. She'll *nay*vuh be any better so long's Floyd's whuh he is —weah-ing a Yankee jacket."

"That *is* queer, isn't it? The queerest thing about it is that he's just been made corporal in the very troop he charged into at Selma. A classmate of mine is second lieutenant in the same troop, and wrote me about it."

"*Floyd* ought to be the lieutenant."

"Miss Walton, you continually surprise, and now you delight me! This is really promising! A Southern girl says her brother ought to be a Yankee officer."

But she flew at him from the door-step, her eyes flashing fire. He seized the kitten and held that struggling quadruped, paws foremost, between him and impending vengeance.

"*Oh!* Ah do despise an' hate you maw an' maw ev'y time you come. You're mean, spiteful, hateful! You know Ah nevuh meant any such thing. Ah'd *sco'n* him if he was! Ah'd tuhn mah back on him—as Ah do on you *now*, an' Ah wish it was fo'*evuh!*"

10*

And, suiting action to word, the tumbling, clustering ringlets which fell upon her pretty shoulders were flouted almost in his face as she whirled about and marched tragically back to the door-way.

"Well," said Lambert, mournfully, "it's an ill wind that blows nobody good. Your wish bids fair to be granted. I think I won't disturb Mrs. Scroggs to-night, and if you'll tell me where to find Miss Ogden I'll bid her come back to you, so that you can resume the fun I interrupted. Kindly say to Mrs. Scroggs that if she has anything to send to Floyd and can get it ready before ten to-morrow morning I'll be glad to take it with my baggage. The hotel porter will come for it. —Good-night, pussy. *You* don't seem to object to Yanks.—Good-by, Miss Katesie. When your wishes are so promptly granted and you so easily get rid of a fellow, you *might* shake hands with him; but pussy 'll have to do."

With that he solemnly took the kitten by a furry paw and with ludicrous gravity gave it a formal shake, then turned deliberately away. He was down the steps and crunching along the shell walk before she started from the stupor which had seized her. Then she sprang to the edge of the veranda, and he, treading lightly now and listening eagerly for the sounding of the summons for a parley, heard, as he expected, the half-tremulous, half-truculent hail,—

"*Aw*, Mist' Lambert!"

"Yes?"

"*Whuh* you going?"

"Oh, didn't I tell you? I'm ordered to Texas."

Then he listened, wickedly, maliciously, and vouchsafed no further word. For a moment not a sound came from the shaded veranda. Slowly, therefore, he turned, and, treading as though on china teacups, went on towards the gate. Did he hope she would call again? Did he know or realize the deep-rooted, stubborn pride of the Southern girl? Slowly, more slowly still, he faltered to the gate. Nearing it, still eagerly listening, he shortened step, only pretending to walk. Still no sound, no summons to return. His hand was on the latch, and there it waited, reluctant to open, but waiting was vain. He glanced back over his shoulder, and, vague and shadowy, he could just distinguish the outline of the slender form he had grown to love with such longing and tenderness and passion. It clung there motionless. At least, then, she had not turned indifferently away. But the word, the whisper he prayed for and craved to hear, and would so eagerly have obeyed, came not to recall him. Fifteen—twenty seconds he waited, then, in sudden pride, or pique, or resolution, threw open the white barrier, slammed it after him, and strode briskly away, startling the mocking-birds into sudden silence with the lively whistling of an old West Point quickstep.

But Esther, coming forth from the open door-way to greet and welcome their friend, saw the erect, soldierly figure marching off in the moonlight; saw her little sister standing as though rooted to the spot; heard the ostentatious spirit and swing and rhythm of "*Buenas noches;*" heard a faint, questioning, incredulous, tearful little voice piping "Mr. Lambert! Mr. Lambert!" and the woman had learned in that instant what the lover would have given worlds to know.

XVII.

"Lieutenant, there's no use trying. We're only twenty, and there must be two hundred of 'em. They've got that stage-load long before now, escort and all. The whole thing's over with. If there were any women 'twould be different; every man of us would go then to try to rescue them; but there were only men. I'm as sorry for Colonel Sweet as you can be, but we can get his body when the Indians have gone. We can't afford to lose any more of our people."

The speaker was the captain of a party of Texan frontiersmen,—rangers they were afterwards called, when their organization was more complete; but these were the days when the Lone Star State was un-invaded by railways and when to its very heart—far as the capital—the savage Kiowas and Comanches often raided in full force, ravaging the scattered settlements far and wide. Lieutenant Lambert, his duty finished with his testimony in the case of the deserter Riggs, had obtained permission to delay his return a few days and taken stage to Lampasas, where Floyd Walton was stationed with his troop. Lambert would not willingly return without seeing him and delivering in person the little packages so hurriedly prepared at the new home. Then, too, there was no man in the army in whom the young officer now felt so deep an interest. Was he not Katesie's brother, and might not that brother have some influence over that obdurate heart?

It was not the porter of the hotel who went for those packages. It was Lambert himself, hoping, of course, to see the young lady whom he had so successfully tormented the evening previous; but his scheme had been checkmated in most absurdly unromantic fashion. The New Orleans evening paper among its military items contained a brief paragraph to the effect that Lieutenant Lambert was ordered over to Austin as a witness before a court-martial there in session, but would return to the barracks in a week or ten days, and this paper he had been careless enough to leave on the veranda. Katesie had gone miserably to her room, Esther had lit upon the paragraph, and in ten minutes Lambert's melodramatic scheme was exploded. Never would he forget the saucy merriment in her pretty face when he appeared upon the scene that morning, hoping and expecting to find her penitent, piteous, and mutely begging to be forgiven before he went away. He had come prepared to be grave, sorrowful, dignified, and then to be disarmed by her distress, to lead her away under the magnolias to the shaded recesses of the old Southern garden, there to assure her she was pardoned, and then to tell her she was loved. A charming *château en Espagne* was that which the boy had builded; a sweet, sad, blissful, ecstatic parting was it all to be as a result of his skilful use of his "sudden orders to Texas;" but, like many another well-laid plan, it went ludicrously aglee. She was there on the veranda, romping with her kitten, when he came, and never made the faintest reference to his departure. He alluded gloomily to the fact that the boat would be along in less than an hour, and she cheerfully responded, "Yes; Ah thought Ah huhd its whistle just a moment ago," and raced pussy to the far end of the gallery. He tried other announcements with no better success, and was bewildered and defeated and stung by her apparent heartlessness and indifference when at last he had to go, and went away miserably jealous and wretchedly in love, fairly beaten at his own game.

So gloomy and unlike himself was Lambert that the two or three classmates who happened to be at Austin were much surprised, and so absorbed was he in his own woes and pangs that not until he reached Lampasas did he learn that the soldierly-looking man who rode all the way from the capital with him was no less a person than the Brevet Lieutenant-Colonel Sweet of whom he had heard so much at Tugaloo, and who, promoted to the rank of major, was now on his way to report for duty at a frontier post. The stage with the colonel rumbled away on its journey after supper. Lambert went on out to camp, only to find that Corporal Walton with four men had gone as escort to that very stage, as there were rumors that the Comanches and Lipans were on the war-path again. It might be four days before they returned. It would be two before a stage went back to Austin, and it was now nine o'clock at night.

The very next morning brought direful news. A big band of hostiles had swooped down on the stage station at the crossing of the Caliente, fifty miles to the northwest, massacred everybody, and run off the stock. The cavalry troop in camp at Lampasas was miles away by the time the tidings reached Lambert at the tavern in town. Then came worse news. A settler rode spurring in from the Concho trail to say that he had seen the Indians when they attacked the stage with overpowering numbers, and had just managed to escape with his own life. He believed that not one soul was left to tell the tale. There were many gallant spirits among the Texans of the frontier,—men who were accustomed to fight at the drop of the hat, and who, in defence of home and friends, were indomitable. Yet even these well knew the hopelessness of the situation as described. They were far too few in number to undertake the pursuit and attack of such a band as this. Moreover, their own wives and children would be left in danger were they to take the field. It was even impossible to persuade two or three of their number to ride post-haste on the trail of the cavalry, who, at the first alarm and on receipt of tidings that the Indians had ridden away eastward towards the Brazos, had taken the road for Waco at dawn in hopes of heading them off or driving them should they attack the defenceless settlements. There were, therefore, absolutely no troops to go to the rescue of the stage party, if, as seemed beyond hope, any of them were still alive, and Lambert, burning with eagerness to do something and tormented with anxiety as to the fate of " Brother Floyd," found himself helpless.

A sergeant and some semi-invalided men had been left in charge of camp, and from these he gathered a little information, but not of an enlivening nature. The nearest posts to the westward from which help might come were McKavett and Concho, each over a hundred miles away ; but Concho, being on the left bank of the Colorado, and doubtless warned by this time of the Indian raid, could be sending cavalry down the valley in pursuit. It was expectation of this, probably, that started the raiders eastward towards the Brazos, where there were no troops, and where, sweeping northward again in wide circle, they might confidently expect to get safely back to their wild fastnesses, leading the cavalry a stern chase all the way. Shrewdest tacticians of modern warfare as they are, they had indeed already divided, one party riding eastward as reported after swooping down on the Caliente station, and driving some of the stock ahead of them, for the sole purpose of drawing the Lampasas troop off in that direction, leaving the settlers along the Colorado to the mercies of the other and larger portion of the savage force. There was no use now in sending couriers after the troop. It had five hours' start. It would be evening before the fleetest horse could overtake the command. Lambert urged the sergeant to give him a horse and arms, mount three or four men, and let them go with him, if only to reconnoitre. Then some of the Texans who had no families to defend might volunteer. But the sergeant dared not take the responsibility of disregarding his instructions, and was wiser than Lambert in the wiles of Indian warfare. "I'd go myself gladly, lieutenant," he said, "but orders are orders, and a party of four or five would be surrounded and cut off and massacred before you fairly realized that an Indian was near you." Then Lambert had appealed to the Texans, and the captain had replied as above; and then, just when he was giving up in despair, a sergeant and two men, dust-covered and with horses in a lather of foam, rode furiously in from the Waco trail.

"Is it true?" cried the sergeant, as he saw the unusual gathering at camp. "We met a feller half-way over to the Brazos riding like hell, warning folks the Indians were to the north, and he said they had jumped the stage this side of Caliente. It's *true?* And you haven't done anything? Mount every sound man you've got, and give us fresh horses."

"My orders were to take care——" began his comrade.

"Damn your orders! I bring later. The old man didn't believe it, and had a sure thing ahead of him, or he'd have turned back with the hull outfit. Why, man, that stage—or what's left of it—ain't thirty miles away, an' you fellers sitting here like so many dam women!" And the trooper flung himself from saddle at the word, and then caught sight of Lambert's forage-cap and eager face.

"Get me a horse, too, sergeant; I'll go with you. I'm Lieutenant Lambert, a classmate of your second lieutenant."

"You'll go in command, sir, and we're with you,—six of us, anyhow. I've heard Corporal Walton speak of you, sir, often. How many of *you* fellers 'll go?" he demanded eagerly of the knot of Texans, while the few troopers hustled about, saddling spare horses and levying on the list of invalid mounts, too sore or feeble for a long chase, but good enough for a thirty-mile dash when it was life or death at the end of it. In an instant the whole atmosphere seemed changed, —charged with ozone, electric force, magnetism,—something,—for the snap and spirit of the new-comer flashed from man to man. Lambert, a stranger and without authority in the premises, could effect nothing; Sergeant Dolan, a war veteran, a man they all knew, and clothed with power as coming direct from that military demi-god "the captain," had a dozen men armed, equipped, in saddle and ready for business, in ten minutes. Six were soldiers, six civilians who half laughingly ranged their raw-boned Texas ponies in line with the mounting troopers, and Dolan sung out to Lambert, who had raided his classmate's tent for extra boots and riding breeches, "We're ready, sir."

In the hot May sunshine, at high noon, they went loping north-westward over the lovely prairie, spangled with wild flowers, the Colorado twisting and turning like a silver serpent in its green bed to their left. Five miles out, a wretched, half-demented creature hailed them from a clump of willows by a little stream : "You're too late, you fellers. They ain't anything left alive from the Paloma to the Caliente, except Indians. The country's alive with them. Good-by to *your* scalps if you venture over that ridge." And he pointed to the long, low line of bluffs that spanned the horizon to the northwest. One man stopped to question, but speedily came galloping on in pursuit. "He's scared out of his wits. He can't prove what he says," was the brief report to Lambert and the sergeant, now riding side by side at the head of the little column.

Another hour, and, closer to the river, they were following the meanderings of the stage-road, and the ridge loomed higher ahead. Two more settlers had been passed ; and they were exaggerative beyond any semblance of probability. The Indians numbered thousands, the dead hundreds. The stage had been warned not to push on beyond Paloma Bluffs last night, but persisted in an attempt to reach the Caliente. Colonel Sweet and party had been butchered to a man,— victims of his own rash effort to aid the poor fellows at the station, and of his criminal disregard of Texan warnings.

"We'll know the truth in an hour, lieutenant, so there's no use wasting time with those beggars. You can see the Paloma from yonder bluffs," was Dolan's only comment.

Just at one o'clock, the foaming, panting horses were reined in and the girths loosened, while Lambert, guided by the veteran Indian-fighter, crawled cautiously up the height in front of them. Half the men, dismounted, were stationed with ready rifle or carbine where they could command every approach. Who could say whether Indians were not even then lurking in every ravine? A young Texan, following the road, pushed on cautiously to the point so as to scout the trail beyond. With drooping heads and heaving flanks the motley herd were huddled in a little swale to the right of the road, their holders eagerly watching the young leader and saying few words. Warily Dolan reached and peered over the crest. They could see him pointing,—could see both him and Lambert shading their eyes with their hands and staring away into space,—could see Dolan suddenly clutch the officer's sleeve and, crouching lower, point as though to some objects far out over the slopes beyond. Then down they came, eager, elastic, with gleaming eyes and glowing faces. "Mount, men, mount! There's a fight not five miles ahead!" sang out Dolan, and, swinging into saddle, with Lambert only a length in lead, struck spurs to his horse, the whole squad clattering at their heels. Young Texas, peering around the point, heard them coming, and threw a long, lean leg over his scraggy pony. "See anything?" he hailed.

"Yes: Indians attacking something or other 'bout a mile to the north of the road: looks like a dug-out o' some kind."

"'*Tis* a dug-out, by Gawd! *I* know the place. Witherell's herd used to graze around there last year, and he and his boys built that dug-out in case they were attacked; and maybe the stage managed to get back there. Some one's alive, else the Indians wouldn't be fighting."

A cheer went up from the foremost men. After all, then, there was vestige of hope. Lambert, eager and impetuous, was spurring off to the open prairie that lay beyond a sweeping bend of the stream, but Dolan hailed him:

"Not yet, lieutenant, not yet. There's some wide arroyos out yonder. Stick to the road, sir, till we can see the hut. It's up a long shallow valley beyond that second divide. I know the place now."

"But they'll see us, sergeant," shouted Lambert, as he bent over the pommel and drove his rowels wickedly at the torn flanks of his poor brute. "I hoped to surprise them, and charge."

"Lord love you, sir, there's no surprising these beggars in broad daylight. They've been watching for some of us ever since sun-up, and they've seen us now. Lucky they haven't guns, 'cept old muzzle-loaders. They've mostly nothing but bows and lances."

The horses were panting furiously now, and some of the squad were stringing out far to the rear. Dolan, glancing back, saw two or three men vainly lashing at their exhausted mounts long musket-shot behind.

"It won't do, lieutenant: we'll have to keep together, or, first thing you know, a hull pack o' them yelping curs 'll burst out of some ravine and cut those fellows off,—kill and scalp 'em and scurry away on their fresh ponies before we could get back to help. Let 'em catch up, sir. We'll get there time enough."

And so, more slowly now, as advised by the veteran plainsman, Lambert led his party, the young Texan ranging alongside and riding on his right. He, too, wanted to charge, and again old Dolan pointed out the absurdity of it. "Their ponies are fresh and nimble. We'd never catch *them*, while they could ride around and spit us with their damned arrows. What we want is a chance with our Spencers and rifles, sir: *that's* the way to empty their saddles and stand 'em off. Look yonder, sir!"

And then, just as Dolan pointed, three mounted warriors, their war-bonnets trailing over their bounding ponies' backs,—the first hostile Indians Lambert had ever seen,—burst from their covert behind a low divide to the right and went scurrying away towards the northward hills in wide *détour* to join their comrades. The road disappeared around a gentle rise in the prairie half a mile ahead.

"Out with you, Lang and Naughton!" said the sergeant, briskly. "Go ahead to that point." And the two troopers, well knowing what was required of them, darted on without a word, Lambert and the main body following now at steady trot. Before the two thus thrown in advance had come within three hundred yards of the bend, a little jet of smoke and fire flashed out from over the ridge, followed instantly by two others; both riders swerved; one horse stumbled and went down, his rider cleverly rolling out from among the striking, struggling hoofs. "That's the way they'd have picked *you* off, sir," shouted Dolan, as the whole party burst into a gallop and drove straight for the ridge. "We'll sweep them aside in a second."

They did not wait to be swept aside. Six or eight painted savages were spinning away over the sward by the time the troopers came laboring to the top, and others, circling, yelling, brandishing their arms, and hurling jeer and challenge over the intervening swale, were in plain view along the opposite slope not half a mile away. Beyond that lay the scene of the siege; and just over it, only a few yards away

F   11

from the road, lay two bloated, stiffening objects, at sight of which every horse in the pursuing party shied and snorted. There lay, bristling with arrows, two of the stage mules. Two hundred yards farther, the smouldering remains of the stage itself, with the gashed and mutilated body of a man only a lariat's length away, greeted the eyes of Lambert and his foremost men. Here Dolan flung himself from his horse, tossed the reins to one of the men, saying, "Hold all you can. Lead 'em to the hollow yonder," and, kneeling, drove a long-range shot at some gaudily-painted warriors clustered about some object half-way up the opposite slope. A pony plunged and reared, and a yell of rage and defiance went up. Man after man, nearly all the little squad sprang to earth and opened brisk fire on every Indian within rifle-shot, and every man for himself, following the general lead of Lambert and Dolan, strode forward up the gentle ascent towards a dingy mound, half earth, half logs, about a quarter of a mile ahead of them, until Dolan shouted right and left, "Cease firing! Stop your noise! Listen!"

And, borne down the wind, faint and feeble, yet exultant, there came the sound of distant cheer, and the rescuers knew they had not risked their lives in vain.

XVIII.

One soft, warm evening in early June quite a family party had gathered on the veranda of the old white homestead at Pass Christian. The air was rich with the fragrance of jasmine and magnolia; a great bunch of roses lay on the little table beside the reclining chair, where, propped up with pillows, Mrs. Walton was placidly enjoying the beauty of the moonlit scene and rapturously contemplating the stalwart form of her soldier son. It was too much—it was too soon— to expect of a Southern woman even so customary a thing as a change of mind, when that change involved a confession of interest and pride in the army blue, but the mother did not live in all the broad and sorrowing South whose soul would not have thrilled with pride and delight, even though hidden and unconfessed, in reading the ringing words with which in general orders a great Union leader had published to his troops the story of the heroism, devotion, and soldierly skill with which Corporal Floyd Walton, Troop "X," Fourth Cavalry, had conducted the defence of the passengers on the Concho stage, saving the lives of Brevet Lieutenant-Colonel Sweet, who was shot early in the engagement, and of two civilians, and, though himself twice painfully wounded, maintaining the defence and inflicting severe loss upon an overwhelming force of hostile Indians, until finally relieved by the arrival of a detachment of troopers and volunteers successfully and gallantly led by Lieutenant I. N. Lambert, —teenth Infantry (wounded), and Sergeant Dolan, Fourth Cavalry.

Sergeant Walton, promoted within the week, had been granted a month's furlough as soon as able to travel, and with his arm in a sling had hastened homeward, where within the forty-eight hours succeeding his arrival he had time and again to tell the story of that fearful day. They had got within five miles of the Caliente before discovering that only a smouldering ruin remained of the stage station. Hearing from fleeing settlers of the raid, Colonel Sweet had decided to push forward at top speed to reinforce the little party of defenders. The driver had urged the same course, and the two civilian passengers had naturally demurred. Then, when they found it too late, they turned and strove to retrace the road to Lampasas, were headed off at dawn, but fought a way to Witherell's old dug-out, the driver and two soldiers being killed, Colonel Sweet and the corporal both shot in the attempt, and the stage abandoned and burned. And there in that stifling hole, without water for the wounded, they had fought off dash after dash of the Indians; but their ammunition was almost gone, and only two men had any fight left in them, when they heard the welcome crack of the rescuers' rifles. Even then the Indians hung about all the long afternoon and night, and Lambert got his painful wound in heading a little squad that ran the gauntlet to a neighboring spring for water for the fevered wounded. Of his own conduct Floyd had little to say ("What else did they expect of a Walton?" was his mother's comment. "Is bravery so rare an attribute in the Federal army?"), but he could not say enough about young Lambert. "We were fighting for our lives: we *had* to fight," he said; "but he risked his to fetch us water. I say *that* young fellow's a trump." And he flashed a significant glance at Katesie, for Cousin Bart, with the imbecility of manhood, had let that domestic cat out of the bag, and then, once started, had told more. Floyd Walton, under pledge of secrecy, was held a spell-bound listener to Cousin Bart the second night after his arrival, when the rest of the family had gone to bed. Bart had been celebrating his cousin's deeds and rejoicing over his return to the extent of tangling his tongue, but

Floyd could not trip him on his facts : "If you don't believe me, you can ask the doctor—ask Colonel Scroggs—or Walton—he'll be hyuh to-mawwo," said his informant. "That's the kind of Yank *he* is, by Gawd, suh ; an' if I thought they was maw like him you bet I'd reconstruct too. But the Lawd don't make too many like him, nor young Lambert either."

And when Floyd finally went to his room that night after the loving visit to his mother's bedside, he sat long at the open casement, gazing out on the soft, still beauty of the moonlit night, his heart touched and thrilled as it had not been for years, and his pride humbled. While he, wayward and forgetful of their needs, had left mother and sisters to struggle for themselves, and had lost himself in vain dreaming of a sweet-faced girl who he had early enough been warned was *not* for him,—while he, reckless, selfish, and weak, had abandoned himself to drink and despair and then to the cold charity of the world, —it was an alien and an enemy, an uncouth soldier in the hated blue, who had stood between the stricken and helpless ones at home and absolute want and privation. The good angel who ministered to them in their distress, even when stipulating that they should never know whence came the needed aid, and who finally became the "purchaser" of the desolate and ruined place, thereby supplying the means to make them so content and comfortable now, was that creature of strong contrasts, Captain Close.

Not until long after midnight did Walton leave his seat by the open casement and seek his pillow ; but there was another watcher whose vigil outlasted his. In the little batch of letters brought by Cousin Bart from the post-office that evening was one which bore the Austin stamp and was addressed in Lambert's hand. Reading it hurriedly, Floyd had changed color and thrust it in his pocket, Katesie watching him with furtive eyes, yet never trusting herself to question. It was Esther who eagerly demanded news of their absent friend. "Oh, yes, he's getting better," Floyd admitted, but then faltered. When was he coming? Oh, Lambert didn't say. The doctors probably wouldn't let him travel just yet. The letter was mainly about—other matters—about Colonel Sweet, who didn't seem to be doing as well as they could wish. His wife was on the way to join him. Didn't Lambert send any word or message? No. He probably wrote in a hurry. And that night Miss Katesie sat with her dimpled chin buried in her pretty round arms, gazing long out upon the flashing waters, a sad, silent, and deeply troubled girl. There was something in that letter that concerned her; and how disagreeable she had been to Lambert! and she just *knew* it! and Floyd was mean and wouldn't tell her! At least this was the burden of her song when at two o'clock in the morning she threw herself sobbing into Esther's loving arms, and Esther, soothing and smiling softly to herself, thought she could soon find means to comfort her.

That week brought other letters, and a telegram to Floyd, and he had business in New Orleans and must go over for a day. Lambert was coming on from Texas, and he'd fetch him back with him. Everybody could see he was feverishly impatient to get away, and a sad smile flickered about the mother's pale lips as she laid her hand in blessing on his head. He went by the morning boat and hastened to the levee where the steamers of the Cromwell line came in from New York. He was there hours before the Crescent came ploughing her way up the swollen and turbid river; and, before she was sighted at English Turn, who should appear but Lieutenant Waring and the general's aide-de-camp who had come to see him during his brief confinement under guard! Floyd, though in civilian dress, had promptly sprung to his feet to salute them, but they recognized him instantly, and heartily shook his hand and congratulated him on his recovery and on the honors he had won. And then it transpired that he, too, had come to see if he could be of service to Mrs. Sweet, and Waring suddenly bethought him of a story he had heard about the Quitman days. A fellow of infinite tact was Waring when he chose to be, and, after a few words of cordial greeting to the fair passengers, he winked at his comrade the aide-de-camp, as he said he must hasten back to battery duty. And so, even when the sergeant would have deferentially fallen to the rear, it was that distinguished non-commissioned officer who gave his arm to the younger of the two ladies in response to Waring's calm " Mr. Walton will take charge of Miss Sweet," and while the mother was led away to the waiting carriage by the staff officer, well knowing that the mother-made engagement was at an end, the daughter's little hand slipped trembling upon his arm. What happened in the elysium of that two minutes' threading of a dusty, crowded, freight-heaped wharf was not confessed by either until two long years after. The ladies went on to Galveston that night, and Walton's face was radiant when, two days later, he came back home; and then he could have hated himself for his selfishness when he saw Esther.

11 *

"Why, where's Mr. Lambert?" was her startled query, as she met him at the gate. Only the moment before as they saw the boat splashing away from the pier had Katesie, with madly beating heart, run from her side to bathe her flushed cheeks and hide in her room until she heard his voice on the veranda and the first greetings were over, and then she would summon up all her saucy spirit and go tripping down to meet him with due nonchalance and levity. She had planned it all, poor child, rehearsed the little comedy time and again, and was steeling herself to act her coquettish *rôle*, when her sister's words and Floyd's reply fell upon her astounded ears :

"He had to go straight on home. His mother's ill."

And not until then did Katesie Walton know that she, too, "had surrendered."

All things come to him—or her—who knows how to wait; even an absent lover, even the era of peace and good will between estranged and warring sections, even the end of a long story. Another year rolled by on clogging wheels and wrought many a change throughout the sunny South. A dauntless spirit had drifted from this to a better world. Reverent hands laid the wasted form of the lady mother under the grand old live-oaks close to the "shining shore," and the Walton household, grieving, yet glad that the long years of suffering were ended, gave up, against his vehement protest, the refuge which the beneficence of a stranger had afforded their beloved in her declining days. The sisters went with Scroggs to his new home in Texas, where a pioneer railway company had tendered him employment. Here Floyd could sometimes visit them, a stalwart sergeant who gratefully declined the offer of influential men to procure his discharge, saying that he meant to serve every hour of his enlistment. Here, within hail of the cavalry trumpets and sight of the national flag, there often came to spend the day a fair-faced girl, a Northern blonde the very antitype to Katesie's Southern beauty, and the blue and the gray looked love and trust when each gazed into the other's eyes, for some remarkable bond of sympathy had linked Genevieve Sweet and Kate Walton in close companionship.

Here, too, were received and answered letters increasing in frequency, and one never-to-be-forgotten day, from a far distant post, there suddenly appeared a very proper young fellow in the conventional travelling garb of the period ; and presently Jenny Sweet bethought herself that important household matters had to be looked after at the garrison, and Esther had her marketing to do and must do it. "Of course Mr. Lambert will dine and take tea with us." (We dined at one and tead at six-thirty in those days in Texas.) And so there was no one left to entertain him but Katesie—and the cat; and even the cat was very much in the way—in Lambert's way, that is, for the girl had the ungracious creature in her arms, covering her with undesired caresses, the instant after Esther's departure. The porch was vine-clad, shaded and inviting, but Katesie perversely insisted on the steps and the hot morning sunshine: pussy loved the warmth and sunshine. Lambert sought to stroke and caress Sabina, since Sabina was held tight over a thumping little heart and close under rosy lips and dimpled chin and soft, flushed cheeks. His finger-tips thrilled at the delicious proximity, and Sabina magnetically perceived it and malignantly set back her ears and hissed, whereat he pinched her ears and was promptly bidden to "Go sit ovuh yawnduh 'f you cahnt leave huh yuhs alone," whereupon he transferred his attentions to Sabina's lashing tail and precipitated a row. Sabina clawed and struggled; the outraged caudal bristled like a bottle-washer; Katesie sought to soothe with more hugs and kisses and those emotional and passionate mouthings which women lavish on their feline favorites. "Oh, um Cattums!—um Kittums!—um Pussums!—um *Tweet*ums!" rapturously exclaimed Miss Walton through her close-pressed lips, as she buried her nose in the fluffy fur; and this was more than Lambert could stand. With sudden quick decision he lifted the astonished Sabina from the damsel's arms and dropped her on all-fours on the grass-plot below. Then, as quickly, he seized her mistress by her empty hands.

"Katesie, do you suppose I've waited all these weary months to see you squandering kisses on a cat? Have you no answer *now*, after all I've told you, after my coming so many hundred miles?"

Her hands were writhing about in his grasp, making every pretence, and no real effort, at getting away. "*Ah* didn't tell you to come," she finally pouted.

"It's no time for trifling, Katesie. I've loved you dearly—ever so long—ever since the first time you leaned this bonny head upon my shoulder."

"Ah didn't!—Ah *nevuh* did!"

"You did; and I've got five glossy threads of your beautiful hair to prove it."

"It was all the fault of that ho'id shoulder-strap. Ah *hate* it, and you 'h hateful fo' reminding me of it!" And still her hands kept writhing in vain, impotent pretence at struggling. He held them with scarce an effort.

"Well," said he, solemnly, "they will never vex your soft cheek again, Katesie. I have worn them for the last time."

"Yo' have?" And now the struggles seemed gradually to cease, or their continuance became purely mechanical, and the big, deep gray eyes looked wistfully up through their long, curving lashes. "Whut —whut foh, Ah'd like to know?" She didn't quite say "*lahke*."

"Well, several reasons have been set before me. Mother is getting on in years, and wishes I could be near her, instead of half across the continent away."

She was looking up at him very solemnly now.

"Ah nevuh could beah you in those things—cits," she said at last.

"Brava! You are mastering army vernacular already, Katesie," he answered, his eyes twinkling. "And do you think you could bear me if I continued to wear the old shoulder-straps? Ah, Katesie, it's too late. Here they are." And, transferring unresisted one snowy wrist to contact with its fellow in the grasp of his left hand, he drew forth from an inner pocket an oblong parcel in which lay the light-blue velvet straps, wound round and round with silken threads of hair. "I couldn't bear to turn them over to any one but you," he solemnly said. "They are mine no longer."

She was silent a moment. Then the deep gray eyes were again uplifted, studying with troubled gaze the soldierly, sun-tanned young face.

"Ah'd—much rather you were going to keep on weah-ing them," she said.

"But I thought you hated the very sight of them—and the uniform?"

"That was befo' Brothuh Floyd woh it."

He had repossessed himself of the little hands by this time. "Then you *do* like the army blue a little? How I wish I'd known this sooner!"

"The army isn't so bad, now that some Southern gentlemen are going back into it," she answered, airily.

"It would be still more attractive with a certain Southern girl I know in it."

"Ah don't see how that would do you any good, 'f you're going to leave it."

" Ah! It was the army I was thinking of just then,—not myself. Thank you for thinking of me, Katesie." And now his eyes were brimming over with mingled tenderness and merriment. He had raised her hands, and, placing them palm to palm, stood clasping them, their rosy finger-tips close to his lips.

" Ah didn't! Ah wasn't! Let go ma hands, Mist' Lambuht." And once again she began to writhe, simply to feel his resisting power. " *Ah* wouldn't live like some o' those women do at the foht—just like gypsies."

" No," responded Lambert, demurely. " That's what a lady friend of yours told me : she said you were only a spoiled little Southern girl, brought up without any idea of housekeeping or care and responsibility."

" *Who* dayuhd to say such spiteful things ?" demanded Miss Walton, all ablaze in an instant.

" She said," calmly resumed Lambert, " that the main reason you didn't care to be a soldier's wife, probably, was that you'd always been made a pet of and wouldn't know how to look after a brute of a husband and one room and a kitchen,—all a lieutenant's allowed, you know."

" *Who* dayuhd to say such things ? It wasn't Genevieve !—Ah'd never speak——"

" Wait till I tell you the rest," pursued Lambert, calmly. " She said she really couldn't see why I wanted to marry you : you were not at all the sort of girl she'd expect a Northerner to marry."

" Ah never hnhd such outrageous impudence in all ma bawn days. Who *was* it? Ah'll never speak t' you again 'f you don't tell me this instant. Ah'll never let you leave this spot till you *do* tell me."

" I'm only too glad to stay. I was afraid you might send me away anyhow, even after you found I had given up the shoulder-straps—for your sake,—since Esther told me I'd find it hard work to make you a soldier's wife."

" *Esthuh!* *She* said such mean things 'bout me? Oh, Ah'll pay huh off fo' that ! Ah could manage just as well as she could, and keep house ev'y bit as well ! Ah've been out theyh often with Jenny Sweet, and seen just how they managed. Ah'd been watching—and studying" (sob) " and now—now"—with sudden inspiration—" Ah b'lieve you're just laughing at me ! Ah *hate* you moh than evuh, and Ah'll *nevuh* mah'y you—*nevuh*—jus' fo' leavin' the ahmy and not havin' sufficient

F *

confidence in me to think I could be a soldier's wife.   Ah might have done it—Ah *would*, perhaps, if you had stayed, but—but——"

But now she was seized and strained to his heart, and the furiously blushing face was kissed again and again, though indignant tears were starting from her eyes.   It was useless to struggle.   She leaned there at last, passive, pouting, sobbing a little, and striving to push herself from his embrace,—but striving so feebly, so very feebly.   "My own little rebel," he murmured, with his lips close pressed to her cheek, "'Esthuh' *did* tell me I'd find it hard work to win you for a soldier's wife,—did tell me you had had no care or experience in the past,—did say she thought a Northern officer would have fallen in love elsewhere; but she never said you were not fit to be a soldier's wife, and *I* never said I was going to quit being a soldier. I love it better than anything in the world—but you——"

"You *did!* You said yo'd done with the shoulder-straps fo'*evuh!*" And up flashed the indignant gray eyes again, and this brought the quivering little mouth, so red and soft and warm, too close for safety to his yearning lips.   Down they swooped upon their prey.   "I didn't," he whispered as he held her close.   "It's the old strap—the second lieutenant's—I'll never wear again.   I've won my bar now,—and my wife."

We were sitting one winter's evening nearly two years later in the Lamberts' quarters at old Fort Scott.   Kinsey was there too, and Floyd Walton with his bride on their wedding tour.   A blazing fire of hickory logs was snapping on the hearth, and under the soft light of the shaded lamp was Katesie, a charming picture of young wifehood, her needlework dropped in her lap, her gray eyes following every movement of her husband, who was declaiming to his guests and pacing up and down in uncontrollable excitement.

It was the January of the "Consolidation Year," when by act of Congress forty-five regiments of infantry were summarily "telescoped" into half their number, and some hundreds of officers and gentlemen who had joined the regular service at the end of the great war in the reasonable hope of attaining suitable rank before they died, found themselves suddenly bereft of all hope of promotion and doomed to remain subalterns and file-closers until they were fifty.   It was the year when to provide for the superfluous officers of the consolidated regiments of foot they were crammed into every obtainable vacancy in the horse and artillery,—when incompetents were ordered before a board of examiners and given a chance to defend their commissions, while—oh, the black shame of it!—others, gallant fellows who had fought all through the war, but had been at some time or other in the past at odds, personal or official, with certain of their superiors, now, without word of warning, without opportunity of defence, without knowing who were their accusers or what the accusations, found themselves summarily dropped from the rolls and their places promptly filled. The needed reduction by fair means proving too slow, the methods of foreign despotisms were resorted to: "confidential reports" were solicited from commanding officers, some of whom, disdaining such *lettre-de-cachet* business, promptly consigned the offending document to the flames or "pigeon-holed" it without reply, while others accepted eagerly the opportunity to undermine the men whom courts had honorably acquitted. In some few instances there were gentlemen thus disposed of who never knew they had been accused of misdemeanor until, amazed, they saw their names upon the published list. Among those thus given their *congé* was Brevet Captain J. P. Close, First Lieutenant —teenth Infantry, at the moment expecting his promotion to the captaincy of Company "C". "The old man," as his soldiers called him, had returned to duty after his six months' leave, with eyesight permanently impaired, and had been received with cordial and avowed esteem by Farnham and Kinsey and with open arms by Lambert. The manly fellows in the regiment followed suit, and they had done much to rub off the uncouth edges, to polish the rough exterior, and so reveal the value of the gem within, and Close was plodding contentedly along as quartermaster of a four-company post, when the blow fell. Minor, now lieutenant-colonel, was in command of the —teenth, the old adjutant and quartermaster in command of him. There was no need of asking whence the unseen allegations came.

An ill wind it is indeed that blows nobody good. In the general "shake-up" there came a colonel to the regiment whose first official act was to accept the resignations of the two staff officers and to appoint Lambert adjutant. "I wish you had gone in for a commission," said he to Floyd, whom he had known in his sergeant days in Texas, but Floyd replied that if this treatment of Close was a specimen of army justice he reckoned railroading would suit him better. Whereupon the new colonel swore that if Close were only back again he'd make him quartermaster and let his oppressors see the other side of his story; but Close never came.

With certain other wronged and astonished men, he had gone to Washington and pleaded his case before a most harassed and unhappy Cabinet official who was no longer able to undo the mischief, the Senate having confirmed the nominations to the vacancies thus created.

"He allowed that he guessed a few mistakes might have been made 'long of his putting too much faith in what some officers told him," wrote Close to Lambert, "but that in nine cases out of ten the thing was all right. I told him I hadn't come to talk about anybody's rights or wrongs but my own : what I wanted was the captaincy I was clean bilked out of. He said he couldn't fix that *any*how. The only thing was to take a second lieutenantcy and start back at the bottom of the ladder again. Some of them—poor fellows who'd been so long in the army they didn't know any other way of living and supporting their families—was fools enough to do it, but I'd see him dumned first, and nigh onto told him so.

"I guess I've had 'bout enough of it anyhow, Lambert. I did my best for the government in the days when if we fellows hadn't done our best there mighty soon wouldn't of been any government 'cept Jeff Davis, and if this here's a specimen of the best the government can do for a man that got plugged pretty full of lead fighting for it, why, next war that comes around I want to be a sutler and nothing else. Lucky I ain't as bad off as the rest. The boys are doing first-rate, and the girls are well hitched to very decent farmers, both of 'em, and 'bout all I've got to look after's my property. They're running two railroads through there now, and it won't be long before I can be a Senator or Secretary, if I can't be a sutler. Now I'm going back to Spirit Lake, where I'm building the prettiest home in the Hawkeye State, and it'll be all ready to welcome you and Mrs. Lambert and—well—just as soon as she feels like travelling again—and you must come and spend a long leave with me. I ain't got any children of my own, and my kindred are kind of wrapped up in theirs, and I took a shine to you the first day you set foot in that old mud-hole of a camp at Tugaloo. So don't you ever fret about the future, Lambert. You stood by me when I hadn't a friend, and—my will's all made, boy, and don't you forget it.

"Yours truly,

"J. P. CLOSE.

"P.S. *Dam* the Cap."

SERGEANT CRŒSUS.

SERGEANT CRŒSUS.

I.

THE colonel was hopping mad. Anybody could see it, and every-body within range of his tongue and temper felt it. Bob Gray, the adjutant, guessed it before he got within sound of his voice, and could swear to it before he got out again. Being only an adjutant, however, he couldn't swear at it, and so keep on even terms with his chief. He bottled his own wrath, as he did the colonel's commentaries, and kept them both for future emergencies. A relic of the vaunted old dragoon days was the colonel; one of the fast vanishing lot of hard-riding, hard-fighting, and sometimes hard-swearing campaigners who had learned their trade under masters of the art long years before the war. He had crossed the Llano Estacado and camped on the Mimbres and chased the Navajoes when Navajoes were monarchs of the Southwestern plains, were bellicose not bucolic, raised sheol instead of sheep,—a statement otherwise expressed by Kit Carson, a keen scout and keener judge of aboriginal nature, who said that when they were not raising hell or ha'r in equal proportions the Navajoes were either dead or asleep. We were having campaigns ten times more thrilling in point of incident, ten times fiercer in point of fighting and casualties, ten times tougher in point of hardship and privation—and the food we lived on—than those of the Navajo days, to be sure, but the colonel would have it the service wasn't to be mentioned alongside that to which he had been accustomed when they scouted with Kearney or Fauntleroy and rode races with the Mounted Rifles at Albuquerque and Santa Fé. "They made cavalrymen in those days," said he. Then with gloomy reference to the losses of the summer just gone by, "Now they only kill 'em, and this set of slummers they are sending out to recruit us is only fit to be killed anyhow. Why the devil did you send me such a wooden-headed idiot for an orderly on this day of all others?" he demanded of his staff officer. "Why, he couldn't speak English!"

Now, when the colonel began to ask questions and invite explanations we all knew that he had, measurably at least, blown off his wrath; was beginning to regret anything sharp he had said; was penitent, and wanted to be mollified and forgiven and taken into good-fellowship again. Nobody knew this better than the adjutant, or presumed on it more. At this stage of the proceedings Bob became downright impudent. But his brown eyes twinkled with fun as he stood facing the colonel and waiting for an opportunity to speak.

"No, sir, he couldn't speak a word of English," repeated the colonel.

"We-ell," said Bob, reflectively, "it wasn't a civil service examination I was running. He was the cleanest man on guard, and your orders are——"

"Then send me the dirtiest so long as we are in the field," burst in the colonel, impetuously. "What I want in an orderly is just what I don't want in an adjutant,—a man who can repeat what I say, and not think."

"Well, anybody ought to be able to do that, sir," began the adjutant, with a twitch under the heavy thatch of his moustache.

"Wait till I get through, young man," interrupted the colonel again, impressively; "then you may be as harmless as you know how. What I need in an adjutant is one who can think and not say anything—except when I tell him to. Now, you sent me a Dutch doll that couldn't even squawk in English. He called me names in some foreign lingo."

"Well, you wouldn't want him to do it in English, would you, colonel?"

"Wouldn't? I didn't—Damn it! where are your wits this morning, Gray? He—he——what was it he called me, Fallon?"

"Sounded like O-burst, was all I heard, sir," said the quartermaster, uncomfortably. "But Sergeant Stein says that's only the double Dutch for colonel."

Mr. Gray's eyes were dancing now. "I never saw the man before in my life, colonel," said he. "He came with that big batch of recruits the other day. Manning's first sergeant marched him on. He looked spick-span neat and clean and intelligent,—by long odds the trimmest and most soldier-like fellow on guard."

"Not excepting the officer of the day and adjutant, I suppose," interposed the colonel.

"No exceptions whatever, sir. Indeed, not excepting any man in the whole command, from the colonel up—I mean down. You were saying yesterday that the only way to tell real cavalrymen from recruits was that we looked like jayhawkers and they like Jew-store dummies. Still, I thought the sight of a man clean shaved, with buttons and buckles polished, would please your eyes after all this campaign's mud, so I sent him. Of course if he could only call you names in Dutch I'm sorry, and will see that you're properly looked after next time."

But even "Old Tintop" began to see the fun under the sedate gravity of the adjutant's words.

"Confound you for a young rascal! What have you been making me say, anyhow? Come back here, Fallon, and stop your laughing, too, sir. You're a nice pair to play it on your old—— What do *you* want, sir?"

Turning suddenly, he addressed a ragged, tattered, hungry-looking party in hunting-shirt, buckskin breeches, and Shoshone leggings, standing attention before the colonel's "shack,"—he had no tent,—with a bare brown hand raised to his rusty brown carbine in salute.

"I'm ordered to report to the colonel as the dirtiest man on guard, sir," was the stolid answer.

For a moment the commander gazed at him in wrath, and then a light flashed across his mental vision.

"Now see what you've reduced me to, Gray, you infernal young sinner. I sent Stein back with the orderly you picked out, and here's the result."

"Well, sir, if dirt's what you want, this——"

"But it isn't," interrupted the colonel. "I want an orderly, and not a scarecrow. Now you see, do you?"

"I think I do, sir. Neither a rag doll nor a Dutch doll, neither the cleanest nor the dirtiest, just a happy medium, one who can call names in English preferred, not so swell as to put our head-quarters to shame, nor so shabby as to make us blush for all—— Well, I think I understand you."

But here the colonel interposed with language so forcible as to put a stop even to Gray's fun, which he would stand, as a rule, longer than anybody else's. Meantime, the discovery having been made that recruit Schramm was but a novice in English, whatsoever he might be in German, that young soldier was told by the sergeant of the guard to "Go on out of this and back to your bunkies. Sure you couldn't tell a

Sioux from a shyster unless he shot you in Dutch," which, being interpreted, was understood to mean that until he had mastered the English language he wasn't fit for sentry duty. And so, much troubled, the young fellow went to Sergeant Schultz, a Prussian like himself, and sorrowfully told his tale.

Never in his life had Private Schramm's blue eyes gazed on scenes and soldiers such as these. Just what he expected to find in the ranks of the American army he had revealed as yet to no one. It was the eventful summer of '76, when, amazed at the force and fury with which the Sioux had fought and baffled the commands of Crook and Custer, Terry and Gibbon, Congress authorized the immediate enlistment of twenty-five hundred men to fill the gaps in the four regiments of cavalry engaged in the campaign. No credentials were required. Eager for a chance to get to the new diggings—the Black Hills of Dakota—at the expense of Uncle Sam, swarms of toughs were enlisted in the slums of New York and Philadelphia and Baltimore, and four weeks later were deserting by the dozen, with horse and equipment complete, as they reached the wasted army in the field. But there was leaven in the lump. "That young feller's a soldier clean through," said the recruiting sergeant when Schramm gave his name, age, nationality, etc., answering promptly so long as the questions were propounded in the German tongue.

"Can't he speak English at all?" said the recruiting officer, doubtfully. "Well, what's the odds, after all, so long as he's only going to be scalped? Swear him in." And so, silent, observant, patient, Schramm was shipped westward with the first lot of victims, turned over to the waiting officers at the cavalry dépôt, was marched out to camp and set to work grooming a horse the very evening of his arrival, and turned out for drill the next morning, when, barring a certain quaint habit of throwing the left foot far out to the front at the command "march," and a queer way of executing "about face," it was found that he was far better drilled in the rudiments, at least, than the corporal detailed as his instructor. The carbine manual was strange to him, but not so the sabre. He handled it like a master. He knew how to clean and polish arms, belt buckles, etc., in a way that the few old hands at the post recognized at once as "expert." He was besieged by German sergeants with queries as to his past history, but said he preferred to keep all that to himself. Yes, he had served. No use in denying that. He had been through certain cadet schools and entered a certain regiment of Hussars ; which one he wouldn't say, neither could they find out by writing. It was nobody's business but his own, anyhow, said he. The United States had adopted him, and he was now an Amerikaner, a "Freiwilliger," too. Long before the weary march to the hills was over he had demonstrated the fact that he was a fine horseman and a good shot. Lieutenant Ray, commander of the big detachment, had more than once spoken of it ; and so, when finally they reached the wild romantic hills and were distributed among the regiments there awaiting them, Schramm looked with wonderment in his soul, if not in his eyes, at the slouch-hatted, rough-shirted, unshaven officers, at the ragged mob of the rank and file, at their gaunt skeletons of horses, and marvelled that his strange fortunes had made him a soldier in so strange a service.

Wisely he kept his views to himself, making no comment even to the Germans who were disposed to be sociable and to question him as to his antecedents. In two days a strong column marched away,—all broken-down men and horses and all raw recruits being left behind,— but with Schramm, evidently an educated cavalryman, riding buoyantly in the ranks of D Troop on the spirited roan he had bestridden all the way from the railway. " Whatever they look," thought he, " these fellows are mightily at home on the frontier." Sergeant Schultz explained that they always left their uniforms in garrison when in the field after Indians, but called his attention to the fact that they never lived better in the old country than these rough-looking fellows were living now. Already the ills of the summer were forgotten.

Whether he forgot or not, Schramm made no reply. He was well content with his rations, for field appetite is a wondrous sauce, and soldier coffee with bacon, beans, "Dutch oven" bread, and antelope steak have a relish in the keen October air known only to the frontiersman. Schramm, from looking pale, peaked, and a trifle pathetic when he stepped from the crowded train at the railway, had sprouted a fuzzy beard, blistered the skin of his cheeks and nose in the hot noonday sunshine, seared his eyelids by intemperate ablutions in alkali water, and was making commendable progress in plains-craft and plains-English. In three weeks' scouting down the South Cheyenne, with the Bad Lands on the right and worse lands on the left, he became so proficient in the cavalry art of pre-empting a good patch of grass for his horse that his troop commander, closely watching his new recruit, remarked that that young fellow would be a valuable non-commissioned officer some day, if he hadn't been already. Like the Germans of his heterogeneous troop, the captain was of the opinion that Schramm had a history.

One evening, far down the valley where not an Indian had been seen or heard of, the outlying sentries reported a bunch of black-tailed deer in the foot-hills to the northwest. Lieutenant Morgan was in command of the guard, and his captain was officer of the day. Morgan took a squad of three or four men, mounted, and rode away down the wind, while a party of officers scrambled up the bank to the edge of the broad prairie to watch the sport. It was just then that Schramm, his blue eyes ablaze, clicked his heels together, stood bolt upright, and began, coloring even redder in combined eagerness and embarrassment, "Bitte, Herr Rittmeister," then, desperately plunging into trooper's English as he had heard it spoken, "Kin I go along mit dem fellers alretty?" and as Manning nodded assent, he saluted with marked precision, bored a hole with his heel in the alkali dust in punctilious execution of the "*kehrt*," sprang bareback on his horse, and rode away, carbine in hand, after his trooper comrades. Half an hour went by, and the herd, still undisturbed, continued to graze. The hunters were out of sight among the depressions of the surface. The captain sent for his field-glass, and other officers joined him and levelled their binoculars on the distant quarry,—just a deer family having a quiet dinner together in a sheltered ravine opening out into the broad bottom of the stream. Presently, one after another, three or four black objects crawled around a point. "Yonder's Morgan," said the watchers. Suddenly the deer family tossed high their heads, then darted away into the hills and were out of sight in an instant. Two or three of the younger officers set up a laugh of derision: "Pretty hunting that is!" But the elders looked grave. "What scared them?" was the query. The black dots of hunters had halted, evidently in surprise. There seemed to be a moment of consultation, and then all three could be seen running back in the direction in which they came.

"Going for the horses to chase the deer," laughed young Leonard, who sneered at Morgan's claims as a deer-stalker.

"Chase be hanged! Look there! the deer are chasing them."

Then uprose every man in mad excitement, for their senior lieutenant, Mr. Ray, had sprung to his feet and rushed for his horse. "Deer, you damned fool! It's Indians!" he cried; and, shouting for some of the guard to follow him, Mr. Ray threw himself upon his nimble sorrel and darted out over the prairie to the rescue. In a minute half a dozen men were stringing along after him, while the alarm sounded among the cottonwoods and the herd-guards came driving in their excited *cavalladas*.

Meantime, there was the mischief to pay. Leaving two men as horse-holders in a little swale, Morgan with three others, including the eager young Prussian, crawled off for a shot at the herd. They were in plain view, and utterly unsuspicious of approach from that quarter, when, all on a sudden, the buck started, stamped, tossed his crest, and away they all flew up the grassy ravine. Rising to his feet to study the situation, after a word or two of caution to his comrades, Morgan was saluted by the whistle of a bullet past his head,—another,—another,—and each coupled with the sharp report of the rifle.

" Back to your horses, quick !" he shouted.

All four ran, only to catch sight of a party of Sioux lashing straight down the slope to head them off, while others, firing rapidly, gave chase from across the ravine to their rear. Before he had gone twenty yards Morgan saw Schramm stumble and fall, face downward.

" What is it ?" he cried, running and bending over him. " Are you hit ? Here, let me help you, man." And poor Schramm could only clasp his hand about his leg and plead in English equally broken, " Lauf'—Roon ! Herr Lieutenant. Ach Gott ! I can it not make." Then Morgan, big powerful fellow, cut him short and swung the little ex-hussar on his back and plunged ahead, heedless of his captive's splutter and struggles. But yelling Sioux and whistling bullets both were gaining. Another minute, and down went lieutenant and man, carrier and carried, and this time Schramm, rolling over and over, never let go of his carbine, but, lying prone, levelled it over a little hummock, and sent a shot square at the foremost Indian, tripping his calico pony in the nick of time. Morgan echoed with another. " Good boy, Schramm ! Give 'em some more," he cried, as the charging warriors veered and opened out. Then came other shots from the swale in rear. Only one man held the horses now ; the others—the whole squad—were blazing away.

" Check to your game, my bucks !" panted Morgan, loading, firing, and missing again. " It's little but lead you'll get out of this outfit." The Indian bullets were biting at the turf all around him, yet mercifully flying wild. Schramm, bleeding fast, was paling, yet keeping up his fire, wondering how it was he could so rarely hit those yelling, painted, feathered fiends darting about them only a few hundred yards away. Then, rising on his knees, he shouted Prussian taunt and challenge.

"Lie down, you fool!" yelled his officer, rolling over to him, and, seizing his shoulder, Morgan forced him to earth. Not a second too soon: an Indian had sprung from his pony, taken deliberate aim, and sent a shot that just grazed the hand that pinned him down; and then came thunder of hoofs far out over the prairie, and the rush of comrades to the rescue, and then the Sioux, firing to the last minute, whirled away up the ravine, and Morgan's deer-hunt was over. That night, while Ray, with his troop, was still out in pursuit, Morgan lay with a shot-hole through the left shoulder at the bivouac fire, and was chaffed and condoled with in moderation over the failure of his venison-chase, and took it all meekly enough. He had bagged no game, had well-nigh lost his own and other lives, had ridden almost blindly into Indian ambuscade, and yet, in point of result, as it turned out, that was about the best day's work he had done in all his life.

II.

"If ever a man came into the cavalry who deserved well of his country," said his colonel, "it is Morgan." He was a good soldier, but a bad manager,—a combination far more frequent than is probably known. He came into the regiment in '66, burdened with a wife and a war debt. A capital trooper, he had won honors with the sabre in the Shenandoah; had risen to the command of his battalion, and was urged to take a commission in the regular army. Famous names backed his application, but he had been held to duty in Texas while earlier-discharged volunteers were picking up the plums in the newly-authorized regiments. He got in eventually as second lieutenant where his own lieutenants had gone in as first. He had the brevet of a lieutenant-colonel of volunteers and the rank and pay of a low-down subaltern of regulars when he and his wife and a little daughter joined the regiment in the South. When he came to the frontier after five years of reconstruction duty, her health was impaired as much as his prospects. Morgan was supporting an invalid wife, three children, a negro "mammy," an egregious folly of a female nurse, and a scattered indebtedness of no one knew just how many hundreds or thousands, all on a first lieutenant's pay, and that hypothecated. He loved his wife and little ones ; he was attached to his comrades and his profession ; but every month found him more dangerously involved. He had no relatives to help him ; she had some who might, but didn't. He wore old clothes, stinted himself in every way, yet saw no light ahead, and, to make a long story short, would have thanked God for the chance to end it all, but for the thought of those helpless little ones, when at last the wife, not he, was taken. She had been practically bedridden for two years, and it would have been mercy to take her long before, but Morgan couldn't see that. He wept sorely over the cold, emaciated form, then roused himself, gathered his children in his strong arms and folded them to his heart. "You must be more than ever 'little mother' to them now, Connie," said he, as he kissed the white forehead of his eldest. She was only fifteen that spring, yet for two years had been more woman than child, trying to help mother, trying to be a comfort to "poor daddy," whose face took on deep and deeper lines with every month, trying to be a teacher and playmate and mother all in one to sister Lottie, only eight, and to burly, brown-haired, uproarious little Billy, the one member of the household whose spirits were unquenchable. There were ministering hands and loving hearts at the rude old frontier fort, and in poor Mrs. Morgan's last days, far from her home and kindred, there was no "lack of woman's nursing," no "dearth of woman's tears." Everybody seemed to go in the solemn little procession when, afoot, they followed the wasted form to its bleak and lonely resting-place in the post cemetery out on the open prairie.

"My God ! to think of poor Carrie's having to be buried in such a dreary waste as this !" moaned the widower that evening as some of his comrades strove to comfort him. He had written to her relatives —she had brothers and a sister married and well-to-do—telling of the inevitable end so soon to come, intimating that she longed to be taken home and to lie by her mother's side in the shaded church-yard, but that he actually had not a cent. The brothers were very sorry. Both in their younger days had freely borrowed the captain's tens and twenties and lived high with sister Cad, to whom the big-hearted dragoon sent each month four-fifths of his pay. Pretty sister Lottie, too, made her home with Caroline, "who would otherwise be so lone-some," much of the four years Morgan served at the front. His pay was the main support of the family, in fact, for the boys were still attending school, and the old man's business languished as the war went on. But all this was something they rather wished to forget in the years that followed. They didn't want to grow up into actively inimical relations with their elder sister's husband, yet having so long lived on his bounty, how could they, being ordinary mortals, help learning to hate him unless they could forget the benefits of the past? Bob and Sam, of whom she so often talked, were prosperous business men now, with wives and olive-branches and vines and fig-trees of their own, and how could their wives or they be expected to want to have her, a dark shadow at the fireside, to linger, languish, and slowly die on their hands? Neither brother felt that he could stand the expense of fetching Carrie home. Each thought the other ought to do it, and both thought that Lottie should,—that is, Lottie's husband. But Lottie's husband knew not the impoverished trooper on the far frontier, nor his wife, nor his children, and Lottie was not particularly anxious that he should. Her beauty had captivated the brilliant young lawyer when professional business called him from Cleveland to Saginaw, but it took all he could command to keep up the style in which they lived now. A gay winter was coming on, and there was very little interest and less discussion among the three over the question which should succor Carrie, and so poor Morgan's humble appeal was fruitless.

It was December when she was laid away. In February a strong column was sent to break up the Sioux strongholds to the north, with the not unusual result of breaking up several households at the fort. The Sioux lost nothing they did not get back; the soldiers got back nothing they lost; in fact, many of them did not get back at all. The savage chiefs held a council to settle on the spot for the next battle, and the soldiers a court to settle on the spot the responsibility for the last, which was a failure. It was found that beyond certain serious casualties the damages were mainly at the hands of Jack Frost to the feet and fingers of the foemen, though several officers were declared to have suffered in mind, body, and estate, and others in reputation, which was odd, in view of the fact, as shown before the court, that the accused had no reputation to lose. Morgan, happily, was spared all participation in this hapless campaign, being retained at the fort because of recent bereavement and his motherless children. He was made commissary to help him out of trouble, and thereby was plunged into worse. When the command went out in midwinter he would have been glad to go and never return, but, as has been said, for those little faces at home. Another column was sent out in May, and others followed that in June, and still Morgan was held at the fort on commissary duty until later the direful tidings flashed in over the wires that Custer and his pet troops were wiped out; then everybody had to go. Morgan strained "Little Mother" to his heart, praying God to guard and bless the babies and bring him back to them in safety. Mrs. Warren, their next-door neighbor, promised they should be the objects of her tender care. They had old Mammy with them still, but the nurse had flitted eastward months before,—one good riddance at least, —and by the end of July Morgan was serving out groceries and taking in money as field commissary. A column on frontier campaign with only the clothes it had on and with never a wagon could hardly be expected to be burdened with a safe in which to secure the commissary's funds. Uncle Sam has a simple way of reimbursing himself in the event of loss: he stops the commissary's pay until the amount is covered, and the commissary may stop the hungry mouths at home meanwhile as best he can,—that isn't Uncle Sam's business. Morgan had over seven hundred and fifty dollars in "greenbacks" in the lining of his canvas hunting-coat when they reached the Southern hills in October, and not a cent of it when they marched out on the 15th. The campaign being virtually over, all danger, hardship, work, and heavy responsibility at an end, a staff captain came by rail and stage to take over the funds and stores of the line lieutenant and charge up to him every cent's worth that had leaked or dribbled from the mule-packs, a species of charging that differed from that expected of a linesman, in that it involved none of the perils, yet promised greater reward.— You may be assured this gentleman did not come without a safe.—And Morgan, riding from the bivouac to the stage station, a mile away, the very evening of his successor's arrival, was lassoed on his horse in Cinnabar Cañon, gagged, bound, robbed of his package of greenbacks, all in the flash of a bull's-eye. Picked up, stunned, ten minutes thereafter, he could not describe his assailants, but certain hard characters with the command, some of the precious gang of recruits just arrived, made off that night with their horses, equipments, and everything. Certain civil officials gave chase. There was still hope they might be overhauled and the money captured before they could reach the mining towns. Meantime, Morgan, not severely hurt, was ordered to join his troop. It was God's mercy that only an hour before the robbery he had counted out every cent for which he was accountable

G   13

in the presence of Old Tintop and his adjutant, otherwise he would have had to stagger under the accusation of having made away with the money and made up the story.

In vain the rough old campaigner had sought to cheer Morgan by assurance that the party sent out in chase couldn't help gathering in the robbers, who, with one exception, were strangers to the frontier. Morgan groaned in spirit. " No, colonel, it is useless. Luck has been dead against me ever since we furled the Wolverine guidons and I joined the regulars. That money will never be found, and I am eight hundred dollars more in debt than I was a month ago, when it was all I could stagger under. It's only worse and more of it." And here this forty-year-old fatalist turned away and buried his bearded face in his hands.

And now, a few weeks later, with a hole in his shoulder and fever in his veins, Mr. Morgan was being borne along homeward in a mule-litter, hopeless and sick at heart, totally unconscious of the fact that one man at least in the long dusty column looked up to him with an enthusiastic gratitude, even while looking down on him from the saddle. Schramm's right leg had been shot through midway between ankle and knee, but the fracture was simple, and the wounded limb was skilfully dressed, set in splints, and Schramm rode in a litter a week or two, as ordered, then his Teutonic prayers took effect on the " Herr Wundarzt," and he was allowed to swing the leg over the handsome roan his captain had promised he should have again as soon as he was able to straddle the beast and settle the question why he had named him Bredow. We had little or no time for war-history in the cavalry in those days.

Morgan could not but note how affectionately Schramm's blue eyes would beam upon him and how full of anxious sympathy were his frequent inquiries as to whether there were not something he could do for the Herr Lieutenant. They sent the two, with others, in together to the old fort on the railway, and Schramm, whose wound was the more serious, was much the sooner recovered, and bustling around as though nothing had happened, while the veteran lieutenant, whose hurt was slight, seemed unable to rally. There are wounds that sap the vital forces worse than knife or bullet. Morgan was fretting himself to death. He broke down utterly when Old Tintop, a month later, came in to see him on his arrival at the post.

" What can I do, colonel?" he moaned. " I am too old to resign and try to find employment at home. There's no room for crippled dragoons there. Yet my creditors are hounding me, my pay may be stopped any minute to settle this commissary business, and then what will become of my children?"

It was too much for Tintop. He had in his desk that moment the fatal paper received from Washington. It was all very well for the board of survey and the department commander to exonerate Lieutenant Morgan from blame, but the watch-dogs of the treasury couldn't allow him to drop that seven hundred and fifty dollars. There was no doubt that he was robbed. The robbers, in fact, deserting recruits *en route* to the mines, were easily overhauled by experienced frontiersmen who "lit out" in pursuit the moment the affair was heard of. It was scandalous on the part of "tenderfoot toughs" from the far East to rob an army disbursing officer—and expect to get away with the swag. Buckskin Joe, Lopsided Pete, and other local celebrities lost little time in overhauling the Bowery gang and recovering such valuables as they had; but who was to overhaul Joe and Pete? The auditor said Mr. Morgan ought to have kept that money in the safe. The department commander, striving to aid a good soldier, pointed out that they didn't carry safes when on Indian campaign; if they did, they would even less frequently catch the Indians. But it availed nothing. What did the Treasury Department care whether Indians were caught or not? Mr. Morgan was held to have violated the spirit of his instructions in that he went to Captain Stone in town to turn over the money, instead of waiting for Captain Stone to come to him. Then the general pointed out that Morgan was ordered to march with the command at daybreak, and therefore had to turn over the money that night. But the bureau officials couldn't see it. Let Lieutenant Morgan get a bill of relief through Congress, said the pragmatic official, well knowing that such bills are the outcome of influence, not innocence. The colonel went to the office, and by way of comforting himself for the weakness which prompted him to blow his nose and wipe his eyes very often before leaving Morgan, and to kiss Connie and Lot several times after, pitched into Mr. Gray, his perennial chopping-block, and Gray, finding meekness and silence not what was needed, fired back. They exchanged volleys a minute, Gray having all the advantage of sense and the colonel of sound, and ended, as usual, by the old man saying he wouldn't give a tinker's dam for an adjutant he couldn't pitch into when he had to pitch into somebody, or that couldn't talk back. "I'm all broke up about Morgan. Can't we do something to pull him out of his hole?"

So they wrote letters, did the officers, to Morgan's wife's relatives, setting forth how brave and deserving and unfortunate he was, and that something must be done for those children. It's all well enough in the eyes of one's wife's relatives to be brave and deserving, but they have no use for a man who is unfortunate. In fact, if he is only fortunate they care very little how brave he may be, and less for his deserts. Robert answered the colonel's missive, but the others did not. Rob said they had already been put to much expense on their sister's account,—which, as they wore no mourning and published no notice in the papers at the time of her death, was an out-and-out whopper. He furthermore said if something had to be done for those children to go ahead and do it,—which was simply indecent. Tintop had a copy made and sent it to a classmate, a distinguished officer of engineers whose office was in Detroit, and whose duties made him well known in influential circles, and the colonel made inquiries and sent reports. The boys were well-to-do, in a paying business, both of them; and as for Aunt Lottie, she wasted more money in six months than would clothe, feed, and comfort her army nieces and nephew as many years. "But," said the engineer, "I fancy her husband owes very much more than Mr. Morgan, and the crash may come any day."

But what Tintop could not do through Morgan's wife's relatives he brought about in other ways. The engineer colonel knew prominent business men who were comrades of Morgan's in the old Wolverine brigade, famous at Gettysburg, Winchester, Five Forks, and Appomattox. Some had amassed wealth, many were prominent, all were sympathetic, and when they took hold it was with a vim. Meantime, however, valuable time was lost, and poor Morgan was breaking down under his load. Meantime, too, ministering angels, army wives and mothers, none so wealthy that their charity entailed no sacrifice, none so poor that it could not and did not help, moved by that boundless pity and sympathy which motherless little ones excite, were lending helping hands about the cheerless quarters and bringing grateful tears and smiles to Connie's anxious face. Mrs. Warren, Mrs. Woods, and others had laid their matronly heads together and organized a committee of ways and means. Of course nothing could be done to excite Morgan's suspicions or wound his pride. Connie, too, was old beyond her years and shrank from what might look like dependence, but she was too young to manage household expenses. Old Mammy had none but extravagant ideas, as befitted the retainer of a good old Southern family, and the father was practically helpless. It was at this stage of the proceedings that Fagan, the veteran striker who had long been on domestic duty for the Morgans, in accordance with the system then in vogue, was taken down with acute rheumatism and went to hospital, and that Private Schramm, who for days had never missed an opportunity of inquiring for the lieutenant and occasionally lending a helping hand, came suddenly into prominence. Somebody had to be detailed as Morgan's "striker." There were always quite a number of the enlisted men who were eager to be placed on such duty, thereby earning five dollars a month, living on better rations, escaping guard duty, drills, and roll-calls, and having only to bring in wood and water, black boots, clean equipments, etc. Schramm was reserved, temperate, studious, a model young soldier, daily acquiring more thorough knowledge of military duty and of the English language as spoken by the blue-coats on the border. Two or three times the doctor, finding him hovering about the quarters, had sent him over to the hospital for medicine, or the like, and Schramm, saluting with Teutonic precision, had obeyed every order with soldierly alacrity. More than once when Fagan, groaning and coughing and wheezing in the keen wintry air, seemed unable to bear his burden of firewood into the house, Schramm had laughingly lent his aid, and one evening he came suddenly upon the tall, slender, fragile form of Connie staggering into the kitchen door, heavily laden with logs. With one spring the Prussian was at her side, the blue eyes kindling, and he who hitherto had never presumed to address the "gnädige Fräulein" except with hand at temple and heels aclick, briskly dispossessed her of her load, and bore it into the sitting-room, where Lot and Billy were squabbling over their blocks in the wintry gloaming, and Connie blushed to her temples as she thanked the stalwart young soldier, once more standing erect and brushing the bark-dust from his overcoat.

"Father sent Fagan to town," she explained, "and he should have been home an hour ago. We are so much obliged to you, Schr-r-r-amm." And Schr-r-r-amm seemed so hard a word to say that she blushed still more, hesitated, and stammered,—she who, garrison-bred, had never heard the private soldier addressed in any other way.

It was that evening, later, that old Fagan declared himself all broke up, which meant just the opposite, that he had broken down and must quit work. Mrs. Turner, a light-hearted and thoughtless young matron, was sitting with Connie at the moment.

"He'll go to hospital, won't he?" she said. "Then how much better it will be! Captain Manning will let you have Schramm." But, to Mrs. Turner's surprise, Connie promptly declared she would not have Schramm.

"Why-y, I thought he was so devoted to your father,—so nice in every way."

"Certainly," said Connie, with decision; "he is devoted to father, and he is simply altogether too nice to be put on any such duty."

"Did you ever know so strange a child?" said Mrs. Turner, telling of the conversation a little later. "She fairly put me down as though I were a chit of fifteen—like herself."

"Ye-es, instead of being old enough to be her mother," suggested a fair rival, mischievously, and Mrs. Turner bridled, but said no more.

But Manning, too, fell into error. Informed by his first sergeant at tattoo that Fagan was down sick and the lieutenant without a striker, in all kindness and desire to help he asked who would be the best man to send, and the sergeant promptly answered, "Schramm. Schramm was all the time over there, and doubtless he would be glad to take the detail." Manning hesitated a moment. He had other views for this young soldier, whose usefulness in the troop could become very great as soon as he mastered a little more English. But he called him forthwith. Schramm was among his comrades, awaiting the assembly signal, and, summoned abruptly, he stood attention in a foot of snow and answered, "Zu Befehl, Herr Rittmeister," before he could catch himself and blurt out "Ca-Capitan." His gloved hand remained, Prussian fashion, in salute.

"Schramm, I hate to lose you from the troop, but would you care to go to Lieutenant Morgan's as orderly?"

"I, Herr Rittmeister?"

The roll of the *r*'s was almost like that of a drum. The blood mounted to his cheeks. He stammered, looked utterly bewildered, stumbled, and between embarrassment and sense of subordination stood meekly mute.

"Don't you want to go?" asked Manning.

"Bitte, Herr Capitan, unless I haf it to do."

"Oh, no, by no means. I supposed you'd really like it," said

Manning. "I would much rather you didn't. That's all." And Schramm nearly fell over himself in the effort to salute and face about in a foot-deep drift and escape before the Herr Rittmeister might change his mind. "Whom can we send, sergeant? I want a good steady man, for Mr. Morgan is far from mending."

"Well, sir, there's Penner: he ain't good for nothing else."

And so it came to pass that Penner, a mild-mannered, moony young barbarian, went gladly to duties with which he was far more familiar than the grooming of frolicsome steeds and the tramping of lonely sentry-posts. And Schramm, redoubling the assiduity of his attention to military duties, none the less kept up his frequent visits to the Morgans' quarters, modestly presenting himself at the rear door and laboriously inquiring how the Herr Lieutenant had passed the night and whether he could do aught to serve him during the day. Penner was soon sufficiently domesticated to answer these queries himself, but not infrequently Constance came to answer the soldier's knock, and then at sight of the gnädige Fräulein Schramm's manner would become simply extravagant in precision and deference. Within the week after he declined the place the soldiers were saying Schramm "wouldn't be dog-robber, but was bossing Penner's job all the same." And certain it was that Penner owed much of his usefulness to the suggestions of his better-informed countryman. Meantime, Mrs. Warren and Mrs. Woods were doing all that lay in their power to help about the house, and another loving woman, who devoted two hours each morning to the lessons of her own little ones, had induced Constance to send Lot and Billy to her as recruits in the kindergarten, and the officers, dropping in each evening to cheer the old man up a bit, still striving to hold from him the fact that the Treasury Department had proved deaf to all martial appeals in his behalf, were made glad one bitter evening by a despatch from the Wolverine Senator. The old Michigan brigade had still "a pull," and Tintop himself went whistling down the line to tell Morgan the glad news that he had friends at court.

"Bill of relief for Morgan will be presented," wired the magnate. "Meantime, no stoppage allowed."

"Who could have fixed this for me?" asked Morgan, gratefully, with glistening eyes.

"Oh, your friends at home did it," answered Tintop, promptly, with pardonable thought of how much stirring the friends at the front had first to do. "What they ought to stir about now is to help you out

with these—these—other claims; I don't mean pay them for you, of
course,—you wouldn't want them to do that,—but fix it so that you
could capitalize 'em someway; raise a little fund that you could repay
at so much a month with six per cent. interest, and then wipe out all
these pressing things."

Poor Morgan! *his* first thought had been that now he could order
a suitable head-stone for Carrie's lonely grave.

III.

The winter went out in storm and bluster. The springtide set in
with reluctant flow. The prairie wastes, swept clean by furious gales
in March, rerobed in glistening white in April, peeped forth through
ragged rents in their fleecy mantle at the soft touch of the south wind,
then, lulled by the plash of warm summer shower, went to sleep one
evening late in May, still thinly veiled in white, and when the rosy
breath of wakening dawn stole faintly over the grassy billows, lo! all
in a night the face of nature had changed, and the foot-hills met the
sunshine clothed in fairest, freshest green. Who can welcome spring
as could the exiles of the old days on the frontier? How those fair
women, those restless little ones, seemed to glow and gladden after the
long, long months of seclusion when, snow-bound, they were penned
within the stockade or limited to the sentry-lines of some straggling
prairie post! Now swarming forth like bees they came to greet the
sunshine, the softening air, the tiny, shrinking little flowers trembling
in the breeze along the southward slopes, and one exquisite morning
late in May, perched on the very verge of the steep bluff overlooking
the stream, Constance Morgan had flung to the winds her rippling
mane of auburn hair and stood stretching forth a pair of long, slender
arms, encased in very shabby and shining serge, as though welcoming
the first sight of the distant lowlands,—the broad, beautiful valley of
the Mini Ska. All the long winter she had borne on her white
shoulders the cares of an army home, and that a home without a
mother. Loving hearts and hands, it is true, were there to aid her.
Morgan's devotion to his invalid wife during her two years of mar-
tyrdom and his grief over her loss were matters that had won deep
sympathy even in a crowded garrison bent on getting all the enjoy-

ment possible out of their few months of home life. All the previous summer, spring, and fall officers and men of the cavalry, at least, had spent in exciting campaign, and no man could tell how soon the order would come returning them once more to the field, leaving the wives and little ones to watch and pray. "Make hay while the sun shines" seemed to be the social axiom of the cavalry in those days. Enjoy the too brief days as best ye may, for soon the summer will come, when all men must work at their appointed trade, and seven months out of twelve and sometimes more it meant separation from the loved ones within the guarded limits of the forts, a separation that, in too many cases, proved but the entrance upon that which on earth, at least, is final. There were music and dancing, play-acting and feasting, therefore, through the winter at Ransom, and frequent exchange of jovial hospitality with the big-hearted townsfolk over and away at the transcontinental road, but there wasn't a day when somebody, from Tintop down, wasn't sure to drop in and have a chat or a game of checkers, or in the evening a hand at whist, with Morgan, who sat up in an easychair and was made as comfortable as willing hearts and hands could devise, and Mrs. Vinton not only taught Lot and Billy as she taught her own, but time and again sent them home in garments newly fashioned, but with pardonable mendacity represented to be something she had that didn't fit her daughter or that her little Jim had outgrown. Connie's clear eyes saw through the stratagem, and her soft red lips quivered as she kissed the fair round cheek of the loving woman who so well knew how to bless and comfort, yet rob the act of every hint of charity. And strangely, too, Connie's scant supply of commissary was eked out by many a dainty sent to Morgan's door from somewhere along the line. No one ever gave a dinner, or luncheon, or supper party, that long winter, without a remembrance of some kind for those motherless kids, oftentimes including some comforting beverage for old Morgan himself. Even the sutler, whom the men damned for a skinflint, found means to "chip in" unknown to Morgan, who didn't at all like him, and the surreptitious dozens of stone bottles of stout, glass dittoes of Bass and Budweiser, that had been smuggled in by the back gate during the last year of Mrs. Morgan's illness, never found their way on the bill. He had sent Connie at Christmas a dress of soft black cashmere over which the child's womanly eyes had glistened, and which, impulsively, she had taken to her father's room, opening it before him and saying, "Isn't it lovely? Wasn't it just

G *

lovely of him?" And then she was brought to sudden realization of this rancor towards the trader by the flush that overspread Morgan's face and the heavy frown between his eyes.

"Connie, child, you shall have it, of course; you need it; but we can't take presents from Curran. He must put it on the bill," he said.

But neither on Connie's slender back nor Curran's bulky bill did those dress-goods ever appear. She sent him a misspelled, grateful little note, saying how it touched them all that he should have so kindly remembered her, but papa was "inflexable" in his views about accepting "presants" from friends they might never be able to repay, and honest Curran,—honest at least in his desire to do a kindness to the tall slip of a girl with the big brown eyes and auburn hair that made him think, he sometimes said, of a colleen he'd lost long years before,— honest Curran mistook her meaning entirely, thought her words Morgan's, and, mindful of some caustic comments the big lieutenant had made anent sutlers' checks he sought to collect at the pay-table several years before, had all his Irish aroused and was made fighting mad. "I'll sind him a resated bill, bedad, and cut his acqueentance intirelee," said Curran that night in relating the incident to some of the boys in the club-room, whereupon that ne'er-do-well and scapegrace Briggs promptly besought him to take like cognizance of the first thing he, Lieutenant Briggs, might say, as he despaired otherwise of ever squaring his account.

But the incident bore its weight of woe to Connie, despite the merriment it gave the boys. Acting under the advice of his colonel and his friends, Morgan was diligently turning over to the adjutant fifty dollars a month of his scanty pay in order that critics and creditors alike might know he was doing all a poor devil of a broken-down lieutenant could do to pay his debts without absolutely starving his household. The balance went to Connie, and with this she was expected to feed, clothe, and comfort the family, pay the cook, laundress, and striker. Morgan had no life-insurance, and in those days could get none. Curran was one of his heaviest creditors, and Curran had been perfectly willing not only to wait, but to open his storehouse or purse-strings still wider for the struggling fellow's benefit. Only so many dollars a month could be parcelled out for the butcher and baker, the grocer and the commissary, and Connie kept her books, and, aided by her lady friends, kept her accounts. But over and above all these necessary expenses were certain dainties and luxuries which Curran had authorized black Mammy to draw for at the store whenever the supply was getting low, and Morgan, insisting now on auditing the accounts, could find no such items on the bills rendered, and the truth came out. Curran went off East to buy goods just then, and Morgan did not write the letter his heart was pouring out when he learned how in secret the rough fellow had been so long his benefactor, but he forbade all such traffic in future, and Lot and Billy howled for oranges and raisins in vain. Christmas found their little stockings filled. Many an army mother, planning for her own brood, had remembered the motherless in the humble quarters down the row. But no one could tell whose hand had sent the rocking-horse and the big wax doll that were found by Penner at the door when he opened the house on Christmas morning. Suspicion attached to several heads, including Tintop's, whose head, by the way, had been cracked by a shell during the war, and a portion of whose skull, so rumor had it, had been replaced by a silver plate, which led to his wearing a nickname and a wig. But one and all the accused established what Mrs. Whaling once pronounced an alibi, "because they had sent something else." Then they thought of Trooper Schramm, now a fine-looking dragoon, consummately at home in his business; but Schramm hadn't been near the house for two weeks. A paymaster's escort was needed to convoy that official to distant winter cantonments, and Schramm had promptly asked to be allowed to go. This time he didn't say "mit dem fellers" as he had in the field the autumn before, neither did he add "once" or "alretty." Schramm was "studying book English," said the first sergeant. The paymaster got home to his Christmas all right,—he needed no escort when his money was gone,—but Schramm and his squad trotted in two days later, after the turkey and cranberry sauce were all devoured, so Schramm could have had nothing whatever to do with the gifts sent out from town. So long as they had them, Lot and Billy didn't care who was the donor. They believed all the more in Santa Claus. It was Connie who thought and wondered; it was Connie, alas! who hoped and dreamed.

Among the daily visitors to the house Perry Thornton, second lieutenant of Manning's troop, had been prominent all winter, and there wasn't a handsomer, blither boy in all the regiment when he joined. He was barely twenty-two, with a face almost womanly fair, and a form as slender and graceful as boy's could be. He rode and danced and sang well. He didn't drink; he wouldn't gamble. He was a soldier's son, an enthusiastic youngster who had seen some years of schooling and travel in Europe, and who had much to tell of soldiers who had won the V. C. or the Iron Cross. "Now in Europe," said he, "the officer is held as a hero who, at the risk of his life, bore off a wounded comrade to whom it meant death if abandoned." The cross for valor, pinned on his breast by royal hands, was the least reward to which he could look. Joining the regiment just at the end of the autumn work, and reading of the narrow escape of Lieutenant Morgan on the way, Thornton's first longing was to make the acquaintance of the gallant subaltern who had so bravely stood by the humble recruit and got his wound in saving him. Down went his ideal to dust when a grizzled, careworn, sad-faced veteran was borne from the ambulance into the homely quarters, and somebody said, "The old man's about petered." Thornton could not understand it. "In England or in Germany officers and men would have been lining the way and standing at salute," said he, "for a fellow who did what Mr. Morgan did."

"O-h, up there when he went deer-hunting, do you mean? Oh, yes, I remember,—helping Schramm out when he got hit. Ye-es, that was all right," said one of the young gentlemen of the regiment, and in so saying conveyed the idea to the new-comer that there was nothing in that sort of thing to excite remark. It was the rule, not the exception, in the American cavalry. "We'd all do just as much,"—as, indeed, very probably they would. But Thornton determined he would cultivate Morgan, decorated or not, and so it had happened that it was the "plebe," the newest comer to the regiment, who spent an hour almost every afternoon before stables playing checkers with the invalid veteran, rarely noticing silent, busy Connie, who came and went, or sat beside them with her needlework, darning the youngsters' stockings or sewing on buttons by the dozen, yet saying never a word. Perry had no end of interest in his new profession, but none whatever in children. It was the proper thing for him to be devoted to the senior subaltern who in other armies, perhaps, would have won such distinction, and he wrote with both pride and complacency to his friends at home of his daily intercourse with a fellow who did what Beresford was V. C.'d for at Ulundi. "But nobody out here seems to think it worth mentioning," he added. He was immensely proud of being second lieutenant in a troop whose captain had won three brevets with the regulars, and whose first lieutenant had done as much with the volunteers, both in the great civil war; but he hadn't been long enough in the service to find out that brevets followed on the heels of the great Rebellion like rain on the boom of a battle, deluging everybody who happened to be around. He found Morgan loved to hear of life in foreign armies, while no one else had time to listen. He loved to talk, and so he came. He loved to hear of cavalry campaigns during the war, and soon got Morgan to telling and explaining, and so, little by little, he came to be looked upon as the sunshine of their day. He was "pulling Morgan out of himself," and when the spring came on the "old man" was surely better, able to sun himself on the southern porch and watch the drills on the broad parade. Connie was but a child. Who could have a thought for her? And so here she stood this exquisite May morning, just bordering on womanhood, as the sweet spring buds were bursting into bloom, and with yearning, outstretched arms, with a deeper, fonder glow in the big brown eyes than mortal yet had seen, gazing longingly away down the distant valley, down along the silver windings of the stream, fringed by the fresh green of the cottonwoods, away from the dull brown buildings of the old frontier post, away from barracks, quarters, and corral, away from its bustling life and cares and sorrows, away from that picketed enclosure far out over the prairie where now the loved mother had been resting long months beyond the twelve, away from aging father, from laughing girl and romping boy, Connie Morgan's heart, shining through her steadfast eyes, was following the fast-fading dust-cloud that told where the squadrons were marching sturdily away to drive the Indians from their old haunts down the wild wastes of the Mini Ska, and Perry Thornton riding on his first campaign.

IV.

The cavalry battalion had been gone only two days. Some few of the officers' families, well assured that it would be Thanksgiving in earnest before they could hope to see the campaigners again, had taken wing to the East and were domiciled with friends or relatives far from scenes which so constantly brought to mind the image of the absent husband and father. In most cases, however, the little households remained at the post, assured by department head-quarters that they should be undisturbed in the tenure of their army homes. Mor-

gan, whose health and spirits had slowly revived as the sun came northward over the line, had striven to convince Old Tintop and the surgeon
that it would do him good to go, but was flatly denied the luxury he
craved and bidden to remain at the post. The department commander
came out to look over the field in early May, and told Morgan that he
meant to keep him on duty at the post all summer, in the hope that
the autumn would find him promoted to his captaincy. Then he
might be able to get an order to go before a retiring board and so home
to the old State and old friends he had not seen for years. Morgan
thanked the kind-hearted chief for all his help and consideration, but
his tired eyes wandered away over the prairie to the lonely grave he
often managed to visit now. If it were only possible to retire for
good and all, how willingly would he go and be laid away there by
Carrie's side, were there only some provision for Constance and the
babies! It appalled him to realize that they were dependent absolutely
upon so slender a thread as his life; that he must struggle on, must
exist, must suffer and try, at least, to be strong that they might not
starve. If only those debts were paid, if only he could retire and
take the children to some quiet Eastern home, however humble, where
they might be sent to school and where Connie might receive the
education thus far so utterly neglected, then Morgan could live on,
grateful and almost content. He could surely get some clerkship,
some desk-work that would enable him to add a few hundred dollars
yearly to the allowance of a retired dragoon. He did not begin to
know, poor fellow, how universal was the theory among business-men
that old soldiers were unfit for business of any kind. He wrote to
Carrie's brothers again, saying nothing, of course, of how often and
how much he had helped them in the past, and begged them to find
some opening that would warrant his retiring. No answer came. He
wrote again. Then Bob sent a few curt lines:

"Yours rec'd, contents noted. Tho't Wm. had ans'd or wld have
done so. Business very slack. Times hard. No opening of any kind.
H'd to dischg two clks last month. Better hang on to your present
situation awhile longer. If anything turns up will let you know.
"Yr bro. aff'y."

Morgan read human nature well enough to see just how much that
meant. He would "hang on to the situation" as a matter of course,
despite the fact that the doctor said the rheumatism would hang on to

him as long as he remained in that climate. Both General C—— and the colonel had again interested themselves in his behalf, and the railway managers said they could place him in their office in town when he got ready to retire. The salary was very small, but would help. The work was exacting, however, and the doctor said he simply could not do it in that climate.

"Never mind, old friend, we'll fix it somehow," said Tintop, cheerily, as he came to say good-by, looking very much the younger of the two as Morgan leaned heavily on his stick. "You just stay here and run the ordnance office this summer. There's bound to be promotion by fall." And so, sadly enough, the veteran trooper had seen the squadrons ride away, and he was left sole representative of the commissioned force of his regiment at old Fort Ransom, and not till they had been gone two days did he note that Connie was drooping.

"What is it, Little Mother?" he said, fondly stroking back the tumbling mass of auburn hair and kissing her white forehead. "Tired out with all your household care? Growing too fast? Lot and Billy too much for you now?"

The big pathetic brown eyes were swimming a little, but she looked bravely up. "Perhaps it's spring fever," she said, with an attempt at laughing it all lightly away. "I'm sure there's nothing else. I'm only a trifle fagged. It will be all right now that we all can get out again in the sunshine every day."

She was fastening his necktie for him at the moment, then, patting his grizzled cheek, she took the whisk broom to dust the worn old fatigue-coat preparatory to letting him stump forth on his halting way to the ordnance storehouse, but there came a rousing rat-tat-tat at the front door just at the instant, and, Mammy being up to her elbows in flour and Penner away at the commissary, Connie sprang to answer, and there, precise and soldierly as ever, stood Schramm.

"Why, Schr-r-amm!" she cried, delightedly. "Why—when—how did you get back?"

"Sergeant Schultz, gnädige Fräulein, was sent back with despatches, and I came with him. Is the Herr Lieutenant within? I bring letters." And he handed her a packet.

"Come right in, Schramm; papa will be so glad to see you."

And thus bidden, yet ever unbending, Schramm stepped to the inner door, and there, hand at salute and heels together, he stood attention, his kind blue eyes alight with fidelity and affection.

"Hello, Schramm!" exclaimed Morgan, limping around the big base-burner with extended hand, which the soldier grasped respectfully an instant, then returned to his invariable attitude. "Well, you must have ridden hard."

"Only forty-five miles, sir. We left them in camp on Bear Fork at midnight. There was news from the agency. We go back this afternoon with orders to catch them to-morrow at Painted Lodge."

Hurriedly opening the packet, Morgan glanced over the contents: two official letters for himself, and a smaller note. "Why, Con, this is for you—from Thornton," he said, in surprise. Then, never noting the eager, almost incredulous light that flashed into her eyes, or the instant rush of color to her cheeks and brow, he tore open the first letter, an order from Tintop to send on certain arms for the use of scouts. He glanced quickly up to send Schramm for the ordnance sergeant, but Schramm had disappeared. There stood Constance, her eyes dancing, her red lips parted, her bosom heaving, languor and pallor utterly banished from her face, grasping in both hands the letter he had given her, devouring its pages with all her soul in her eyes, utterly lost to him and to the world at large in the rapture of a young girl's first dream of love. For the first time in his life Morgan saw that his child was beautiful. For the first time it dawned upon him she was no longer a child. For the first time in his life the father called her to his side and she did not hear.

"Connie," he said. Then at last, almost sternly, "Constance!"

"Oh! what, papa dear? Forgive me, I was so—I was——"

"Yes," said he, vaguely, feeling all helpless and bewildered yet. "Yes. What does he say? Why does he write to you?"

Another rush of color, a new flash in the great brown eyes, yet more hesitancy, more embarrassment.

"Why, there's a letter for you, papa,—he says so; but—this is about something else."

Slowly Morgan turned, unwilling to think, reluctant to believe, unable to wound. It was all so sudden, so utterly unlooked-for. What on earth could Thornton have to say to her? Where was the letter to him? Oh, here, inside Gray's despatch. He tore it open: "Dear Old Man,—In the mail sent forward to catch us there comes a welcome letter from father. He says that Wall, of the Ninth, and Clinton, of the Sixth, have applied for retirement. You are sure of your double bars then before September, and we are all rejoicing. I couldn't help writing, as I wanted to be the first to tell you. Please give the enclosed to Connie. Love to the kids, all three. Yours, P. T." Give what to Connie? He turned the envelope inside out, and there was no enclosure other than the letter. Mechanically he stretched forth his hand.

"Let me see your letter, Connie," he said, and to his dismay she for an instant shrank back. Then, seeing the pain in his eyes, she sprang towards him.

"Oh, do, papa; read every word," she said. "Indeed, I'd rather, —only he—only they didn't want you to know it—just yet." But he did not seem to hear her.

"I only asked to see if it could go inside here," he said, slowly. "Thornton speaks of an enclosure, and probably that was it.—Here, Schramm," he cried, hastening to the door, "will you tell the ordnance sergeant I want him right off? I'll meet him at the store-room. Wait a minute; just give me your arm down the steps." And, leaning on the blue-shirted, muscular shoulder, Morgan stumped away out through the little gate, out across the grassy parade where the infantry companies were busy at drill; and there was a cloud on both faces now, as, saluting at the gate, Schramm fell respectfully to the rear.

And yet, an hour later, when Morgan returned to his quarters and Lot and Billy came tumbling tumultuously to greet him, and he, moody and troubled, sent them off in supreme content to buy a nickel's worth of gum-drops at the store, then came slowly to his door, a vague sense of new trouble was tugging at his heart, a doubt as to what he ought to do or say numbing his faculties. Pausing at the threshold, he heard Connie's voice, low, rich, tremulous with happiness, singing one of her mother's old dear songs, a thing she had not done since the bitter day they followed the mother to her grave, and the instant he entered she came to throw her arms about his neck and raise her glowing face to his lips. He took it between his hands and looked down gravely, fondly, yet with such a world of trouble in his eyes. The song was hushed. Once more the color mounted to her temples, but the big, soft eyes never flinched nor faltered.

"Read that letter now, papa dear," she simply said. "I want you to read it." And then when he would not, but sank wearily in his chair, she went and fetched the letter she had placed upon his desk, and perched herself upon the arm of the chair and nestled her soft cheek against his weather-beaten jowl, and opened the note before his eyes, which in turn he promptly shut. Then she strove to pull them open by means of the lashes, and then he turned his head away.

"I don't want to read the letter, Con," he said, remorsefully. "I never meant to let our Little Mother think I——"

"Then I'll read it, papa," she began, interrupting him, whereat he clapped his hands to his ears. "Well, at least you must see the picture," she cried, and, jumping up, she ran to the mantel with a tin-type, a likeness of a tall young fellow with a downy moustache, arrayed in cavalry scouting garb, with prairie belt and holster, a very present-able young dragoon, too, the second lieutenant of Manning's troop; but the eyes of the first lieutenant thereof looked less kindly on this counterfeit presentment than ever they had upon the face of the original.

"Where was it taken?" he asked, rather abruptly, feeling that he must say something.

"Mr. Thornton says an itinerant artist drove out from town and met them at the first camp and took quite a number and some groups. He had two of them taken just like this, to send home, and dropped the odd one in here, saying it was a philopœna and a bribe."

"Bribe? For what?" demanded Morgan. "Why should he bribe my little girl?"

"Oh, there was no need," she laughed, blithely. "He—they all, he said, wanted something your Connie was only too glad to get and give. Now you must read it and see for yourself, papa."

But he would not. He was ashamed of the fear that for a moment had possessed him, that she had consented to a correspondence with Thornton without once asking her father's counsel,—she, his little Connie, his first-born. True, she was older at fifteen than many town-bred girls at twenty, for her childhood had been nipped in the bud, and since those slender shoulders had borne the care and burden of woman for two long years, was it to be forbidden her to know aught of woman's glory? Only, had he been blind all the time? Day after day had Thornton been their visitor, yet never in all that time had the father seen or suspected in the young officer any more interest in Constance than he displayed in Lot or Billy. True, she was almost always a silent attendant at their daily game, or an absorbed listener to their talk, rarely leaving them except to go into the other room to moderate the clamor of the youngsters, who, being burly and aggres-sive, were too often involved in a game of give and take in which they were fairly matched. But Thornton's manner to her, which was at first simply kindly and jovial, as it was to the other children, had certainly changed to greater deference as the winter wore on. Little by little he saw how her father leaned upon the girl, how thoughtful, how devoted she was. He had been reared a gentleman. He had a mother and sisters whom he dearly loved, and from earliest boyhood he had been taught by his soldier father the lesson of gentleness, courtesy, and consideration. From the other officers in the regiment, most of whom had known her in pinafores, her greeting was simply "Hello, Con!" or "Morning, Connie; how's dad to-day?" Thornton's impulse from the first when he met this tall slip of a girl in solemn black was to call her "Miss Morgan," which made her blush furiously. Later on, laughed at by the veteran sub., he had compromised on "Miss Connie," but not until he had been a daily visitor for several months had it come to "Connie." Morgan never knew how she had fled to her room and nearly cried her eyes out the morning the battalion marched away. It was after breakfast that Mrs. Woods had come for her and, with other ladies, had driven out to the butte south of the post, from whose side the Mini Ska could be traced for miles, but to whose summit Connie alone had been bold and active enough to climb. All he saw and realized now was that his darling had been pale and languid, plainly drooping for a while, and then all on a sudden, at the coming of that little note, sunshine, gladness, gratitude, joy, all had beamed from her speaking eyes, had bubbled from her girlish heart in song. He had mourned the mother's loss before, but it was as nothing compared with the helpless yearning that possessed him now. Who was there to counsel, who was there to take his beloved child to her heart, and with mother love and sympathy, with mother kiss and clasping arms, in the sure haven of mother's changeless love win from the virgin soul its cherished secret, then guide and guard and counsel as only mothers can?

Poor Morgan! He would not read the boy's frank letter. That might imply doubt of his little girl. He could not consult such friends as Mrs. Freeman; she had taken her babies and flitted away to the sea-shore for the summer. Mrs. Stannard, once his wife's kind friend and adviser, had gone long months before, when the major went to his new station. There were loving women, kind women, motherly women, at the post, yet not those to whom he could speak of anything so sacred. Neither could he bring himself to the faintest reference to the matter in talking with his child. There was simply one thing which he could do, thought Morgan. All the winter he had been growing fond and fonder of the bright-faced, glad-voiced, soldierly young fellow; but now, now, if it should transpire that all this time Thornton had been laying siege to Connie's innocent heart, he could hate him and in time crush and punish.

At noon the sergeant came to say the stores were boxed and ready for shipment. Would the lieutenant sign the invoices? Over at the adjutant's office the infantry bugler had just sounded mess and orderly call. The companies were going in to dinner, the noise and bustle around the barracks contrasting strongly with the silence and desertion over there across the parade where stood the cavalry quarters. As Morgan came forth into the bright sunshine of the first June day, he noted how the snow-belt on the distant peak had lifted higher in the last forty-eight hours, and thought with a heavy sigh how care and trouble had sunk so much deeper around his heart. Major Rhett, of the infantry, temporary commander of the post, was standing by the sundial as Morgan and his sergeant came trudging along. One or two officers were with him. A telegraph message was in his hand, and he was looking strangely worried. All of the group ceased their talk and glanced at Morgan as he neared them.

"The ordnance stores are ready for shipment, major," said he. "The colonel will have a couple of wagons at Alkali Station to meet the freight to-night. We have billed it there."

"How far were they camped from Alkali last night, Mr. Morgan?"

"How far, sir? Well, they were on Bear Fork, probably fifteen miles north of west of Alkali. They camp to-night at Willow Springs, and to-morrow under Painted Lodge Buttes, and——"

"Yes, I know," interrupted the commander, "and it was at Willow Springs Major Graves was to meet and pay them, I believe?"

"So I heard, sir. Though at first I rather imagined they wouldn't be paid now until after next muster."

"Well, they won't. Graves was robbed at Minden Station, early this morning, of every dollar, and the robbers wore cavalry uniforms."

V.

Old Curran, the sutler,—for sutler he was long years before his designation was changed to post trader, and longer still before his occupation was wiped out entirely by the civilizing process which made bar-tenders of "blue-coats,"—old Curran had been losing money all winter, and was growling about it. He looked to the payment following the April muster to recoup him for his losses, as many a good soldier was deep in his books. The payment should have been made in May, but for some reason it was postponed, possibly in order that the paymaster might make the circuit of the cordon of posts in the bright weather of early June; but a pack of young rascals and malcontents at the Indian reservation had been turbulent all spring, and no sooner was the snow out of the Mini Ska valley than the cattle came after the budding grass and the Sioux came after the cattle. They were hungry, no doubt,—the Sioux sometimes are, despite the fact that they are excellent providers and know how to take care of themselves, and the difference between them and certain tractable and therefore systematically ill-treated tribes is, that when they are not given what they want they take it. Heaven helps those who help themselves, and in their dealings with the wards of the nation the United States of America have this resemblance to heaven. The Sioux helped themselves so liberally to cattle—and herders—this particular spring that Tintop, with six troops of his devoted regiment, was hurried forth to brush them out of the Mini Ska, and then to go on and help some comrades four hundred miles away who were too few in number for the work in hand. To Curran's disgust, the battalion marched out leaving its score at the shop unsettled. Not that the soldiers could help it at all, but because they themselves were creditors who couldn't collect. Then, to Curran's delight, it was announced that Major Graves was sent out by rail to pay them before they got too far away. Curran rejoicingly set forth to meet him and be present at the ceremony, and thereby, doubtless, collect large portion of the dollars due him. Curran thoughtfully, too, loaded up a couple of wagons with pies, cakes, cheese, pickles, crackers, canned fruits, bottled beer, whiskey, and tobacco, lest the boys shouldn't know what to do with what remained of their money. This load he pushed forward on the heels of the command. Then his own fine team and spring-wagon were sent down the valley to Alkali Station, whither he proposed to follow by rail and meet the paymaster on his arrival, and to entertain him royally on the drive out to the Springs. It was estimated that the battalion, breaking camp on Bear Fork at 5.30 A.M., could unsaddle and pitch its tents at Willow Springs by noon. It was estimated that leaving Alkali, say at six A.M., after a hearty breakfast, the paymaster would be trundled away up the valley of the Dry Fork and be landed at the Springs, twenty-five miles north of the railway, in plenty of time to meet them, and Tintop was ordered to detach a sergeant and ten men to ride over to Alkali from their camp on Bear Fork to bivouac at the station over-night and escort the paymaster up the next day. Graves left department head-quarters on the westbound express, his clerk, his valise full of funds necessary for the payment of the battalion, and he himself, all comfortably ensconced in the Pullman car. They were due at Alkali at four A.M. They could retire early, have a good night's rest, and be called by the porter in plenty of time to be up and dressed and to enjoy a camp breakfast with their escort at the little station—a mere siding with some cattle chutes and pens—before starting on their drive.

Standing where Constance had stood on the summit of the high, precipitous butte that lay southwest of the fort, one could see the valley of the Mini Ska stretching away to the eastward a distance of nearly fifty miles. Then the stream seemed to bring up suddenly against a line of bluffs that turned it off to the northeast, and this general direction it followed another fifty miles. The land was low and undulating along the left bank, while on the right, between the stream and the bold line of bluffs to the south, there was barely room for the railway. Fordable here near the fort, the Mini Ska speedily deepened and widened and became sluggish in flow as it rolled out into the lowlands after its tumbling rush through the mountain-chain at the west. Every year since its establishment had a cavalry column marched away from Fort Ransom to straighten out matters between the Sioux and the settlers who were venturing too close to the reservation. The first year or two the trail led along the west bank, hugging the stream, but, as it was found that this was the longer, hotter, and dustier way, a new route was decided on, cutting across the big bend and winding along over the foot-hills of the range, from which several streams of clear, cool water came pouring forth, speedily to become murky and turbid on reaching the broad plain below. The first day's march lay almost due east from Ransom and parallel with the Mini Ska, the next veered around towards the northeast, and camp was always made at Bear Fork. Not until the fourth camp at Painted Lodge did the trail and the stream again come together, and from that point down to the disputed territory, the pet raiding-ground of the restless " young men," the two were never far apart. West of Painted Lodge the Sioux did not often venture, though the broad bottom-land within this elbow of the Ska was a fine grazing-ground.

The railway, coming up from the southeast and over a high plateau, dropped down to the valley by means of a long, winding ravine scooped out for it by the Antelope, a little tributary that joined the Mini Ska just at the elbow, and here, at the point where the rail and the river after running parallel for eighty miles suddenly quit company, the line shooting eastward, the stream northeast,—here stood Alkali Station. Cattle-men had built a low bridge over the stream at this point, with the intention of making Alkali the shipping station for their beeves, and from this place a sandy road ran down the left bank to Painted Lodge Butte and away to the agencies. Once upon a time the mails were carried that way, and a stage ran twice a week between Alkali and the reservation, but when a rival railway sent a line across the Missouri and tapped the lands of the Dakotas far up to the northeast, the agency freight, mail, and passengers were sent around that way, and Alkali became a deserted village. There stood the old stage-house, the cattle-chutes, and the rickety dépôt, but no trains stopped there now except on signal, and the telegraph instrument and operator had been moved to Minden, some twenty-five miles farther west. Here, too, was a bridge over the Mini Ska and a cattle-shipping point. Here the ranchmen who did not care to take the extra twenty-five-mile gallop to Butteville had all their mail addressed, and Minden speedily assumed the mild and modest importance which Alkali had lost.

And it was at Minden, said Major Rhett, that the paymaster was robbed that morning soon after dawn, and robbed by men in cavalry overcoats. Morgan listened a moment, simply stunned.

" When did the news come in, sir ?" asked he of the major.

" Ten minutes ago, as soon as they could repair the wires which were cut. The sheriff is on his way out here now."

" Where is the paymaster ?"

" They're coming up on a freight from Minden this afternoon, he and his clerk."

"But—I don't understand," said Morgan: "how on earth did he get to Minden? Why did he come so far west? The escort was to meet him at Alkali, so I was told."

"That's just what nobody understands, and what he'll explain later, I presume."

An orderly came hastily from the direction of the office, and, halting, saluted the post commander.

"The sergeant-major says they were assigned to C Company, sir, for rations."

There was an awkward silence a moment. Finally the commander wheeled on Morgan:

"You've known those couriers some time, haven't you, Mr. Morgan? What is their reputation?"

"Our men, sir? Schultz and Schramm, do you mean? Why, major, the sergeant is one of our veterans, a man we all trust. Schramm is not a year with us yet, but he's as good as they make 'em, I think, in Germany. Surely they are not suspected? They came in with orders and despatches."

"Very true, but they passed within sight of Minden if they came back by the trail, and through it if they followed the stage road. They may have seen or heard something. At all events, I wish to question them," was the major's answer. "What time did they reach the post, Mr. Adjutant?"

"Just at guard-mounting, sir."

Rhett pondered a moment. "The colonel's note says he was aroused at midnight by couriers from the agency who had had a hard ride and could go no farther. But for his orders to meet the paymaster at Willow Springs to-day, he says, he would have pushed on to Painted Lodge,—made a forty-mile march. It really looks very threatening down the valley, and now that the money's gone and the paymaster can't reach him I'm in hopes he will push ahead. Already people are wiring out here from town, asking whether the Indian rumors are true. They've got a story there that ten people were killed yesterday."

"Yes, sir," put in the adjutant; "our market-man brought it out here an hour ago. It's going all over the post. They say in town one reason there's no chance of catching these robbers is that the cavalry has been ordered to come on with all speed, and that a courier rode out to them from Minden before daybreak this morning. Despatches were sent them before the line was cut."

Away on the winding road to the southwest towards the distant frontier town a couple of wagons could be seen slowly moving towards the post. Beyond them little dust-clouds, rapidly sailing over the plain, told where fleeter horsemen were speeding. The men coming out from their dinner were gathering in groups on the verandas, chatting in low tones and watching the group of officers. Presently the orderly came hurrying back alone.

" What orders did you give those couriers, Mr. Wood?"

" Nothing especial, sir. Schultz asked if they were at liberty to start back as soon as they wished, and I said yes."

" Then they must be taking a nap," said the major. " What with being up most of last night and having to ride all to-night, they need it. Their consciences are clear if they can sleep all the morning."

The orderly reached them as the major concluded, halted half a dozen paces away, and reported :

" Sergeant Shea says the couriers left nearly an hour ago, sir."

" Left an hour ago ! Which way ?"

" He doesn't know, sir. Private Burns says he saw them ride away after the quartermaster's corral at 11.30,—going towards town."

VI.

It was one o'clock that afternoon before the sheriff reached the post. Butteville, the thriving county seat, lay just five miles away to the southwest, and a hard prairie road connected it with the post. As a distributing point to the mines and a market for the ranchmen the growing town had shot rapidly into importance. Two banks, both reliable, two hotels, well patronized, and shops and stores in good number, were barely able to supply the demands. Dozens of bustling men breakfasted every morning at the big eating-house of the railway company, where the west-bound express was supposed to find ample sustenance for its passengers before pushing on for the long day's run through the mountains. The sheriff and the coroner, as was the case in most frontier cities of the day, were by long odds the hardest-worked officials, and just now the sheriff was fairly used up. The first inti- mation of anything wrong east of Butteville was the sudden stop of

H   15

the wires. Up to daybreak train-despatchers and night operators sitting, red-eyed and weary, over their instruments, after the long hours of vigil, found everything working smoothly. The night had been still, neither storm nor excitement anywhere along the line, until just about four o'clock Butte, called up by Pawnee Station, was asked, "What's afire at Alkali?" Butte didn't know,—hadn't heard. Pawnee explained that a despatch for Paymaster Graves from Minden met No. 3 at Pawnee, and said bridge was down at Alkali. Two ranchmen from over Painted Lodge way rode into Pawnee at three A.M. and said hell was broke loose down the Mini Ska,—Sioux scalping and burning everything in sight. Where were Colonel Winthrop and the cavalry? Butte answered: The colonel and six companies had marched for Painted Lodge two days before, couldn't be far from Alkali now. Sioux wouldn't dare come that far up the valley. Who said the bridge was down and burnt? Pawnee replied: Hold on a minute. More refugees from valley are reported hurrying to the railway, and Pawnee wanted to see the ranchmen who first came before they got good and drunk and couldn't talk reliably. Perhaps Minden could tell about the bridge at Alkali. Butte called Minden accordingly. Minden said some of the cavalry had come up from Alkali an hour before, said they'd been sent to Alkali in the first place to meet the Paymaster on No. 3, but they found the bridge across the Mini Ska afire, so the ambulance, escort, etc., were all on the way up to Minden, and these two rode ahead with a despatch for Major Graves, explaining the situation and telling him to keep on and meet them here. Minden sent it to Pawnee, and Pawnee gave it to the porter of the sleeping-car. That's all Minden knew about fire or anything else. Butteville was the west end of the division, however, and Butteville demanded further particulars,—told Minden to ask the cavalry if any of the buildings at Alkali were reported afire. Minden said wait a minute, he'd find out: No. 3's head-light just coming around Buffalo Bluff. The soldiers had gone out to meet the lieutenant as soon as assured that the despatch had been delivered to No. 3, and they were now watering their horses at the creek. It was just light enough to see them out there. Then No. 3 reached Minden, was duly reported in and out, and then the wires went down. No. 3 came into Butteville at breakfast on time and all right. The division superintendent asked what was the matter at Alkali Station, and the conductor replied, nothing that he knew of. They had come lively down Antelope grade and struck the Mini Ska valley, running forty-five miles an hour, which they didn't check, as Major Graves's telegram said, "Come on to Minden." Had he seen the despatch? Why, certainly. It was all right, signed by some lieutenant or other, commanding escort. Had he seen no fire at Alkali? Oh, yes, over on the bank of the stream five hundred yards or so from the station there was some fire. Thought it was only a camp-fire or two. There were two or three men, soldiers, he thought, on the old platform, but it was barely dawn, and the engine left such a trail of smoke and steam that the men were enveloped in it, and he couldn't make them out distinctly. No. 3 dropped the major and his clerk at Minden, where other soldiers met him, and then hurried on. "What's the trouble?" "Well," said the superintendent, "since the moment you pulled out from Minden to this moment, Mr. Hart, we have been cut off. Not a word can we get from the east."

By the time the express pushed on for the west again a couple of hand-cars had been despatched eastward in the vain hope of finding the break near town, and these were overhauled ten miles out by the engine and caboose sent scouting down the valley. Not until they were within a mile of Minden did they find the gap, and along there the wires had been clipped in half a dozen places. The superintendent gathered the particulars while his men were patching. Here at the station, surrounded by a knot of excited ranchmen and settlers, were Major Graves and his clerk, but all they had to show was the telegram. It read plainly enough :

"Minden Station, June 3, 3.05 A.M. Major Graves, U. S. Army, on No. 3, Pawnee Station. Bridge down at Alkali. Cannot cross Mini Ska. Come on to Minden : escort meet you there.
"EDWARDS, *Lieutenant Commanding.*"

Never suspecting anything wrong, Major Graves sent his clerk to notify the conductor and show him the despatch. The porter made them coffee and a light breakfast at the *buffet,* so as to enable them to start at once for the longer ride that their going on to Minden would necessitate. They were met as they jumped off the car by a couple of troopers in overcoats, thimble-belts, and the slouch-hat then much affected by the cavalry on campaigns. "This way, sir," said one: "the lieutenant says the escort's ready to start the moment the major is." He made a move to take the valise, but instinctively the major held on. The train pulled out as they stepped around to the rear of the dépôt. Graves could see a little knot of horsemen close to the stream. "The boys will be glad to see you, sir, and we've a long ride ahead of us," said his conductor, and in another moment Graves was tripped, thrown heavily to the ground, bound, and gagged, and there he lay helpless, while his clerk was similarly handled, and away went the valise with its precious thousands, he had no idea whither. He saw only three or four men in all, but they were all in cavalry overcoats, and the horses and equipments, so far as he could judge in the light and distance, looked like those of the regulars,—not cowboys or road-agents. They vanished in the twinkling of an eye, and not until they had been gone fifteen minutes or more did the station agent discover the plight of the paymaster and release him. Meantime, the wires had been cut. Pursuit was useless. No one knew who the robbers were, or which way they had gone after crossing the bridge. But an early bird around the station said he saw two soldiers galloping west along the north bank of the stream, and all Minden—what there was of it—was ready to swear that soldiers were at the bottom of the whole affair.

It was ten o'clock before they could send a despatch to Butte. It was barely 4.45 when the robbery took place. It was noon, as we have seen, when the news reached the fort, and one o'clock when the sheriff got there.

"Cowboys! Road-agents!" said he, indignantly. "No, sir. We hung the last of them two months ago. There isn't a road-agent left in Latimer County. Those robbers were soldiers,—cavalrymen, deserters from Colonel Winthrop's command. Fisk, the operator at Minden, will swear to their identity, at least of the two who came in with the despatch. Of course he sent it when he saw Lieutenant Edwards's name signed and they told him so straight a story. You send couriers after Colonel Winthrop, find out who are absent from the battalion, and you'll know who your robbers are. Then I can do something."

"Did you pass any of our men on your way out from town?" asked Rhett, after a moment's pause.

"Your men? Soldiers? Nothing but the ordnance sergeant and some wagons. Who were they, and where'd they go?"

"I don't know that they did go—that way, at least. Two couriers came with despatches this morning from Colonel Winthrop and left at 11.30 to rejoin him. Some one said they didn't go east, however, but struck out for town."

"What were their names? What were they like?" asked the sheriff, eagerly.

"They are two of our best men," answered the major. "Mr. Morgan, here, knows them well. They are Germans,—about the last men likely to become highway-robbers."

"Humph! I'd stake my commission on their innocence," said Morgan, briefly.

"Oh, of course all men are innocent until proved guilty," said the sheriff, crushingly. "All the same it's my business to look after them. You say they went to town instead of back on the trail of the battalion, major?"

"I did not," was the major's chilling reply. "I said somebody else said that they had struck out for town. Very possibly they had business there; and they were not under my jurisdiction, anyhow."

"No; they're under mine," said the sheriff. "Men need funds, as a rule, to transact business in Butte, and soldiers without money have little business so far off their track. If they have money when their comrades haven't, where'd they get it?"

"Well, Schultz, the sergeant, has been in service some twenty years, and is reported to have saved up much more money than I ever hope or expect to," said Rhett. "I presume his bank-account can be ascertained at the First National. Schramm, the other, isn't a year in service."

"Schramm?" exclaimed the sheriff. "A good-looking, blue-eyed little Dutchman?"

"A good-looking, blue-eyed, medium-sized, slender young German, if you like, Mr. Sheriff," said Morgan. "What have you to say about him?"

"Oh, I'm saying nothing. I want you gentlemen to talk. That young fellow gets nearly thirteen dollars a month, doesn't he, major?"

"Well, rather less than that, Mr. Sheriff."

"Does he own a mine or a faro-bank hereabouts, or is he in cahoots with Curran?" asked the civilian.

"If he is, he's a dead loser this time," said the post adjutant, shortly,—he being a young officer deeply imbued with the proper idea of deference to a commanding officer and resentful of civilian impertinence, even on the part of a sheriff. "Old Curran was at Alkali waiting for first pick at the paymaster's dollars. Now his beggars on horseback are off for six months' service against the Sioux, and he'll lose most of their accounts."

"So he has no means outside of his pay, this young Deutscher? Well, that's what I wanted to know."

"Fortunes outside of the pay are not often to be found in the army," answered the major. "What makes you think Schramm has one?"

"Oh, I don't," said the sheriff. "But I believe he has more money than he can easily account for, and the sooner he is overhauled the quicker we'll know something of this morning's work." And with that the sheriff whirled his cayuse about, and, giving him a touch with the quirt, went bounding lightly away to the corrals.

"Tha' fellow's a brute," said Mr. Woods, presently. "You don't suppose he really suspects Schramm, do you, Morgan?" But Morgan, gripping his stick, was already trudging angrily away.

That night the paymaster himself arrived at Fort Ransom, leaving his faithful clerk in conference with the officials in town. Graves was soon the centre of an eager gathering at Rhett's quarters. By this time, too, Curran was back, coming up on the afternoon freight. He had gone down to Alkali by the east-bound express the previous evening. The escort was already there, bivouacked for the night at the edge of the stream. They were up betimes and had a hot breakfast all ready for Graves, and were surprised to see the train shoot past instead of stopping to let him off. Not until the engine sent out from Butte came steaming down at noon did they know what had taken place at Minden. Then there was nothing left him but to return by the first opportunity. The sergeant and detachment remained awaiting orders, as the paymaster might draw funds from the bank at Butte and come on again. Just as he was leaving on the afternoon freight a courier came to Alkali with orders for the sergeant, and the messenger said that the battalion had reached Willow Springs and was surprised to find no paymaster there. News from the lower valley was so threatening that Colonel Winthrop had determined, after resting a couple of hours, to push on for Painted Lodge, upon the supposition that the paymaster had missed No. 3. The escort was ordered to wait for him until next train from the east, and then, whether he came or not, to rejoin the battalion by the shortest route, following down the left bank, and bringing the extra ammunition shipped from Ransom.

Curran was utterly disgusted with the whole affair. "Ten chances to one," said he, "them fellows will never come back to the post, and I'll never get a cint of me money." Curran, as the party most interested, was persistent in his cross-questioning of the major, who was eager enough to explain, but not to Curran. In brief, he said he had brought in that sole-leather valise nearly twelve thousand dollars with which to pay Winthrop's command. The rest of his funds, sealed in his little iron safe, were turned over to the express company to be forwarded to Butte, two days later on, by which time he had expected to return to pay the infantry at the fort and then go on to the outlying posts to the northwest. By evening, too, Rhett had received telegraphic orders to hold his little battalion of foot in readiness to take train to Pawnee and thence march across the range to the lower Mini Ska. Although exaggerated, the reports of rapine and murder were only too true. The Sioux were indeed at their devilish work. In the subdued bustle of preparation the paymaster's excitement and distress of mind created less sympathy than would ordinarily have been the case. Eagerly he was showing his despatch to officer after officer, and asking whether any one would not have acted just as he did under the circumstances and on receipt of so genuine a message, and gentlemen who under other circumstances would unhesitatingly have said yes were now disposed to be a bit conservative, to look judicial and suggest inquiries. Wouldn't it have been better to stop the train at Alkali and see if the report were true? The bridge was only half a mile from the station, and somebody would have been sure to know. These are times when everybody's backsight is so much better than his foresight. Everybody could see with half an eye that had the paymaster caused the conductor to stop the train at Alkali some of the escort would have been on the platform to meet him, and they would have told him that there was nothing in the world the matter with the bridge, that the whole thing was a plant. But Graves pointed out that he didn't own the road and couldn't make the train stop unless he meant to get off, which he didn't. Lieutenant Edwards had wired him to come on to Minden. Everybody knew Edwards. He had escorted Graves on the winter trip to the Black Hills cantonment. It was most natural Edwards should have been selected to escort him this time. He was with the battalion, first lieutenant of Captain Frank Amory's troop. True, as matters turned out, Edwards had not been sent at all. Old Sergeant Daly, with eight troopers, was considered amply sufficient. Of course it was a plant, a most successful plant, and more than likely, said the paymaster, somebody closely connected with the cavalry had engineered the whole scheme. Everybody knew there were some very shady characters among the men enlisting during the Centennial year. Everybody knew what train would fetch him out from department head-quarters. The plotters would not wire in time to admit of his making inquiries, but waited until the last moment, then, dressed and equipped as the cavalry were dressed and equipped, they had sent two of their number in to Minden Station with a despatch signed by an officer whom they reported a mile or two behind, coming up with the wagon and main body. Everything looked straight to the operator, and so it was sent to Pawnee and there handed to the Pullman porter. What could have been more complete? The troopers who met him at the platform addressed him confidently and respectfully, saluting exactly like old soldiers. Of course he hadn't a personal acquaintance with the entire regiment, but this he would say and did say, that he believed Mr. Lacy, his clerk, was willing to swear that the two men who met him at Minden were *bona fide* members of the Eleventh Cavalry; Mr. Lacy had seen them before, and could identify them if he were to see them again. The sheriff's people were already working on the clue.

It was nearly tattoo that evening when Morgan left the major's and went slowly homeward. Voices in eager conversation were audible in the kitchen as he entered, then became as suddenly still and the door was quickly closed. It was his custom to go to the children's room and kiss and pet them a little after Connie had prompted them through their prayers,—devotions over which, in their infantile depravity, they were far more apt to fall asleep than during the subsequent ceremony. But the sounds from aloft as he entered were those of lively contention rather than adoration, lively controversy rather than the lisping prayers of childish lips. Lot and Billy were still up and astir, it was evident, and so engrossed in their tilt that the father's slow coming up the creaking stairway failed to divert their attention. Halting at the door and looking in, the veteran trooper enjoyed a *coup-d'œil* of the scene. Perched on the bed in the bifurcated vestment of canton flannel referred to as his "nighties" was the burly son and heir, barefooted, flushed, truculent, bouncing up and down on the bed-springs as he conversed with his sister, who, equally flushed, if a trifle less confident in mien, and just about half undressed, was standing with one of her spring-heeled, buttoned boots in hand, half concealed, half disclosed, as though she lacked determination to hurl it after its mate, now reposing on top of the bureau beyond the bed, surrounded by the wreck of a glass toilet-set, once their mother's,— Aunt Lottie's one present to her army sister.

"I don't care," said Lot, sturdily; "you did it."

"Oh, you're worse'n Annanice Afire! I didn't!"

"You did, too! and you shan't call names."

"I shall if you 'cuse me again," said Billy, stoutly. "You fired that shoe at me when I wasn't even lookin' at dolly, and it smashed everything."

"I don't care," reiterated Lot: "it was all your fault. It never would have hit 'em at all if—if you hadn't dodged. So there!" And then Lot, triumphant, turned, saw her father's grave face, and lost her nerve. Running to him, she burst into tears, whereupon Billy began to whimper sympathetically.

"Hush, Lottie. Never mind who did it now," said Morgan, taking her in his arms. "Hush, child. We'll settle that some other time. Where's Connie? Where was she when this happened?"

"Mammy called her to the kitchen. Sergeant Hinkel's wife comed," sobbed Lottie, "and she told Billy not to step on my dolly, and he— he—just danced it off the bed a purpose, and I—and I——" and here the sobs overmastered her, and Billy came tumbling off his perch in dire dismay. And this was the situation when Connie's low voice and fleet footsteps were heard on the stairway, and Little Mother came hurrying in. One glance told her what had happened. She flew around the bed to the bureau.

"Oh, Lottie, Lottie, how could you?" she cried. "Our dear mother's set,—Aunt Lottie's present!"

"Never mind, Connie, never mind it now, dear. She wasn't aiming at it," said paterfamilias, with his patient smile.

"She was aimin' at me!" burst in Billy, whose distress at sight of Lottie's grief was suddenly tempered by the prospect of her getting off scot-free, as was too often the case when the father administered justice, "and then she said I did it 'cause I dodged."

"Well, he called me names," sobbed Lottie,—"said I was worse'n Annanice Afire."

"What on earth is Annanice Afire?" asked Morgan blankly of his eldest.

H *

"Nothing, father dear. I read them the story of Ananias and Sapphira when Billy told a story the other day. Let me undress Lottie, now.—Come, child."

But Morgan noticed instantly how nervous and flurried was her manner, how tremulous and cold her hand. His little Connie, his big tall Connie now, so tenderly, so fondly loved. Not until the little ones had forgotten their squabble, had begged each other's forgiveness at Connie's knee and cried themselves blissfully to sleep, did the father see her again. She seemed to busy herself a long time aloft instead of coming down to his den. Meantime, Fenton, officer of the day, came hurriedly in :

"Here's the latest, Morgan. Schultz and Schramm took dinner together at Conway's restaurant, leaving their horses at the Empire stable, and didn't start until nearly three o'clock. The sheriff has sent a posse after them. He claims that Lacy's description of the robbers fits them both."

"Blatherskite !" said Morgan.

"Well, that isn't all. Rhett's got a despatch from the chief. We go at daybreak. Special train. You'll be K.O. here to-morrow. The despatch from Pawnee says ranchmen report an officer and his orderly killed and scalped not twenty miles from Painted Lodge. Better come over to the office awhile."

"I'll be there in a minute," said Morgan, rising stiffly. "Connie !" he called at the foot of the stairs. "Connie !"

No answer. Slowly, wonderingly, he climbed the little stairs. Her door was open, the room dark ; the night-lamp burning dimly in the children's room threw but a faint beam through the connecting door-way. Groping in, he became aware of something dark upon Connie's white bed. It was his child, her head between the pillows as though to shut out every sound.

"Constance !" he exclaimed, distressed, dismayed. She started up, her hands clasped to her temples. Then, as though overwhelmed with the realization of some haunting dread, she bowed her face upon his arm, quivering from head to foot, and with one low moan of "Papa," —the old baby name seeming to come most readily to her lips,— "Papa, they've killed him !"—sank back upon the pillow.

VII.

The doctor was needed for Constance that night, and Mrs. Fenton and Mrs. Woods, loving women both, came in to minister to her, so utterly was she unnerved, unstrung. Morgan knew not what to say or think. It was no time now to ask to see the letter she had begged him to read. It was no time to torture her with inquiry as to why the belief in Thornton's death should so utterly prostrate her, even were the belief itself justifiable,—which he did not at all concede. Ranchmen reported an officer and his orderly killed in the Mini Ska valley far to the north of Pawnee Station that evening about dusk. Ranchmen were proverbially sensational. Even if an officer had been killed, why should it be Thornton? True, Winthrop's was the only command in the valley at the moment. True, the Indians knew of their coming, for what movement of troops did they not know all about as soon as the troops themselves? If an officer had been killed, it very possibly was one of the Eleventh. From the landing at the head of the stairs Constance had heard the abrupt announcement of Captain Fenton, and, waiting for no explanation, had rushed to her bed. Why should she believe Thornton to have been the victim? And, even if he were, why should it so affect her?—the apple of his eye, his loving, winsome, loyal Connie, his "Little Mother," as he had so long called her? Morgan wrung his hands in distress and perplexity.

The doctor came in after his brief examination.

"The child has been running down all winter," he said. "She is in a low, nervous condition, the natural result of the long strain. She has had a woman's cares on a child's shoulders, Morgan, and any shock was likely to upset her. The sudden news that one of her friends was killed was quite enough to floor a stronger woman, let alone Connie. We'll have her up again in a day or two; but she ought to have rest and change."

Rest and change! how glibly the words fall! How leaden they light on the ear of husband and father impoverished in the service and bound to the wheel! How was he to offer rest and change to any of his brood? If rest and change could have saved the life of his beloved wife, how could he have won it for her?

"I've given Constance soothing medicine. Better not disturb her to-night," said the doctor, as he left: so Morgan ventured not to bend over his sleeping child, fearful of breaking the spell. Yet at dawn, when the little battalion of foot marched off to Butte, she was up and at the window, importuning him for latest news from the front. Hours that morning he had to be at the office, for despatches were coming in thick and fast, ordering ordnance stores and ammunition sent hither and yon, and up to noon nothing whatever was heard from Winthrop's command, and the big eyes that questioned him, when he came to kiss Connie's white forehead, were rimmed with mourning circles, as though already she believed him gone and for him mutely wore her weeds. At three P.M. came a despatch from Rhett, six miles out from Pawnee, *en route* for the Mini Ska, dated at twelve : " Report of killing of officer and orderly untrue. Lieutenant Thornton's horse accidentally shot while scouting. No other casualties heard of. Winthrop reported forty miles northeast of Painted Lodge already."

Morgan took this over home at once. Mrs. Woods, bonny little army wife and mother that she was, came from Connie's room, and to her he gave the message. He would not permit any one to think he supposed his child could be, at her tender age, unduly interested in the fate of any man. Yet he found himself listening at the foot of the stairs. Would she cry out in relief and joy? No; whatsoever she might have betrayed to him, Constance was on her guard now. She was her mother's daughter for " pure grit," said he.

" Connie is so glad it wasn't true," called Mrs. Woods, tossing the brown paper down the stairs. " She wants to know when you are coming up to see her ?"

" After a while," answered he. " I must go to the storehouse first." He hastened to his stock of arms and munitions of war, thinking little of them, it must be owned,—thinking little of anything just now but Connie. Not yet sixteen, an innocent, ignorant, garrison-bred girl, yet so like her mother in her own girlhood, so gentle, unselfish, thoughtful for others; could it be that all unsought she should have given her girlish heart to the bright-eyed, merry young fellow who had so suddenly left them, and that it was known—noted by others? If not, why should Rhett have taken all the trouble to send that message telling of Thornton's safety? Sorrow, trial, trouble of nearly every kind had come to him during the last year or so, but this was something so utterly unlooked for. What could he do? What should he do?

At the storehouse, the ordnance sergeant, aided by one or two semi-invalided troopers, was packing cavalry equipments to be sent to a distant command. The glad June sunshine was pouring in at the open door-way, and the mountain breeze was fresh and bracing. The men were chatting in low tones over their work, and the talk was only of the robbery. Graves was in town, in consultation with the civil authorities. The local morning paper had but two topics to discuss, the Indian outbreak and the robbery. It had but one theory : the Indians were the malefactors in the first case, and the soldiers in the second. That cowboys or settlers, ranchmen or road-agents, could be the real culprits was not for an instant to be believed. Two soldiers closely answering the description given by Mr. Lacy, the paymaster's clerk, had been in town for several hours the previous day, patronizing stables, saloons, and restaurants, and liberally supplied with money, had ridden away as soon as details of the robbery were being circulated about the streets, and they were now "at large,"—that expressive term which is used by the press when it desires to imply that the party enjoying his constitutional rights is probably a fugitive from justice. The sheriff, with efficient " posses," was scouring the country in pursuit. Officials at the fort, professing to doubt the evidence laid before them, had refused to co-operate with the civil authorities in securing their arrest, and had insisted that the men were merely returning on the trail of Colonel Winthrop's command. Morgan had read many a screed in similar strain. It was what his own men were saying that aroused him to sudden interest.

" Who was that red-headed chap was out here last night asking to know where was Schramm's trunk?" inquired Private Geohegan of his comrade.

" Oh, he's wan of the sheriff's gang. I misremember his name. Sure the quartermaster-sergeant told him Schramm carried his trunk, like the elephants, on the end of his nose. But he said he knew he'd left a box or trunk in somebody's care,—Mrs. Hinkel's, I think, or the wife of some of the sergeants. He was nosing around the landresses' quarters half the evening."

" Was he? Did he get anything?"

" He did. He got some important information. Mrs. Clancy tould him she'd black his eye for him if he stuck his red head inside the door, and while she was entertaining the gentleman Mrs. Hinkel ran up to the post with a box, and when she came back the feller was talking about a search-warrant. It's little of Schramm's they'd find at ould Hinkel's now. She's took it up to the officers' quarters, whatever it is."

16

And then Morgan remembered the eager voice in his kitchen the night before, and Lot's announcement that it was Mrs. Hinkel who begged to see Constance, and a new light flashed across his mind, a new shadow fell athwart his path. What if the authorities were now to ask him where Schramm's effects were hidden? What if they should demand the right to examine them? Morgan was no longer simply a subaltern officer, he was the commander, *pro tem.*, of the big and important post of Fort Ransom, and bound by every consideration to act in conjunction with the civil officials in the enforcement of law and in the aid of civil process.

Even as he was pondering over the matter, a horseman appeared in the broad glare of the sunshine on the bare open space in front.

"I'm looking for the post commander," said he, and handed him a telegram. Morgan mechanically unfolded it and read:

"To the Sheriff, Latimer County, Butteville. Commanding officer Fort Ransom instructed to give every assistance in his power. You will be allowed to make all proper search."

This was signed by the adjutant-general of the department, and was presently supplemented by another which the operator at the post handed in. He was in conversation with the deputy sheriff at the moment, and, excusing himself, Morgan opened and read:

"Commanding Officer, Fort Ransom. Civil authorities report they are hampered in search for money stolen from Paymaster Graves. Render every assistance and allow all proper investigation."

"Do you mean that your people think any of this money is hidden here at this post?" he queried.

"Well, sir, that's what some of 'em say. Two of our officers will be out here in a moment. I rode ahead while they were jogging along in their buggy. They were here last night, and Mrs. Hinkel was seen toting a box up into the post just as soon as she heard they were inquiring for her shanty."

Morgan turned away. Far out across the winding ribbon of the road, twisting and twining over the rolling surface of the prairie, he could see the black dots in the light dust-cloud that told of the rapid approach of the officers of the law. Officially he had no knowledge of the whereabouts of that box, nor even of its existence; personally he had now every reason to believe that it was secreted under his own roof. Confident of Schramm's innocence, he had faith that nothing criminating could be found in Schramm's belongings. But suppose that the box contained papers,—personal and family documents which dealt with nobody's business but his own. What right had they to turn his letters inside out, possess themselves of his secrets, and parade them in the columns of the press, as paraded they certainly would be? It was an embarrassing question.

"What gave rise to the suspicion that Schramm had left valuables in the hands of Mrs. Hinkel?" he asked.

"Oh, that was easy to find out," answered the civilian. "All the soldiers, all the laundresses, were full of information about Schramm, and the mere fact that he held aloof from all but a few of their number was sufficient to make them suspicious of those with whom he did associate. Mrs. Hinkel and Mrs. Schultz were sisters, I am told, and Schultz and Schramm became very friendly. Schramm, it appears, spent many an evening at Hinkel's, and took a box there when the battalion was packing for the field, and went there with a small bundle the moment he got in from the front, the morning of the robbery. Now we know just what those two men did in town, and what we want to find out is what they did out here, what that packet was and what became of it. To-morrow we expect to have the men themselves."

"You do? Where?"

"Oh, well, down the Ska somewhere. They doubtless think that the safest route. You see, they couldn't go in any other direction without their being headed off and its being open admission of their guilt. Possibly they mean to catch the regiment, go through the campaign with it, and by and by, when the thing has blown over, pull out the money that they've hidden hereabouts, and have a good time. We have two parties out after them now: one, to head them off, went down to Pawnee by rail and rode north from there; the other follows their trail. I suppose you know we found the valise?"

"No. Where?"

"On the north bank of the river, not more than a mile west of Minden, sliced open with a bowie and rifled of whatever paper money there was in it originally. Nothing else was taken, so the paymaster and clerk say. They even left the nickels and dimes. Evidently they were in a big hurry."

Morgan's sad eyes wandered again over the prairie. The buggy was not a mile away, and another was following. If he could only see Mrs. Hinkel a moment before the inquisitors came. "Sudsville," that bustling suburb of the army post of those days, nestled along under the bank of a little tributary of the Mini Ska, while the cavalry stables and corrals occupied the broad low ground that skirted the stream itself on the southward side of the garrison. He had known the woman for years. She was an honest, sturdy, stout-hearted "frau," devoted to her husband, the Hanoverian sergeant, and proud of her brother-in-law, the Prussian Schultz, whose wife had died some years before. She held herself above the run of the colony of soldiers' wives, therefore they were not as ready to lie for as against her. Nevertheless, she had won even their respect; but the gabble of the laundresses' quarters had been amply sufficient to direct the scrutiny of the officials to her doors. Schramm, who left the box with her when the battalion marched, had left also a small package with her the morning he and Schultz rode in. Where were box and packet, and what did they contain? That was what the sheriff was determined to find out, and so certain was he of being on the trail of the robbers that he had bidden Graves and his clerk to follow and identify the money that might be recovered. When Morgan saw the occupants of the second buggy, as they drove in by the south gate, he went straight to his quarters.

"Is Constance asleep?" he asked of Mrs. Woods, as she met him at the stairs.

"No; she's awake, and anxious to see you," was the answer.

Still undetermined what to do, the father slowly climbed the steep stairway. Oh, how fondly and trustfully the big eyes beamed upon him, as he tiptoed in! Already his child was looking better, almost happy. She stretched forth her arms as he bent to kiss her.

"Dear old daddy! All the worry seems to come to you now, and Connie's forbidden to get up and help you. Is there any further news —of the robbery, I mean?"

"Yes." Then he paused a moment. "Constance, dear, the civil authorities claim that they know the robbers,—that they are of our regiment and that we are shielding them. The general orders me to aid in the search. They say Mrs. Hinkel had a box which belonged to Schramm and contains now some of the stolen money. What box did she bring you last night?"

"Schramm's box, father, and begged me not to let it go. It contains no stolen money. It holds papers and personal——" But he interrupted her.

"No matter what it may hold, we cannot hold it now. I do not blame Mrs. Hinkel for fetching it to you, but I must have it and the key."

"The box is in the lower drawer of the bureau, father. I have no key at all; Schramm has that. I did not tell you, because we knew that if you were questioned about it you would have to tell the truth, and then poor Schramm's letters would be no longer sacred."

"They shall touch none of his letters if I can help it," said Morgan, "but they must be allowed to examine for themselves."

A quarter of an hour later, in the office of the commanding officer were Graves and his clerk, the sheriff and a deputy, Morgan and the post surgeon, the latter officer having been summoned at Morgan's request. On the table was a stout sole-leather case about two feet long and six inches deep, shaped something like a despatch-box, something like a valise. It was evidently of foreign make, strong, durable, yet showing signs of service and wear. Such name as had originally been painted on its end was long since carefully scraped and painted out. In addition to its straps, a strong brass clasp and padlock secured it.

"It seems a pity to burst such a lock and spoil such a case," said the doctor, gravely. "I suppose you gentlemen feel that it must be done?"

"Oh, I never had a straighter tip in my life," said the sheriff. "I am betting on finding important evidence right here, if not the swag itself."

A soldier entered with some tools.

"One moment now, gentlemen," said Morgan. "This box is the property of a comparatively new soldier of ours. I believe he occupied higher station abroad than here. If money be found herein, well and good, I've nothing to say; but I protest against any prying into his personal secrets. This isn't Russia."

But the very first thing lifted out of the leathern box, as, its clasp shattered, it lay open before their eyes, was a long, official envelope. The sheriff tore it open, and therein lay ten fifty-dollar bills, national currency, crisp and new.

"My God!" exclaimed Lacy, pale with excitement. "I believe I could almost swear that those are some of the very bills we drew from the First National."

"Do you ordinarily pay enlisted men in fifty-dollar bills, Mr. Lacy?" asked Morgan.

"Certainly not," was the prompt reply. "There were over twenty

16*

officers with Colonel Winthrop's battalion : so we brought a thousand in one-hundreds and two thousand in fifties." And Lacy counted the bills over again with trembling fingers. The sheriff's big red hands were dragging out other packets now, bundle after bundle of letters, old, faded, and stained, several little books in German, three or four parcels wrapped in silk, each of which, when unrolled, proved to contain portraits. One of a soldierly, gray-moustached man of fifty-five or thereabouts, in the conventional broad-breasted undress uniform of the German army. Another,—on ivory, this, and in costly frame,—a painting of a lovely face with deep blue eyes and a fond, tender smile about the lips,—a mother face, which appeared again, with more of silver and less of gold in the curling hair that framed it, in two or three photographs. There was a photograph, too, of a stalwart young lieutenant in the dress of the Uhlans. Another, a boy not more than eighteen or nineteen, in the uniform of the foot-guards, with the iron cross on his breast. There was a sword-knot or two, and then some documents, closely written in German, filed, docketed, and trimly wrapped, and these, one after another, the sheriff was searching through and swearing over because he couldn't understand them, when again Morgan interposed :

"There's no more money there, Mr. Sheriff. Surely there's no reason for prying into the man's family affairs. When the arrest is made that will be time enough. You've got what money there is. Kindly give me a memorandum receipt for that, and then seal the case up again. I say again, I'm ready to bet anything both Schultz and Schramm will be able to account for every moment and every dollar. All you have to do now is to get them, which your deputies can effect as soon as they reach the regiment."

And, seeing how much Morgan seemed to take the matter to heart and that the officers evidently agreed with him, the sheriff finally consented :

"All right; only we've got to take this with us. We ought to hear through Pawnee from the parties sent to make the arrest by to-morrow night."

And hear they did, late the next evening. The party sent out from Pawnee rode north to the Miui Ska until they struck the cavalry trail near Painted Lodge, then followed the battalion on to camp. Schultz and Schramm had neither been seen nor heard of by the battalion since they were sent back from Bear Fork.

VIII.

It was on a Wednesday morning that Old Tintop marched away from Ransom. It was on Friday morning at dawn that the robbery occurred at Minden, Friday at guard-mounting that Schultz and Schramm reached the post, Friday noon that the news of the robbery came to Major Rhett, by which time the two couriers were again up and away, going, as we have seen, to have a quiet dinner by themselves in town before starting to return to their detachment. Fanning, proprietor of the Empire stables, said they had unsaddled in his corral about half-past twelve, had told him to feed at four, as they purposed starting in the cool of the evening; but they came back hurriedly just before three, saddled up, paid their reckoning, and left. He knew Schultz well; the other was a stranger, twenty years younger. Conway, keeper of the thriving restaurant, said the sergeant and his friend came in about one. He knew Schultz well also, and Schultz ordered a good dinner to be served, with a bottle of Rhine wine, as soon as convenient. They were shown to the curtained alcove at the rear end of the house, farthest from the bar, and were waited upon by the Mongolian combination cook and waiter. Meantime, everybody coming into the bar was talking of the robbery, and finally about half-past two Conway went himself to the box occupied by the Germans, and told them the news. They got up at once, left their wine and coffee unfinished, and hastened out to get further particulars. A few minutes after three they were seen riding briskly away on the Minden road, north of the river. It was Saturday morning when the sheriff's officers were sent in pursuit, one party going by rail to Pawnee, as has been said, then taking horses and riding over to the lower valley of the Ska; the other followed the trail. On Sunday evening members of both parties met near Painted Lodge, one coming back from the command to report that Schultz and Schramm were not there and hadn't been there, the other riding eastward hard as they could to catch the malefactors whom they believed still ahead of them. Between the two the Germans had slipped out somewhere and gone none could say whither.

When Monday evening came there was news indeed. Tintop, by a forced march, had jumped between the Sioux raiding-parties and the agency, whither the renegades were now returning, and there had been

a battle to the death. The fight had come off somewhere among the
breaks on the north side of the Ska Sunday afternoon, ninety miles
from the agency and a hundred from the nearest railway-station. The
news came from Indian sources entirely, but neither agent, interpreter,
mission priests, nor soldier guards could tell by what means they got
the tidings, and no Indian or half-bred *would* tell. That they believed
it authentic was evident from the wails and lamentations of certain
bereaved squaws. All the agent could telegraph was that a collision
had occurred and the losses were heavy on both sides. Tuesday morning dawned with no further particulars worthy of credence. But
when No. 3 came in for breakfast at Butte, Colonel Rand, inspector-
general of the department, stepped briskly off and inquired for
despatches at the office of the hotel. Receiving several, he was shown
at once to Major Graves's room.

With the paymaster at the moment were the sheriff and a brace of
reporters. Mr. Lacy was away on some mysterious errand which was
to result, so it was said, in the recovery of a large portion of the stolen
funds. He had been gone since Sunday night. Rand thoughtfully
read his telegrams as he mounted the stairs. The bell-boy's rap was
answered by the sheriff, who was seated nearest the door, a proceeding
at which Graves reddened ; it smacked of proprietorship, an indefinable
air of authority and possession on the part of the sheriff having become
more and more noticeable to the paymaster ever since their visit to
Ransom. It galled him, yet was manifested in so intangible a way he
knew not how to resent it. The fact of the matter was, Graves didn't
know how to do anything when Lacy was away. He had been in
service only a year, despite his gray beard, and was the nominee of a
man to whom neither Executive nor Senate could afford to say nay.
He simply leaned upon Lacy, who for his part was unquestionably one
of the ablest and most accomplished assistants a government official
could expect to have.

"What do you want?" said the sheriff, gruffly. "Nobody rang."

" Don't want nawthin'," was the answer, as the boy's eyes wandered
past the bulky form which was too familiar to be of interest, and
sought out the party who had been "held up." "There's a feller here
askin' for Graves," he proceeded,—the use of a handle to a man's
name being regarded in many far Western communities at that day as
a virtual admission of personal inferiority. The paymaster heard his
name and hastened to the door. Rand, swinging coolly along the

corridor, reading his despatches, glanced up, gave no sign of recognition of the sheriff, but held out his hand to Graves, whose face lighted with relief and hope at sight of the staff-officer.

"Come right in, colonel," he exclaimed. "I'm mighty glad to see you. I've been hoping you'd come. My God! did you ever hear of a more perfect plant? Come in; I want to talk with you."

"Had your breakfast?" asked Rand, briefly, and barely glancing at the other occupants.

"Not yet. I—haven't much appetite to speak of, and these gentlemen came up to see me the first thing. Let me present——"

"Well, come and take breakfast with me, then. I'm hungry as a wolf, and I can't talk until later," interposed Rand.

"All right, colonel; I'll go with you in a minute. As I was saying, the sheriff and these gentlemen——" again indicating his friends.

"Don't let me intrude now, Graves. I'll order for two. Finish your business with your friends, and then join me as soon as you can." And, before the paymaster could present the sheriff or introduce anybody else, Rand whirled about and went striding slowly down the corridor, engrossed apparently in another despatch.

"Give me my old room, if you can," said he at the office, "and order breakfast for two at once. Give us a little table by ourselves: I'll be back here in ten minutes."

The colonel was not in sight when Graves, still accompanied by the sheriff and the correspondents, came down to the office. Nor did he reappear in the hall. Graves, nervous, anxious, and fretful, kept glancing at the main entrance, and finally led his faithful attendants to the porch without. Here they could command a view of the street both ways. In fifteen minutes a waiter came out to say that Major Graves's breakfast was getting cold, and the other gentleman was half through his'n; wanted to know if the major's friends wouldn't excuse him long enough to let him come in and get a bite. The correspondents saw through the scheme and took it all laughingly. The sheriff said he'd go with him. Rand looked neither surprised nor annoyed when the big fellow came bulging in. He bowed civilly, but continued his engrossing work of tearing a territorial chicken to shreds, simply saying they must excuse his apparent haste, he had had no supper the night before and a long day's work was ahead and he was ravenous. The sheriff grimly watched the well-known officer (every town and settlement in the department knew the general's right-hand adviser, Rand),

and twice essayed to open talk on the subject of the robbery. Rand listened with every manifestation of polite interest, but vouchsafed not a word of his own. Suddenly pushing back his chair and tossing his napkin thereon as he rose, he said,—

"Now excuse me, major; finish your breakfast, and I'll write a letter or two. Join me in the office as soon as you're ready."

Of course Graves was ready in three minutes, and the sheriff also. Rand looked up, nodded cheerily, and went on with his letters. These he presently read over, folded, addressed, and stamped, with easy deliberation, and by this time the correspondents rejoined the major. Rand glanced at his watch, picked up his letters and took them to the desk. Graves and party followed. Then out came Rand's big cigar-case.

"Smoke?" he said, tendering the bunch to the sheriff, who pulled one forth in his pudgy fingers while Graves was presenting Messrs. So-and-So, of such and such papers, to both of whom Rand extended cordial greeting and his cigar-case, then took Graves by the arm, nodded cheerily a good-day to the party, and popped the paymaster through a side door. For an instant, only, they were too surprised to act. Then, with a "Well, I'll be damned!" the sheriff jumped to the door. There at the side entrance stood Fanning's best bay team and open buggy, Graves just being hoisted in. Rand sprang lightly after him, and, without a vestige of triumph on his face, blithely waved his hand to the party at the door, and away went the bays and the buggy.

"Well," said the sheriff, "if he isn't a cool one may I be—double damned!"

Not until afternoon could he, or any one else, for that matter, get at either Rand or Graves. Making a long circuit, and keeping him in constant chat, the colonel drove the unhappy paymaster out over the hard prairie roads, and towards noon reined up at the fort, where the team was turned over to an orderly, and the two staff-officers were welcomed by Morgan and regaled with lunch. Rand swore the canned lobster and commissary crackers and cheese, washed down with Budweiser, the most delicious things he ever tasted, and was full of sympathy with Morgan in his anxiety about Connie.

"Here's what you've got to do, old fellow," said he. "You must let that brave little woman come and pay us a visit. Send Lot and Billy, too. I've got a great big house, and my wife will be only too glad to hear child voices in it again. I like Connie. She's a brick.

I'll send passes for the whole party, and the change will do her good. Now, speaking about Schramm : had he never told her about his antecedents?"

No, Morgan knew he hadn't. So later Rand went down to see Mrs. Hinkel, and thus it happened that he was still at the fort when along about three P.M. the wires began to warm up with other and graver matter. Rand was wanted at the instrument if by chance he was still at the fort, for it was necessary that he should be placed in immediate communication with the general, who was at department head-quarters, and presently the soldier operator's cheek began to pale, as he checked off and jotted down, name after name, the list of the killed and wounded in Tintop's daring fight against the combined war-parties of the reservations. The gallant old dragoon himself was safe, but Morgan's captaincy had come. The flag went down to half-staff unrebuked by the lonely officer in command, for brave Manning, his long-time troop-leader and friend, had fallen fighting hard. The list of the dead, though large, was exceeded by that of the wounded, and supplemented by that of a party of whose fate no man could hazard more than mere conjecture. In addition to the names of Schultz and Schramm were those of ten other troopers reported among the missing. It was the roster of a little detachment sent out on the trail of alleged road-agents or robbers. They had started only a few hours before the fight, and were under the leadership of Lieutenant Thornton.

<hr />

IX.

A special engine and car took Rand, the doctor, and certain hospital attendants eastward to Pawnee that evening, but meantime, on his return to town, the colonel had gracefully surrendered to the press. He had so much to tell about the action of Winthrop's command that it left little room for his views or theories as to the robbery. He won the hearts of the correspondents by offering to take them along with him and tell them all he could on the way, and thus get time to look into certain other matters with which he was charged. He asked the sheriff for a description of the bills found in Schramm's box, and the sheriff allowed him to see the packet and make memoranda for himself. He asked to see Mr. Lacy. In fact, he asked twice to see Mr. Lacy ; but, though that gentleman had returned to the hotel at noon, he could not be found. He had gone out again after hearing that the major was driving somewhere with Colonel Rand. Up to the minute the special was reported ready, Mr. Lacy did not reappear, and when it was time to start Rand told the telegraph operator to send the following:

"BUTTE, Tuesday, 5.30 P.M.

"GENERAL C——, on No. 3:

"Just starting for Pawnee. No news here of Thornton's party. Rhett's battalion escorting wounded. Shall push forward to Mini Ska to-night. Ordered Graves to return with clerk to head-quarters by next train. Funds in safe by express. Shall stop to question Minden."

The run to Minden along the level valley was made in thirty minutes, and the agent was on the platform, a green flag hanging from the signal-arm overhead. The engineer, therefore, had orders to stop anyhow. A little knot of loungers had gathered, and with genuine frontier curiosity swarmed about the colonel as he took and opened the telegrams awaiting him. He read as he moved to the door of the station, and some of the party prepared to do likewise. Once inside the office, however, Rand shut and snapped the door behind him and turned on the agent:

"You were ordered, I believe, to send a written description of the two men who came to you with a despatch for Paymaster Graves and lured him on here Friday morning last. Have you done it?"

"Yes, sir. Sent it up to Mr. Burke at Butte to-day,—the division superintendent. I couldn't describe much. You see, it was still darkish, although—at least it was kind of dark in here, though it was after dawn outside. They wore their slouch-hats down low, and their collars up. I didn't suspect anything. They were both bearded, and in the prime of life, I should say,—about thirty, perhaps. Looked as much like soldiers as any I've ever seen, out here, leastwise."

"Do you think you'd know 'em again?"

"Well, no, sir; to be frank, I don't. I didn't notice them particularly. They were so quiet, had so little to say. Only one of them spoke to me at all,—gave his message right out soldier-fashion, and said he was instructed to notify the lieutenant of the time it was wired. I sent it right off quick as I could get Pawnee, and then they went out again, leaving me at the desk. When they came back, just as the train hove in sight, although it was broad daylight I was paying attention to the train and not to them,—hardly heard a word, or more than even glanced at them, when No. 3 came in. I saw a little clump of men over by the stream watering their horses, and all had on army overcoats. These two fellows who met the paymaster were the ones that first came in ; I'm certain as to that."

"Are you? Well, why? What was there to make you certain?"

"Because the fellow that did the talking used good English,—better than most soldiers,—and he ordered the other fellow around. The other called him 'sergeant,' the time he spoke."

"Good English, eh? Out-and-out Yankee, do you mean? or plains English, or Boston English? At all events, it sounded like a Yankee talking, not a foreigner, didn't it,—a German, for instance?" said Rand, eying him keenly.

"Well, now you speak of it, colonel, the fellow called sergeant had just a little accent,—German-like. But I mean he didn't use slang nor cuss words. He talked what we call book English."

"And you thought him only thirty?"

"Certainly not more than that. He looked so light and spry. But he had a pretty heavy beard. It covered all his face."

"No sprinkle of gray in it?"

"Well, sir, not that I noticed in that light."

"Where did they leave their horses, and what were the horses like, —bays? sorrels? chestnuts?"

"I didn't see their mounts at all, sir, except in a clump at a distance. They seemed mixed colors then."

"Exactly. Not all one color, as they would be if they belonged to one troop of cavalry,—bays, or sorrels, or grays?"

"Well, they were a good way off, colonel, and I can't be certain. Mr. Long, here, saw two men riding up along the north bank not more than twenty minutes after No. 3 pulled out."

"Yes. What colored horses were those two riding, Mr. Long?"

"Roans, sir. I could see plainly in the slanting sunshine. Cleanlimbed little fellows, too. They were no plugs or bronchos. They were genuine cavalry horses."

Rand compressed his bearded lips, as he turned away, signalling to the conductor, "Go ahead."

That evening a little party pushed away northward from the quartermaster's field dépôt, established close to the railway-station at Pawnee. A long ride was ahead of them, as the doctor was sorely

I 17

needed. About the same hour, over in the Mini Ska valley, Rhett had pitched his few tents and posted his sentries and outlying pickets to guard the wounded and the helpless against possibility of Indian attack. True, Indians of the plains rarely attack at night, and are scary and superstitious as so many negroes. True, the hostiles were all back under the wing of the agency by this time, probably. But Rhett had never before been on Indian service, and, whether he had or not, determined to neglect no precaution. He had met the convoy returning from the scene of the fight, had relieved the cavalry guard, sending it back to overtake the battalion,—now fourscore miles away *en route* to a still more threatened point,—and, under the orders flashed after him by wire and swift courier, Rhett was coming back to Pawnee, bringing the sufferers with him. The killed had been buried, temporarily at least, at the scene of the savage fight. There were thirty wounded in his care, borne mostly on travois and drawn by captured Indian ponies. When he halted at the end of his day's march Painted Lodge Butte bore southwest by west perhaps fifteen miles away, and the stage-station at the bridge over the Mini Ska lay probably five miles from their up-stream picket. A group of officers, chatting in low tones around the camp-fire among the cottonwoods, dispersed about ten P.M., and all but the commander of the guard rolled into their blankets, one or two of the number enjoying a good-night whiff at their brier-roots as they stretched themselves on the sod. Beyond the heavy breathing of some sleeper and occasionally a feverish moan among the wounded, who, with their attendants, were sheltered in a little hollow out of reach of possible shot, the camp was very quiet. The few horses, the mules and Indian ponies were securely hoppled and guarded where they could graze at will on a bench just to the north of camp, and when the moon came riding up the eastern sky and faintly picturing the bluff-bordered valley, the scene was one of calm and placid repose. Fenton, the officer of the day, could not help remarking upon it, as he went trudging out over the grassy slope for a midnight visit to his pickets. They had been talking of the strange and successful scheme by which the outlaws had lured the paymaster on to Minden and there robbed him, for the theory of the civil authorities that cavalrymen alone were the perpetrators had received something of a set-back when these gentlemen from Ransom met the wounded and the guards from Tintop's command and learned that the only absentees at the time of the robbery were Schultz and Schramm, who could hardly have effected it by themselves; and what opportunity had they had of learning the paymaster's movements? True, the sheriff's people, unable to find out what had become of the two, forbidden to invade the confines of another Territory, which they would do if they followed the cavalry, afraid to linger in the valley after the cavalry had gone, and utterly averse to searching among the Sioux trails for their prey, had returned to the railway. Among the wounded was Lieutenant Edwards, the paymaster's friend, and no one was more interested about this affair in which his name had been so recklessly and effectively misused than Edwards himself. The young doctor with the wounded told him he mustn't talk so much, but Edwards was bound to find out all he could, and so it happened that this very night, catching sight of the officer of the day as he started out on his rounds, Edwards feebly hailed him, on the shallow pretence that he had something to tell.

"Say, cap., I wanted to ask you if you knew we were just about opposite the gap that Thornton and his fellows took to pursue those road-agents?"

"Certainly. They went right up over yonder," said Fenton, pointing to where, dim and shadowy, a ravine seemed to pierce, wedge-like, the barrier of the northward range. "But what do you mean by lying awake and asking conundrums when you ought to be asleep?"

"Because I'm a damned sight more interested in old Graves's predicament than I am in our own, though I may yet have to convince a vigilant treasury that some other fellow, not I, sent that despatch. We were only some twenty miles east of here when that courier caught us with the news of the thing and the statement that the gang had scattered, some coming our way. The courier himself saw two of them, he said, as he came across the bridge, far up across the prairie, riding for Wagon Gap for all they were worth. Then he sneaked over and struck the trail and said that not two but six, at least, had gone to the Gap. That's how Thornton came to be sent back with orders to pursue and punish, capture, recover, and all manner of things that Tintop knew perfectly well he couldn't do, yet had to order him in compliance with his own instructions. He must have ridden right across the line of flight of the Sioux we whipped on Sunday, and, if so, God help him and his! There's nothing left of 'em but wolf-bait now."

"Oh, you're a little used up, Edwards. They'll squeeze through all right, I think. Quit your talking, and go to sleep."

"I can't sleep. 'Tisn't that this hole hurts me so, or that I'm so thirsty, but I can't get that confounded business out of my head, and I'm worried about Thornton."

"Well, shut up," said the captain. "Listen." And he stood holding out a warning hand.

"What do you hear?" asked Edwards, presently.

"I can't hear anything, thanks to your clatter. I thought I heard a challenge 'way up-stream where our picket is. Do be quiet now."

Both men listened with strained ears. Over at the edge of the bench to the northeast where the drowsy animals were scattered, a slowly-pacing sentry had halted, turned about, and, with the moon-beams glinting on his rifle, he too was listening, as though his attention had been attracted by some sound on the up-stream side of the camp.

"What was it, Lucas?" asked the officer of the day, coming up out of the hollow where the wounded were lying.

"I don't know, sir. The noise off yonder awhile ago was coyotes, but this cry came from up the bank."

"So I thought. It sounded like a challenging sentry. Who are out there?"

"Corporal Rafferty, sir, and two of B Company. I couldn't see anything, yet about ten minutes ago six or eight of them mules were pricking up their ears and looking out across that stretch of prairie yonder like as though they'd seen or smelt something."

The captain waited no longer. Turning away from the sentry, he walked rapidly out upon the bench which overlooked the river-bottom. Up here the moon illumined his way, while underneath the low crest there were fallen cottonwoods and more or less jungle and tangle to trip over. A camp sentry, well hidden under the bank, waited until his senior was close at hand, then challenged in muffled tone.

"Have you heard anything unusual off yonder?" asked the officer of the day as soon as he had been formally advanced and recognized.

"There's voices out there, sir, and horses. Rafferty's party has got 'em, whoever it is."

Presently two horsemen, piloted by a soldier afoot, came slowly through the timber towards them.

"Don't challenge," said Captain Fenton. "I'll hail.—What have you there, corporal?" he sharply asked, when the party had come within a dozen yards.

"That you, cap.?" queried a voice with the Western twang in it.

"Good Lord, but I'm glad to git yere! We've ridden seventy-five likely miles since morning, and ain't had a drink for twenty-four hours. Say, any of our other fellows yere? We're the posse sent out from Butte."

"Oh! I thought you'd given up and gone home," said Fenton, shortly, disappointed somehow that it was not a courier.

"Well, we did start, till we got word of Lieutenant Thornton's striking the trail, then we turned round and followed him. Luckily, the Sioux headed us off."

"Why luckily?"

"Good Lord! ain't you heard? The lieutenant and his men were corralled up at Slaughter Cove. I don't reckon there's hide nor hair of any of 'em left by this time, 'cept what the Indians have got on their scalp-belts."

"Slaughter Cove, man! why, that's not more than thirty miles north of us,—through the Gap."

"That's all true, perhaps, but we had to ride around a whole county to work our way out. The Sioux have got the swag by this time, robbers, troopers, and all."

X.

A proud boy was Perry Thornton the night the details of the robbery reached them. Finding no paymaster at Willow Springs on Friday noon, and alarmed by reports of Indian outrages down the Mini Ska, Tintop, as has been seen, decided to push on for Painted Lodge as soon as men and horses had enjoyed an hour of nooning; and so by sunset of the long June day the cavalry had put some forty-three miles to their credit and gone into camp once more, close to the stream, and not more than ten miles from the bridge over which was carried the broad and once well-beaten trail from Pawnee to the agency. Thornton, eager to win his spurs, and being a prime favorite with Tintop, as indeed he was with everybody, had been accorded the bliss of a side-scout, and was sent over to the stage-station at the bridge to gather news. There was no difficulty in loading up with rumors. The air was full of them. Perry found at the station half a dozen cowboys, ranchmen, and the like, most of whom had escaped

17 *

by the skin of their teeth and the performance of prodigies of personal valor. The old telegraph-line from Pawnee to the station was intact, but north through Wagon Gap and so on to the agency there had been no communication for a week, and no one was venturesome enough to go out and discover why. Around by way of Bismarck and Yankton it was easy, though slow work, to communicate with the agency people, and the situation warranted the belief that the Sioux had slashed the wires running southward from their reservation, and therefore towards the railway and the coming soldiers, but had left the northeastward passage open, under the natural impression that no tidings could ever get to the enemy by a road that ran the opposite way. Perry was urged by his informants to get back to camp and bring up the cavalry, and had not gone a mile before the accident happened which led to the shooting of the horse he was riding. The telegraph company, thinking to be enterprising, had sent a young man out with an instrument only the day before, and reopened the old office at Ska Bridge station, and when a cowboy came running in to say the lieutenant and his party had been jumped on the way back to Painted Lodge the despatch was sent at once which so alarmed the good folk at Ransom and which Rhett found means to modify on the following day; by which time, however, the truth was learned at Ska Bridge, as the cavalry battalion, "going for all it was worth," passed on downstream in a cloud of alkali-dust. Perry was ready for another ride even after a long day's march when, late Saturday night, as they slept far down the Ska, a courier rode in from the stage-station behind with full particulars of the robbery and the news that some of the gang were unquestionably striving to escape towards the Indian agency to the north, and had been seen spurring through Wagon Gap. The telegraph operator at the station had told Old Tintop all that he knew of the affair during the brief moment that the colonel halted, but now despatches and authentic news came after them.

"We've got to send an officer and ten men on the trail of those beggars," said Tintop, sitting up in his blankets and reading by the light of Gray's lantern. "Whose turn is it?"

"Mine, colonel," sang out a cheery voice from a roll of bedding under an opposite cottonwood, and in a moment Thornton, fresh as a daisy, was pulling on his boots and girding himself for the ride.

"You've just got back, you young cub, and the horse you killed was worth the news you brought ten times over," growled the colonel.

" Well, that's why I want to have another go, sir," was the prompt, laughing answer. And Tintop would not say him nay.

It was this way that Thornton came to miss the stirring fight of the battalion on the Sunday noontide, and to stumble into a siege of his own beside which, in point of peril and pluck and long-continued strain, the fierce, brief hour of battle of his comrades was but a bagatelle.

At one A.M. on Sunday he and his little squad rode away on the westward trail, guided by the couriers who brought the news. Two miles back from camp they left the river and edged away to their right over the moonlit valley towards a rift in the boundary hills just faintly visible in the dim and ghostly light. An hour after dawn they halted in a deep ravine to water their horses, and then went loping on again, Thornton eager and exultant, proud of his trust and determined to overhaul the robbers if riding could do it. By noon Sunday they had pushed northward out of the Gap with the fresh trail leading on ; by one had halted to feed, water, and unsaddle awhile in the midst of the wild scenery at the head of Fossil Creek, the ten-mile pass out of sight behind and the rocky walls of Slaughter Cove no great distance ahead. It was here that Sergeant Jeffers, instead of lying down and resting, as did the others, was seen bending double and examining the tracks of their predecessors all along the bank and among the trees. Wherever a horse had stepped in the mud and the hoof-print remained unbroken he bent closer and studied it with mingled interest and anxiety. At last Thornton, watching him as he munched his bit of hard bread and chocolate, took his tin mug to the brook for a drink and turned on the non-commissioned officer.

" What are you studying so closely, sergeant ?"

" These hoof-prints, sir. There are two I've seen this morning that worried me at first, in view of the charge made that the robbers were cavalrymen."

" Why so ?"

" Just this, sir. Two of these horses we're after wear the government cavalry shoe. Look here, and here. I could almost swear those shoes were fitted and every nail driven and clinched by D Troop's farrier."

" And do you mean that some of our fellows are actually mixed up in the robbery, after all? Why, man alive, there's no one out but Schultz and Schramm."

"That's just exactly what I don't believe, sir, if by being mixed up in the matter the lieutenant means they belong to the gang. No, sir; for the last hour it has been dawning on me that we are not following one party, but two. An Indian would have told us this before now. The first party went through the Gap hours ahead of the second, and we're as many hours behind. The first party probably were the road-agents; the second, chasing as hard as they could, were Schultz and Schramm."

"How do you make it out?" asked Thornton, his bright eyes ablaze with interest.

"Well, everywhere through the Gap, lieutenant, these cavalry hoof-prints showed atop of the others. In every case where there was soft ground you could see that our print was the last made. The first party camped here, fed, watered, ate, and smoked, and finally went on; our fellows merely fed and watered and hastened after them. You can see where their horses were tethered, where the cooking was done, where they lay and smoked. Some of them had cigars. I picked up three stumps. Our fellows never stopped more than to give their horses what grain they had left in their nose-bags, and a good long drink. It was Schultz and Schramm, simply because they alone were away from the command. They had gained on the gang considerably, too, through the halt of the former right here, and I believe we'll hear from them yet."

Two hours later, pushing on in grim determination still on the trail, with the opening of the strange, wild, heavily-timbered rift in the hills named but the previous summer Slaughter Cove, just to their left, the party rode suddenly out from among the pines to where a bare, treeless shoulder of the mountains towered between them and the east. Northward up a steep ascent among scattered timber went the trail, and Thornton and Jeffers dismounted to lead and rest their panting horses. The others in silence followed their example. Slowly they clambered up the winding path, each moment nearing the crest, and at last within half a dozen yards of the top Jeffers signalled with his bare brown hand, tossed his reins to the nearest trooper, and then, bending low and removing his scouting-hat, went crouching towards a little cairn of stone, an old Indian guide-post made to keep their runners from losing the way in the depths of a Dakota winter, when all the face of nature was veiled in snow. One after another as they closed up on the leaders the weary men halted, and some at once threw themselves upon the sod; all allowed their horses to graze. For a moment Jeffers lay flat, peering over the crest; then of a sudden he seemed to catch sight of something that set him all of a quiver. He shaded his eyes with his hand and stared, slowly rising to his feet, the muscles of his lips and jaws twitching with suppressed excitement. Thornton, busily engaged at the moment in opening the case of his field-glass, did not at first see him. Just as he had drawn out the binocular and wiped the object-glass with a silken handkerchief, one of the troopers muttered, " Look, lieutenant, he's beckoning." And in a moment, with beating heart, the boy had crept to the veteran's side.

It was a wonderful view that opened before his eyes. They were halted on the eastward slope of a bold, rock-ribbed, pine-covered range that seemed to stretch away northward without pass or break for many a league until lost in a maze of similar black-crested heights that, perhaps forty miles away, veered around to the east again, curtaining the intervening slopes and foot-hills and valleys until it was merged in the general haze of the far eastern horizon. All the rude, rugged chain of hills bristled with its growth of pine and cedar, glistened here and there with its outcropping of boulder and quartz, or glinted when the searching sunshine fell on the duller hues of gneiss and granite. All the rolling foot-hills, a tumbling sea of spotless green, shimmered in the unclouded rays. Far as the eye could reach, northeast, east, southeastward again, a glorious stretch of upland prairie, of wind-swept, woodless turf, once the roaming-ground of countless thousands of the wild cattle of the Western world, the now annihilated buffalo. Far away to the southeast, dim and indistinct, a dark winding fringe told where the Mini Ska rolled smoothly through its wide and open valley. Far away to the northeast, among rounded bluffs and palisaded buttes, a shining blue ribbon turned and twisted, dove out of sight under grass-grown walls, only to come gleaming into view again still farther on, the Wakpa Wakon,—Spirit River,—curling through the heart of the reservation, the sacred lands of the Sioux. There, some-where to the north, sheltered from the fierce wintry gales by the grand curtain of bearded mountain to its west and north, hidden from sight by its surrounding citadels of bluff, lay the substantial settlement of the agency, a long day's march away. There in every deep sequestered valley, along every babbling stream, lay the lodges of the pampered tribes,—old men and children, old women and young, living indolently and in plenty at their guarded homes, while the sons and brothers and

I *

braves, the war-chiefs and the turbulent young men, swarmed into the forbidden grazing-grounds of the settlers, far beyond the treaty line, and in rude and bloody foray found their sole content. The trail the cavalry squad had followed in the early morning along the windings of a feeble tributary of the Mini Ska had left the broad valley thirty miles away to the south, and, bursting through a dividing ridge by way of Wagon Gap, left the old beaten road at the Springs where they made their noonday halt, plunged into the timbered ascent close to the backbone of the ridge, while the road, by a sweep or détour to the east, climbed gradually to the level of the upland and could be faintly seen in places five or six miles away like a dun-colored ribbon gartering the green carpet of the prairie. To their left and rear a frowning gorge in the heart of the range opened the narrow way that led to the basin or cove among the pine-covered hills,—the Slaughter Cove the guide had pointed out at noon. To their right, therefore, all was bold, open, undulating, smiling in unclouded sunshine; to their left—the west—all was dark, frowning, and forbidding; and yet the one was the path of death and danger, the other the only line of escape.

"By Jove, what a magnificent view!" is Thornton's exclamation after a moment's gaze. "What did you see, sergeant? You looked as though something lively was up. Any sight of the chase?"

But Jeffers, crouching low and pointing over along the slope not a quarter of a mile away, simply said, "Look there, sir."

Two lithe, painted objects, crawling slowly on all-fours, with feathered war-bonnets trailing along their bare red backs, were rapidly nearing a third, who, bareheaded, seemed peering over the ridge in his front at some other objects in the ravine beyond, at something out of sight from where the troopers lay. Behind the two crawling creatures first seen came, at ten or twelve yards' distance, others of their kind, eagerly gesticulating and signalling to others still. All on a sudden three or four ponies, placidly cropping the turf down the slope behind their creeping masters, pricked up their ears and glanced nervously around, and in a moment there rode into view, full tilt, one after another, half a dozen more wild warriors in the full panoply of their craft. And—it was his first campaign, he was only a boy—Perry Thornton's heart leaped up in his throat, for the sunshiny, breezy, billowy upland was simply alive with war-parties of Sioux.

"I am willing to do my share of fight,—fight double my weight of Indians, gentlemen," the guide was saying a moment later. "God only knows what's set them on to us, but the whole Sioux nation's coming up from the Mini Ska, and we're cut off. I can't fight all hell, neither can you. The one chance of getting out of this is by way of Slaughter Cove. There's a game-trail over the range back of it. They ain't seen us yet. Now is our time."

"Whom have they seen? What are they watching over there?" asked Thornton, his lip trembling a bit despite himself.

"I know without waiting to see. It's your fellers coming back from their chase after the road-agents. They have either got the money or they haven't got it. In either case it'll be of no earthly use to them in ten minutes. Those Indians are laying to lay 'em out as they climb the trail. See?"

See? It was plain enough now. Creeping like panthers, the lithe, sinewy fellows were scurrying up to line the crest. Others, dismounting at the run, were hastening to join them. Others, signalling, were conveying some tidings to another party that, three miles away, could now be seen sweeping at full gallop across the Pawnee road.

"Come, gents," said the guide, sliding back to his horse and quickly mounting. "My partner had more sense'n I when he swore he wouldn't trust his scalp north of Wagon Gap. If you want to save your souls alive, mount and follow while there's yet time. I'm bound for the Cove and back to God's country beyond."

A nervous young trooper started to follow as the frontiersman went sliding and sprawling back down the trail, but a stern voice checked him. One glance in the sergeant's eyes was all the reassurance Thornton needed. The spirit of his soldier father spoke out on the instant:

"Stay where you are, men! Let that d—d coward go. We're here to save Schultz and Schramm."

XI.

A moment longer the two soldiers, boy lieutenant and veteran sergeant, remained crouched at the ridge, peering over, and in low eager tones making their plans. The actions of the Indians clearly indicated that they were, as the guide remarked, "laying" for some party coming back along the trail. There could not be more than four or five in the party, or the Indians would not attack at the moment, but wait until they had more of their kind to back them. There could not be less than two or three, or the warriors would have been down on the poor devils before this, six to one. The one dread now was that they might shoot from the rocks before their friends could interfere. All this was hurriedly discussed, then up spoke Thornton: "We'll charge at once. We can drive them off, get Schultz and Schramm out, and then all retire together into the Cove. Mount! Tumble up there, you men. Drop carbines and draw pistols. Keep watch, sergeant. Wait till we're ready."

And now the intense excitement of the moment seems to communicate itself even to the tired horses. Eagerly they begin to toss their heads and paw the earth and sniff and snort. "Smell the Sioux, do you?" mutters one trooper, as he braces tighter the cinch of his saddle. There is indeed "mounting in hot haste," yet without noise or confusion of any kind. Perry's young heart is beating like a forge, and for the life of him he can't prevent a trembling at the knees as he swings into saddle and looks to the chamber of his revolver. It's his first fight, yet so constantly has he studied and pondered over all the experiences of his comrades that he feels certain his plan is the right one,—to burst from their covert, stampede the dozen Indians close at hand, then slip away with the victims that were to be, before the more distant warriors can reach the spot. Once back within the natural fortress of the Cove, they can bid defiance to five times their number. Meanwhile, the men, some a little white and tremulous, others, veterans at the business, cool and imperturbable, have mounted, slipped the muzzles of their carbines into the ready sockets, and, like their young leader, are testing their pistols. Jeffers raises his hand in signal. "They're getting ready, sir. Two of them are sighting now."

"Then we haven't a second to lose," says Thornton. "Just follow me now, full dash; but don't yell till I do. Keep quiet till we get right on 'em. Then gather in our fellows and get back here quick as you can. Forward now. I shan't give any commands."

Up the slope they ride in column of twos. There's no space to form "front into line." Perry's heart and Perry's horse alike are bounding. Ten seconds, and they are over the crest and in full view of their foemen four hundred yards away, between them only the open, rolling surface of elastic turf. Quick as each man reaches the summit he plunges ahead, "opens out," and rides up on line with the leaders, Thornton, still curbing his excited horse, riding at plunging lope and glancing back to see his followers out of the ravine. Then Jeffers comes tearing up to join him. Then comes a loud, resonant, Indian warning, shouted from somewhere down the sunny slope, and then there's no time to think. Every man at the instant claps spurs to his horse's flanks and sets up a yell, and then down they go in sweeping charge, straight at the painted, feathered bipeds leaping for their ponies along the opposite rise. Distant Indians let drive long-range shots, in hopes of downing a horse and breaking the impetus of the cavalry dash. There are three or four of these who have reached their ponies, leaped into saddle, and, as they scurry away, bend low and send a wild shot or two at the rushing horsemen, but all to no purpose. Thornton and his followers come cheering, charging on, straight for the second crest, and in an instant one luckless warrior is tumbled over by the leaders, while Jeffers and Malloy, long used to hunting in couples, have run down another, who, farther to the left, had sought to mount and escape. The ping and crack of revolvers and Winchesters echoing back from the rocky range are suddenly dwarfed by the louder bang of the Springfield rifle. Dashing up and over the ridge, occupied but an instant before by the red men, Thornton comes into view of a little party away down the trail ahead of him. Two of their horses are already shot, one stiffening out in death, one rolling in agony. Two white men, dismounted, are battling for their lives against a circling rush of Sioux, and, borne by the mad impetus of the charge, Perry and the half-dozen at his heels swoop headlong down among the combatants, and the Sioux, amazed yet never bewildered, bend low on their ponies' necks and go sweeping away up the farther side of the long ravine, then, circling about, spring to earth and at long range resume the fight. Their bullets are whistling about Thornton's ears, as he reins up in the midst of the rescued party. One man, with the film of death already glazing his eyes, a stranger, lies gasping on the turf. Over him, piteously crying his name, a mere boy is bending. Sergeant Schultz, grave, yet with quivering lip and trembling hand, gives greeting to his young officer. "We were surprised, sir, and cut off. We had no hope of rescue," he is saying, while the men are rapidly dismounting and running out to kneel and return the fire now coming in from almost every side, Schramm, cheering with delight and enthusiasm, leading them on.

Then comes the up-hill fight to gain the Cove. Not an instant can be lost. Already, with soldierly appreciation of the situation,

18

Sergeant Jeffers has dismounted two or three men to hold the ridge over which lies the line of retreat, and Thornton, directing two men to lead back the horses, disperses his little force as skirmishers. "Get your wounded back up the hill," he says to Schultz. "Jeffers knows where we are to make our stand. Fall back, fast as you can. We'll keep 'em off." The bullets are nipping the bunch-grass all round them, and the old German sergeant's face is very grave and white, but he never wavers. Schramm, after hoisting the wounded stranger into saddle and giving the reins into the hands of the weeping boy and calling for some one to steady his father, runs back to join the firing line. Slowly up the trail now Schultz marshals the led horses. Back slowly between them and the yelling Indians, now each moment reinforced, comes the little band of defenders. Over to the left, a young trooper, under fire for the first time, suddenly drops his carbine, claps hands to his leg, and sets up a howl of misery.

"Help him if you can, Schramm," sings out Thornton. "Keep your places, the rest of you." Thicker come the hissing bullets from front and flank. Only Jeffers's forethought saves them from attack in rear. At last the horses, snorting and plunging, have reached the ridge and are led safely over into the swale beyond. At last the German sergeant has convoyed his wounded across the barrier, then turns for one or two shots over the heads of his comrades now backing up the slope. It is the instinct of battle, the impulse of the soldier,— and the last of his soldierly life. Finger on trigger, muscular hand grasping the brown carbine in the act of aiming, down, face foremost on the sward, poor Schultz has tumbled, a Winchester bullet tearing through his loyal heart.

Five minutes later, in a little amphitheatre among the rocks, two hundred yards to the west of the ridge from which the Indians first were sighted, the well-nigh breathless detachment is regathering, and the fight goes on. Here, stretched on the ground, stone-dead now, lies the civilian,—the stranger found in company with Schultz and Schramm,—while sobbing over him kneels his boy. Here, badly frightened, the wounded recruit has been dropped and told to quit his noise. Here, badly wounded, lies Corporal Treacy, an Irish trooper whose five years in the cavalry have known many a scene of death and danger, but whose only worry now is that he cannot fire another shot. Here Jeffers is posting the men among the rocks as they arrive, so as to cover the retreat of the lieutenant and two or three still out at the front and for the moment invisible. Schramm, having dropped his wounded comrade under a sheltering boulder, has run up to Jeffers just as two men come drifting in, one supporting the other, who is bleeding and deathly white.

"They have killed Bredow, my horse," he cries, his blue eyes snapping and great beads of sweat starting from his face. "Where is the lieutenant?"

"Back there, trying to lug in Schultz's body," gasps the wounded man. "Only two fellows left. Hurry—save——" and down he goes in a dead faint.

"Schultz's body! Gott in Himmel!" cries Schramm, as with one bound he is over the boulders and rushing out to the front again.

Two hundred yards away, just over the ridge, with whoop and yell and flashing rifles, the Indians have concentrated their energies on one devoted little squad. Stumbling up the slope, Thornton has come upon the prostrate form of the veteran soldier, stone-dead, yet in mute appeal seeming to beg that he be not left to the savage mutilation of the Sioux. "Here, Connor!—Help me, Fritz!" he shouts to the nearest men ; and so, desperate and daring, the three join forces to save their friend. One drags, the others fire, and they have just got the senseless clay to within ten yards of the crest, when with triumphant rush and yell the mounted Sioux come charging at them. Poor Perry! All in a flash he sees that hope has fled,—that here on this wild upland, far from home and loved ones, just at the opening of the career so long sought, so proudly entered, his gallant, manful, soldierly effort has cost him his life. But he has lived like a Thornton,—like a Thornton he'll die ; and, kneeling by Schultz's lifeless form, he drives the last shot from the sergeant's carbine, tosses it aside, grips tight his beautiful revolver, a proud father's gift, and with a last prayer on his lips, and mother's face swimming before his eyes, braces himself for the shock. There is sudden clamor of shots behind him. Straight in front, not forty yards away, a charging Sioux plunges head-foremost to the ground, his pony veers wildly, so do two others, and the well-aimed shots have taken effect. "Courage!" he shouts. "They haven't got us yet." For, checked by this unlooked-for salute and dreading more, the warriors duck and swerve and circle away. Then down comes Schramm, with Jeffers a close second.

"Quick, lieutenant! Quick! Back to the ridge! We'll bring Schultz."

Too late. Seeing how puny in numbers are the little party of rescuers, the Sioux come on again, firing as they dash, and then for the first time Thornton finds his hands and arms covered with blood. A deadly faintness overcomes him. The earth begins to swim and rock and whirl, and he only knows that Schramm has swung him on his broad and muscular shoulders before he swoons away. They are holding his flask to his lips when—safe for a time at least—he reopens his eyes among the rocks at Slaughter Cove.

"Where are the Indians?" he faintly asks.

"It's what I can't understand," says Jeffers. "We could see whole troops of them riding away like the wind, southeastward towards the Ska. There ain't more'n a dozen round us now, I reckon,—not enough to attack, yet too many to admit of our getting out, with all our wounded. Thank God, sir, we got you back in time to check the blood. That bullet just missed the jugular, but you bled like a stuck pig. Schramm says you were all covered with it when he reached you."

"I didn't know I was hit—more than a mere graze," said Thornton, faintly.

"Hit twice, sir. You got the other when they dashed on us at the crest and Schramm had to drop you for a minute."

"Did Schramm carry me out?"

"Every foot of the way, sir. The little Dutchman is made of steel: only he's heart-broken about Schultz. We couldn't fetch him in, sir. They got the body, after all, and I had to order Schramm under arrest to prevent his going out a second time."

Thornton closes his eyes a moment. Faint from loss of blood, the realization of the peril of the past hour and the danger of the present, he knows no pain from his wounds, he realizes that he is in command, responsible for all, and that there may yet be a demand for his every energy. He needs to think; yet everything seems awhirl.

"Take another pull at this, lieutenant," says Jeffers. "You're very weak yet, but we're all right now." And he holds the flask to the boy's lips and raises him on his arm. "It's my belief the battalion has struck the main body of these beggars over near the river, and flash-signals have been going for the last hour. We can see 'em with your glasses. If they have, we're well avenged, for there isn't an old hand in all the regiment that isn't just mad for a fair fight with 'em. They won't bother us more this day, so long as we keep inside and under cover, and if the colonel's after them the rest won't stop to inquire for us to-morrow either."

" How many are wounded ?" asks Thornton, feebly.

" Well, sir, there's yourself and Corporal Treacy,—you're the only ones seriously hurt. Little Reddy there is shot in the leg, and three or four are scratched. Schramm's shirt is full of holes, and I thought he must be hit, he was so covered with blood. Between losing Schultz and Bredow, he feels pretty well broke up; but there won't be anything too good for him in the regiment when we get back, sir. Here he comes now : he's been over at the spring, washing off the blood."

Thornton feebly turns : " Schramm, my brave fellow ! it seems I owe my life to you. Where would I have been but for your courage ?"

And Schramm, apparently not seeing the hand feebly outstretched, stands at salute and replies,—

" Where would I have been, sir, but for the lieutenant ?"

***

XII.

" Head-Quarters Detachment —th Infantry,
Camp at Slaughter Cove, June —, 187—.

" Post Adjutant, Fort Ransom :

" Sir,—I have the honor to report that in compliance with the verbal orders of the major commanding the battalion I marched with four officers and seventy men of Companies E and H, —th Infantry, to the relief of Lieutenant Thornton's detachment of the 11th Cavalry, reported besieged by Indians at this point. Leaving camp of the battalion on the Mini Ska at 1 A.M. on Wednesday, with three days' cooked rations, we reached Buffalo Springs soon after dawn ($6\frac{1}{2}$ miles), pushed on through Wagon Gap, reaching the head-waters of Fossil Creek ($27\frac{1}{2}$ miles from camp) at 10.45. From this point our advance was slow, as Indians could be seen along the heights, and we had reason to expect attack. They drew off at our approach, however, and we reached the besieged party near Slaughter Cove about 1 P.M., much to the relief of its members, who, though at no time suffering for food or water, were without surgical attention for their wounded, and had had a sharp fight with a large force of hostiles on Sunday, and had been under fire much of the time ever since. Fortunately for them, the general engagement between their comrades of the Eleventh and the main body of the enemy, forty miles to the southeast, had the effect of drawing all but a small number away from their front and of driving them thence to the agency. There is every reason to believe, however, they would have returned by this time to finish their bloody work had we not been hurried to the scene.

"The killed are Sergeant Schultz and a civilian by the name of Stearns, whose son, a lad of eighteen, is with us, but seems so distracted by his recent experience that his mind is unbalanced. The civilian was one of a party of four who had ridden northward and were pursued by Sergeant Schultz and Private Schramm on the supposition that they were connected with the paymaster's robbery at Minden and had the money with them. Schramm reports that these two met them close to the scene of the fight, galloping back, saying they were attacked by Sioux, and their comrades, who were some distance ahead, were probably killed. The speedy appearance of the Indians proved the truth of part at least of their story. Lieutenant Thornton's prompt charge saved the lives of the two troopers, but in the engagement which followed Schultz was killed, and the other casualties were the result of an attempt to save his body. Lieutenant Thornton, who appears to have behaved with great gallantry throughout, being twice wounded in the effort, was himself saved from death by the devotion of Private Schramm, who bore him away on his shoulders in the face of a dozen enemies. Among the other wounded are Sergeant Jeffers, Corporal Treacy, Troopers Reddy and Gross. Dr. French reports that they can speedily be moved to Pawnee, and urges that as soon as possible ambulances be sent to meet us.

"After the wounding of Sergeant Jeffers, the active command of the defence was vested in Private Schramm, whose bravery and skill were so marked as to win from his superiors the most unstinted praise. He is now threatened with fever as the result of exposure and exhaustion and grief over the death of his friend, but Dr. French hopes that it will prove nothing of great gravity.

"We begin the homeward march, carrying the wounded on litters, to-morrow morning. The body of Sergeant Schultz, fearfully mutilated, was found and afterwards buried by our men this afternoon.

"The conduct of the detachment under my command was excellent: every man was in his place at the end of the thirty-five-mile march.

"Very respectfully,
"Your obedient servant,
"D. G. FENTON,
"*Capt. —th Infantry, Commanding.*"

Such was the official report which had followed Rhett's command back to Ransom and brought a gleam of sunshine through all the gloom. The death of Captain Manning, an officer of sterling worth, and that of so many good men and true, three of whom had families at the post, could not but weigh heavily on the spirits of one and all. The home-coming of the wounded, however, called for the active services of many hands as well as the liveliest sympathy of every heart, for the journey by field and rail had been a trying ordeal in the fierce heat which for seven days after Winthrop's fight had seemed to hard-bake the broad valley of the Ska even to the westward mountains. Then the grief aroused by the casualties in the main engagement had been supplemented by keen anxiety as to the fate of Perry Thornton and his party. Rhett was a cool-headed fellow and had done about the right thing: even Edwards and other cavalry cranks were ready to admit that. Aroused soon after midnight by his officer of the day and the demoralized deputy, he had little time to think. Orders required him with his battalion to march back to Pawnee as escort for the wounded. Communication with department head-quarters in the dead of night would have involved hours of delay. The deputy might be lying, yet the chances were in favor of the truth of his stories. Rhett knew the bulk of the Indians must have scampered for home in order to show up at the muster sure to be made, so as to convince the agency officials, at least, of their presence, and that they therefore could have had no part in the recent outrages. The general had taken the field, going 'cross country after Winthrop, and was now far beyond telegraphic reach. If the Sioux had surrounded Thornton near Slaughter Cove, the sooner help was sent the better. Fenton, always ready for anything and keenly relishing the idea of footmen marching to the relief of cavalry, was promptly told to take his own company and Company E and "get there." The cooks were up, coffee boiling, and bacon sizzling, before the order was fairly out of the major's mouth, and the command marched away towards the gap in the far blue hills under the twinkling pole-star within the hour.

"God speed you, old man! Send us word quick as you can," said Rhett, as the dusky little column went swinging away out of camp. "Give 'em a lick for me, Mickey," called Private Toohey to a chum in a luckier company than his own. And that was the last heard of them for twenty-nine hours. Then two of the lately-besieged troopers, Fritz and Reuter, came trotting in among the travois just as the convoy broke camp at the mouth of Pawnee Gorge, twenty miles nearer home. Leaving the Cove at dark the previous evening, they had ridden all night with the news of the rescue, had routed out the telegraph operator at Ska Bridge and sent away certain despatches with which they were charged, had learned that the major and his command had passed on about nine A.M. and would be found somewhere to the south along Pawnee Fork, and then pushed ahead with the glad tidings. Everybody, therefore, at Ransom knew the main facts long before Rhett and the wounded got home. Everybody mourned for Schultz, a veteran of nearly twenty years' service in the regiment, and rejoiced for Schramm, who had covered himself with glory. Everybody was proud of Thornton's spirited behavior in his maiden fight, and full of genuine distress over his wounds. Edwards, badly shot and a veteran of many a tough cavalry campaign, wasn't the object of one-tenth the sympathy that was lavished on "Pretty Perry," one of whose hurts—that slit along his neck—was a mere scratch, that would be an ornament to him all the rest of his life, while the hole bored by the little Winchester in his side was something that would soon heal and seldom hurt him. But who can paint the sensation at the Thorntons' happy home? Delight and dismay intermingled! Telegram followed telegram, that which came from the general late in the day blinding Colonel Thornton's eyes: "The regiment glories in your gallant boy. We'll send him East on leave at once. Full report by mail."

Then with what eagerness they waited the coming of letters and particulars! with what emotion did they read Perry's modest pencil scrawl, bidding them ascribe all credit to Jeffers and give all gratitude to Schramm! with what fluttering hearts, what tearful eyes, did they strive to read Fenton's letter telling the story of Perry's dash to the rescue of the imperilled troopers, of his heroic effort to save poor Schultz's body, of the daring and devotion of Trooper Schramm, of the enthusiastic praise the little detachment lavished on their young lieutenant! Here at least there was no division of sympathy or sentiment. Here at least was Perry the hero of the Indian campaign, the future leader in many another. Stopping only long enough to drop in upon a little coterie of old campaigners, receive their hearty congratulations, and read them the despatches from the seat of war, the veteran colonel left by first train for the far West to meet his boy and to bear to that brave and devoted Prussian trooper the blessings, the gratitude, and the assurance of the fervent prayers of mother and sisters for his own happiness and prosperity for all the years of his life—and beyond.

Four days and nights of ceaseless travel it took the colonel to reach Pawnee. By that time the general with Tintop and the regiment was far to the northeast, straightening out another squabble, the army as usual acting as buffer between the Indians and the people and getting hard knocks on both sides. By that time Rhett with his command was back at Ransom, and Fenton with the wounded from Slaughter Cove was on the homeward march. They were breaking camp in Pawnee Gorge, thirty miles north of the station, just about the time that No. 3 went whistling down the grade, shooting the sharp curves of Antelope Fork after leaving the colonel to be received by the quartermaster at Pawnee Station. His first question was for news of his boy, who was doing splendidly, said the officer, when they passed Ska Bridge yesterday. "Fenton's going to send him with one or two others ahead in the ambulances this morning. They'll be here before noon. Schramm comes in at the same time, poor fellow. He's got an ugly touch of fever, Dr. French wires, and they want to get him to hospital as soon as possible. The death of his friend Schultz seems to have been a hard blow."

"I wish they'd let me take him home with us," said Colonel Thornton, with glistening eyes. "I know a little woman who followed the drum many a long year with me, and two pretty girls as ever were born under the flag,—if it is their father who says it,—who would be only too happy to spend nights and days for weeks to come nursing that young gentleman back to life. Do you know him at all?"

"Only by sight, sir. He was quite a character at the post, owing to his devotion to Captain Morgan, who helped him out of a close call last year just after he enlisted. They all agree that he is a gentleman by birth and breeding, whom some freak of fortune has landed on our shores. He'd get the Iron Cross at home for this exploit."

"Well, we'll show him here that if we have no decorations to offer, we Americans know how to appreciate heroism and reward it. There's nothing much too good for such a fellow, in our eyes."

An hour later, the sun just peeping up over the eastern verge of the plateau and the colonel and his host being comforted with early coffee, the quartermaster could not help but note how wistfully the old soldier's eyes kept turning to the northern road. An inspiration seized him.

"Look here, colonel, it's going to be a hot day, and those fellows would be glad of a little ice. Suppose we take my buckboard and drive out and meet them?" And Thornton, after the proper amount of hesitancy as to taking an officer away from his duties, gladly assented. So the quartermaster ordered out his team, and by six o'clock they were bowling over the magnificent prairie road, with the sun clambering higher every minute, and with a couple of buckets of ice, blanket-swathed, swinging under the rear axle. Two hours later, rounding a bold shoulder of bluff among the bends of the Pawnee Gorge, they caught sight of white wagon-covers halted at a little clump of willows half a mile ahead. "Hurrah! Yonder they are at the Springs," said the quartermaster.

And there they found them. Two or three soldiers were passing cups of the cool, sparkling water to the fevered hands under the canvas screens. The young doctor, dismounted, catching sight of the coming buckboard, sauntered forward to meet it, in hopes of letters. One glance at the gray-moustached soldier by the driver's side was enough.

With extended hand he hastened to help him alight, as the quartermaster reined in his braying mules.

"Colonel Thornton, I feel certain," said he. "Yonder's your boy in the ambulance,—jolly as any Mark Tapley you ever heard of." And Thornton, unable at the moment to speak a word, grasped and shook the doctor's hand, bowed his gray head, and passed him by.

"There's a meeting that would disarm the cynicism of a Carlyle," said the doctor, an instant later, though both men turned their backs and looked away, for under the lifted curtain of his trundling litter Perry had peeped and seen his father's face,—the father whom he supposed two thousand miles away.

Just before noon that day, under the doctor's careful supervision, the wounded were being lifted from the wagons and borne beneath the canvas flies stretched for them in the coolest and breeziest part of the quartermaster's guarded corral. Perry, boy-like, had insisted on scrambling out on his feet, partly to show how lively he was, partly that he might be close at hand when there was borne with measured tread and gentle hands the prostrate form of a trooper whose flushed face and twitching hands and glittering eyes proved him to be in the clutch of burning fever. About his litter, anxiety in every look, hovered the colonel and his wounded boy, for there lay gallant Schramm, blind to their solicitude, deaf to any word of cheer.

"I think we can bring him round in a few days of quiet here," said Dr. French, "but quiet we must have."

"Well, sir," said the colonel, decidedly, "we don't leave here until you do. There are mother and sisters hungering at home to get at Perry, but neither my boy nor I can turn a back on a soldier like Schramm. Let me know just what he needs, and every cent we've got is at your service."

"It is a serious fever, I fear," said the doctor, "but what he needs most now is absolute repose. We've got to guard him against disturbance of any kind."

"Do you mean he can't be moved at all, doctor?" asked a man who, with one or two other civilians, had entered the enclosure despite the efforts of the corral-master, who, positive at first in his refusal, had stepped back bewildered at sight of a formidable paper.

"Certainly," said Dr. French, shortly, with the "Who are you?" expression that comes into the faces of the most even-tempered of men when disturbed in the midst of their duties.

"Then we've simply got to camp here till he can be,—me and my party."

"You have? I'd like to know why."

"'Cause I don't mean to lose my position through losing him. Here's my warrant. That man's wanted for the Minden robbery."

XIII.

It was July before the sheriff of Latimer County would have been allowed the undisputed custody of the person of Trooper Schramm, and by that time the sheriff began to wonder whether he really wanted him or not. To begin with, the young German lay at Pawnee for nearly a week in about the hottest fever Dr. French had ever encountered. The infantry went on home to Ransom with most of Thornton's little squad and the wounded, but Colonel Thornton's influence with his old comrade the adjutant-general of the department was amply sufficient to have the doctor and some attendants remain there with his son and Schramm. There were days of delirium in which the young Prussian babbled of the Rhineland, of home and mother, of old days in saddle with the Hussars on the sunny slopes beyond Metz, of mad envy at sight of Bredow's squadrons riding away eastward from the heights of Tronville, down the sheltering ravine, then up the slopes again and, in headlong charge, full on the front of the battling French. Then, exultant, he seemed to hear the longed-for order for his own fellows, to recall the keen soldier rivalry between Uhlan, cuirassier, and hussar as the three regiments "lined up" for their charge, with dragoons and hussars in support, and with the August sun just sinking in the west they swooped down upon the arrayed divisions of Montern and Clerambault to the north of Mars-la-Tour. And then he lived again the perilous hour of his first experience with the Sioux, and poured out his heart in gratitude to the officer who so pluckily saved him. Old Thornton, sitting by his camp cot, his father-heart yearning over his own boy lying in placid slumber close at hand, learned enough to guide him in a letter to the American legation at Berlin,—a soldier father's letter to another soldier father in a foreign land, angered at and estranged from the son of whose very existence, perhaps, he was in doubt. The letter was posted before Thornton heard him babble of other names, and tell of the gnädige Fräulein, Morgan's oldest child, and with grave face the colonel rose and looked at his sleeping boy, and went out upon the breezy prairie, walking for hours before his return. Many things did Schramm mutter and murmur and reveal that Thornton could not understand at all, but he knew enough German to divine much of the soldier's past, and to demand of his son what letter was that he sent to Constance Morgan; whereat Perry, looking much amazed, answered, with all promptitude, "Letter to Connie Morgan? Why, certainly! I wrote to her the second day out from Ransom to tell her what you told me about promotion and to ask her to send us the measures for her father's belt and helmet. The men of the old troop were bound to send him his captain's shoulder-knots, and some one suggested that it might be a pious idea to chip in and order a complete new outfit, helmet and knots and belt and all,— just to surprise him. Some thought he might take offence, but old Tintop swore he shouldn't." And Thornton *père* walked out again. Perry had never lied to him in his life. Would it be fair to ask the boy if he had been making love to Morgan's motherless daughter?

But within the week the crisis was over: Schramm was out of danger. Mother and sisters were clamoring for Perry at home, so eastward went the colonel and his boy, and presently, by easy stages, westward went Schramm, his escort camping at Alkali, crossing to the north bank and going on to Minden, where camp was made again, and where Mr. Fisk, the agent, came over, ostensibly to see if he could be of any service, and then went back to his office and said to a deputy sheriff that if that was one of the men who came in with the despatch that Friday morning of the 1st of June he'd changed so he couldn't tell him.

Meantime, Rand had been clear around to the agency by the other route, and turned up again at Butte the day Schramm was returned to Ransom. "Don't you disturb him, Mr. Sheriff," said he; "and just take my advice now, don't go too fast on this trail; you may get in so far you can't get back—with credit to yourself." And out at the post the doctor had given strict orders that nobody should breathe in Schramm's hearing what everybody knew,—that he was "wanted" for the Minden robbery. "My first duty is to see him restored to health and strength," said he: "then the law must take its course." And so, with the regiment long miles away, Schramm lay patiently in hospital, tenderly thought for by every one, frequently remembered through the mails by the distant family of Thorntons, promoted corporal of his troop in regimental orders promulgated from head-quarters in the field and read to the whole assembled command both there and here at Ransom, reciting the heroic nature of his conduct in the affair at Slaughter Cove and the skill and bravery with which, his superiors being disabled by wounds, he had conducted the defence. All this was very pleasant to Schramm, whose eyes lighted with joy when Morgan, his captain now, and Jeffers, invalided by wounds, and Treacy ditto, all came in to congratulate him; but the sweetest thing in life to the convalescing soldier was the sight of Connie Morgan's pretty face when, regularly as the day came round, the gnädige Fräulein appeared with some little bunch of wild flowers, some little dainty or cool drink, but always with her gentle voice and soft brown eyes and sweet, serious smile, to ask how the corporal was feeling this bright day. The only trouble now was that he began to get well too fast. His fellow non-commissioned officers, Jeffers and Treacy, limping in one day, said there was a big row among the railway people all over the East. "Riots and ructions" had followed. The militia and police were whipped. The regiment had been whisked in from the field, piled into passenger-cars, and sent away towards Omaha, and they, the wounded of the Indian war, were losing this trip to civilization and beyond. Next day Rhett and his men were suddenly telegraphed for, and again was Captain Morgan both ordnance- and commanding officer.

And then one beautiful day Schramm sent for Mrs. Hinkel and his box, and she, weeping, came to Constance, and together they appealed to Morgan, and then the old man in the new shoulder-straps realized that the matter could no longer be hidden, and before nightfall Schramm learned that he was under the surveillance of the sheriff, charged with being accessory to the robbery of Paymaster Graves, at least to the extent of receiving and concealing a certain part of the money. And Schramm, speechless with wrath and amaze, stood attention to his captain on the hospital porch, and simply quivered and shook and clinched his hands. Morgan made him sit down, and, prefacing his statement with the assurance that no one who knew him believed him in the faintest way connected with the robbery, went on to say there were certain matters that, unexplained, seemed to point to him with the finger of suspicion. He and Schultz left camp on Bear Fork toward half-past twelve A.M., and though they started back by the trail of the regiment they had probably left it and borne away over to the south so as to ride along the bank of the Ska, in plain view of Minden, ten minutes after the departure of No. 3 and just after the robbery. A Mr. Long had seen two troopers on roans riding briskly west at that time. The operator said the troopers had come in before-hand with the false despatch, and he thought they might have looked like Schultz and Schramm. The paymaster couldn't be sure,—couldn't identify him; but Mr. Lacy, the clerk, had described the two who met them at the train and led them back from the dépôt while he followed in rear, and Lacy's description certainly pointed to them. Then on reaching the garrison Schramm had gone to Mrs. Hinkel, got his box, put a package in it and charged her on no account to let it fall into other hands, and this box the sheriff had opened in presence of the commanding officer, and the first thing found was an envelope containing five hundred dollars in fifties, which Lacy was ready to swear was some of the lot taken from the paymaster's valise. Then they were in town together and hurried away the moment they learned that the robbery was known and soldiers suspected, and instead of returning to the regiment they had turned off and gone away northward through Wagon Gap until met and run back by the Sioux. This, said Morgan, was the case against him as far as he knew.

Schramm's first question was as to the letters and papers : where were they? "Sealed up and safe," said Morgan. "We have the officer's pledge as to that. So is the money sealed up." But Schramm didn't seem to care about the money. That was of little consequence. He could explain at once where it came from. A draft from the old country had reached him early in May at a time when he wished to use money, and Schultz cashed it for him. Schultz would not put his savings in the Butte banks. His money was in Chicago. He had had money sent out to him by express. This could be verified at the express-office, and the draft could doubtless be traced back through Schultz's Chicago banker. As for their taking the Minden road, it was not much longer, they had plenty of time, and the road near the river was prettier. Close to the bridge on the south side they had seen some horses held by one or two men just as the train pulled away. Then away over by the dépôt were some fellows who appeared to be wearing cavalry overcoats, ranchmen probably who were going to drive out some distance, as troopers wouldn't think of wearing overcoats in June. They were interested watching the distant train, however, speeding away westward, and they rode at a brisk lope up the valley, never thinking of the party of men and horses again until that afternoon. Then, hearing of the robbery, it flashed upon them that they had seen the perpetrators, and back they went, heard of them down the stream drinking and quarrelling among themselves, were close on their trail opposite Wagon Gap, and decided to follow, thinking they might possibly overhaul and recapture some of them, at least, with the result already known. Beyond the Cove they came upon Stearns and his boy racing back for their lives, pursued by Indians. No time to ask questions then. It was fight for life against the common foe. The man was killed before he could tell his story, and now Schultz was gone. Schramm had to face it alone.

"No, not alone," said Morgan. "We believe you guiltless and

mean to see you through." And then Colonel Rand came out to see him. What Rand wanted was to know what had been done with the papers, etc., taken from the civilian who died of his wounds at the Cove. All Schultz's effects, of course, were in the hands of the officers whose duty it was to take charge of the papers and property of deceased soldiers. Rand said the boy had been taken to an asylum and was recovering, but had neither money nor papers of any kind. Schramm could hardly be persuaded to sit in the presence of an officer of such distinction as Rand, but succumbed to orders. A wallet with letters and papers and a little money, a silver watch, and a tobacco-box, had been taken from the body before burial. These were all turned over to Captain Fenton when he came. The man's name was Stearns, and his post-office address Minden. And then up jumped Rand with light in his eyes.

"That's what I wanted to know," said he. "I thought I'd seen that poor boy before.—Now, corporal, don't worry about this matter. We could acquit you easily enough, but there's something else to be done. We want to nail the real perpetrators and get that money back if possible: so the trial can't come off just yet."

"But—pardon, colonel," said Schramm, rising again. "May I not my box have? There are letters, portraits,—home-gifts." And Rand said he was going in to see the sheriff then and there.

A month the troops from the plains were kept on duty in and around the railway-centres of the West. Four long weeks the garrison at Ransom consisted of Morgan, the surgeon, the band, the ordnance-sergeant and clerk, quartermaster, employees, and so on, with the hospital steward and attendants, the sick and wounded. Schramm, convalescing rapidly now, was assigned to daily duty at the adjutant's office. Jeffers, still limping a little, with Treacy and others, became the nucleus of a species of running guard, and did patrol and watch duty. The railway company, grateful for the services of the troops in saving their property, sent a sleeper to Butte and an invitation for such of the officers' families as would like to go to Chicago, Omaha, or wheresoever the husband and father might be, as the guests of the road, and many went, and Rand wrote asking for "Connie and the kids" to come on and pay Mrs. Rand a visit, but Connie wouldn't go. Who would take care of daddy? she asked, nestling her face against that veteran's stubbly cheek; and Morgan gave it up.

The sheriff, who had been a frequent visitor, quit coming out to the post, and began to talk around town about the way the fort people had behaved from the start in this robbery business. He would have had the robbers at the time, only the cavalry had interfered. He and his posse would have nabbed those fellows skipping for Tomahawk Range if it hadn't been that those d—d meddlers of troopers drove them beyond his jurisdiction. The Tomahawk was the name given the black-fringed spur that came down from the mountains west of Wagon Gap almost to the valley of the Ska. It was famous for bear, elk, and black-tail deer, and all its length, except a few miles at the southern end, lay within the Sioux reservation, and no one could go thither to shoot except by previous arrangement with the agency people. Nevertheless old Stearns, the recent victim of Sioux vengeance, had for more than a year kept a shooting-box somewhere in the mountains, where with his half-witted boy he lived a hermit life, coming down to Minden very seldom, yet frequently being seen about the agency at the north. Keen sportsmen of Omaha, Yankton, and Sioux City, it was said, sometimes made up hunting-parties, and, having properly and previously "fixed" the Sioux chiefs through agency interpreters, went up by way of the Indian villages and, with Indian guides, had many a day of famous shooting, and came home, the envied of their kind, with a baggage-car-load of carcasses they could not always even give away. The strikes and riots ended, it suddenly occurred to Colonel Rand that he hadn't shot a bear in years, so he went up around by the all-rail route, taking a couple of friends, and such was his enthusiasm that he could not hear enough about what other parties had been doing in that line. Game-laws did not obtain on Indian lands in those days, except such as the Indian and his keepers agreed upon, and even late in May, it seems, some eager sportsmen had come out from the Missouri and gone into the Tomahawk Range, guided by a clerk in the agency and "Lame Johnny," a half-bred Sioux. For a man so interested at the start, it must be owned that Rand tired rather soon of the sport. He left his friends at the agency after a day or two of desultory shooting, and went back to head-quarters.

Then the troops began to reappear at their old station, as their services were no longer needed; and the August suns were beating hot and dry on the valley of the Ska; and presently Old Tintop and the Eleventh were once more restored to Ransom, and began the work of straightening out their quarters and stables, and the new first lieutenant of Troop D saluted his predecessor, its present captain, and Schramm blushingly invited his brother non-commissioned officers, all who could be spared, one evening after their duties at the post to meet him at Conway's restaurant in town, where a bountiful supper was provided, and where each man was regaled with such drink as he most fancied, and where Schramm in a very effective little speech proposed the health of their new captain, which they drank with cheers, and the memory of their gallant comrade Schultz, which they honored in soldier silence. Nothing like this had happened in the annals of the regiment. "Why, it must have cost him sixty or seventy dollars," said Sergeant Bowman, as they rode back to the post that night. One of their number in jocular mood thought it appropriate to ask Schramm had he been "holding up" another paymaster, or was this what was left of the last one? whereat Schramm looked his interrogator full in the face a few seconds without so much as changing color or saying a word, and then, turning calmly away, resumed his chat with their first sergeant, who as the senior guest at the feast was placed at the right hand of their host. It was evident that Schramm would have no witticism on that head.

But if Schramm took it in dignified silence, the sheriff did not. It grew to be the popular thing for the troopers just then to hail this magnate with the query, "Hullo, sheriff, when's the trial coming off?" The "boys," as they sometimes called themselves, had much resented it that the officials and the public were so ready to accept the theory that only members of the Eleventh Cavalry could have planned and perpetrated the deed. Hence, as time wore on and the evidence against Schultz and Schramm wore off and the sheriff seemed drifting further from a solution of the mystery, the boys took keener delight in chaffing the civil authority on the public streets and inspiring him to mighty blasphemy and portentous threat.

"You fellows had better keep civil tongues in your heads," said he, with many a lurid expletive, the night after the Schramm supper. "You may think it d—d smart to chaff about this. Perhaps you soldiers can turn to now and catch the fellers that ran off with your money. If it wasn't soldiers that did it, by —, I'll lay any bet no soldier can say who else done it."

A week later, however, when the story of the sheriff's wager, "with weeping and with laughter," was being told at Ransom in connection with the liveliest episode in Ransom annals, there fell from the oracular lips of Mrs. Whaling, the relict of a former commanding officer and now a prominent figure in Butte society, the memorable words, "Well, I guess he wishes he hadn't been so precipitous."

XIV.

Pay-day at the post! Old Curran had ordered an extra **stand** put up in the bar-room, an extra load of keg beer out from Butte, and a choice supply of *cabbageros* for the defenders of their country's flag, who on these occasions deemed it their duty not to be seen out of ranks without a weed in their teeth, no matter how high in price nor how low in grade. The laundresses, arrayed in their best bib and tucker and smiles, had spread the cloth in their shanties down under the hill, with the bucket of punch and dozen of tumblers in readiness for callers,—it being one of the unwritten laws of the rank and file in the good old days to square with the laundress if you didn't square with anybody else. The non-commissioned staff, the band, and the troops had all been ordered to hold themselves in readiness,—the one function of the military year in which such orders were totally unnecessary, even the sick in hospital manifesting a strong desire to get up and go to duty, on that day at least; and Lieutenant Phipps with twenty troopers had met Paymaster Graves as he and Mr. Lacy stepped forth from No 3, bustled them into the waiting ambulance and around the corner to the express-office, where they receipted for the little iron safe, and then at spanking trot set forth across the prairie and were deposited at the hospitable door of Old Tintop, where breakfast awaited the major, where his safe was stored *pro tempore* under the vigilant eye of the officer of the guard, while Mr. Lacy, pleading previous engagement, begged to be excused and went to take his sustenance under the Currans' roof. Guard was mounted in full-dress uniform at the usual hour, everybody being out for to see, and Gray being in his glory. Even more than usually jubilant and stirring were the strains of the band as, to the rollicking airs from "Arrah na Pogue," the yellow-crested column came swinging around in review, for it was "Cavalry Day,"—one of Tintop's fads being that it spoiled the ceremony and ruined the guard to have foot and troopers march on together. "Uniform, arms, and manual are all unlike," said he, "so what's the use? They no more mix than oil and vinegar: we're the oil and you're the vinegar." And so, being a favorite at department head-quarters, the old fellow had been sustained in his idea of having alternate guard, cavalry one day and infantry the next,—a system which worked in with the "percentage" fairly well and which the colonel pronounced a triumphant success, "and anybody who don't believe it had better not say so."

Then, right after guard-mounting, in their full-dress uniforms, with gloves and side-arms, the garrison was paraded for payment. Graves sat beside a table in the administration room, big stacks of greenbacks,—tens, five, twos, and ones,—and cylindrical columns of silver and nickel, in front of him. Off to his left, muster- and pay-roll of the first detachment, head-quarters staff, and band open on the table before him, his keen eyes glancing about the room and studying every face, sat Lacy. The adjutant took a seat at another little table, midway between the paymaster and the door, with his duplicate roll, and, all being ready, called the sergeant-major's name. Mr. Lacy called out the amount due. The paymaster rapidly counted out the money and handed it to the soldier who stood attention in front of the desk. The staff and band were speedily settled with and sent about their business. Then came the senior captain with his company, a change of rolls, and so for three hours, without incident of any kind, the interesting yet monotonous ceremony went on. Not until near noon did it come the turn of the captain youngest in commission at the post, and then at last D Troop came swinging across the parade from their barracks, and gray-haired Morgan took the little table just left vacant by Captain Prime. The windows were open, and a soft air was blowing through, and yet it seemed hot and oppressive.

"This is the last company, is it?" said Graves. "Thank God! I'm about tired out now. All ready, captain?"

"All ready, sir," answered Morgan, and then called "First Sergeant Warren."

A buggy drove up in front of the office, and some of the men nudged one another. It was the sheriff who alighted, followed by Colonel Rand. Behind them came another, and a deputy or two in the saddle. D Troop, standing at ease along the gallery in front of the administration building and from there to the walk leading to the gate, exchanged remarks in an undertone as to the cause of this sudden and suspicious arrival, but no one within the building apparently took notice thereof. A long hall ran through the building from east to west. The men entered the room by the door at the east end, and, receiving their pay, passed out through the other, and so to the rear porch. The paymaster and his clerk sat facing the door at the eastward end of the big room, with their backs to the northern windows, and so took no note of a party passing around on that side of the building. Several officers, clerks, etc., were grouped about the room west of the pay-table, and these were presently reinforced by the new arrivals,—Rand entering, followed by the sheriff and others, but signalling to the officers who greeted him to make no unnecessary to-do. By this time Morgan had read down among the names of his corporals. Rand, quietly suppressing the greetings accorded him, made it known that he wished to listen a moment. Corporal Treacy had just picked up his money, faced to his left, and made room for the next man. "Corporal Hugo V. Schramm," called the captain, and, straight as an arrow, quick, lithe, soldier all over, in stepped the man of Slaughter Cove, hand at visor in salute as he halted. Lacy glanced quickly, curiously up and studied the clear-cut face an instant with his steely blue eyes, then as quickly dropped them. Graves, too, looked up in mingled interest and embarrassment. Here stood the soldier virtually branded by him and his as a robber, yet pronounced by officers and comrades a hero. Graves felt that his first impulse was to hold forth his hand, but it occurred to him that that would hardly be in accordance with military propriety and etiquette. "I should like to see you, corporal, after we finish," said he, in a most conciliatory tone. Schramm thrust his money into the palm of his left-hand glove, saluted precisely, and, merely saying, "Yes, sir," strode away to the west door, but there his name was called in low tone and he halted. An officer beckoned to him to wait, and, wondering not a little, he stopped, then turned to a vacant corner behind Rand.

Rapidly the list was finished, the last man paid. The paymaster stretched his legs and arms and looked around for some one to suggest an adjournment to the club-room, and the first thing he saw was Rand, with the sheriff in his trail, and Graves's eyes began to dilate. Lacy was repacking coin and paper money at the instant and bending over a leather satchel which he had placed on his chair. A strange and sudden silence had fallen upon the crowded room. Old Tintop from his office across the hall, with faithful Gray at his elbow, came lounging to the door, and, catching sight of the civilian garb, stopped short and glared. Lacy, just snapping the clasp of his bag, felt the sudden fall

K *

of a muscular hand on his shoulder, and, with a perceptibly violent start, looked up. The bearded face of Colonel Rand was close at his side, the dark eyes sternly fixed upon him, and Lacy turned ashen and his limbs began to tremble and quiver, despite his fiercest effort, for there confronting him stood the sheriff of Latimer County, a pair of steel wristlets in his extended hands.

XV.

The sensation caused by the arrest of Mr. Lacy, the paragon of paymasters' clerks, as he had been described in one of his letters of recommendation, ended not with the going down of the sun that day, nor many thereafter. Graves himself sat in a state bordering on collapse for a few hours after the occurrence.

"Why, that gentleman was recommended by half the Senate, and almost insisted on by my bondsmen," said he, with tears in his eyes. "What will they say to me? Why, Rand, he actually had to be named as my clerk before I could be confirmed at all." To which the imperturbable inspector-general responded, "Yes, no doubt. You see, Graves, they had to get him out of Washington: he knew too much;" and when Graves besought him to say why he suspected the paragon, Rand serenely answered he didn't; he *had* suspected him a month ago, perhaps, but now he *knew:* so should everybody else just as soon as the case could be brought to trial. But meantime other entertainment was provided for the cavalry. Even while Lacy was frantically sending telegrams and letters to officials of high degree all over the East, demanding investigation, vindication, etc., there came an order for the immediate detachment of three of Tintop's companies to take the field far to the northwest. D Troop went as a matter of course. This time Schramm did not have to ask "to go along mit dem fellers." It was their veteran captain who was left behind.

Just as Perry Thornton had told his father, the men of the troop, thankful for, yet declining, the proffered subscription of the officers, had ordered from the East as handsome an outfit of belt, helmet, spurs, shoulder- and sabre-knots, as money could buy, Connie alone of the household being in the secret. Her father never again had asked to see Thornton's letter, and she, who once had been so insistent, ceased all mention of it or of its writer. The glow of delight with which the child had received and read that jolly, warm-hearted, yet utterly unsentimental note had opened the father's eyes no more than it had her own. Constance Morgan stepped from girl- to womanhood in the day and hour which taught her how, little by little, there had been kindled in her heart a tiny flame of tenderness that burned as incense at the altar,—an offering at the shrine wherein the boy sat installed, the hero of a girl's imaginative and impulsive nature. With what burning cheeks did she own it to herself! With what womanly shame did she realize that she had betrayed it ere she herself fairly knew of its existence! She!—an army girl, a soldier's daughter, with Lot and Billy to look after, with dear old daddy to nurse and comfort,—she, Constance Morgan, daring to indulge in idle day-dreaming over a boy in his first uniform! It was simply shameful. She could have scratched the eyes out of any woman who saw her poring over that letter, had there been any there to see. She raged within herself to think that for that moment she had been blind and deaf to her father's presence and lost in reading Thornton's laughing words. No one on earth ever knew what pangs of maidenly wrath and shame "Little Mother" endured for several days, but whenever after that initial exhibition Morgan looked for further symptom of sentimental regard for the absent lieutenant, he failed entirely, and wished that he might write himself an ass for ever having believed it.

The presentation came off at the assembly-room one lovely evening in July, Sergeant Jeffers being spokesman for the troop and utterly routing Morgan, who knew not how to formulate reply to words so rich with soldierly trust and affection. Close behind the speaker stood Corporal Schramm, his glistening eyes fixed on Connie's beautiful, blushing face, with its swimming eyes, for Jeffers's voice was tremulous when he went on to say how for ten long years the old hands had soldiered under Morgan and never once could recall a harsh or an unjust word, never once a day when his voice or heart or hand had failed them when they looked to him for leadership or aid. The old fellow was worn and ill and heavily laden, and this unlooked-for tribute from his men completely floored him. "Why, men," he stammered, "I—always stood by you as a matter of course. I never dreamed of doing anything else. What's an officer for, if it isn't to be a friend and leader to his own troop first of all? I'm more obliged to you than you can imagine. This isn't strictly according to law and regulations, I am afraid, and if I'd got wind of it in any way before, I should have stopped it; but precedents seem to be plenty of late, and I only wish I might think it would be my luck to wear them as your captain for years to come, but your old lieutenant makes an older captain, and I'm soon to step aside for a younger soldier and better man; but so long as I live, men, this gift of yours and these words of Jeffers's will—will—— God bless you all, lads, I can't finish it."

And then the men in their full-dress uniforms had escorted their captain and Connie and the invited guests homeward that night, and the first thing when father and daughter were left alone old Morgan turned to Connie.

"So that was what Thornton's letter was about, was it, Connie?"

"Certainly, father," she replied, looking straight into his eyes with those clear brown orbs of hers. "What else could it have been?" And that was the last mentioned of the subject between them.

Each and every one, the men had shaken hands with their captain and pledged his health in the foaming beer old Curran had insisted on "setting up" for the occasion. They swore, soldier-like, they'd never let the captain retire; but that was a matter beyond their jurisdiction. Wind and weather and many a worry laid the veteran by the heels, and his old enemy, rheumatism, took fresh and forcible hold. When D Troop rode away to take the field, poor Morgan was groaning both in flesh and spirit, and when late that autumn Schramm came posting homeward under subpœna to testify *in re* The People *vs.* Lacy, the chevrons of a sergeant decked his sleeves in recognition of a ride of over a hundred miles through Indian-haunted wilds to bear despatches to a distant command, but neither captain nor Connie was there to bid him welcome. The lonely grave out on the prairie lacked the bunch of wild flowers which formerly decked it every Sunday morning. The old quarters down the row were peopled by strangers to the German soldier now. The sweet face of the gnädige Fräulein smiled no more from the dormer window over the veranda: the Morgans, one and all, were gone. A retiring board had pronounced the old dragoon unfit for further service, and with his own fuel and quarters to furnish now as best he could, with no more medical attendance or supplies from Uncle Sam, with all the brood to feed and clothe and educate, without a word of aid or welcome from the kinsfolk in the East, poor Morgan meekly took his discharge and his retired pay, and a tiny two-storied cottage in an out-of-the-way street in Butte, and strove to set up housekeeping with Connie at the head and a Chinese man-of-all-work at the foot of the new establishment. Rand had been to see them and urged their all coming eastward awhile as his guests at home, but the railroad company had offered Morgan a little berth which he considered it his duty to accept at once, and Connie scouted the idea of her being in need of rest or change; she could not think of leaving father; and within the month it seemed as though her vision were preternaturally clear, for presently poor Morgan could not leave the house at all. It was at this stage of the proceedings that as Connie, broom in hand, and an old silk handkerchief over her head, was sweeping out the hall one sharp October morning, the Chinaman having been discharged as the result of a strike for more wages and less work, she sent a whirl of dust upon the glistening boots of a statuesque trooper with hand at salute and blue eyes beaming in delight at sight of his friend the captain's daughter.

"Oh, Schr-r-r-amm!" she cried, throwing down her besom and joyously grasping his gauntleted hand. "Where did you come from? Come right in; papa will be so glad!—Here's Schramm—Sergeant Schramm, daddy dear;" and, first closing the outer door, she opened that which led to the Den, and ushered the sergeant in and watched with glistening eyes the greeting of the two soldiers. Schramm must stay and take luncheon with them. "We are no longer on duty, lad," said Morgan, with a sad smile, "and if you'll have a bite with us and tell us all about the old troop it'll be a comfort." And Connie's eyes and lips were even more insistent. Off came the blue overcoat, and there in all the glossy sheen of the new, snug-fitting blouse, with the triple bars of his sergeant's chevrons, the athletic frame of their soldier guest stood revealed, and they made him sit, and Connie poured his tea and bustled in and out of the kitchen, and Schramm sat with his old captain and talked by the hour of the troop, and how well Jeffers held his own now as first sergeant, and what a fine soldier Treacy was, and yet—he did not say how or why, but fast as their term of service expired the old hands took their discharge, and then "took on" in some other troop. And all the time he talked, whensoever she flitted in or out or by, the blue eyes would follow and were full of light and reverence and watchful care. It was as he walked slowly away, two hours later, eagerly promising to come again, that those same blue eyes were clouded with deep anxiety,—Morgan was failing so fast.

The trial, he told them, was to begin forthwith; but it never did.

In some of Lacy's appealing letters to former employers in official station in Washington reference was made to the malignant hatred of Colonel Rand as the inspiration of all their proofless and damnable accusations, and these getting to the War Department and so coming to Rand for remark, the placid colonel finally waxed indignant. It was bad enough, said he, that Lacy should be an expert thief and blackleg, but that to cover his own tracks and those of his pals he should seek the ruin of innocent men was rather too much of a good thing. Then the general came back from the field about this time; Rand made his report, and on went a four-page letter to Washington reciting briefly the evidence now in their possession as affecting Lacy. This was shown to the ex-clerk's friends at court, and two letters from the East, after being opened and examined by the sheriff, were handed in to Lacy's cell the day after Schramm's arrival. That night the prisoner asked for more paper and permission to write till late, and when morning came the neatly-folded document proved to be the final statements of the clerk who had cashed so many papers of that name within the past year—but would cash no more. What was left of Lacy lay stiffening on the narrow cot. The night-watch had not even heard him groan.

A fellow of much inventive genius was Lacy, and of uncommon usefulness until luck turned. Cards, mining stocks, wheat, wine, and women all combined against him. He had to cover the money abstracted to pay his losses and put up more margins. He owed still more, and his creditors, gamblers like himself, said, "Pay or we peach." There was just one way to "raise the wind" without reaping the whirlwind: the paymaster must be robbed on the very next trip; and the plan was to have the train "held up," until the sudden move of the cavalry suggested an easier way. Out went two of his sportsmen friends with letters of introduction to the hunter hermit in the Tomahawk Range. Down they went with him as their guide and companion and scout. Cavalry overcoats and slouch-hats and equipments such as were worn in the field in those days were to be had almost anywhere. Armed with their bogus despatch, they rode to Minden, dodging Sergeant Dolan's escort from Bear Fork to Alkali. Leaving their horses with the boy at the bridge, the three men received the paymaster and Lacy at the station to which he had been lured, and the rest was easy until it came to getting away with the money. The hermit forbade their returning by way of his hut, as they would be trailed thither and he and his boy instantly suspected. They must go farther east, by way of Wagon Gap, and back to the agency with their game, as though from innocent and successful hunt. But, in dodging the troops and certain couriers they saw, time was lost, in which they got to drinking and quarrelling. Lacy's friends were two well-known contractors for Indian supplies, long accustomed to agency ways, well versed in Indian affairs, and often suspected of being knaves of deeper dye than mere swindlers of the aborigines, which species of crime was not bereft of virtue in frontier eyes. They were known to the trade by the names of Stein and Wirtz, and their intimacy with Lacy and certain employees of the quartermaster department had attracted Rand's attention to them months before the robbery. Hearing of their absence from town, he traced them to the agency, thence to the range beyond, and found that the date of their return that way corresponded exactly with that of Thornton's fight. Young Stearns had at last made a coherent statement. Promising to give his luckless father his share as soon as they got back within sight of that harbor of refuge, but plying him with liquor all the time, these men rode to Fossil Creek in company, then gave their dozing guide the slip and dashed rapidly ahead. Being aware of the Indian outbreak, they probably studied the country with their glasses and saw the commotion among the distant war-parties, and so dodged into the range away from the road, and by a wide détour got safely in, while their hapless guide, following in drunken pursuit, ran foul of the Sioux, was chased and killed. Wisely they hid such of the money as they did not need at the moment, and kept away from head-quarters and Lacy awhile, until the announcement in the papers that the crime had been definitely fixed on the soldiers Schultz and Schramm gave them courage to unearth their plunder and fetch it nearer home. Not that they intended to divide with Lacy by any means,—he was in their toils now, and could be further bled,—but to hold him with mingled threat and promise. And all the time Rand was weaving his web about them. The more coherent statements of the half-witted son, now being gradually restored to such intellect as he possessed, had given ample clue, and the arrest of Lacy at Ransom was the result of a despatch to Rand that his confederates had been pounced upon the previous night at Yankton with over ten thousand dollars of the stolen money in their possession. So long as they did not peach, however, Lacy was still safe, and he played the indignant and wronged and faithful servant, and played it well, for just six weeks; then "Dux femina facti"—the woman who was leader—by the nose—of the triumvirate, and the recipient of much of their stolen plunder, was also arrested when on the wing to the East, and—she couldn't keep a secret; her circumstantial confession of the whole business from beginning to end, made when hoping to win exemption for herself, ended the battle. Then Lacy's own hand penned his parting words and freed his shame-stricken soul.

"It was a well-planned job," said Rand, "on Lacy's part at least, but it had its leak so long as there was a woman in it."

And now, as his evidence was no longer needed, Sergeant Schramm had no further business at either Butte or Ransom. "But you don't want to go back that long distance alone," said Old Tintop. "We can assign you to duty here until your troop comes home next month." And, to the adjutant's infinite surprise, Schramm eagerly assented.

October went, and keener winds from the mountain-gorges and fiercer twinges in Morgan's legs reminded them that winter was at hand. Often now the post surgeon found means to ride over to Butte and see the failing soldier, and many a day officers or their wives contrived to visit town and dropped in to see Connie and offer aid and comfort to her father, but Connie declared she needed no help. She had an excellent servant now, a German woman whom Mrs. Hinkel brought to her, who cooked and washed and did almost everything for so small a sum that when the amount was mentioned I fear me there were women who were sorely tempted to offer the paragon twice as much to quit the Morgans and come to them, but they deserved the more honor that they promptly dismissed the unworthy thought. Connie said Mrs. Hinkel, too, was kind and useful in making things for the children, and Miss Franzen of the public school, who lived in the next block, took such interest in Lot and Billy and taught them so much. Why, they would really be in clover, were poor father only better. And then one evening when Schramm had ridden into town and left his horse at the Empire and had come promptly around to see the Herr Rittmeister, he was amazed to find a tall, gray-moustached, soldierly man seated by the captain's side, while there—right by Connie —in civilian dress stood a tall, slender young fellow at sight of whom the sergeant's eyes clouded, and he would have retired, but was too late, for with one leap Perry Thornton had him by the hand.

"Schramm, by all that's glorious! Father, look here!" And

before the Prussian ex-hussar could realize it, a veteran colonel of dragoons was wringing one of his hands, while the lieutenant clasped the other. Nor would they or the Morgans let him go.

"I have a letter from Berlin which I am charged to give you, Herr von Rhetz," said Thornton *père*, and at the name Schramm's lips quivered and twitched and he turned very white, but straight in the colonel's kindly face looked the unflinching eyes of blue.

Yet even then he would have asked to be permitted to retire,—the soldier in him shrinking from what he deemed intrusion, and a strange restless gnawing at his heart impelling him to go and leave them to the joy of a reunion in which no doubt he had really no place,—but, one and all, they forbade. Constance held in her hands two cabinet photographs, and Perry stepped forward, took one of these, and, holding it forth, said to Schramm,—

"If you need more reason, sergeant, here it is, for this is the picture of a young lady who says she must have yours, and quickly too."

"The young lady is most gracious, Herr Lieutenant,—and most beautiful," said Schramm, studying it attentively ; then, glancing up, "The lieutenant's sister?"

"Not quite," laughed Perry, blushing, "though that's what my sisters are beginning to call her—rather prematurely."

And then in his perplexity Schramm gazed past the handsome boy and sought Connie's face. It was beaming. "Pardon," he said, "I am so dull. Does the lieutenant mean it is his betrothed?"

"Yes, and we are here to drink her health,—we five."

For one moment Schramm's eyes sought doubtfully the eyes of the maiden who stood there so unflinchingly and smilingly before them, and then his hand went out in earnest.

XVI.

A winter of unusual severity was that which followed upon the heels of a summer campaign that had been full of lively excitement for Tintop and the regiment. Once more, however, the spirit of social gayety was abroad, and the Christmas holidays were merry with many a charming function. Hops, germans, dinners and luncheon-parties, theatricals, minstrels, and soldier balls, day after day and night after night, were in full career at Ransom, while dense and

blinding snow-storms blocked the roads and soon succeeded in making
the trip from fort to town more of a venture than the winter passage
of the Atlantic. Starting from town with sunshine and sleigh-bells,
one might encounter storm and tempest before half the distance was
traversed. December, though sharply cold, had been bright and
beautiful until about the 15th; then came the succession of blizzards
that cut communication almost entirely and caused a wail of dismay
from the shopkeepers of Butte, most of whom had laid in goodly
store of toys and trinkets for the delectation of their best customers,
the people out at the fort. The stage had to be taken off, and for days
the mails were carried to and fro in saddle. The doctors, senior and
junior, found plenty to do at the fort and little to tempt them elsewhere, so their visits to Morgan became infrequent. There was just
one man at the post whom no gale could daunt, no storm could con-
quer, and that was Schramm.

Every one knew that Morgan was slowly growing feebler. "He
ought to have gone to the Hot Springs long ago," said the doctor,
"but now it is too late." He could not stand the journey without
special attendants and accommodations, and those were things he could
not, and Uncle Sam would not, pay for. Knowing that he would have
nothing to leave, and deeming him near dissolution, his creditors were
hounding him again. If he lived, the fifty dollars per month would
gradually pay them off, but if he died there was nothing: hence the
renewed clamor for immediate settlement. The weather was bitter,
the little house cold and draughty, fuel was horribly expensive, and
there was the veteran dragoon, a helpless cripple, looking death in the
face and imploring him yet a little while to hold his hand, not that the
broken-spirited soldier might recover his strength,—he was past all
that,—but that he might linger on even in labor and sorrow, that with
his annuity he might save his children from utter destitution. Hours
he sat in loneliness, for it was impossible, save at rare intervals, for his
old comrades to reach him now. He wondered how Connie could sing
so happily about the house. Surely she and Bertha, the middle-aged
maid-of-all-work, had accomplished wonders with the little sum he
could devote to household expenses. Lot and Billy looked hearty
and rosy and well fed and clothed when they came tumbling noisily in
from school. Connie's sweet face and slender form were rounder. The
dark circles under the big brown eyes were gone. Here he was, hardly
daring to eat, thinking how soon they might be left without bite, sup,

or cent. Yet Connie smiled and sang, and was picking up little house-hold words and phrases in German, and blushingly accosted Schramm in his native tongue when Schramm came, as he rarely failed to come, twice, thrice, or oftener during the week, to pay his respects to the gnädige Fräulein, and to see what he could do for the Herr Rittmeister, who, ever since the day of the Thorntons' coming, had vainly protested against the further use of the name Schramm, had insisted that the time had come for the German sergeant to drop his punctilious observance of the deference due all superior officers, and had informed Connie that he should be addressed as Herr von Rhetz; but it was all to no purpose. Schramm forbade. "I left my name with my past when I came to enlist in this army," said he. "I had to win a future for myself, and so took my mother's name meantime. Call me by that so long as I wear the blue." Indeed, he couldn't bear to have the gnädige Fräulein address him as "sergeant" at all. He said that from the first he loved to watch her lips as she struggled with the combination that finally gave utterance to a Sch-r-r-ramm. There could be no question that he loved to watch her lips, no matter what she might be saying, and small blame to him either.

But out at Ransom Schramm was becoming a notability in earnest. Despite his plea to Colonel Thornton to keep secret as yet the story of his difference with his stern old father, his retirement from the German service, his practical banishment from home, and then the proffered forgiveness and reconciliation, there were so many suspicions that the Thorntons were plied with questions they could not altogether dodge. Every one knew by this time Schramm had money in plenty, and that it was deposited in a German bank in the East. "Yes," said Thorn-ton, "that was his mother's fortune, which had become his own;" but the colonel refused to tell more, saying the soldier had a perfect right to serve out his time as Schramm and nothing else. Everybody saw, however, the courtesy and distinction with which the Thorntons, father and son, treated him,—Perry, in fact, waxing hot and wanting to fight an ill-conditioned, cross-grained subaltern who sneered at him. Schramm's box was kept in the vault of the First National now, where the cashier and other officials would fain have treated him with greater deference than they showed his officers, had Schramm per-mitted it. He would never enter the bank when an officer was there, and should one happen in, even the veriest cub in the whole garrison, Schramm would spring back from the counter and stand attention and at salute, never presuming to come forward again until the shoulder-straps had vanished. This naturally gave umbrage to the public, which, very properly, preferred moneyed sergeants to mortgaged subs, but no one at the post could truthfully say that Schramm ever in the faintest way failed in the respect and deference due his superiors in grade.

On the other hand, there were those who saw that Schramm's new captain was taking frequent opportunity to treat the young German with scant courtesy; it was apparent from the moment of the return of the troop from the field. They had already begun the homeward march when Schramm was ordered by Tintop to await their return to head-quarters, but Captain Bragg declared that Schramm had shirked his duty with the troop. The medal of honor awarded him was presented by Tintop and pinned on Schramm's breast in presence of the whole command, and Bragg sneered at the colonel's commendatory remarks, and sneered again in Thornton's presence as the troop marched in from parade. Perry was already disgusted with having to serve longer in D Troop, but no transfer could be obtained. Schramm's duties in barracks and stables were most scrupulously performed, but never to the extent of winning expression of satisfaction from Bragg. Schramm rarely asked to be excused from duty, but often put in for a pass to go to town. There was no good reason for refusing so good a man, so Bragg growled and grumbled, and finally said he couldn't have his horses ridden all over creation, and Schramm must walk thereafter or hire a coach-and-four. Schramm never by word or sign showed irritation. He received the blunt, ill-natured reply with silent salute. He hired Curran's buggy, and then, an evening or two thereafter, just before stables, came loping back from Butte on a splendid bay, Lieutenant Edwards's favorite horse, which that officer had vainly asked three hundred for when he needed money to go East on sick-leave, and failing to obtain his price had sent him to the Empire stables in town. Schramm, it transpired, had bought the entire "outfit," equipments and all, but had the bridle and housings stored and replaced by modest black leather and dark blue blanket. Bragg forbade his keeping the horse in the troop stables, and Schramm, flushing slightly, replied, with the utmost self-command and respect, that he could not presume to think of such a thing. Mr. Curran had kindly consented to take charge of his horse in his private stable, where Schramm, you may depend upon it, paid roundly for forage and grooming. Then it next transpired that Schramm had named his new ac-

quisition "Rand," and, as Rand in his capacity as inspector-general
had frequently rapped Bragg over the knuckles, this gave greater
offence to Bragg. Then a famous opera-company, crossing the continent, struck a blizzard and were snow-bound in a special car at Butte.
There was a big hall with a fair-sized stage in town. The owner urged
a performance, and the manager agreed to give "Faust" on a guarantee
that took the owner's breath away. He braved the drifts, however,
and galloped out to the fort and told his story. "Go ahead," said
Tintop. "You shall have the band, and we'll all take seats." But
when he heard the price, Tintop retracted. "We can't stand the
figure—that is, I can't, and few of my officers can." Nevertheless the
owner found means to give the front row of the gallery, all around, at
a reduced rate, and there the fort contingent looked down on the two-
dollar seats in the so-called parquet, and just before the overture began
in marched forty sergeants, cavalry, infantry, and staff, from Ransom,
each man in his nattiest dress uniform, and took possession of the rows
of chairs reserved for them, and after the opera was over did these
non-commissioned officers adjourn to Conway's, where another bountiful
supper was spread in his big room, and then back to the fort in the
dawn of the frosty morning to the tune of soldier songs and merry
sleigh-bells. "Schramm's stag-party" was the talk of the post for a
week thereafter. Bragg thought it an outrage that enlisted men should
be allowed to sit in public entertainment in presence of their betters.
Tintop, on the contrary, said he was proud to see so many of his men
intelligent, soldierly, and so thoroughly capable of appreciating such
music and such a company. As for the opera people and the local
manager, they were enraptured. Connie, you may be sure, was there
to see. She and her friend Miss Franzen had been brought thither
and taken home in a carriage from the Empire, and invited and
escorted by the principal of the public school, to whom, it transpired
later, tickets as well as instructions had been sent beforehand, and it
was just about this time, just before Christmas, that somebody started
the new name for the blue-eyed Prussian, and Schramm, to his manifest
concern, was hailed as "Sergeant Crœsus."

The snow blockade was such that many children at the fort lost
their faith in Santa Claus. He who rode the snow-drifts and the
storm was barred at Ransom, yet seemed to swoop in force on Morgan's fireside. Brand-new sleds were there for Lot and Billy, and
another doll, and such stacks of furniture and boxes of leaden soldiers,

besides valuables of more practical sort. All these, together with
fruits and candies to be stuffed in their worn stockings, had been
smuggled in through the kitchen and the connivance of Bertha, and
with them were some costly books, Schramm's gifts to his honored
captain and brown-eyed Connie. He dared not offer half what his
heart longed to lay before them. They had a Christmas dinner, too,
that Bertha swore was her own production and inspiration. They had
remembrances from the fort that Schramm "packed" in on horseback.
Perry Thornton and others had by no means forgotten them, and
Schramm had blushingly called upon such kind friends to say he should
be only too glad to carry in anything they might wish to send. There
was no lack of Christmas cheer, even where one heart was so heavy as
poor Morgan's, and no one was allowed to dream how very much of
all this holiday feasting was due to Schramm. And so all through
the long hard winter, patient and reserved, assiduous in every duty at
the fort, yet finding frequent opportunity of visiting his friends in Butte,
Schramm held his way. Old Hinkel was made an ordnance sergeant
along in March, and with his wife and olive-branches took departure
for a far southern post, Schramm seeing them to the train and receiving tearful warmth of blessing from the honest frau by way of
good-by, and in April the doctors made more frequent trips to town,
for Morgan rallied but little with the lengthening days. It was evident that no bill of relief could bring lasting benefit here.

But, despite pain and hopelessness, Morgan clung to life with great
determination. Live he must for the babies' sakes, he said, and once
more now his days were brightened by visits from old friends, once
more in the sunny afternoons Perry Thornton dropped in for checkers
and campaigns or to show a new picture of his lady-love, Connie
sometimes sitting contentedly by, but generally busying herself with
Bertha about the house. And then, just as was sure to happen, came
the order for summer's work. "Away to the Big Horn!" said the
colonel, as he reined up one day at Morgan's open door, catching
Schramm in the act of blocking out a flower-garden for Lot and Billy.
And that evening before parade the regimental adjutant, seated at his
desk, was surprised by a visit from Sergeant Schramm, who begged of
that influential officer a few moments' interview.

"Young man," said Tintop to his staff officer, as he espied the
latter tripping around from the club-room just before first call, "that's

the third time I've seen you coming out of Curran's since four o'clock."
To which Gray promptly replied,—

"Yes, sir. You see, last week you remarked upon my going in
there so often that I thought it time to reverse the process." And this
afforded the colonel the opportunity of giving Gray the good raking
down he deserved, and, just as Gray had hoped and planned, brought
on the reaction that always followed an outburst. That evening Tintop
came over to the office to "make it up," and then, when the skies were
cleared, Gray broached the subject of Schramm's interview. It seems
he wanted a fortnight's furlough to go to New York and other points
on urgent personal business, and had reason to know that Bragg would
forward the application disapproved; and Bragg did. Bragg's endorsement read, "This young soldier has been the recipient of so many
indulgences already as to seriously impair his usefulness as a sergeant.
He succeeded in evading field duty with the troop last fall, and seeks
to shirk it again. For a man not yet two years in service, he has been
promoted over older and more deserving men so rapidly as to turn his
head." And Tintop considered the whole thing a reflection on him as
regimental commander, and so sent for Bragg and so told him, and
said, furthermore, that if Bragg didn't like Schramm and could find
one man in the whole regiment who was willing to transfer to D, now
that Bragg was its captain, he would be glad to order an exchange;
and this gave Bragg the opening he hoped for and a chance to reply
that, so far from wanting to get Schramm out, his remarks were con-
clusive proof that he was only striving to keep him in. It was hot
shot, give and take, for ten minutes, a warfare in which it must be
owned that Tintop rejoiced even though he did not excel, and it ended
in his ordering Bragg to leave the office and coming in, all in a tower-
ing rage, to ask Gray if he ever in all his life knew such a cantankerous
ass as Bragg,—"unless it's me for letting him rub my fur the wrong
way." Gray said that he really didn't like to draw invidious com-
parisons; but Schramm got the furlough, was back at Ransom in ten
days, and caught the regiment before it camped in sight of Cloud
Peak. He had a long conference with Bertha before he left, and his
good-by to his captain and Connie was very brief. The day after he
left there drove up to the door a low-wheeled phaeton that Connie
instantly recognized as Mrs. Amory's. Mrs. Amory was the wife of
one of the officers of the Eleventh, who, with her children, had gone
back to visit their Kentucky home as soon as the regiment was ordered

away, leaving the phaeton for sale. Bertha came in with a note addressed in Schramm's peculiar cramped and precise hand:

"Will not the gracious Miss Morgan do me the very great honor of the occasional exercising of the horse and carriage which must be left at the Empire stable during the summer without other use? The groom will call each morning for the orders of the gnädige Fräulein, whose acceptance will much honor and deeply oblige both 'Rand,' at her service, and the gracious lady's

"Most humble and grateful

"SCHRAMM."

And when the doctor happened in and found Connie with tear-brimming eyes and saw through the situation at a glance, he said it was an inspiration. On those smooth hard roads, in that low, couch-like, soft-rolling carriage they could give her father air, sunshine, a sight of the distant mountains, a look at the old fort, an occasional visit to the now neglected grave. Constance took "Rand" on a preliminary spin, and found him, as was to be expected, perfectly bridle-wise and reliable, and between Dr. French and Bertha the dear old daddy was presently bundled in by her side, and the only mar to the exquisite joy and harmony of that sunshiny morning was the indignant howl of Billy-boy on their simultaneous return, he from school, the elders from their blissful drive.

And now frequently in the fair June weather they came bowling out to the garrison, Morgan contentedly reclining in the phaeton and chatting with old friends among the infantry officers, while Constance ran in to see Mrs. Woods and other lady friends who had been so kind to her in their dark days, and often they drove to the neglected cemetery, and the mother's grave, adorned now with simple head-stone, was put in order, turfed and trimmed, and often decked with wild flowers. But there was greater surprise in order. A letter from Aunt Lottie said their uncle had business requiring a visit to the far West, and that she would come with him. And they came, and spent two days in Butte, and Aunt Lottie urged her brother-in-law to make an effort and move to the East, for Connie's face was a fortune. "She will fall in love with and marry some penniless officer if she stays here," said the experienced woman of the world, and was aghast when Morgan calmly answered that he hoped she would, if the man was of the right sort, as only in the army had they found friends in the days of their sorest need. As for himself, he looked forward to the time when he could be laid away by Carrie's side. All he prayed for was that his children might not be left destitute. Already, indeed, two young gentlemen at the post, subalterns of Rhett's battalion, were noticed casting sheep's-eyes at Connie's lovely face, and were beginning to be assiduous callers at the little house in town, but Constance seemed to have no thought for any man but father. Aunt Lot went East again with distinct sense of defeat, but her husband took matters less to heart. The doctor had assured them that the long journey was hardly possible, and that Morgan would do fairly well until winter again set in, and then, "Should anything happen, Connie," he said, "you must come to us."

But Connie's reply was politely indefinite. Something did happen late that autumn, and Connie did not go.

XVII.

Letters came only at rare intervals and by roundabout and devious ways from the command in the Big Horn, but early in September there was news of interest. Sergeant-Major Hunter, covered with service chevrons and scars, took his honorable discharge and final papers and went into department head-quarters as clerk. Tintop and Gray had talked the probabilities over and were fully prepared. To the wrath of Bragg, the grumbling of a few who disapproved of giving first prize to a two-year-old trooper, and yet who would equally have criticised any appointment Gray could have made, but to the outspoken satisfaction of nine-tenths of the regiment, Sergeant Schramm was named sergeant-major, the senior non-commissioned officer of the Eleventh. Modestly he accepted, for already his colonel and other officers had bidden him look even higher. "You are on the road to a commission," said Perry Thornton, when the young German came to tell him of the offered sergeant-majorship and to beg the Herr Lieutenant's kind advice. "I only wish the commission might come in time for you to stand up with me. Congratulate me, Rhetz: the wedding is to be in December."

One chilly October afternoon Connie had driven Mrs. Woods into town after a brief visit to the fort. Daddy was ailing again since the frost set in, and beginning to house himself still more. She had left

L 21

her friend at Mrs. Whaling's, and, turning "Rand" about, was spinning up the main street towards their home at the westward skirt of town, when, striding along in front of her, slender, erect, in the most immaculate of yellow stripes and chevrons and a natty blue uniform, she caught sight of a well-known form, in an instant had reined up at the curb, and her glad voice, eager and joyous, rang with the old name.

"Schramm! Why, when—how did you get here?" she cried, throwing down the reins and holding forth her slender hand. The street was full of people, and who that saw could fail to note the sudden flash of delight in the face of the soldier addressed? Instantly he whirled about, sprang to the curb, and was on the point of clasping the proffered hand, when as suddenly he seemed to remember, straightened up instantly, raised the forage-cap from his curly blond head, and answered, respect, homage, admiration in his fine blue eyes,—

"Only this morning, gnädige Fräulein. The adjutant and I were sent in by way of Green River. The regiment is marching home."

"Oh, father will be so glad! Have you time—can you run up to see him now?"

"Assuredly, Miss Morgan. I was on my way there."

"That's simply lovely. Come, let me drive you now. You can't imagine what pleasure 'Rand' has given us all." And, edging back to the right side of the phaeton, she eagerly made room for him beside her. Schramm flushed to his very eyes.

"Oh, gnädige Fräulein, I thank you, but I could not. I will come——Pardon! I must stop on the way. Please drive on, Miss Morgan. It cannot be that I should drive with an officer's daughter." And, seeing rebellion in her eyes, he abruptly turned and strode away. He reached the little home only five minutes behind her, but the next day and the next "Rand" stood unused in the stable. "It's your own doing, Schramm," she said, with flashing eyes, when at last he meekly came to ask why she would no longer honor him by driving his horse and phaeton. "If there is any military impropriety in my driving you, there's every impropriety in my driving your horse and phaeton." And argument was useless. She refused to enter it again. This was the first break. Then came a second. On three occasions within the ten days after his return, the sergeant-major, calling to see how fared his captain and the family, found Lieutenant Renshaw, a very presentable young infantryman, seated in the little parlor. Once it was Renshaw who opened the door. At sight of him the soldier had become rigid, like a pointer. His inquiries were made on this occasion with hand at salute, and he faced about and left at once, but Constance pursued and caught him at the gate, and Renshaw, watching from the window, saw him at attention, punctilious as ever, and saw that Constance was pleading. She was flushed and ready to cry when she came back. Schramm came seldom now, and Renshaw more frequently, and the third winter opened in chill and gloom.

Thornton came to say good-by just before Thanksgiving, and went blissfully away to his wedding, leaving Renshaw haunting the invalid's room and swearing to himself at Connie's ceaseless household duties. He began to realize that she was actually striving to avoid him, and so did Morgan. One night Morgan called her to him and gently, fondly began to plead with her. "He has asked my consent, Constance. He is a gentleman. He loves——" But she would hear no more, and with a burst of tears fled to her room. Poor Renshaw was told that Constance could not listen to any proposal: she would not leave daddy.

"But daddy must soon leave her," the father urged again, "and then what is to become of you and Lot and Billy? Renshaw said he would only be too glad——" But here the slender white hand was placed on his mouth, and further words were impossible.

He took it sorely to heart, did Renshaw, and he said some ill-advised and peppery things the day of Mrs. Fenton's tin-wedding reception when waltzing with Connie down the long hall. "If nothing but a German baron will suit, why, I suppose you can have him; but the least the fellow can do is to wait till he gets his commission, and not be——"

But he never finished. With one low cry of "Oh, shame, Mr. Renshaw!" she tore away from him and into the dressing-room.

It was just dark that evening when the ambulance from the post landed her at their door, and Mrs. Whaling, who had matronized the little party of town girls, drove on with her brood. Connie stole, as usual, to her father's side to bend and kiss him and murmur some fond inquiry. But pent-up indignation, the strain and misery of the long ride during which she had been compelled to listen to brainless sallies and congratulations on Renshaw's devotion, all proved too much for her. No sooner did she feel the father's arms around her than her girlish strength gave way, and she lay sobbing on his breast. There was the sound of a rasping chair, of some one striving to hurry from

the room, but she did not hear. " He—he dared to speak of Schramm !"
she cried, " of Schramm, who—who is truer gentleman—truer hero—
than any—any—any officer they've got."

And the shadowy form striving to find means of exit from the tiny
den in which reclined the invalid and his clasping, sobbing child was
that of Sergeant-Major Schramm, who, all unnoticed and unseen by
her, was thus become the hearer of his own perfections. Renshaw's
hapless outburst had proved his own undoing and swept away the last
barrier to his rival's approach. " The least he can do is to wait till he
gets his commission," indeed ! After Connie's outburst it was more
than mortal man could do to wait at all.

L'ENVOI.

It seems very long ago, that bitter winter in the heart of the
Rockies, yet one of the old regiment, enjoying with his wife and
children the first blissful taste of foreign travel, stood one exquisite
summer morning on the forward deck of the oddly-modelled " dampfer"
that was churning the blue-brown flood of the Rhine, and thus replied
to the query of his better half:

" Know her? Why, you'll know her instantly. Connie can never
grow old." Yes, rounded indeed is the sweet face of the woman
standing with her soldierly husband close to the railing of the landing
under the beautiful, vine-clad heights ahead, her soft brown eyes fixed
in eagerness upon the approaching steamer. The slender form we
knew in the shabby old black serge is almost majestic in its proportions
now, yet how fair and sweet and smiling is the dear, bonny face once
so piteously sad amid the snows of far-away Ransom ! Happy wife
and mother,—the idol of her soldier-husband's heart,—the " gnädige
Fräulein" whom he won in distant America long years ago had speedily
found her way into the love of the old retainers of the ancestral home
to which, summoned to succeed the stern old father whose last words
and thoughts were for his banished son, he bore her so soon after the
last volley was fired over Morgan's head as they laid him away, as he
had prayed, by Carrie's side. He died without a lingering fear for
the children's future, one hand clasped in faithful Schramm's. The
commission had indeed been tendered, but gracefully, courteously
declined because of family duties at his old home in the fabled Rhineland. Again he wears the uniform of his famous corps, all the better
officer for his experience in the American cavalry. Already Lottie

had cut a wide swath among the bachelor subalterns of the hussars before finally bestowing heart and hand and a Schramm-provided *dot* upon a totally different party, though an eminently sound one. Already Billy has won distinction (as a skylarker and *schläger* and all-round scapegrace) at Heidelberg, where he sports a yellow cap and a monocle, a straggly moustache, and some ridiculous slashing scars, of all of which he is inordinately vain, and with genuine American enthusiasm he prattles of "my brother-in-law the baron," who laughs at his stories, chaffs him about his duels, quizzes him as to his scientific attainments (for Billy, be it known, is going back to America this fall to offer his services to capitalists as an expert mining engineer, and says for the first year a salary of five thousand dollars will do); but the Herr Graf pays his debts and provides his pocket-money, and the only secrets Connie does not share are those concerning her hopeful brother and his affairs. As for Connie herself, she is happy as the years are long, happy as even an army girl deserves to be.

THE END.

www.ingramcontent.com/pod-product-compliance
Lightning Source LLC
Chambersburg PA
CBHW030813020726
47499CB00006B/1894